# THE HILLS OF HOME

## THE SONG OF THE ASH TREE - SECOND EDDA

# THE HILLS OF HOME

## THE SONG OF THE ASH TREE - SECOND EDDA

# T L GREYLOCK

Grass Crown Press

Copyright © 2016 T L Greylock

Cover design by Damonza
Map by Gillis Björk

All rights reserved.
No part of this book may be reproduced, scanned, or distributed in any printed
or electronic form without permission, except in the case of brief quotations
embodied in critical reviews and certain other noncommercial uses permitted by
copyright law.

This is a work of fiction. Names, characters, places, and incidents either are the
product of the author's imagination or are used fictitiously. Any resemblance to
actual persons, living or dead, events, or locales is entirely coincidental.

ISBN 978-0-9965366-3-9

*For H&H, who knew how to live.*

I learned it from men, | the men so old,
Who dwell in the hills of home.

*Harbarthsljoth, Poetic Edda*

Ragmoor
Finngale
Danew
Axsellund
Vannheim
Ba
Bergoss
Silfravall
Karahull
Garhold
Narvik
Ingis
Innrivik
Wayhold
Grudenhavn

Norfaem
Hullbern
Darfallow
Skolldain
Ver
fell
Gornhald
Ulfgang
Lillevall
Freywyn
Thollgrim
Ruderk
Kolhaugen
Ervard
Kollumheim
Finnmark
or
Othmund
-Midgard-

# ONE

THE WINTER SEA was thick with foam and the air was sharp with brine. Waves crashed against the rocky shore, sending the salt spray leaping to the clouds. Gulls wheeled in the sky, buoyed by the gusty air, their cries calling their brothers and sisters to join the dance.

It was their eyes that saw the sail on the horizon, saw the ship valiantly riding on the rough seas to make the shore. The sail was the black of a starless, moonless night and the dragonhead prow, the color of blood, barred sharp teeth.

Only the gulls saw the ship reach land, saw the hooded figures jump into the shallows and splash to shore, hauling the ship onto the sand and snow behind them. One figure lingered a moment and when he, too, jumped from the prow of the ship, the oil-slick deck flared and hungry flames leapt up behind him, eating through the dry tinder, charring the oars. Sparks soared into the air and at last the sail burned bright.

On the snow-strewn shore, the sailors watched the ship burn. The gulls circled overhead until the smoke drove them away but the watchers remained until the ship was wreathed in flames. Only then did they turn their backs to the sea and, as they ventured further onto land, the wind threatening to tear their cloaks away, no one was there to witness.

# TWO

RAEF LOOKED TO the horizon, as far west as west goes, and for a moment imagined he could see the ocean. The high peaks and deep valleys, the rushing rivers and sun-speckled forests that lay between him and the salt shore of Vannheim vanished as his mind, far ahead of his body, raced across the distance and brought him to rest. Home. If he closed his eyes, he would see it all before him but Raef kept his gaze on the cloud-streaked sky over the high moors of Axsellund. Tomorrow, they would reach Vannheim soil and Raef would step foot on it as the lord of Vannheim for the first time.

Night would be upon them soon, and Raef looked back to the east to the sliver of rising moon. It hovered over a cliff face, suspended just above a waterfall, a delicate boat on the verge of tumbling over. Another night, another moon rise. Raef tried not to wonder if it was the last, but he could not help but imagine the wolf, Hati, chasing the moon, his slavering teeth drawing ever closer, his hot breath befouling the air. For eighteen days Raef had watched for the dawn and for eighteen days he had seen the night sky grow light, the tendrils of pink and orange announcing the arrival of Sol and her chariot. Raef cherished those golden rays slipping over the horizon each morning.

"The moon will rise again tomorrow, Raef. And the sun after him." The voice was Gudrik's. The poet limped to Raef's side, wincing with every step, leaning on a stout pine stave. They had spoken of this before.

"How can we know?" Raef took his gaze from the moon and looked at Gudrik.

"When the gods battle for the fate of all nine worlds, it is not a small thing. We will know. And there is much that will happen before that final battle begins."

"So it is said. But I hear Thor's fury when I sleep at night and I see the bolts of his anger and grief behind my eyelids. The storm that heralded Balder's death still echoes within me." Raef shook his head. "How is your leg?"

"Much the same. The pain is less, thanks to the herbs we found at the last farm, but it is rest my body needs to heal."

"When we reach my home, you will have all the rest and care you need."

Gudrik grinned. "I shall grow fat and lazy."

Raef laughed and watched his small party set up camp by the waterfall's pool. Vakre was tying the horses. Siv and two men were encouraging a young fire. They were only twenty in number, the last of the Vannheim warriors to return home from the great battle of the burning lake, the battle that had brought the Valkyries down to Midgard, that had seen the defeat of the Palesword and Freyja's deathless host. After six days of travel, when he was certain Brandulf Hammerling's wrath was not hounding their steps, Raef had sent the rest ahead to bring word of their arrival and remained behind to travel at a pace more suited to Gudrik's broken leg. Raef looked back to the west.

"See those twin peaks?" Raef gestured to a pair of barren hills settled between the higher granite summits of their neighbors. Gudrik nodded in response. "That is where we will enter

Vannheim." Raef knew the place well for it was the most accessible passage into Vannheim from the east. A smooth approach, not too steep. The ground beneath the snow was easy to travel by horse or foot, free of the fallen rocks and boulders that cluttered so many of the lower slopes to the north and south. He had stood at that spot between the hills with his father more than once, the wind blowing at their backs. The first time, he had been a small boy and it seemed to him the edge of the world, for he had never yet ventured far from the Vestrhall. Later, as the rugged hills and vast forests of Vannheim had become a second home to him, Raef had come to that place between the hills alone. Sometimes he imagined himself a great hero, the last defender of Vannheim against a horde of invading warriors, and he had held that gap single-handedly to save his people. Other times he simply watched and listened to the world around him and he came to know the feel of the breeze as it curled up the slope beneath him, the silence of the streaking eagles as they dove from the sky to snatch their prey from above, the path the sun took in high summer, and the sound of spring rain falling on dry winter grass.

Raef could feel his heart beat a little faster in his chest as thoughts of home swelled in his mind. They would rise early, with the sun, and they would reach the narrow, swift stream before midday. After crossing it, they would climb, first through thick trees before rising above the tree line and coming to the gap. And then he would be home and at last he could put his mind to the vengeance he had sworn to have. His father's murderer was yet unnamed, no more than a shadow, and duty, honor, and blood demanded retribution. How he might discover the source of the treachery that ended with Einarr Skallagrim's death, Raef did not know. But time was against him. The Hammerling would bring the war to Vannheim, justified by Raef's desertion after the battle of the burning lake. And soon Heimdall would blow his great horn, summoning the warriors in

Valhalla, the Einherjar, to the last battle, and the nine realms would fall first into chaos and then darkness and oblivion. He would be the last Skallagrim to sit in the high chair in the Vestrhall. But if the gods might grant him the chance to see his vow fulfilled, to see Einarr avenged, he would take it.

A hand brushed against his shoulder and Raef turned to see Eira at his side. He began to point to the peaks as he had done with Gudrik, but her eyes showed that her mind was elsewhere. She took his hand and led him away from the lookout and around the pool until Raef felt the spray of the waterfall on his face. There she dropped his hand, unclasped the bronze pin that kept her cloak in place, and kicked off her boots. Raef watched her while she dipped a toe into the water. She grimaced, the cold water giving her second thoughts, and Raef took advantage of her hesitation, grabbed her around the waist, and jumped into the pool.

The water cut off Eira's shriek, but she surged to the surface ready to fight, her eyes now dark and determined. Raef, laughing, checked her wild swing and pulled her close to him. He kissed her and felt the tension leave her limbs.

"Come," he whispered, "the water is too cold."

"Catch me," she said. Wriggling free, Eira burst from the pool and dashed into the trees, pausing once to see if he followed. Raef, laughing again, raced after her, his eyes on her wet hair, dark and glistening in the moonlight. She was quick, though, and he lost sight of her between the heavy branches. Stopping, Raef listened for a moment and then, hearing rustling to his right, turned to follow the sound. He called her name once, aware that his own wet clothes were a danger to him. Her game, and his willingness to play it, was risky on a cold winter night. Pain in his side caused Raef to pull up. The ribs that had broken in the battle throbbed, awoken by his exertion. Clenching his teeth and holding his hand to his side, Raef leaned against a tree until the pain was more bearable.

"Eira," he called. "Let us be done with this." His ribs flared again and Raef bit his lip against the pain. He closed his eyes and listened for any sign of Eira, but the forest was quiet. The cold caught up with him, and Raef began to shiver, his soaking clothes clinging to him. Cursing the persistent ache in his side, Raef pushed off the tree and began to retrace his steps back to the others, all desire chased away by the cold and the dizziness that threatened to overtake him.

He had not gone far when a sound behind him caused him to turn and look. His eyes saw nothing, but he sensed someone was there. "Enough, Eira." He continued on, hunched over, his arms clutched across his ribcage as though they might still the fire that raged in his bones. The noise came again, but this time Raef ignored it, no longer in the mood for games.

When it came a third time and still Eira did not show herself, Raef stopped, alert now. He drew the longer of the two knives on his belt, the only weapons he had. The broken axe, nearly useless, was wrapped in his blanket at the camp and he had not yet found a replacement for his shattered sword. Raef's gaze darted among the trees and once he thought he saw a shadowy figure just outside his vision. When he turned to face it, there was nothing.

The rope slipped over Raef's head and was around his neck before he could protect himself. His hands came up, scrabbling uselessly, and he twisted hard to his left, trying to throw his attacker off balance, but whoever held the rope was prepared and did not falter. Desperate for breath, Raef lashed out behind him with his knife but the blade only sliced through empty air. Still Raef flailed as his vision darkened, but his strength began to fail and he slumped to the ground, the knife falling into the snow at his feet. His attacker let him fall but the rope remained tight. The snow seemed to rise up to meet Raef's face, and then all was dark.

# THREE

GENTLE MOVEMENT WAS the first thing Raef became aware of. For a time, his whole world was that movement, side to side, up and down, uneven, unpredictable, but familiar. As Raef's mind emerged from darkness, he latched onto that, clinging to it until he had drawn himself far enough from the depths to know that he had truly awoken. His eyes refused to open, but his other senses began to return to him.

First he felt the wood grain beneath his fingertips. It was smooth and well-worked, not the rough wood that has just been chopped from a tree. His fingers moved against the grain, stretching, reaching, trying to place himself somewhere other than the void of his mind.

It was warmth that Raef knew next, not the warmth of a hot fire on a winter night, but the warmth of the sun. It caressed the backs of his hands and then at last he became aware of its full embrace along the length of his body. This embrace fulfilled him and for a time Raef was content to soak it in and felt no need to know more.

After a time, though, it was no longer enough to just be warmed by the sun and at last Raef's small world of wood and sunlight grew to include the sound of water. It was not the sound a waterfall makes, nor the sound of a coursing river, and at length Raef came to understand that the gentle movement he had first known was tied to the sound of the water. This revelation seemed important to Raef, but he could not quite fathom why. There was no fear in this understanding, only peace.

The world cracked open around Raef when the cry of a bird came to him and light and sound and smell came rushing back to him on the wings of a gull, for he knew beyond a doubt that it was a gull he had heard. He was at sea.

The movement, familiar and peaceful, was a boat riding the gentle swell of a calm sea. The wood beneath him was the well-worn deck of a ship. The smell of the salt water flooded his nostrils as he took his first lung-stretching breath. And if he opened his eyes he knew he would see a brilliant sun overhead.

When at last he did open his eyes, the fierce light of the sun forced them closed again. He drew two deep breaths before trying once more, this time squinting until his eyes began to adjust and he was able to open them fully. The blue of the sky was overwhelming, conquering all of Raef's vision but for the corner of white sail that rose up behind Raef. Moving slowly, Raef sat up, his ribs aching with even that little movement. He tested his legs, drawing his knees up and back, and then felt his neck for injury, remembering the rope that had choked him into unconsciousness. The skin was raw to the touch but otherwise intact. Other than the broken bones in his chest, his body functioned as it should. Whoever had attacked him had done no lasting damage but Raef knew he was weak from lack of food and water. His clothes were his own, dried in the sea air, but his belt held no weapons.

Turning his head, Raef ascertained what he had already known. The ship was empty. The prow caught his gaze for the dragonhead was familiar. This was one of his father's ships, a small one rowed by only six men and holding a crew of no more than ten. A rover, sent ahead of the fleet to feel out the enemy, or to slip into a cove in the dead of night to kill a man and steal his gold. Now it drifted on a sunlit ocean and Raef was the only crew.

Struggling to his feet, Raef's head spun and he gripped the mast for support. His mouth was dry and his lips stuck together. There was no barrel of water, no sign of food. Raef knelt by the mast and pulled up on the iron ring attached to the planking there to reveal the ballast chamber and the small, dark belly of the boat, but it was empty. Rising, Raef tried to wet his lips. The sun was high above, making it difficult to determine east and west, but land was in sight beyond the prow of the ship. The shore was not far off and Raef scanned it for a landmark he might recognize. But among the green hills and rough cliffs, there was nothing familiar. Wherever he was, it was not the coast of Vannheim.

Turning, Raef grew dizzy and the mast seemed to sway out of his grip. He slipped to the deck, cradling his damaged ribs, and dropped back into the darkness.

When he awoke a second time, the ship was still and the sky was growing dark. Raising himself to his elbows, Raef saw the small vessel had run up on a sandy shore. The warmth of the sun had faded, leaving Raef in twilight and at the whims of a night breeze. But this was no winter night. The shore was free of snow and the air, while cool to Raef's skin, was the air of a summer's eve. There was no time to contemplate the season, or where he was, or even who had attacked him. He needed food, shelter, and a fire. Above all, he needed fresh water.

Raef found his feet and stumbled to the ship's rail. Even this effort increased his heartbeat and he felt his legs shake beneath him as he clutched the side to stabilize himself. He was weaker than he had realized. Steeling himself, he slid a leg over the edge, then the other, but his arms would not hold him and he fell to the sand below. The impact jarred every inch of him but most of all his ribs, which exploded with fresh pain. Gasping for breath, Raef lay still, fixing his eyes on the stars above and listening to the water lap against the sand until the pain subsided to a glowing ember that would not burn out.

Summoning his meager strength, Raef forced himself to rise. The sand stretched far into the distance, pale in the moonlight. Beyond the shore, the land was green and covered in thick ferns, larger than any Raef had ever seen, until it rose up in a range of hills. Even in the gathering dark, Raef could see the hills were lush with green trees. He did not have the strength to reach the trees, he knew, but he had to search for water in the flat lands off the shore. Taking one tentative step and then another, Raef made his way to the ferns and examined the large leaves for water. Even a mouthful would bring relief. The ferns were dry, but the ground beneath them was damp to Raef's touch and he continued through the ferns, looking for any sign of a stream or pool.

His progress was slow but Raef did not let himself rest, for he feared he would not rise again if he succumbed to the desire to sit. Twice he almost fell and it seemed will alone kept him on his feet. He touched the hammer amulet at his neck and asked Thor for strength.

When at last Raef heard the sound of water trickling over rocks, he thought it imagined by his desperate mind. But as it grew louder there was no denying it. Raef stumbled ahead until the stream was at his feet. Falling to his knees, Raef put his whole head under the water, then gulped in three deep, eager swallows. Though he longed for more, Raef knew better. Too much at once could make him ill. He allowed himself several small sips, then lay back on the damp earth, his energy spent. The stars shone above and Raef marveled in their bright joy. But as he felt sleep, true sleep, the sleep of a man who knows he will wake, rise up to consume him, he knew a tinge of fear. Nowhere among those vivid orbs was there a star known to him.

ᚠ ᚠ ᚠ

Dawn brought a delicate rain on Raef's skin and a violent hunger in his belly. As he eased the stiffness from his limbs and drank his fill from the cool stream, he racked his memory for a sense of what had happened to him. But beyond the rope that had choked the breath from him, there was only darkness. His hunger told him it had been at least two days since he had chased Eira through the trees. His thirst and the weakness in his limbs told him it had been much more. But from the border between Axsellund and Vannheim it would take a minimum of four days on horseback to reach the sea, five if the winter snows were deep. Add to that the time it would take an unmanned boat to drift far enough to place him in unfamiliar territory, and Raef judged at least seven days had passed since he had been attacked under the sliver of moon. He chose not to think of the strange stars and what that could mean. How he had remained unconscious for so long, Raef did not know, but he had become aware of a strange burnt sensation in his nostrils and knew that certain herbs could induce long bouts of sleep.

They would have searched for him. And they would not have moved on until all hope of finding him was lost. Vakre would have made sure of that. After being certain he was not lying dead at the bottom of a ravine, they would have searched for a trail, but Raef felt in his heart that there was none to find. At best, they might have found his knife, the one he had drawn to defend himself, if the attacker had not retrieved it from the snow. Blame would fall on Brandulf Hammerling, for he above all would wish Raef harm, and Eira would swear bloody vengeance against the lord of Finngale and would-be king. Vakre would maintain an outward calm and counsel patience while an inner fury burned bright. Siv might think of Fengar and wonder if the other king had a hand in Raef's disappearance. But all this would avail them little. Raef knew if the Hammerling or Fengar had captured him in the night, his blood would be staining the snow on that hill in Axsellund and his head would sit atop a spike. His attacker had left him alive and taken great pains to put him on a ship.

Weary of these thoughts, Raef turned his attention to his stomach. Across the stream, a bush heavy with red berries caught his eye. It was unfamiliar to him but the lush berries, gleaming in the morning rain, promised sweet satisfaction. Raef waded through the knee-deep water, plucked one from the bush, and held it close to his nose. The scent of it was rich and heady. Raef's stomach rumbled and he ached to crush a handful with his tongue. But he did not intend to die on this strange shore and a red berry was just as likely to bring death as relief. The ferns would have to do.

The young fronds, curled still against their larger siblings, were bitter but safe. Raef ate slowly, chewing well to avoid upsetting his stomach. The raw greens made a poor meal, but until Raef could find meat, they would provide vital energy. Though his stomach demanded more, he ate only four. After a brief rest, Raef felt strong enough to explore his surroundings.

The morning rain had ceased and the sun emerged from behind thin clouds to shatter the grey light. The raindrops on the ferns sparkled like gems and with the new brilliance came the sounds of forest life. Birds chattered, hidden away in the foliage, and a rabbit, startled by Raef's intruding feet, bounded away, passing within a spear's length. Even had he been prepared with an arrow, Raef could not have made the kill. But the sight of birds and small game was encouraging.

Raef pushed inland. The ground began to slope upward and the trees grew taller and thicker there. Raef kept to the flattest ground he could find to preserve his strength, but a fallen tree, its dead trunk resting against its neighbor, provided an opportunity to reach a vantage point without a long uphill trek. Scrambling up the trunk until he reached the limbs of the living tree, Raef sagged against a thick, sturdy branch and waited for the dizziness to abate. The pain in his ribs stirred, flaming to life and making it difficult to breath, but Raef pushed it away and climbed higher until the branches would no longer support him.

It was not a great height, but it was enough to show where he had come from and what lay ahead. The sun had risen above the forest, not the beach, so Raef knew he had made landfall from the west. The stretch of sand was visible behind him, but ahead the trees grew too close together to see much of the land. And yet, from that height the sound of a waterfall came to him.

For a giddy moment Raef thought of the waterfall in Axsellund and if he just hurried down from his perch, he would find Vakre and the rest gathered around its pool. So strong was the feeling that Raef, leaning out in a mad attempt to hear the voices of his friends, nearly slipped down the rough trunk. He caught himself in time, grabbing a nearby branch to steady himself. Still the feeling lingered and Raef had to close his eyes to shut it out, or he knew he would tumble to the ground.

When he opened them, the madness had passed and Raef, after surveying the scene one last time, descended from the tree. On the ground, the sound of water was faint but knowing it was there allowed Raef to follow it. Again, a rabbit crossed his path and Raef reached for the knife that wasn't there. His stomach rumbled and he plucked another curled frond from the closest fern to appease it.

Not long after, the waterfall came into view. Narrow like a knife, it tumbled down into a shallow pool surrounded on three sides by rocky cliffs twice the height of a man. On one side, a recess in the rocks offered respite from sun and rain. Raef examined it closer and found it dry and larger than expected. With fresh water so close and abundant, it would make a fine shelter.

The sun had warmed the forest and Raef removed his boots and the thick layers of wool and leather he had worn to protect against the snow and winter winds and tucked them into a corner of his small cave. Inspired by the sunlight and perhaps with a faint thought of Eira in his mind, Raef continued to strip from his linen shirt and wool pants until he stood naked at the edge of the pool. He waded in and then submerged himself, lingering just beneath the surface for a moment before rising and floating, arms and legs spread wide. His silver arm rings, one on each wrist, glittered. He closed his eyes, feeling peace for the first time since arriving on this strange shore. The sun warmed him from above and the water revived him from below.

How much time passed, Raef was not certain, but when he opened his eyes, the sun was higher and the skin of his fingertips had begun to wrinkle. Rising, Raef pulled his shirt into the water and rubbed it between his hands until it seemed cleaner. Then he spread it on a rock to dry and did the same with his body. He did not doze, did not let his mind drift. He was alert in a way he had not been since first awakening on the ship. He had evaded the threat of imminent death, but that was no longer enough. It was time to take further action.

By the time the sun's rays had dried his skin, Raef was ready to get to work. The hunger gnawed at him, but he did not allow it to take hold. After drinking his fill from the pool, Raef pulled on his pants, fastened the worn belt, and slipped his boots on, then retraced his steps to the place where the second rabbit had crossed his path. From there, he methodically surveyed the land, walking in increasingly large circles and taking note of every torn leaf, every pile of scat, every track in the dirt. After a time, Raef ceased to walk and instead climbed again into a tree, where he settled in to watch the forest floor below.

The sun had traveled nearly a quarter of the sky before he descended from his leafy hideout but his patience would be rewarded. Rabbits were far from scarce and he now knew what paths they liked to tread. Raef suspected several burrows lay just north of his position among a grouping of boulders and dense bushes. His own pool was the closest source of water and he had detected two distinct paths between the dens and the waterfall.

It had been several years since Raef had constructed a snare from scratch, but he had done it so often under his father's watchful eye that he felt it had been no time at all. Milkweed and elm bark to fashion the noose, a sturdy sapling to hold it, and a twig, set just so to keep the loop open. Raef made three nooses and positioned them with care on the rabbit runs. By the time he finished, the sun was sinking and Raef resigned himself to a hungry night. The snares required patience. As he returned to the pool, collecting supplies to build a fire and more curled ferns, Raef came across a patch of mushrooms nestled beside a fallen log. Some were foreign to him, but others, to his relief, were the same he had foraged for in the forests of Vannheim. Using a large frond as a basket, Raef gathered all the mushrooms he knew were safe and returned to his waterfall.

In the growing dusk, Raef set to work creating his instruments of fire. So intent was he on his work that a deer approached the pool and began to drink before he took notice. She watched him and Raef made no move to frighten her. Perhaps he would build a bigger snare in the morning. When the tools were complete and the first spark blossomed in the darkness, Raef smiled and dropped the ember into the carefully formed tinder nest. Bringing his face close, Raef blew gently until the ember grew and engulfed the tinder in small flames. Soon the kindling began to crackle and the light of the fire sent shadows dancing across the waterfall's pool.

Raef speared several curled fronds and held them over the flames until each was charred on the outside. The taste mellowed with the heat, making the ferns more palatable, but the mushrooms were a welcome change. When the moon was high in the sky, Raef checked his snares. All were empty, but he had not really expected more. Morning would tell if he had positioned them well.

Sleep came in fits that night, for though Raef was weary and had expelled precious energy that day, his hunger was a beast that woke him often. He lay awake listening to the sounds of the forest compete with the waterfall. An owl was close and something larger than a rabbit stirred the underbrush more than once. The fire had burned low and Raef did not bother to keep it up, but he wondered what he might do to protect himself should something with teeth and a taste for flesh come prowling too close. Several sturdy branches were close at hand. He stirred the coals enough to send up a shower of sparks and hoped that the smell of man and fire would keep any curious predators at bay.

When Raef stirred before dawn, he knew he would not sleep again. The promise of meat beckoned, and he rose to check the snares. At the first, the rabbit had broken its neck and lay still on the earth. Raef disengaged it, reset the snare, and moved on. The second rabbit was not so lucky. It squirmed at his approach and Raef could see its pulse beat under its fur. Grasping it carefully to keep his fingers out of reach of desperate teeth, Raef ended its suffering with a quick twist to the neck. The third was the same.

The fire grew quickly and though it was easier to skin rabbits with the aid of a knife, it was not long before Raef had pulled the skins from the meat and gutted the small bodies. Skewered and set over the fire, the smell of cooking meat made Raef salivate. But he remained patient, knowing that undercooked meat could upset his underfed stomach. He judged them ready when the exterior had grown black and crispy. The first bite burned his tongue, so hot he nearly spit it out, but the taste of the meat was sweeter than any mead Raef had drunk and he chewed with abandon, finally giving in to the hunger he had held at bay since awakening on the beach.

The pile of bones at Raef's feet grew until he stripped the last bit of flesh from the third rabbit's leg. Thirsty now, Raef gulped down handfuls of water from the pool and then leaned back against the cliff wall. The sun was warm on his bare chest and the sleep that had evaded him that night crept back like a shadow stealing across his mind. Raef let his eyes close. There was much to do, questions that needed answering, but for the moment he let himself be content with no longer feeling hungry.

If he slept, he did not know, but a shadow that was not sleep came between him and the sun. Raef opened his eyes.

The silhouette above him was lithe and lean and that of a man. At first, the brilliant sun that threatened to spill out from behind his head masked his features, but as Raef's eyes adjusted he saw a pair of pale grey eyes in a bronze, sun-browned face. He blinked, drowsy from sun and food.

"You are a man." It was not a question but there was curiosity there. His voice was low and cool. Raef said nothing. "And a warrior." He leaned down and stretched out an arm until he could touch the fresh scar that ran down from Raef's left shoulder and then the burned scar across Raef's right side. Raef flinched and knew he should back away from the stranger, but his arms were heavy at his sides. The nearly colorless eyes drifted to the rings on both of Raef's arms and then his fingers slid up to Raef's ribs. There was no mark there, Raef knew, but he found the damaged bones with ease. "You have pain here." He withdrew his hand and pushed back the long, pale hair that had fallen over his shoulder. "You should sleep." And Raef did.

ᚾ ᚾ ᚾ

When he awoke, the stranger was gone and for a time Raef was not certain he had not dreamed of the visit. Though he had a man's shape, his hair, skin, and eyes marked him as something other than what Raef knew, something from the stories he had learned as a child. Raef shook that from his mind. He had a hill to climb.

As Raef reached the top of the hill that fed his waterfall, he discovered it was a false summit. A much higher, rockier peak reared above and to the south, but the distance Raef had traveled was enough, for the view below him revealed much. His ribs had protested the entire climb and he knew he could not have gone much further. Sinking down on the rocky earth, Raef studied the land.

The world was green and full of life, a world on the brink between spring and summer. A pair of narrow lakes hiding between steep hills to the east sparkled in the sun. Beyond, more hills, more trees. To the south, the peaks grew more rugged, though none were true mountains, and tall, thick-trunked trees dominated their slopes. Their bark was dark, nearly black and Raef was sure each leaf stretched across a distance greater than his height. A flurry of wings drew Raef's gaze in time to see a flock of birds emerge from the hillside below him. Up, up they rose, pumping their wings hard and fast until they reached a draft of air. Then they soared up the hillside, sweeping higher, silent now, a rush of orange, black, and sharp beaks. They passed over Raef's head and disappeared down the western slope, a final confirmation of what Raef's heart had already known. The unfamiliar birds, the peculiar trees, the green land when it should be winter. And above all, the stars whose names he did not know and the bronze-skinned stranger. He had crossed the boundary of Midgard. He knew not how or which of the nine worlds he now gazed upon, but he knew he had left the world of men.

# FOUR

RAEF TOOK A deep breath and let it out. He felt his heart begin to beat as fast and hard as the birds had pumped their wings, but he forced away the panic, knowing he could not let it wash over him. It was not like the anticipation of battle. That would be welcome. The tingling skin on the back of his neck, the surge through his muscles, the battle-roar that worked its way up from deep within, an echo of his ancestors. These things he knew, these things were ingrained. And though battle was a promise of blood and death, there was no fear for Raef. But this was different.

There was no enemy here, no screaming warrior worthy of his wrath, no sword, even, with which to show his strength. He was alone and his opponent was the unknown. Raef's mind raced with the stories of the nine worlds. Fire, ice. Treacherous giants burning with hatred for the gods. Secretive alfar, both dark and light. No safe place for man.

A clear thought penetrated the tumult of his mind and held the creeping fear at bay. It came on the wind of his father's voice. "There is still a sun in the sky and earth beneath your feet, Raef." Raef closed his eyes and he was on a jagged cliff in Vannheim. Above, his father waited, his expectant face peering down from the safety of the summit. Below, the world dropped away into a deep, dark fjord and Raef's arms were beginning to tremble with exhaustion from the climb. He heard his younger self, a boy of nine, protest that it was impossible, that he would surely fall, that he could not do it. His father had not smiled, had not insisted the way was easy and that Raef would do it. At the time, Raef had seen only sternness in his father's features. He recognized now that fear had been there as well, that Einarr had not been certain his son would survive the challenging climb.

"Look around you, Raef. This is the world and it is often harsh. You will be a warrior of Vannheim and then its lord. There is no easy path for you. You must learn to survive. And then you must learn to flourish."

Raef had conquered the cliff that day and the exhilaration of feeling so close to the sun and knowing he alone had put himself there had stayed with him. As he grew in years and strength, the cliff became an old friend and a tangible reminder of what he was capable of.

His father's voice died away and Raef opened his eyes. He touched the Thor hammer around his neck. Though his heart still thrummed in his chest, there was something other than fear driving it. Perhaps this was not so very different from a battle after all. He knew not what lay ahead, but there on that hilltop, Raef made a vow, to himself, to the gods, to his father. Let the gods be his witness, he would find his way home.

ᛞ ᛞ ᛞ

The shadow came from above, spiraling out of the blue until darkness fell across the sun. Raef turned, an instant too late, and was thrown back to the earth. He sprawled face down in the dirt, his chest riven with pain. Raef clutched his ribs and struggled to rise and face his attacker, but his pain turned to astonishment.

The creature that stared down at him seemed to Raef as painted wood made flesh. Bright, pulsing eyes the color of a sunset arrested any movement Raef might make. Hot breath blew from narrow nostrils and a slender tongue snaked out from between sharp teeth. It was a familiar face, for it and its kind adorned the prow of every Vannheim ship.

The beast held Raef's gaze for a long moment then folded its immense wings into its body. It was only then that Raef noticed the rider on its back.

"You are not afraid." The rider was as Raef remembered, only now Raef could see his pale hair was twisted behind his head and streaked through with many shades of blue. He rode tall, unaided by saddle or harness, his head held high.

"I never thought to see a dragon."

"There are no longer dragons in this world or any other." He smiled a little at Raef's confusion. "What you and your kind carve in your ships is a memory, nothing more."

"Then this is?"

"A younger, smaller cousin, you could say."

"What do you call it?"

"That is not for you to know." It was said without threat or judgment.

The creature stretched its neck and the rider patted it twice before sliding to the ground. He stepped closer to Raef but said nothing, his eyes roaming over Raef from head to toe.

"Am I as strange to you as you are to me?" Raef asked.

"No one who calls Midgard home has set foot here since the early days, long before your histories begin."

"Where is here?" Raef's voice was soft.

"Alfheim."

Home of the light alfar and only sparsely recounted in the stories from Raef's childhood. He knew little of the place or those who dwelled in it. "And what do you want with me?"

"What makes you think I want something from you?"

"You ride that creature across the sky and descend on me as a falcon does its prey. How could I think otherwise?"

The light in the alf's grey eyes faded. "I must bring you to the others."

"Then I am your prey."

"I bear you no ill will. We do not allow strangers to roam freely."

"Why now? Why not drag me off when I was half dead? I could not have stopped you."

The alf looked at Raef as though this were an odd question. "You needed to live first."

"And if I refuse to go?"

He whistled sharply and the creature rose up, spreading its wings wide. "Would you refuse him?"

The creature's smooth, leathery skin shone under the sun, the color of the ever-changing ocean splashed with burnished gold. The sunset eyes watched Raef and a low sound emanated from deep within the beast's throat.

"If I had a sword, I might."

"But you do not," the alf said, his voice now harsh. He whistled again, a different call this time, and the creature was upon Raef, wings and clawed feet extended. Raef ducked and tried to roll under its belly, but the beast twisted with ease and pinned Raef to the ground with one foot.

"I do not want to hurt you."

Raef kept still, one sharp claw pressed into his throat. "There is more you do not say."

He nodded. "I do not know what will happen to you. But still I must bring you. It is our way." The alf touched the creature's neck and it released Raef in one fluid motion. Raef stood, not removing his eyes from the stranger's.

"What do I call you?"

"For now, nothing." He did not ask Raef's name but instead reached up to his mount's back and pulled himself astride. Raef took his extended hand and climbed up behind him. The creature rolled its shoulders and unfolded its wings in anticipation of flight. Raef, despite his predicament, felt a tremor of excitement. If a command was uttered or the creature urged in any way, it was invisible to Raef. He only knew that one moment the ground was close, the next it was vanishing underneath them as strong wings propelled them toward the sun.

They soared, they dove, they danced, and for Raef it was over all too soon, though they had covered a great distance. They descended into a narrow valley, closed on all sides and guarded by sentinel trees that rose above the rest. It was quiet there and it seemed to Raef a forest full of memory as they dismounted from the creature's back. The beast took to the air at once and soon disappeared from sight.

"This way. We continue on foot from here." The alf led the way and the forest seemed to come alive with every step he took until Raef was certain he heard singing. The voices were soft and wordless and Raef stopped and looked for them among the treetops.

"What is that singing?"

The alf seemed surprised. "Do not your trees sing to welcome you home?"

Raef raised his eyebrows and shook his head. "A sorrowful welcome, is it not?"

"Sorrow? I hear only joy." The alf furrowed his brow for a moment but then motioned for Raef to continue. "I should warn you. Others will not be as friendly as I have been."

Raef wanted to laugh. "Friendly?"

The alf frowned, not understanding Raef's amusement. "We are not comfortable among strangers."

"Even strangers who have done no harm?" Raef asked. The alf offered no response. "Do they know I am here?"

"No." The alf paused and took a moment to turn in a circle, his gaze taking in everything both high and low around them. The singing had stopped. Raef began to speak but he silenced him with a raised hand. "You must go first, now."

Raef hesitated. The alf carried two weapons, a pair of knives. One lay on his hip, the other at the small of his back. Every step Raef took lessened his chances of escape and the absence of the creature made the alf less formidable. He took two steps, as though to pass in front as he had been directed. Neither took their eyes from the other but Raef was quick, grabbing the alf's right wrist, twisting, turning, extracting the second knife and spinning away before he could react.

"You have done me no harm and I do not wish to do you any. But I am leaving."

The alf's eyes showed surprise that Raef had disarmed him, but his features smoothed over quickly. He did not draw the other knife. "You asked if they knew you were here. I lied. They know. There are eyes upon us even at this moment. You will not get far." The planes of his face went still and hard, and the pale eyes were unforgiving.

Raef shrugged. "I must try." He turned and began to retrace his steps. The alf did not follow.

"You may call me Aerath."

Raef paused but did not face him.

"If you go beyond my sight, I cannot help you. The dragon-kin will come for you. It will not be painless."

Raef turned and met Aerath's gaze. "Can you guarantee my safety?"

"No. But I can guarantee your death if you go."

Not a leaf stirred above them and not a sound could be heard, but Raef sensed predatory eyes and knew Aerath spoke the truth. He closed the distance between them and handed the knife back to him, hilt first. The blade was sleek and cool in his palm and he was loath to part with it. It had felt good to hold a weapon again, even for so short a time. Aerath pulled it from his hand and returned it to its home. His eyes held neither trust nor suspicion.

"I have given you my name," he began.

"Not your real one, I think."

Aerath acknowledged this with a nod. "It is not something we share with those outside our blood ties. Only those closest to me in our clan know my true name. But perhaps you will share yours with me."

"Raef." He did not elaborate.

"Then come, Raef, the Guardians await."

"The Guardians?"

Aerath nodded, his face solemn and respectful. "Our guides, our most sacred council."

The moss grew thick under Raef's boots as they walked deeper into the valley, sinking beneath him and then springing up in his wake, silencing his every step. Raef thought of Vakre and his skill at moving through a forest. Vakre would have enjoyed this place. Though the trees were high all around, light still filtered to the earth, illuminating the brilliant green moss that marched up every tree trunk.

Aerath was quiet behind him until he reached out to touch Raef's shoulder. "Stop here." He gestured ahead to where a steep knoll rose up from the forest floor. "Just there, over that rise, they will be waiting. You will see the six Guardians and it will be up to you to know who ranks first among them."

"How will I tell?"

"Use your eyes, your ears, but make up your mind quickly. They will not be patient. Do not look any of them in the eye. When you have decided, make eye contact only with the one you have chosen." Aerath hesitated. "You must not be the first to look away."

"And if I am wrong?"

Aerath shrugged. "Their moods are changeable."

Raef nodded and continued on. Beyond the knoll, was a hall. It was open to the air and the sky and the rain. Dozens of slender tree trunks framed three curving sides and a canopy of leaves arched overhead. Though filled with Aerath's people, all of pale hair and warm, brown skin, it was silent but for the chatter of birds overhead. At the far end, occupying delicate wooden stools, six tall, graceful figures watched Raef, each with eyes so faded, so light that Raef, from his distance, could see no traces of color in them. They watched him, unblinking and impenetrable.

Raef approached, his steps slow but unafraid. The crowd parted before him, whispers in long robes, but he had eyes only for those ahead, his gaze roaming over each, trying to decipher their challenge.

"Midgardian." The speaker was the farthest to Raef's right, male and owner of a clear, ringing voice. "How is it that you have come here?"

"Not by my own will," Raef said. He did not linger on the speaker but looked down the line at each in turn. "I bring no trouble." Not the first to speak, too obvious. And not the most imposing, a male on the left, for the same reason. "I wish only to return to my own land."

"Where there are strangers, trouble follows."

This one was female and she did not bother to hide her displeasure.

"Is it the stranger's fault, or is it of your own making?" Not her, too antagonistic.

"Speak no insult, Midgardian." She spit out her name for him as though it was a vile word. "You should be honored to be among us."

"Should I? You have done me no great courtesy." Raef continued to look between the three who had not yet spoken, focusing on their chins to keep from making eye contact. "You have given me no reason to honor you. I have been brought here against my will and you do not even give me your name."

She rose from her seat and advanced on Raef, restraining herself only when she was within arm's length. Only then could he see flecks of brown in her eyes.

Raef spread his arms out wide. "And now I am threatened and unable to defend myself. Is this the hospitality of Alfheim? The gods will not forgive it."

She came no closer but stalked in a circle around him, gaze narrowed in disdain.

"Why are you here, stranger?" The voice was gentle and came from the other female among the six. Too kind.

"I have said. I do not know." Raef knew he was running out of time. Two males had yet to speak and he looked between them. Their faces were impassive and betrayed nothing. At a loss, Raef said the first thing that came to mind. "Perhaps Odin has sent me." There. A twitch under the eye of the man just left of center. Raef made his choice and locked eyes with him.

"Fool!" The final male, the one Raef had not chosen, broke his silence. "You have chosen ill, Midgardian." Raef did not look away from the eyes he had chosen. "You will pay for your ignorance." He, too, left his seat, but still Raef refused to take the bait.

"Peace, Second. I do not think you frighten him." The pale eyes blinked, slid away to the Second, and then back to Raef. Raef exhaled. "I am First among the Guardians. You have chosen well." The words were meant as praise but Raef did not think it sincere. The First's voice was too calm, too detached. He looked beyond Raef. "Aerath. Come. You have much to answer for." The six Guardians stood and the hall began to empty until only Raef, Aerath, and the Guardians remained. Aerath did not look at Raef as he walked by, head held high, shoulders stiff, and followed the Guardians. Raef began to do the same but the kind one held up a hand.

"Not you," she said. She smiled and though it was not warm, Raef thought she meant well. "You must wait." She, too, turned away.

"Here?" Raef called after them but got no answer and they soon filtered between the trees and out of sight. Raef threw his hands up in the air. "Odin's eye, why will they not just say what they mean and mean what they say. Insufferable and arrogant." Raef raised his voice, half hoping they would hear. "A blind mountain troll would be a better host than you!"

A rush of wings behind him made Raef turn just as a dragon-kin settled to the ground. It stretched out its neck and sniffed at him, then cocked its head to one side and stared.

"What did you do wrong to get the job of watching me?" Raef asked.

The narrow tongue flicked out once, twice, three times and then the creature's whole body shivered, a great ripple under the smoke-colored skin streaked with silver and shades of twilight, as it let out a loud breath. Though different in color from the one Aerath rode, this dragon-kin had the same sunset eyes and they looked at Raef with something he could only define as expectation.

"Should I run just to give you something to do?" Raef settled on the mossy earth instead, legs crossed. "I should have when I had the chance."

The daylight was getting old and Raef had not eaten since his three skinny rabbits that morning. When his stomach grumbled to remind him of this, the dragon-kin's tongue flicked again and it inched closer to Raef, peering at his belly now.

"Do I sound good enough to eat?" Raef plucked a tuft of moss from the earth and held it to his nose. It smelled of spring and he placed it on his tongue. Earthy, green, bright. He rolled it around, then chewed and swallowed. It nearly stuck in his throat. Despite that, Raef made himself eat another, then another, for he did not know when he would eat again. All the while, the dragon-kin watched, its eyes following Raef's fingers from earth to mouth. "I once had a dog like you," he said. Raef tore a larger chunk from the dirt and tossed it at the dragon-kin. The beast caught it with ease but its nostrils flared and it flung the moss, wet with saliva, from its mouth. "Yes, well, you are free to come and go as you wish. You probably have a fine goat waiting for you somewhere. I cannot be so demanding."

They stared at each other for a moment and then Raef, not sure if it was recklessness or boredom that propelled him, got to his feet. The dragon-kin sat up taller at this movement but did nothing else as Raef closed the short distance between them until he could feel the dragon-kin's breath on his chest. This one was smaller, he realized, than the one he had ridden, but he knew the creature could overwhelm him in an instant if it chose. The muscles beneath the skin were lean and strong, the teeth and talons just as sharp and threatening.

"My dog enjoyed a good scratch behind the ears." Raef held a hand close to the dragon-kin's snout. The beast leaned away, the sunset eyes wary, but Raef held his ground. "Would you like the same?" Neither moved. Birds flew overhead, the shadows shifted, but at last the dragon-kin, without moving any other part of its body, extended its neck just enough to come within an arm ring's breadth of Raef's hand. Raef felt it inhale, its eyes never leaving his, and then it snorted the breath out and retreated from Raef until the original distance between them was restored. The eyes narrowed and the talons dug into the mossy earth. Raef kept his tone even. "Do I smell that terrible?"

Raef broke eye contact, then, and resumed his seat on the ground. His fingers found a small twig and he began to strip the bark from it until it was smooth and bare to his touch. He stretched out on the moss, his eyes on the sky, and remained that way until

Aerath's face came between him and the blue. Though Raef knew him only a little, he sensed trouble in that face.

"They will speak with you now."

Raef got to his feet. "Are you coming with me?"

Aerath shook his head, his lips tight. "No." He gestured beyond Raef. "There." Raef looked to where he pointed. The Guardian who had spoken kindly waited for him at the edge of the hall. When Raef turned back to Aerath, he was gone. The smoke-colored dragon-kin watched him until he was at the Guardian's side, then it took to the skies.

The Guardian was not very old, Raef realized as he came to stand in front of her. Thin lines radiated from the corners of her eyes, but they were the only obvious sign of age that Raef could see. She did not speak to him, but led him away from the hall. The sound of running water came to Raef's ears and soon they passed by a rocky stream. Raef paused and knelt to drink, but the Guardian grabbed his arm before he could dip his cupped hand into the water.

"You must not defile these waters."

"Defile. Am I such filth as that?" Raef felt anger build within him but forced it away. He extracted his arm with as little force as possible. "I have traveled far this day and I am thirsty." He tried to keep his voice polite.

The Guardian was silent for a moment and then seemed to make up her mind. She plucked a large leaf from a nearby bush and caught water in its deep well. Raef took it from her, spilled most, and tipped the rest up into his mouth. Though he might have asked for more, she was already on the move. For a moment, he considered dipping the leaf in again himself, but he still possessed some measure of restraint and knew his survival and any chance he had at returning to Midgard might depend upon following their rules. Until it suited him better not to.

The remaining Guardians waited for him in a clearing. They stood straight and tall, hands crossed in front of them, long robes brushing the tips of the tiny white flowers that blanketed the earth in that place. Three standing stones towered above them, nearly three times the height of the tallest. They were smooth and well-worn with age and any inscription they might have carried was lost to time.

The Guardians were silent at Raef's approach and his guide joined them by the pillars. As the silence wore on, Raef ventured to speak.

"My name is Raef Skallagrim and I am a lord in the realm of men."

"You give your name freely." The First Guardian spoke quietly.

"Where I come from, we share such things as a gesture of good will. Even in the hall of my most hated enemy, I would be granted the courtesy of food and drink if I came there in so desperate a state as you see me now." This was a stretched truth. Raef could think of many halls where the name Skallagrim was loathed, the product of generations of dislike between two families.

"Your people are not strangers to me. I have great knowledge of Midgard." The First seemed to hesitate. "You will have food and drink when we have finished." He said nothing more.

"Finished with what? What is it that you want?" Raef was losing his patience and he was glad of the sharp pain in his ribs that sprang up when he raised his voice. The pain might serve to keep his temper in check.

"The truth, Midgardian. Long ages have passed since one of your kind came to Alfheim. We wish to know how you have done so."

"I have given you the truth. I do not know. I was attacked. When I awoke, I was in sight of your shore and my ship made landfall."

"Then the Allfather did not send you?" There was a hint of relief in the First's voice.

It was a question Raef had asked himself more than once. "I do not know."

"You spoke his name before. Do all Midgardians speak of him with such familiarity?"

Raef was surprised by this line of questioning. "I thought you knew my people well."

The First's eyes narrowed and Raef could see his pulse quicken in his throat. "Do not speak of that which you know nothing."

Now Raef let the anger flare. "Now you accuse me of being ignorant of my own people. Or is it Odin One-Eye you speak of? Why do you fear him so?"

"Enough." The bellicose female Guardian stepped between them. "I have had enough of your insults. Speak again in that manner and they will be your final words."

"I only give in kind what is given to me."

She lunged at him, her hands reaching for his throat. Raef stepped to the side, took hold of her forearm, and pulled. Off balance, the Guardian lurched sideways toward him. Raef snaked an arm around her neck and pulled her close, keeping her between him and the others, who were just beginning to react to the violence. The Guardian gasped for air, but Raef gave her little. The others demanded her release but seemed uncertain of what action to take. At last, two of the male Guardians advanced on him and Raef pushed her to the ground to meet their attack.

Though one was powerfully built, neither was a trained warrior. Their swings were clumsy and ill-timed. Raef evaded them with little effort and circled to keep them off his right shoulder. The taller one tried to move behind Raef and was rewarded with a kick to his knee. He buckled to the ground. The other, his eyes on his fallen companion, dropped his guard, and Raef soon had him on his knees.

Raef, his breath coming faster now, stood to face the rest. "I am not your enemy, but I will defend myself. I have done nothing to deserve this." The commotion had drawn onlookers and then Raef saw the now-familiar shadows of four dragon-kin descend on the clearing. Riders jumped from their backs, all armed with long blades, and the creatures swooped low over Raef's head.

Raef, his eyes on their sharp swords, did not resist the riders, knowing his life would end if he did. Using the hilts of their swords rather than the blades, the warriors descended on him. The first blow struck his temple. Raef grit his teeth and did not cry out. The third found his broken ribs and the pain darkened Raef's vision. The fifth, aimed at the back of his knee, brought him to the ground. When at last the beating stopped, Raef's world was reduced to his own heartbeat and the blood he could taste on his lips.

He was dragged, that much he knew, but only a short distance. Words were spoken but Raef could not focus enough to understand them. Raef felt a knife put to his cheek and a fresh trickle of blood to the corner of his mouth told him it had made a mark, but so complete was his pain, he did not feel it. More words, angry ones this time, and then he was pulled in a different direction, his arm wrenched so hard it nearly released from the socket.

The ground slid underneath Raef, moss and mushrooms, dirt and tiny white flowers, then he was hoisted up and slung over a shoulder. Their pace quickened, each bouncing step jolting his throbbing ribs. More than once he felt himself slip into the dream world, but each time he pulled himself back from the brink, determined to stay conscious, though why he did not know.

The sun, descending to the horizon, cast long shadows ahead of whoever carried Raef, fleet footed giants they seemed, their strides smooth and swift. On and on they went, tireless and surefooted, until the sun began to drip below the horizon. Only then, in the first moments of twilight, did they halt. Raef was deposited on the ground, his hand left to trail in flowing water. In the gathering dark,

Raef heard voices, soft whispers, some urgent, others calm, and then a cool, wet cloth was pressed to his forehead and another began to clean the cut on his cheek and the blood from his nose. Raef, unable to open his eyes completely, could only see that the figures leaning over him were hooded, their features swallowed as much by Raef's exhausted mind as by darkness. Fingers prodded the swollen lump at his temple and a pair of hands roaming over his chest discovered the true source of pain and elicited Raef's first reaction.

Raef thrust the hands away and squirmed on the ground, trying to shield his ribs from further examination. Strong hands gripped his wrists and, though he struggled, soon pressed him against the ground. The hands probed no more but the cloth was returned to his forehead, this time smelling of flowers that bloomed under a summer's moon. Sweet and rich, the odor seeped into him, stilling his mind, filling him with drowsiness. He knew that scent and it seemed important that he remember its name, but it slipped away from him, lost to the clutches of scented sleep.

# FIVE

THE TREES WERE singing again. Raef opened his eyes to see green leaves and golden light above him. He lay on the ground, surrounded by purple flowers, but he had been moved in his sleep. His hand no longer rested in the gentle stream though the sound of water was still close. Instead, he was nestled between two protruding roots of a towering tree and his stained clothes had been exchanged for fresh linen, a loose shirt with a deep, pointed neckline and pants dyed to a dark green and tucked into his battered boots. His silver arm rings still curled around his forearms, the wolf heads gleaming softly in the light. Raef's pain was dulled, but every part of him ached. Still, he pushed himself up onto one arm, anxious to see his surroundings.

He was not alone. A female figure sat on a tree stump across the small clearing. The purple flowers were thick on the ground between them. If she noticed Raef's movement, she did not show it, keeping her eyes on the blade she was sharpening. Only when Raef spoke did she look up.

"Is that the weapon I am to be executed with?" Raef did not try to hide the bitterness in his voice. To his surprise, the stranger laughed. The sound was bright and strong and true.

"It is not your blood I wish to spill with this sword. It is intended for other purposes." She sheathed the blade and rose from the stump. Her skin was darker than Aerath's, rich and warm.

"What fate can I expect, then?"

"Only the Norns know the answer to that." The stranger walked toward Raef and he saw faded blue in her eyes. "Though perhaps I have played some part in it." Her gaze scanned over Raef's battered body. "I have tried to save your life."

Raef frowned. "What do you mean?"

The stranger squatted down to Raef's level. Her eyes were hard but when she smiled again, her eyes smiled, too. "I will answer your questions. But first we must look to your recovery." Turning her head, she whistled and two smaller figures, young alfar, Raef realized, emerged from beyond the clearing carrying wooden bowls filled with food. These they set before Raef and then filled an empty one with water from the stream. Raef glanced at his host and then started with the warm, flat bread, tearing off large chunks and washing them down with gulps of water. The small eggs soon followed, along with the plums and berries, and at last Raef cleaned the whole fish from its bones.

When he had drained the last of the water from the bowl, the stranger filled it again, then sat down cross-legged close to Raef. She placed the bowl between them.

"I am called Finnoul."

Raef had not expected to be given a name so readily.

"I have heard you are called Raef."

Raef nodded.

"My people have done you grievous injury, Raef, but I do not ask you to forgive them. I wish now that we had come for you sooner."

"What do you mean, come for me?"

"We watched Aerath bring you to the hall of the Guardians but did not intervene."

"And why would you intervene? What am I to you?"

Finnoul took a deep breath. "I and those who follow me seek to undermine the Guardians, to remove the yoke they have chained us with."

"A rebellion."

Finnoul nodded. "The Guardians have ruled Alfheim since light first shone on this soil. They were wise, once, strong, too, but benevolent and just. Leaders we could be proud of. But that changed, long before my lifetime. They are as you have seen them. Petty, arrogant, suspicious, fearful, and quick to anger. My people, ancestors of those you see today, swallowed this change as you would water, without any realization of what they did, until our traditions twisted into a sullied version of what we once knew and we became a shadow of ourselves." Finnoul paused and took a drink from the bowl. "A few families held onto the truth, the memories, and passed down dreams of the past to their children. Thus was my rebellion born."

"No word of discord in Alfheim has spread to us."

"Nor would it. In a history as long as ours, we are but a tiny moment, a speck of dust on the wind. We are a child. But we are growing. For now, though, the Guardians do not fear us. They hardly acknowledge our existence. But they do not know our true numbers, they do not understand our conviction." Finnoul looked at Raef for a long moment. "But enough of that. It is time we took greater care of your wounds. Can you stand?"

"Yes." With Finnoul's arm keeping him steady, Raef got to his feet and took a deep breath.

"We have a skilled healer. Come."

Though the beating had taken its toll, Raef felt better with each step. They passed out of the clearing, crushing purple blossoms beneath their feet, and Finnoul led him along the small stream, taking care to steer him clear of slick rocks and fallen branches. In time, the forest fell away and the land opened into a wide meadow in full bloom. Flowers of every hue spread out in front of Raef. Deep, rich reds, translucent yellows on slender green stalks, pinks with wide petals streaked with white, tiny blues that pointed at the ground rather than turn their faces to the sun. And the scents. Sweet like honey, a hint of spice, and underneath it all, dark, good earth. Beyond the field of flowers, the forest marched on and the land began to rise, shaping into hills and, in the distance, mountains.

A single tree, tall and ancient, rose up in the meadow, its branches sprawling out from a wide, sturdy trunk, and it was there that Finnoul led him. Vines creeping up the bark concealed much of the trunk and Raef began to ask if the healer was meeting them there when Finnoul reached out and pushed the vines aside, revealing a narrow opening in the wood. Finnoul slipped into the crevice in the trunk and pulled Raef in after her. So thick was the tree that they could both fit with ease, and, as Raef's eyes adjusted to the dim light, he saw that the ground and roots gave way to a spiral staircase that had been carved out of the interior, descending deep into the ground. Faint, flickering light reached up from the darkness below.

Raef peered over the edge. "You live underground?"

"This is our haven, should the Guardians come looking. But you will see that it is more than a hole in the ground."

Finnoul spoke true. The staircase dropped them onto a stone ledge. Beyond and below, a great cavern opened up, so large, Raef could not fathom how far it spread. Though torchlight illuminated some, the dark recesses were shrouded from sight. The ceiling was covered with sharp protrusions of stone that hung down, some fat and thick, others narrow and impossibly long. They reflected the firelight, a glittering roof to this underground world. Finnoul followed Raef's gaze.

"Our own starry night." Finnoul pointed far to the left. Between the pillars of stone that stretched from the ground to the ceiling, Raef could make out a small lake. "Fresh water. And room enough to house any who wish to join us." They descended again, much farther this time, on a narrow staircase hewn from the cave's wall. Raef moved slowly, careful not to antagonize his ribs. When he did reach the bottom, the enormity of the cavern was even more astonishing. It was largely empty. A few figures moved between light and shadow but in greater numbers were the crates, barrels, and sacks in neat stacks and piles.

"Supplies. Gathered over time and with much sacrifice." Finnoul turned and called out. "Ylloria. Our guest is here."

Another female approached Raef. She did not once look in his eyes, but instead assessed every part of him that was swollen, bruised, and bloody. "I could have done much more last night." Only then did she meet his gaze. "You should not have resisted."

"You should not have prodded so hard."

Finnoul laughed but Ylloria did not seem amused. She turned and retreated the way she had come. Raef looked to Finnoul, who, still grinning, motioned for him to follow. "Only once have I seen Ylloria smile. But she does good work."

Ylloria settled Raef on a blanket on the cavern floor. He stretched out and soon her cool hands went to work. There was no tenderness, only skill, as she placed a warm compress on the bump on his temple, rubbed the juice of a crushed plant on the slice on his cheek, and smoothed a waxy substance on the biggest, blackest bruises on his torso. She left the broken rib bones for last.

"These are not new," Ylloria said. She kept her touch light but seemed to glean all the information she needed from just that.

"No. A battle."

"How long ago?"

"It is hard to say." Raef thought for a moment. "I have known the sun to rise twenty-two times since the battle ended. But of my travel here, I have no memory. It must have taken time."

Ylloria accepted this without comment. "The healing process

has been interrupted. It will take longer now. But I can give you something to help the strengthen the bones." Ylloria began to prepare something in a small pot over her fire. Of the many ingredients, Raef recognized only two but Ylloria was intent on her work and he did not ask of the rest. The healer did not speak again until steam rose from the contents. "I will give you some now, but it will be stronger by nightfall. Return to me then." She dipped a cup into the liquid and handed it to Raef. It smelled of a forest after a summer rain. Raef blew on it to dull the heat and then emptied the cup in two swallows. It was both sweet and bitter, but not unpleasant. Raef thanked her and then he and Finnoul made their way out of the cavern and back to the world above.

"Does she stay down there always?" Raef blinked in the sunlight after emerging out of the tree. The flowers around him waved in the gentle breeze.

"Ylloria? No, though she enjoys the peace and quiet of the earth. She says it is a good place for healing and spends more time below than the rest of us. I would rather the cavern remain our last refuge than our home. We belong in the light."

"Where do you live, then?"

Finnoul smiled. "I will show you." She whistled and a dragon-kin swooped out of the sky a moment later. This one was the largest Raef had seen yet and its skin was a deep orange.

"You have dragon-kin as well?"

Finnoul's brow furrowed in confusion. "Of course."

"I thought the Guardians might keep them from you."

"It would not be wise for them to try. The bond between dragon-kin and rider is strong and not easily broken." Finnoul climbed on to the beast's back and helped Raef up. "Have you flown before?"

"Once, with Aerath."

"Good. But this will not be the same."

The power of the dragon-kin's wings as they lifted from the

ground was astonishing and Raef's heart had beaten only twice before they were above the tree. Rather than rise higher, they skimmed just above the highest branches, picking up speed with every pulsing beat of the wings. And then the meadow was gone and the forest rushed by beneath them, followed by hills, green at first, then stony and unlike any Raef had ever seen. The rocky surfaces were striped with layers of color as varied as the flowers in the meadow. In Vannheim, streaks of dull reds and browns and even a bit of green were common enough, minerals built into the rock, but here it was as though countless rainbows had come to rest after a spring storm and Raef stared in wonder.

But then the painted hills were gone, replaced by dark, grim granite peaks that pushed upward to dizzying heights and it was into this realm of stone that the dragon-kin flew, sweeping over slabs of black rock, twisting around jutting, scraping spirals that threatened to knock them from the sky, diving and darting, never straying far from the slopes of the mountains. Death, it seemed to Raef, was but a hair's breadth away, a tiny mistake would send him tumbling to the unforgiving stone. But it was a thrill beyond anything Raef had ever experienced and he was grinning when the dragon-kin finally slowed its pace.

They had climbed high, though the summits were still far above, and the dragon-kin landed on a wide ledge that curved out over a deep ravine filled with roaring water. Finnoul leaped to the ground and spread her arms wide. Her joy at such a place was clear. "My home." A hall clung to the mountainside, much of it carved from rock and larger than Raef could have imagined for something perched so high. Though hewn from rough stone, it was all curves and delicate arches, and the beaming sunlight made it beautiful. "This place is old and was nearly forgotten to us. I have made it mine."

Raef turned to look out on the land below. A gentle breeze

caressed the ledge and the air was quiet, undisturbed by voices or the chatter of birds. So exposed, it would be a violent place in a storm. Beating winds, lashing rains, bolts of lightning. And the thunder would roll across the stone and make it tremble. But Raef suspected that Finnoul would cherish her home even in such weather. It was a home unlike any other.

"Do others live so high?"

"A few. Most of my people keep to the trees below."

"Do the Guardians know where to find you and yours?"

"They do not see the need to look. Not yet."

"What of Aerath?" It was a question Raef had wanted to ask for some time.

Finnoul sighed. "Aerath has yet to make his choice." Raef could hear that the name was unfamiliar on her tongue, that she would have called him by a name closer to her heart, his true name, were it not for Raef's presence.

"But you have asked him to join you?"

"Yes. He is at war with himself. I think he sees the truth but does not wish to confront it." Finnoul took her gaze from the valleys below and looked at Raef. "His father was a Guardian." She looked away again and Raef heard sadness creep into her voice. "I must give him time."

"You care for him."

Finnoul turned sharply, her pale eyes brittle with the hardness Raef had seen in the eyes of so many of her kind. Though she had shown herself to be different, he could not forget that Finnoul, at her core, was one of them. Finnoul blinked and the hardness fled. "I do. I would share this place with him, if he would let me." She turned away from the overlook. "Come, let me show you my home. It is yours while you are our guest."

Raef did not follow Finnoul but called after her. "How long?"

Finnoul turned, a question in her eyes.

"How long am I to be a guest?" Raef had seen nothing but hospitality from Finnoul, but he did not know the alf's intent. What seemed like kindness could mask hidden motives. Raef was inclined to trust Finnoul, but there had been no talk of returning to Midgard.

"So we have come to that." Finnoul came to stand in front of Raef. "Have I not saved your life?"

"Perhaps." It was not a kind answer, but it was the truth.

"I could have you on your knees before the Guardians in but a moment. The flight would not take long."

"You could. But you will not."

Finnoul was silent for some time. "I can show you how to cross the boundary. I can help you journey back to Midgard."

"I must earn it."

Finnoul acknowledged this with a small nod. "I am bound to my cause, Raef. Surely you would not blame me for using any means to further it."

"I would do the same. But I do not see what use I am to you."

"You say you do not know how or why you came to Alfheim. I wonder if there is a reason you landed on our shores, if you have some part to play."

"What do you mean?"

Finnoul seemed about to speak, but stopped herself. Instead, she gestured for Raef to follow her and they entered the mountain hall.

It should have been dark and bleak in the hall of stone. The door opened into a room that soared up into the mountain. Beams of light shone down from above, bringing warmth to the grey walls, and the pillars were covered with small pieces of colored glass that reflected onto the polished floor, a vibrant mosaic in celebration of light. Finnoul did not linger in the hall of stone and glass, but continued on, passing through one of six arched doorways that led out of the hall. The doorway took them up and they climbed a steep staircase that wound around in wide spirals until it opened up onto a terrace. Finnoul would have carried on, but Raef hesitated, his bruised body worn from the many steps. He put one hand to the stone and the other to his ribs.

"You are in pain. Forgive me. I should return you to Ylloria."

Raef took a deep breath. "No. She said after nightfall."

"Very well." Finnoul chose another door and they were climbing again, this time in tight circles. Light was scarce and the walls pressed in close. Raef was glad, for his head was swimming and the lump on his temple pulsed with every step. He stayed close to the inner wall and kept his eyes on each step as he passed it by. He did not want to look up and see how far they had to go.

When at last they emerged into the light, Raef was dizzy and sweat trickled into his eyes and down his nose. He wiped it away with his arm but the motion threw him off balance and he swayed into Finnoul. The alf caught him with a firm grip under Raef's arms.

"Steady." Finnoul lowered Raef to the stone floor, stretching him out. Raef kept still, his eyes closed until the pounding in his head retreated. When he opened them, the room came into focus. Above him, a domed ceiling was punctured by a single round hole. A shaft of light hit the floor two steps away from Raef, its width the height of a man. It was the only source of light and the rest of the round room was poorly illuminated. The only entrance to the room was the door they had come through. Raef raised himself up on one elbow.

"What is this place?"

"I have asked myself that many times." Finnoul offered Raef a hand and helped him back to his feet. "Look closely at the walls."

As Raef's eyes adjusted, he began to see shapes and colors, all faded by time. Figures dressed for battle, dragon-kin diving from the sky, other creatures Raef did not recognize. Raef's gaze followed the drawings upward and saw they stretched from the floor up to the hole in the dome.

"What are they?"

"Some scenes are known to me, pieces of our history. Others, I am not so sure of."

Raef caught sight of a figure riding an eight-legged horse. He carried a mighty spear and was missing an eye. "Odin." Raef stretched out his fingers until they grazed the stone.

"All the gods are depicted in some form." Finnoul let Raef wander around the walls for some time. Raef saw images of Thor crushing giants with his mighty hammer, Mjölnir, of Odin hanging himself on the gnarled branches of Yggdrasil, the world ash tree, of Tyr, lord of battle, offering his hand to Fenrir's teeth, of Freyja riding her boar across a battlefield strewn with corpses, of Frigg veiled on her tall throne. And of the Valkyries riding across a night sky, sparks flying from the hooves of their horses. His gaze lingered on the nine fierce faces, remembering their unrelenting fury in battle and the cold eyes that had stared into his. Finnoul broke into his memory. "There is one scene I wish to show you most of all."

Raef joined her in front of a battle scene. Half the figures were small and hard to make out, but their opponents were much larger. "Giants."

"Yes. But it is not just my people who oppose them." She pointed to a group of warriors riding horses and wielding spears.

"Who are they?"

"They are men, Raef. And they fight alongside my people."

"How can you be sure?"

"There are no horses in Alfheim. Nor have there ever been. And we do not fight with spears. This is a weapon of Midgard." Finnoul turned to look at Raef. "We were allies, once."

"And you think we shall be again. That I have been sent here to aid your rebellion. What if I was sent here to end it?" Raef turned away. "The drawing means nothing. Do not pin your hopes on it. Or me."

Finnoul did not seem dispirited. "No Midgardian has set foot on our lands in thousands of years. Your presence here at this time cannot be void of meaning."

Raef snapped. "It can." His voice rang off the stone walls. "I have my own war to fight and it is not this one. I have to find a way home."

Finnoul's face stiffened and her chin rose. The eyes that had been so open and honest closed off. She could have taken a place beside the Guardians and Raef would not have questioned it. "Then go."

SIX

THE DESCENT WAS less painful to Raef than the ascent, but he would have welcomed the pain in exchange for the guilt that owned his mind. He had spoken the truth to Finnoul. The rebellion would live or die with or without him and Raef had a responsibility to return home, to avenge his father. How he would do so without Finnoul's aid, Raef could not fathom, but he would not abandon Vannheim and he would not renounce the vow he had made in sight of the gods. The alf was mistaken and clung to something Raef could not give her. And yet Finnoul had been a friend when it would have been easier to turn her back.

The main hall was as they had left it but light had bloomed in one of the other passageways. Fearing the Guardians had discovered Finnoul's hidden home and had sent someone to kill the rebel leader, Raef ventured into the passage. The light was faint and flickered as a fire would, but it did not grow more distant. The tunnel was straight as an arrow and Raef, pausing every few steps to listen, felt as though he were headed into the heart of the mountain.

The air grew warmer the further Raef went. It was not the dry heat of a fire, but the damp warmth of steaming water heated for a bath. Here and there a trickle of water ran down the wall, staining the stone. At last the source of the light was revealed. A single torch was set deep into a recess in the wall. It was all but spent but no end to the tunnel was in sight. Raef took the torch and continued on, the floor of the tunnel now sloping downward beneath his feet. The descent became steeper and then at last the tunnel came to an end.

The room was small and roughly hewn from the mountain. Every other surface Raef had encountered had been smooth, but these walls were ragged and unpolished. In the dim light of the torch, the room at first appeared to be empty, but then Raef looked up.

Suspended above him, seemingly floating in the air, was a sword. The blade was dark in color, the steel folded time after time into deep ribbons, and its shape was different from the curved blades Raef had seen the alfar warriors carry. The hilt shone in the feeble torchlight, a glimmer of the moon in darkness.

Raef reached up until his fingers curled around the hilt, and it was then he saw the sword was cradled by four silken threads, visible only from the right vantage point. The delicate strands bore the sword's weight with ease. Raef could not begin to guess what they were made of. Raef extracted the sword from its sling and tested the edge. Sharp. Deadly. It was lighter than swords he had trained with, and the balance different.

The torch gutted out when Raef was only a few steps into the tunnel. He cast it aside and found his way easily enough in the dark. When he emerged, clouds had covered the sun and the colors in the main hall had dimmed. Finnoul stood with her back to Raef, gazing out a window on the far side of the hall. She turned at the sound of Raef's footsteps and did not at first notice the sword held at Raef's side.

"I thought perhaps you would need a way off the mountain," Finnoul said. Her voice was pleasant but less lively than before and she did not smile. "Where were you?" Raef held up the sword and let it be his answer. Finnoul's eyes widened and she closed the distance between them with quick steps. She stretched out her hands as though to take it, but then withdrew them. Her eyes did what she did not permit her fingers and roamed over the elegant blade.

"Take it," Raef said.

Finnoul shook her head. "You found it."

"In your home."

"A home I have borrowed from the clutches of time. I am not its master. How did you find this?"

"I followed a light." Raef pointed to the doorway he had taken. "Down there."

"A light where none should be." Finnoul's brow furrowed. "You saw no one?"

Raef shook his head.

"A gift, then, from the ancients of Alfheim and perhaps from Freyr. I have never seen its like. Daegon will have a sheath for it. Come, we will return to the forest."

Wind whistled across the ledge outside the hall, heralding a coming storm. Dark clouds swirled above and already the stone was spattered with drops of rain. The dragon-kin appeared at once and Raef had barely found his balance on its back when it pushed off, tucked its wings, and dove. They skimmed the sheer face of the mountain, taking a straighter course than they had on the way up. Rain pelted Raef from above, fat drops that soon soaked his hair. The air had cooled and Raef felt his skin prickle under his light shirt as they rushed through the sky.

The ground loomed ahead and the dragon-kin spread its wings wide just in time, halting their free fall. They soared above the trees for a moment, as lightning split the sky and the first roll of thunder crashed through the clouds, but before they could drop in beneath the trees, a second dragon-kin, then a third, rose up to meet them.

"Finnoul!" The rider's voice was nearly lost to the wind. "They have taken Annun and Thannor."

Finnoul's dragon-kin veered to the right so hard that Raef nearly lost his seat. Whatever speed the creature had shown, it was nothing compared to how they raced over the treetops. The world was a blur around Raef.

"I thought you said the Guardians did not feel threatened by you," Raef shouted into the wind.

"They do not. But not all who follow them are so blind." Finnoul said nothing more and it seemed to Raef the dragon-kin was urged to even greater speed. Raef looked over his shoulder and saw four winged shapes following them. The dense trees gave way beneath them to open land and a narrow lake. The dragon-kin dropped down close to the lake's surface, so close Raef felt he could touch the water, then spiraled upward as they reached the far shore where a cliff reared up out of the water.

"How do you know where to go?"

"There is only one place he would bring them."

The scream came from above, winged fury plummeting to meet them. Finnoul's orange dragon-kin twisted and launched itself up to meet the attacker, letting forth a scream of its own. Raef clung on but the impact of the two beasts colliding was too much and suddenly there was nothing but air beneath him. He began to fall back to the earth, the dark sword somehow still in his grasp but useless to him now. Above him, the dragon-kin were locked in battle and the storm raged. Raef closed his eyes and waited for the ground to swallow him, but a dragon-kin swooped in and grabbed his foot. Dangling now, Raef was lowered to the top of the lakeside cliff. The dragon-kin released him and Raef dropped to the stone, contorting his body just in time to avoid landing on his head. Above him, the sky battle continued as Finnoul's companions engaged other dragon-kin.

"Midgardian!" The voice pulled Raef's gaze from the sky and he whirled around to see three alfar advancing on him. Behind them, two figures were on the ground, bound and still. Raef brought the dark sword up and began to circle to his right. "Would you throw your life away for these traitors?" The closest alf sneered and drew his sword.

Raef did not respond but continued to mirror their movement.

"They deserve death," said another. "Since the beginning of days, traitors have been thrown from this cliff. You will not deny us our right."

"What has Finnoul promised you, Midgardian? Is it worth your life?"

At last Raef spoke. "It is."

The first alf came from Raef's left in a smooth, fluid attack. The strange sword sang in the air as Raef met the advance, but the unfamiliar weight and shape propelled the blade ahead of what should have been well-timed footwork. The blades glanced off each other and only a desperate dodge kept Raef from losing an ear. He recovered just in time to duck under the second alf's slicing sword and, though his momentum carried him behind his opponent, he lashed out and was rewarded with a cry of anger and pain.

The third attack was fast and furious and drove Raef backward toward the edge of the cliff. His opponent fought with precision, his face expressionless. Every attempt Raef made to change his direction was met with vicious defiance until at last he was but steps away from falling into the air.

The knife flew so close to Raef's ear he could feel it and at last he had a reprieve. The alf staggered back, the knife buried up to the hilt in his chest, and Raef did not hesitate. Unimpeded, the dark sword found a home in the alf's belly and Raef ripped through the flesh until the body fell away, nearly severed in two.

Raef looked around and saw the two remaining warriors were close to death. One choked on his own blood as it poured out around the knife in his throat. The other bled violently from the wound Raef had given him, a wound Raef knew he would not survive. Above him, a dragon-kin roared in triumph and then landed on the cliff top. The rider jumped to the ground, a pair of knives ready to finish the work he had started. Only when he was certain his victims were dead did he look at Raef.

"You do not belong here." Aerath was soaked through, his pale, blue-streaked hair dark with rainwater. "They would have killed you."

"I am grateful for the life you have saved."

Aerath seemed not to hear, his gaze now on the sky. Only two dragon-kin and their riders remained, higher now than they were before. Raef could not tell if Finnoul was one of them but the look on Aerath's face said she was. He went to mount his creature again, but without warning the beasts broke apart and one began to tumble to the earth, one wing madly trying to slow its fall, the other weak, feeble, and only half-extended. As it plummeted and then disappeared behind a rise, Raef saw that the wounded dragon-kin was not orange, that Finnoul still flew.

The alf was not unscathed, though. She brought her dragon-kin to a gentler landing than her opponent, but she bled from a gash on her arm and the orange beast was riddled with slashes. Finnoul did not speak, but raced across the cliff top and over the rise the injured dragon-kin had fallen behind. She stopped at the top and did not go farther. Aerath knelt to examine the dragon-kin's wounds but he stood at Finnoul's return. She bent over the bound captives, whose chests rose and fell in gentle breaths, oblivious to the storm around them.

"Gone," Finnoul said.

"He survived that fall?" Raef found that hard to believe.

"The dragon-kin, no. But Lorcan is gone."

"Who is Lorcan?"

Finnoul's mouth tightened. "You would call him a captain. He fights for the Guardians."

Aerath broke in. "He fights as he should. As is right."

Finnoul did not look at Aerath but Raef saw her jaw harden. "He sees what the Guardians will not. He understands as few do what I and those who follow me have undertaken."

"You have undertaken death, Finnoul," Aerath said. "The Guardians have ruled for uncounted years and they must continue to do so."

Finnoul met Aerath's glare at last and Raef saw pain in her eyes. "Then why are you here, Aerath? Why did you save him?" She glanced at Raef.

"Your folly is not his. He has no place in your rebellion."

Aerath's words echoed his own but they sounded wrong to Raef's ears. Raef looked at Finnoul. "I do not know what strength I can give you, but I know what it is to fight against unwanted rule. I will help you if I can."

Finnoul's shout was joyous and her grin wide. Aerath looked away as Finnoul clasped Raef's forearm.

"You have said nothing of my promise to you," Finnoul said.

"My words would mean little if I gave them for a price."

"Nonetheless, I will show you the way home." Finnoul knelt again before the unconscious alfar. "We need to get them to safety. Take Thannor." She hoisted one over her shoulder but before Raef could follow with the other, Aerath stepped in front of him.

"I cannot promise that I will help you a second time." The rain had eased up and the clouds were thinning, letting grey light filter through and reach Aerath's face.

"I know."

"Then you put your life in her hands?"

"My life is in my own hands, Aerath. But I believe she is right."

"She seeks to destroy everything we know."

"She seeks freedom. And I know you see it. As you see the way she looks at you." Aerath's cheeks flushed with color and he turned away. Raef walked to the orange dragon-kin, who looked ready to fly once more despite the damage it had sustained. Finnoul waited on its back, Annun resting in front of her. "Is it safe to travel with them like this?"

Finnoul grinned. "We are capable of flying slowly when we must."

The journey to the underground cavern was peaceful and uninterrupted. As the dragon-kin floated through the damp air, Raef watched the sky change around them, a burst of purple and orange revealed behind the wake of the storm. Underground, Ylloria's medicine burned his tongue but the heat was welcome after the chill of the storm. Food was passed and Finnoul found Raef a pair of blankets. They ate in silence, each absorbed in his own thoughts, until Raef's eyelids grew heavy and he felt the strong pull of sleep. He drifted off to the sound of water dripping and under the light of the stone stars twinkling above.

# SEVEN

"THERE."

Raef squinted into the blue sky and dazzling sun, try-ing to pick out which dragon-kin Finnoul had in mind. "The red one?"

"Yes. He is strong-willed. Fierce." Finnoul grinned. "And dangerous."

"And what must I do?"

"Ride him," Finnoul said, as though it were a simple task.

Raef watched the beasts, a dozen or more, circle above, calling to each other and catching the wind beneath their wings.

Finnoul pointed south. "See that ridge? They like to catch the last rays of sun up there before twilight. We will wait for them there."

The rocks were warm to the touch when Raef sat down to wait for the dragon-kin to land on the ridge. They came quietly, their raucous cavorting in the air now subdued. One by one they stretched out, wings spread wide to soak in every last drop of sun-shine. Raef waited near the trees with Finnoul, who had sent her orange beast away.

"Approach them slowly. They already know you are here but forceful movement will spark their anger." Finnoul looked at the red one, draped across the rocks and seemingly asleep. "He will watch you and he will let you get close. Only when you touch him will he show his strength. Then you must be quick."

"You speak as though you have seen this before."

"I have seen others try and fail."

"Is there not a better quarry? One less likely to bite my head off?"

Finnoul grinned. "He would be worth it. He has ruled here since the day I first rode a certain orange kin who did not wish to be ridden."

"You call them dragon-kin because of me. Will you tell me their true name?"

Finnoul's face turned serious. "No. Forgive me, Raef, but this I will not do."

Raef nodded. "And yours?"

"You already have it."

"It is a strange thing that you would share one name and not the other, but," he continued as Finnoul began to speak, "I will not question it and I am glad to have the one I have."

"It is time, Raef. You must act before the light fails."

Raef's steps were slow and steady, his feet light on the ground. He thought of Vakre in that moment, as he walked across the rocks between the drowsy creatures, of the way Vakre moved on the hunt, and wondered if he would live to tell the son of Loki of this moment.

Though the gathered kin stayed still, eyes that mirrored the sunset followed him along the ridge. The red watched, too, unblinking, as Raef approached. When Raef was four paces away, he stopped and the beast lifted his head from the ground. They stayed this way for some time, the kin's back rising and falling in even breaths. Raef remembered the eyes of the smoke-colored kin, the curiosity there, and saw none of that in this one, only calculation. At last Raef moved again, easing his way alongside the creature. Raef inhaled once, then leaped onto the kin's back.

He was upside down before he knew it, but somehow clinging to the smooth skin. The beast twisted and writhed, eager to throw the unwelcome weight from his back. When Raef got his bearings, he saw they were no longer above the ridge. Empty sky yawned beneath him and he was losing his grip.

Raef caught sight of the jutting, half-dead tree too late to avoid it. Swooping in close to a sheer wall of rock, the kin twisted at the last moment and the tree tore Raef from the kin's back. Feeling nothing but air beneath him, Raef grasped at the branches, but they crumbled in his hands and gave way. Above him, the red dragon-kin screamed in triumph and Raef began to fall.

An answering scream sounded and Raef was caught up in the outstretched wings of another kin. They tumbled together for a moment, wings clutching Raef tight to its belly, the ground drawing ever closer, but then a foot latched on to Raef's leg and with a sharp snap the wings caught air beneath them once again. Only then did Raef see that his rescuer was the color of smoke.

The kin returned him to the ridge, setting him down gently on the rocks while hovering above. Raef could see Finnoul in the distance, clambering over the rough ground. The orange kin flew nearby, but it was the grey one that had come for him in time. Their eyes met and Raef stretched out his hand, just as he had while in the hall of the Guardians. The kin backed away and showed its teeth, then took to the sky. It dove into the valley.

Finnoul ran to Raef's side. "Are you hurt?"

"Only a little." Raef kept his gaze on the grey kin far below. It soared along a river and then disappeared into the trees.

"I have never seen a riderless kin act in this way."

"We have met before." Raef explained to Finnoul how he tried to share moss with the smoke-colored kin while waiting for the Guardians. Understanding came to Finnoul's eyes.

"She is once-ridden."

"She?"

"Yes, I recognize her now. Her rider died not long ago. Some kin return to their kind, to the wild, when this happens. Others remain among us."

"Do they accept other riders?"

"Not often." Finnoul looked at Raef. "Perhaps she is seeking one."

"Then why not stay? She fled."

Finnoul shrugged. "She may be unsure about what she wants. She may not understand what you are. But if she is drawn to you, you will see her again."

"And the red one?"

"Was not meant to be. I have seen him refuse many. You need not be ashamed."

Raef felt many things at that moment but shame was not among them. "You do not wish me to try him again?"

Finnoul laughed without humor. "To do so would be certain death." She hesitated but Raef's frown seemed to prompt her on. "They accept the first confrontation. It is as much a part of their understanding as it is ours. We were made to test each other and to form the bond if it is right. But they do not tolerate a second confrontation with the same rider."

The sun had dipped below the horizon, leaving the world in twilight. Raef took a deep breath. "What now?"

"You have risked enough this day. It is time we had a feast under the stars. There are many who wish to meet you and there is much to talk about."

↑ ↑ ↑

The feast was held on an island in the middle of a shallow lake north of the painted hills. Sleek, narrow boats took them across the water, poled by silent, hooded alfar in dark clothing. Torches burned bright and fiery reflections danced in the water alongside the stars. There was laughter and music and all of it carried over the water.

"Do you not fear attack?" Raef asked Finnoul as they stepped from the boat onto the island.

Finnoul pointed to the night sky. Raef saw nothing at first, then spotted several winged silhouettes. "We are more protected than you know. But more than that, we are far removed from the lands my people know best. The core of our homeland is to the west, the forest you saw when Aerath took you to the Guardians. I have known some of my people who seldom venture beyond those trees. We are well away from them, isolated, and they do not know where to look." Finnoul accepted a shell, wide and shallow and unlike any Raef had seen, and handed it to him. The liquid within caught the moonlight as Raef brought the shell to his lips. It had a strange but not unpleasant taste, and it tingled on Raef's tongue.

"Lorcan. Does he search for you?"

"He does. He is determined to prove that we hide out in the fells of the north." Finnoul seemed pleased with this fact.

"Something tells me you have helped him reach this conclusion."

Finnoul grinned and took a shell for herself. She held it out and the grin vanished. "To victory." Raef touched his shell to Finnoul's and downed the contents, but it was not victory that occupied his thoughts. In his mind he drank to home and a summer's eve in Vannheim.

The food was plentiful, the drink even more so, and the faces around him were bright and joyful, but as the night went on, Raef realized he did not feel as cheerful as he should have. Finnoul's people were kind and polite, but their eyes remained distant when Raef was near. Finnoul was swallowed up in the crowd and Raef found he was content to remain on the fringe. He was an outsider, and even Finnoul's friendship and trust would not change that.

Raef slipped away to the water's edge, the noise of the feast fading as his mind traveled far across the nine worlds to Midgard. He thought of Vakre, Siv, and Eira, and wondered where they were and if they believed him to be dead.

It was there that Finnoul found him much later. The island had grown quiet and many of the torches had burned out. Raef had watched the boats traverse back to the mainland, quiet shadows walking on water. With their departure, the shadows in the sky also disappeared and it seemed to Raef the stars were now vulnerable and exposed.

Finnoul appeared next to Raef and sat on the cool grass beside him. She said nothing.

"I have been a poor guest," Raef said. "Forgive me."

"There is nothing to forgive. It is my fault. My people did not welcome you as I had hoped."

"They were kind."

"Kindness is not enough. But it is not in our nature to embrace strangers."

"Would you have embraced me if you had never seen the carvings in your mountain home? If you did not think I, a Midgardian, was brought here for some purpose?"

Finnoul did not shirk from Raef's gaze. "No. I will not lie to you, Raef." Finnoul plucked a stone from the shore and tossed it into the water. The ripples spread and sent plumes of green and blue across the water. Raef looked to the sky and saw it blossom with color that seemed to move and flow like the lake below.

"What is that?"

"You do not have this in Midgard?"

Raef shook his head and stared in wonder.

"It is the aurora."

Raef watched the green and blue play across the stars, expanding, receding, dancing. The night sky was alive.

"A gift from Freyr, who is most dear to us of all the gods."

"It is beautiful."

They watched the lights in silence until they faded and all was darkness once more.

"Come," Finnoul said. "The others wait for us."

The alfar who remained on the island sat in silence around the last burning fire. They were thirteen in number and the joy of the feast was gone from their faces. Finnoul went around the circle, touching each on the forehead and calling them by name. When she at last took a seat, she placed Raef by her side and though the pale eyes around them were wary, not a word of protest was heard.

Finnoul looked to one alf and spoke. "What news, Maelys?"

"The day has been set." Maelys, seated across from Raef, answered in a low voice. "Four nights will pass. Then the Guardians will make the journey to the barren land."

"Who goes with them?"

"The wardens will accompany them. Even now the Guardians seek the sacrifices that will please the gods most."

"Thank you for this information, Maelys. You have done well." Finnoul looked around the circle. "They will be vulnerable on the journey. It is our best chance to strike."

"Lorcan will expect an attack." This came from the oldest alf in the circle. Her white-blind eyes stared hard at Finnoul.

Finnoul nodded. "He will. We will have to be precise and quick. Annun, are you well?" The alf Raef had helped retrieve from Lorcan's grasp nodded. "You must discover the route they intend to take. There are many ways into the barren land. We cannot spread ourselves thin to cover them all. We must be able to concentrate our strength."

Annun smiled. "It will be done."

"Our time is at hand." Finnoul was solemn but Raef could see the eagerness that wanted to leap from her. "We have waited long for this. We need only endure for four more days." A shell, larger than all the rest, was passed, starting with Finnoul and moving left. Each took a sip until it came to Raef, empty but for a drop to wet his lips. The liquid burned as it trickled down his throat and seemed to set fire to his chest. He gave the shell to Finnoul who threw it onto the ring of stones that contained the fire. It shattered with a crack, like thunder in a storm, a promise made to the gods.

Little more was said. The alfar went their separate ways, some on the backs of dragon-kin called out of the skies, others across the silent waters until at last only Finnoul and Raef lingered.

"You mean to ambush the Guardians?"

"There is a day that is sacred to us. It comes perhaps once in the lifetime of a man such as you."

"Perhaps?"

"The date is never set. The sky must be read and the earth heard. I have heard that once this day did not come for nearly three hundred years. But it is upon us now. In time, it has been twisted from its original purpose. What was a celebration of life has become a demonstration of power. The Guardians now choose sacrifices to be sent to the gods." Anger simmered in Finnoul's face, and alongside it, grief.

"Your own people?"

Finnoul nodded rather than give voice to her assent. "Worse, most go willingly, believing the vile lies the Guardians tell them, believing they go to save us."

"Do you mean to kill them?"

Finnoul did not answer right away. When she did, her voice was quiet and ragged, as though she had to tear the words from within her. "I do not know."

"And my part in all this?"

Finnoul was quiet again, this time for so long Raef began to wonder if she would speak. "I will not keep you against your will, Raef," she finally said. "Tomorrow, I will show you the way."

"I gave you my word. Willingly."

Finnoul brought a hand up to Raef's shoulder but did not touch him. "Your heart sings to you of home. I should have helped you there long before this. Instead I have burdened you with my own grieving heart, my own songs of the home I dream of."

"I gave you my word," Raef repeated, firmly this time. "If I cannot help us both, let me at least help you."

Finnoul frowned. "You speak as though something is lost to you, as though time is slipping through your fingers."

Raef shook his head, trying to take back the words he had let loose. "I meant nothing by it."

"Tell me." There was no question in Finnoul's voice and the faded blue eyes demanded the truth.

Raef was uncertain where to begin but the words began to flow from him. "I have seen dead men walk, I have burned a frozen lake, and I have looked into the eyes of a Valkyrie and seen my death reflected there, but all this does not compare to what is coming. Shining Balder is dead, Finnoul. The events that lead to the end have been set in motion. The wolf-age is coming."

Finnoul was still for a long moment, her eyes not leaving Raef's. "You are certain?"

"Have I heard it from the mouth of Odin? From the crones sitting at the roots of Yggdrasil? No. But I know it in my heart." And Raef told Finnoul of Loki, of Freyja's army woken by Torrulf Palesword, and of the storm that showed him Thor's raging grief. "No man can know how much time is left to us."

"If what you say is true, your time is better spent in Midgard, not wasted here."

"I do not count it wasted. I have but one desire that I wish to see fulfilled before the sea swallows the earth. But even that is far out of reach and I know not where to begin. Perhaps this is where I am meant to make my end."

"What is this desire you speak of?"

The words caught in Raef's throat, as if disuse made them more difficult to say. "Justice. Vengeance for my murdered father. But I have only ghosts to chase. The man responsible is faceless and nameless."

"If our time is short, you ought to be with your people."

"If I go back on my word, I will regret it. I will stay."

Finnoul accepted this with a nod. "We will visit the kin again tomorrow. It is time you flew."

⚡ ⚡ ⚡

The rocky ridge was deserted when Finnoul and Raef returned at sunset the next day. The red sun warmed the rocks but the sky was free of winged shadows.

"Strange," Finnoul said. "Only in storms have I seen them give up their favorite place to sun bathe."

"Are we early?"

"No. The sun has nearly set. Perhaps they are hunting." Finnoul shrugged her shoulders. "Come. I will show you the way to the barren land so you might be familiar with it when the time comes." They remounted Finnoul's orange dragon-kin and headed south. A stiff, relentless breeze assailed them from the west as they flew over green woodland. Small lakes pocked the land but it was not long before Raef could see that ahead lay a very different landscape. The trees ended abruptly, cut off by dry ground that rose and fell in small, ragged peaks and then tumbled down into deep, twisting crevices where the sunlight would not reach. There was no water in sight. The kin slowed and hovered high above the barren waste.

"Does it end?"

"Yes. Far to the south lies a great canyon with a rushing river and beyond that the world is green again."

"What happened here?"

Raef could not see Finnoul's face but he could hear the pain in it. "A battle was fought here. Long ago."

"Fire?" It did not make sense, for the wounded land would have recovered over time, but Raef could not see what else might do such damage.

"Giants."

Raef looked again and saw the scarred earth with new eyes.

"Do you see that plateau?" Finnoul pointed ahead of them. It was hard to miss, being the only level surface in sight. "The sacrifice will happen there. We will take them before they leave the trees. The Guardians will be on the ground. They will be defended, of course, but the greatest protection will be up here. Lorcan will be able to see any attack that comes from the skies and we will give him one. Thannor will lead it. When they have engaged, those of us hidden among the trees will launch our assault on the Guardians." Finnoul turned the kin north again. "We should not linger here. Lorcan has many eyes."

It was not until they had nearly reached Finnoul's mountain home that Raef was certain they were being followed. Something darted beneath the treetops, staying out of sight, but Raef, peering over his shoulder, could see leaves and branches stirring in the absence of wind. He whispered this to Finnoul, who changed course, not so dramatically as to make it obvious, but enough to keep distance between them and her home. Instead, though it was dark, they returned to the ridge where they had started the evening and landed on its highest point.

In the dim light, their pursuer abandoned the protection of the trees, guiding a kin up the slope to the ridge. Raef was not surprised to see Aerath's face.

Finnoul exhaled and a low grumble came from deep within the orange kin's throat as Aerath's blue kin circled above them. Finnoul reached for the bow she kept strapped to her kin and notched an arrow on the string. She did not draw it back but her intent was plain.

"I will shoot you from the sky if I must. Did Lorcan send you, Aerath?"

"He does not command me." The blue-green kin hovered now and Aerath's voice was sharp in the gathering dark.

"But what will keep you from telling him where I have been this night?" The bowstring inched back.

A delay, this time, before he answered, and his voice was less brittle. "If you have to ask, then perhaps I was wrong to come at all."

Raef saw Finnoul close her eyes but the bow stayed up. "Then come down here, Aerath, and let me look you in the eye."

"Your words are folly. We both know I will not join you."

"I know no such thing." Finnoul's voice was soft.

The silence between them was deafening. When Aerath did speak, Raef was glad for the swift twilight that had consumed the alf's features, for it seemed to him the words were meant for only one pair of ears.

"I will not. But neither will I tell Lorcan where I saw you. Good-bye, Finnoul." His kin rose up, its wings fanned against the shape of the moon, and then plunged down into the valley. He was out of sight in an instant.

Finnoul did not speak again that night and Raef did not venture to draw her into conversation. His own mind was filled with thoughts of Eira, of her careful distance, of her lips on his. He tried to push those thoughts away, summoning instead the image of his father and the vengeance that simmered within. He had to hold onto it, had to put it before all other thoughts of home, but it shamed him to find that the spark of anger did not flare as it should have, that it was content to murmur in the darkness.

‹ ‹ ‹

Another day passed, another day of Finnoul's quiet. She kept to herself, wandering far afield and leaving Raef among her followers. Raef watched Ylloria prepare medicines, watched her choose her plants with care, learned how to gather the roots without causing damage and which flowers were best for masking foul-smelling compresses. He practiced with his unwieldy, unfamiliar blade, trying to establish a measure of comfort with its balance and its lightness. The ambush drew near and it would have to serve, but Raef, though Finnoul's friends seemed pleased, impressed even, that he carried it, found that his heart was not in the blade. Thannor gave him pointers and they crossed swords at dusk until Raef felt he could defend himself.

Finnoul returned that night but had still not regained her former vitality. The rebels shared food and drink but this was a grim meal without the joy of the island feast. The alfar went their separate ways, filtering into the night until only Raef and Finnoul were left to fly up to their mountain roost. Before they took to the sky, a dragon-kin screeched above them and dove into the clearing. The rider was Annun and he nearly stumbled to the ground as he vaulted from his dragon-kin's back. Catching himself, he tried to speak but could only suck in air. Finnoul rested a hand on his shoulder.

"Breathe. Then speak."

"We are lost. There can be no ambush."

"What do you mean?"

"No worthy sacrifices have been found. The Guardians will not make the journey to the barren lands."

Finnoul's face fell and uncertainty clouded her normally clear gaze. Raef, standing to the side, said nothing but watched them both.

"I see Lorcan's cunning behind this," Finnoul said. "He thinks to keep them safe by keeping them at home. He has made certain no sacrifices are found."

"What can we do?" Annun asked, desperate for guidance from his leader. Finnoul did not have an answer.

"I will go." Raef spoke quietly but there could be no mistaking his words. Finnoul turned to him, already shaking her head, but Raef went on before she could speak. "You yourself said I must be here for a purpose. Let this be my purpose. They will not pass up the chance to put me to death."

"No, I will not ask this of you."

"You do not ask. I offer it to you freely. I do not intend to die in your barren land, Finnoul."

Finnoul remained reluctant. "Even so, there is great risk."

"There always is, when something matters." Raef kept his eyes on Finnoul, not looking to Annun, who watched with curiosity. "Remember what we spoke of."

"I do not know what happens to a man of Midgard if he dies in Alfheim. I do not know if the doors of Valhalla will open for him," Finnoul warned.

"I am prepared to take that chance. Regardless, those who dwell in Valhalla will soon pour forth into the world again." It was perhaps unwise to speak so plainly in front of Annun, but Raef was determined not to let Finnoul find a means to keep him from following through. Annun looked away.

Finnoul's eyes remained unwilling, but she kept this to herself. "Very well. Tomorrow we will see that you fall into the hands of the Guardians."

# EIGHT

RAEF SLEPT WELL. If he dreamed, he remembered none of it, but he woke to Finnoul shaking his shoulder. The mountain hall was dim yet with the grey light of dawn, the stone floor cold on his bare feet.

"Is it time?" Raef stifled a yawn and went to look out the narrow window of his chamber.

Finnoul joined him and Raef saw that her long pale hair was pulled back, twisted at the crown of her head, and streaked now with rich orange hues. The change had sharpened her cheekbones and brought even greater strength to her face. The scent of the fresh dye tingled in Raef's nostrils. "Almost. There is something I would show you first."

The mountains slept yet, great, grey, hulking shapes blanketed with deep purple shadows and tinged here and there with the first rays of pink light. Even Finnoul's orange beast seemed to dwell yet in the realm of sleep, his eyes were half-closed and his wings thrummed the air with languorous ease as they lifted off from the mountain hall. The sky began to glow with golden light in the east and it was there that Finnoul pointed the kin.

Beneath them, land that was becoming familiar to Raef rushed by, but they soon reached the edge of the confines he had come to know. The great forest spread on and on into the distance, seemingly without end, and the sun was above the horizon before the landscape changed. The trees gave way to thick, wet marshland and then at last a great lake opened up, reaching so far to the east and north that the shores were faint lines obscured further by heavy mist.

A single peak rose out of the lake not far from the western shore, rearing up above the calm waters, and it was this that the orange dragon-kin circled around.

"What is this place?" Raef asked. The mountain was smooth and dark in color and the summit was truncated. Instead of a high point, a deep bowl was cut into the black rock.

"It is what I have promised you. Long ago this mountain served as a path between our worlds."

"And does it still?"

"So we believe. Long has it been since my people sought to make such a journey. But it is important that you can find your way here alone. Tomorrow brings much uncertainty. If the battle goes ill, I may be unable to help you on your journey."

"But what am I looking for?"

They circled lower for a better look and Raef could see clouds of vapor rising from the mountain's cauldron. "In truth, I do not know. We do not venture here. As long as you keep your bearings, reaching the lake on foot will not be difficult. Crossing the water and climbing the mountain is another matter."

"Then let us hope I am not on foot."

They turned back to the west and met with Annun and Thannor at the foot of Finnoul's mountain. There would be no goodbyes, though Raef would have liked to thank Ylloria. Raef knew what purpose the two alfar were there to serve. He handed the ancient sword to Finnoul, stripped down to his bare skin, pulled on the ragged clothes he had arrived in, and did not flinch away when they began to beat him.

Their strikes were hard, but their precision would keep Raef from suffering serious damage. To the eyes of the Guardians, he would appear bruised and forsaken. Raef endured the beating without a sound, then folded and returned the borrowed clothes to Finnoul, who completed Raef's transition by drawing her knife lightly across Raef's chest. Blood welled, staining the fabric of his shirt, and then began to trickle down, but the cut was not deep.

"A little blood tells a good tale," Finnoul said, her gaze appraising Raef's appearance. Finnoul hefted the strange sword. "I will have this for you when we meet again." Raef dragged his hands in the dirt and smeared the damp earth on his cheeks and neck. Finnoul grinned. "You are ready."

Finnoul left Raef atop a bald hill in the forest. The sky had grown grey and flat, the air thick and warm, and the trees that spread before them promised dark places. "You will have to walk from here. I dare not take you closer." Finnoul pointed down a thickly treed valley that meandered below them. "A stream runs its course there. Follow it and they will find you." Finnoul looked as though she might say more but instead she nodded.

"Until tomorrow," Raef said. He turned from Finnoul and the orange kin and began his descent into the narrow valley. The sound of water soon reached his ears and he followed it until the stream was underfoot. It was a tiny, rambling thing filled with small silver fish that fled from Raef's shadow and chased the spots of sun that filtered through the trees to the water's surface.

The sun was reaching its peak when Raef felt certain he was being watched and followed. He kept his gaze on the streambed in front of him, but his ears told him of two hunters, one to his left and one to his right. Raef wandered on, pretending obliviousness, kneeling to splash water on his face at just the right moment to give one of the hunters a chance to approach from behind. The sword landed against his bent neck just as he expected.

"Midgardian." The voice was full of satisfaction. "The gods have returned you to us."

Raef stayed low and turned slowly, hands out to show he was defenseless, the blade sliding against his skin. He did not recognize the face that peered down into his. A pair of feet splashed through the stream and the hands of the second hunter grabbed his shoulders and shoved his head down. Raef held still as his hands were bound and murmured a feeble "Where are you taking me?" as they pulled him to his feet. The hunters did not answer as they shoved him forward, each keeping a hand on Raef's arms.

They plunged through the trees, leaving the water behind, and it wasn't long before Raef, though he kept his head down as a show of meekness, saw other warriors join them, silent, light of foot, deadly shadows flitting between the trees. One must have run ahead for, though their pace was fast, the Guardians were awaiting their arrival in the roofless hall.

Raef had thought to see the hall crowded with onlookers, thought to hear voices calling for his death, but the Guardians were the only ones there to see him flung to the earth at their feet. At a word from the First, the warriors slipped back into the forest, save two who stood guard. Raef stayed on his hands and knees.

"Midgardian," the First said. Raef raised his head just enough to meet his gaze. "How fortunate that you have found your way back to us."

There were no questions about Finnoul, her location, her numbers, what she planned. One of the female Guardians, the one Raef had thought kinder than the rest, stepped forward and raised him to his feet. She looked at his face, searched his eyes as though seeking an answer to an unspoken question. Apparently satisfied, she lifted the hem of his worn shirt and let her gaze wander down his chest, prodding at some of his older wounds. She kept her distance from the fresh slice Finnoul had given him. Without a word, she gave a nod to the First and returned to her seat.

The interview was at an end. The First signaled for the guards to take him away but they had taken only two steps when a stranger burst into the hall. He was tall and strong, but what Raef saw above all was the crystal that glimmered where his left eye should have. The stranger bore down on Raef, a long knife in his hand, and grabbed a fistful of Raef's hair. Twisting and pulling, he forced Raef back to his knees and held the knife at his throat.

"Where is the traitor Finnoul? Tell me where she hides!" There was savagery in his voice and Raef knew this was Lorcan.

Raef kept silent and let his head roll back and his eyes close. Lorcan yanked on his hair and then planted a foot on Raef's chest and pushed him over.

"Lorcan!" The First's voice was commanding and through shuttered eyes Raef could see it had the desired effect. Though Lorcan did not take his gaze from Raef, he held the blade at his side and came no closer. "No further harm is to come to the Midgardian. He must be fit for tomorrow."

At last Lorcan's gaze shifted to the First. "Sacrifice be damned. He must tell me what he knows." Lorcan lunged at Raef again but the First bellowed and he came up short, seething.

"He knows nothing. There is nothing to know." The First kept his voice low and calm but Raef could see his pulse beat in his temple. "The lost one is no threat to us. When she grew tired of her play thing," the First gestured to Raef, "she cast him off. That is all that matters." Raef saw frustration burn in Lorcan's good eye and the extent of the Guardians' blindness became clear to him. They had at their feet a chance to learn Finnoul's secrets, but their pride and arrogance had woven them a cocoon of oblivion, and they would rather live and die in a lie than acknowledge the truth. For a moment Raef pitied Lorcan. He was a strong warrior who had seen through the Guardians' veil. Raef could only imagine what he might accomplish if he sided with Finnoul. But that was both his fault and his strength. He had chosen his side and was too stubborn to let it go.

The First continued. "Take him away. See that he is fed and prepare for the morning's journey." He rose and the Guardians began to leave the hall.

"You mean to make the sacrifice, then?" The anger had vanished from Lorcan's voice. In its place was obedience and acceptance.

"Of course." The First looked back over his shoulder, confusion marring his smooth features. "The gods will be pleased," he said, as though nothing else could matter.

And with that Raef was left alone with Lorcan. Their gaze met for a brief moment, Lorcan's jeweled eye glittering, and Raef could see the loathing and questions buried there. Lorcan glanced away and at last sheathed his blade. Raef kept his head bowed as the warrior dragged him from the hall but he paid attention to every tree they passed, each turn they took, mapping out in his head where he was in relation to the hall, to the parts of the forest he had crossed with Aerath, even to the east and the safety he would find with Finnoul's people. Though the First's authority held sway here, in the dark of night, Lorcan might find a path to disobedience and Raef did not intend to succumb to the forest's web should he need to escape. They traveled north and west of the hall, though the distance was not far, and Lorcan deposited Raef within a clearing. Five bare trunks rose up from the earth, each cut short just above the height of a man. Raef's arms were unbound and then retied with one of the trunks at his back. The tough, abrasive bark bit into Raef's skin.

"Water," Raef murmured. He kept his eyes half-lidded and licked his dry lips for effect, but his thirst was real. Lorcan grunted and held a skin up to his mouth. Raef swallowed eagerly until it was empty. "Where am I?"

Lorcan grunted again, this time with derision. "Are you so weak, Midgardian?"

"What are you going to do with me?"

"I would see your knowledge of Finnoul plucked from within you, drawn out like poison. And just as painfully. But you will get better than that, better than you deserve." Lorcan called out to three warriors who were watching from the edge of the clearing. Quiet words were exchanged and then Lorcan left. Two of the warriors went in the opposite direction, leaving one to watch the prisoner. Now they were alone, Raef dropped his act of exhaustion and eyed the remaining alf more openly, taking note of his weapons, his lack of scars, his nervous eyes. It seemed not all of Lorcan's warriors were comfortable in Raef's presence. The guard was young, Raef thought, though his time among the alfar had not made it easier to determine age. He kept his pale eyes averted from Raef, glancing here and there among the trees but not willing to linger on the defenseless stranger.

It was not long before the two warriors returned bearing food. They untied Raef, who sank to the ground, and stayed close while he ate at their feet. The food was cold and plain but Raef was glad the First had insisted on this meager hospitality. He would need his strength. When he had finished, he relieved himself in one of the bowls they had brought, an act that drew looks of disgust. He grinned and offered his hands up for binding.

The ropes were tighter this time, his arms wrapped more securely around the rough bark, and Raef knew he would feel the effect in his arms in the morning. The blood flow would slow to a crawl and it would be a painful night. The youngest warrior drew the task of removing the used bowls. He looked at them disdainfully for a moment and then his face lit up, malice replacing nerves. Using his foot, he upended the bowl and let the urine spill onto the grass next to Raef's feet. Raef kept his eyes on the alf's face and grinned again, returning the nerves to their rightful place.

There was no further interaction between Raef and the warriors that night. They were content to ignore him and Raef was content to watch. Lorcan came and went, as did others, but darkness came and swallowed them all, bringing the sounds of night with it. The clouds that had accompanied the sun dissolved in the cooler night air and the moon was bright enough to bathe the clearing in pale blue light. At times, Raef closed his eyes, resting both his mind and body as best he could, but there was no sleep to be had and the night was long. His thoughts, never far from Vannheim, fled there and Raef let these waking dreams embrace him until Lorcan cast them into the dark. The sky was not yet light with hints of dawn when the warrior approached, but Raef felt the morning was not far off. Lorcan untied Raef's arms. The heavy limbs fell to Raef's sides, the sudden rush of blood painful but also welcome. Lorcan indicated that Raef should remove his ragged shirt.

"Do you know pain, Midgardian?"

Raef wanted to laugh but he kept his face still. "You can see that I do." Lorcan did not glance down at the scars, old and new, on Raef's chest and arms.

"Then let me spare you some. This day, your death comes. I can make it easy, painless."

"How?"

"This." Lorcan held up a small vial filled with an amber liquid. "Take this and you will feel nothing."

"And in return?"

"You will tell me everything you know about Finnoul and the wayward ones who follow her."

Raef pretended to consider, letting his gaze rest on the vial for a moment. "No."

Lorcan's face grew dark, his nostrils flared. He unstoppered the vial and poured the contents onto the forest floor, drop by golden drop. "You will regret that, Midgardian. I will make certain your death is slow and full of agony."

Raef held Lorcan's gaze and said nothing, though he itched to taunt the warrior about Finnoul. It would not do to arouse suspicion. Lorcan strode away and Raef was handed a bowl of clear, sweet-smelling broth.

"This will clean your blood," the warrior said. The taste was cloying and Raef found it hard to swallow, but the warriors watched him closely to be sure the bowl was emptied.

"And fill my belly?"

"You have no need for a full belly, Midgardian."

When it was time to exit the clearing, Raef made a show of struggling, of clutching at the Thor hammer that hung from his neck and begging so he would not appear eager to go to his slaughter. A few sharp blows descended and he fell in line, hoping it was enough to convince them of his reluctance. Lorcan reappeared at the head of a large group of warriors, the most Raef had seen in Alfheim. He could not count them all. The Guardians were among them, stone-faced in the morning air and dressed in white. They did not glance at Raef, did not even speak to their own people but for a brief, murmured conversation between the First and Lorcan. Not long after, Lorcan and many of his warriors took to the skies and the progression set off to the south just as the first rays of sunlight slipped through the trees to warm Raef's face.

ᚱ ᚱ ᚱ

The path was gentle and easy and the trees seemed to hum around them, greeting the day with a quiet song. Raef would have liked to think the trees would sing a different tune if they knew what the day would bring, but he let the song bring him external peace.

Inside, he thrummed with anticipation, eager to do away with the pretense he had created for himself, eager to clash swords and spill blood, to show the Guardians how mistaken they were.

The day grew hot and Raef was soon slick with sweat despite the tree cover. The Guardians in their long robes seemed unaffected, but Raef, noting that their pale eyes were too bright and their pupils large, wondered if this was an unnatural thing brought on by something they had eaten or drunk in preparation for the sacrifice.

They stopped at midday in a small glen that offered cooler air and shade from the hot sun. Water trickled from the rocks and came to rest in a shallow pool. The Guardians took their fill of the water and then one by one the warriors did the same, scooping the liquid to their mouths with a dipper that was passed from one to the next. Raef kept his eyes on the sky, but of Lorcan and his winged warriors, there was no sign and he knew they were likely patrolling far afield. He was not offered the dipper and the rest was short.

The underbrush grew thick and tangled and their pace slowed to accommodate this as warriors hacked at vines and bushes to clear something that might resemble a path. It grew hotter. Sweat trickled down Raef's nose and he tried not to think of the water he had been denied.

It was difficult to determine distance. The flight to the barren land with Finnoul had been short and Raef, deep within the trees, had little way of comparing the terrain they were covering with what he had seen from above. He knew not if the ambush would come at any moment or if they had far yet to travel.

When a dragon-kin swooped out of the sky, Raef felt a twinge of unease in his chest. The rider dismounted and spoke quietly to the First, who nodded, said something in return, and then continued on. They did not stop, they did nothing, and the kin left as quickly as it had come. It could have been meaningless, but Raef gave silent thanks to Odin that Lorcan had left his hands unbound.

There were weapons all around him. He need only get his hands on one.

When the trees thinned and the ground grew dry beneath their feet, Raef knew something had gone wrong. Finnoul had said they would attack before the progression left the shelter of the trees and Raef could see the desolate waste ahead of them. He kept his eyes forward and plodded on.

With the trees behind them, the relentless sun beat down, baking the ground until it cracked. Before they descended into the maze of rock, Raef could see the plateau in the distance. There was no easy path. They wound among sharp spires and bottomless clefts, the shadows of dragon-kin passing over as their sentries kept watch from above. Raef risked a glance up into the blue. It was enough to tell him that there were fewer warriors above them than there should have been. Others must be engaged elsewhere and that could only mean Finnoul had been discovered.

Two steps and Raef could have a sword in his hands. And another six at his throat. It was tempting, the blade that hung on the hip of the warrior just ahead of him, just out of reach. If he drew it, the odds would be impossible but he suspected the Guardians would demand he live long enough to complete the sacrifice. Resistance on Raef's part could give Finnoul time. Or ensure Raef's death. He thought of his father, of his promise of vengeance, and tried to imagine what Einarr would do. He did not know, and in his uncertainty, he waited.

Soon the plateau came into sight again, taller than all else, smooth and flat in a ragged, scarred landscape. They began the ascent, winding up a steep path that had been walked before. Raef was only steps from the top when the screams reached his ears. In an instant, all eyes were on the sky and at last Raef knew what had happened to Finnoul and her warriors.

Far in the distance, a battle raged amid the brilliant blue. The dragon-kin were tiny shapes, diving, clawing, killing. The sound of their screaming was the only noise of battle that reached the plateau and for a moment they all watched in silence. Then the kin that hovered above them answered the calls and the quiet was broken.

Hands seized Raef and dragged him to the top of the plateau. Some kin tried to fly to join the fight, but were held back as orders were shouted for the warriors to remain in place and protect the Guardians. Raef was shoved to his knees, his head forced down so he could see nothing but the cracked, dusty ground, but a warrior strayed too close and Raef's hands found the hilt of a sword. Swinging wildly, Raef came to his feet. The warriors jumped back to avoid Raef's blade, but one was too slow and the edge ripped open his chest. Frozen, he swayed, his eyes wide, then fell on his face. The others overcame their surprise and drew their weapons. They came at him with speed. One, two, Raef evaded, and buried his sword in the third, but then, as Raef could hear the First screaming to keep him alive, they fell on him from all sides. Immobilized and forced to the ground, the sword was wrenched from him as his face was shoved into the dead warrior's pooling blood. Spitting, Raef tried to rise, but it was no use.

When he lay still, the First came to stand by his head. The Guardian bent over and laid a cool hand on Raef's cheek. The fingers ran over the blood that covered Raef's jaw and then came to rest under his chin, forcing Raef to look up at him. The First's colorless eyes were calm.

"You should not resist, Midgardian," the First said. "You should be honored." Taking his hand from Raef's chin, he wiped the blood in Raef's hair and then stood straight, his face disappearing from Raef's view. "Get him up. It is time."

Hands tugged Raef to his knees and he was dragged across the plateau. Then he was lifted and laid flat on a raised rock. The rock's surface was smooth but for a narrow channel that extended from the middle, right at the height of Raef's neck, to the edge. Twisting but held down by strong arms, Raef could only watch as the Guardians gathered. A dish was held to the edge of the rock where the channel dropped off and Raef knew it was meant to catch the blood that would pour from his throat. The First drew a knife from within the folds of his robes. The blade gleamed in the sun and he held it aloft.

"Freyr, best of all the gods, long have you waited for a gift. Take it and take joy of it." The knife descended and Raef, straining against the hands that held him, let loose a roar of useless defiance.

As his scream rose to the sky, a new sound followed in its wake, terrible and fierce, and the First hesitated, the knife suspended over Raef's exposed throat.

The dragon-kin dove out of the sky, a streak of smoke in the blue, and slammed into the First. The knife spun out of his hand as he hit the ground and the kin twisted in the air and landed on the smooth rock next to Raef, who had scrambled to his feet the moment the grips of the warriors had relaxed.

The smoke-colored kin screamed again, daring any to approach, but Raef saw only shock on the faces of the alfar. The First lay flat, gasping for air, but Raef could see he would never stand again. His back was broken. The kin swung her neck around and looked at Raef, her sunset eyes boring into his, and though it was but an instant, it seemed like a lifetime. She blinked and Raef climbed onto her back. The ground dropped away beneath them and he was free.

For a moment, there was peace. Raef closed his eyes and took a deep breath, letting the wind pull at every part of him as though it could wash away the coating of dust and blood. The great expanse of blue called to him but it would have to wait. Finnoul needed his help.

The dragon-kin did not need to be asked to join the fight. Angling back to the north and the edge of the forest, her wings took them to the fray with all speed. It was a battle of both land and sky, Raef saw. Kin and their riders dueled in the air while the ground below heaved with warriors intent on savagery. Among them Raef could see Finnoul. Spiraling to the ground, the kin found a place to land and Raef, though unarmed, leaped from her back.

His presence in the chaos did not go unnoticed for long and Raef had just enough time to snatch a long, slender knife from the grip of a fallen warrior before he was set upon by one of Lorcan's followers. The alf was severely wounded, his left arm hanging useless at his side, and his movement was clumsy. Raef evaded a wild swing and answered with a quick stab that found soft flesh. Twisting the blade, Raef wrenched it from his opponent's chest and moved on, his eyes searching for Finnoul or Lorcan even as a new attacker approached. This one Raef recognized from his capture the day before. The warrior's blade was long and his face spattered with blood.

"You would deny the gods, Midgardian?"

"No, only you."

The alf lunged, his long sword eating up the distance between them. Raef ducked at the last moment and lashed out with his knife, slicing at the back of the elf's thigh as he went by. Unfazed, the warrior attacked again, forcing Raef to retreat and deflect with his shorter blade until Raef was pinned up against a boulder. The sword bore down on Raef, barely kept at bay by the knife, until the alf's free hand drew a small knife and made to stab down into Raef's shoulder, but not before Raef thrust the fingers of his right hand into the alf's eyes, causing him to scream and loosen his grip on the knife just as the tip of the blade pierced skin. Raef wrapped his own hand around both the little knife's hilt and the warrior's fingers, then rammed it home in the side of the warrior's neck.

Gurgling, the warrior stumbled back, clutching his neck, but his body gave out and he fell to the ground, still trying to curse

Raef. Raef leaned over and retrieved the small knife, silencing the bloody mouth.

He had found Finnoul. Armed now with two blades, Raef darted through a gap in the fighting to reach her only to come face to face with Aerath. For a moment he did not know Raef. His eyes were bright with battle, his blade streaked with gore, and Raef could not tell if he was friend or foe.

"Aerath."

He blinked, his blade still raised, but came no closer. "You live."

"For now."

His gaze drifted from Raef to his sword and the blood that covered his hand and dripped down his forearm. "I came to save her." He seemed unsure, on the verge of breaking down.

"And we will."

Together they surged into the wall around Finnoul, who, along with Annun and Thannor, was pressed on all sides by Lorcan and four warriors. Raef quickly dispatched one from behind and then he was in the thick of it, knives flashing. Aerath went down but found his feet. Thannor, bleeding heavily from more than one wound, lunged for Lorcan. He was cut down with ease, but this left Raef an opening and he threw the smaller blade into the chest of the warrior on Lorcan's right. Though Thannor was down and dying, Lorcan was now outnumbered and he and his final companion hesitated, taking stock of their situation.

Lorcan moved first, his sword arcing toward Finnoul, but Raef anticipated this and threw himself in Lorcan's path. His long knife shivered off the larger sword, but it was enough to deflect Lorcan's momentum away from Finnoul. Instead, the blade bit into Raef's upper arm, but it was the last blood it would draw. Finnoul seized Lorcan by the throat and hacked down on his sword hand, severing it at the wrist. Screaming, Lorcan fell to his knees and the sound of their captain's pain brought his remaining warriors to a halt.

Finnoul circled Lorcan, the tip of her sword tracing across the alf's broad shoulders and chest. She leaned close and whispered something in her rival's ear. Whatever it was, it caused Lorcan to close his eyes. When he opened them again, the crystal one flashing in the sun, he did not look away from Finnoul's gaze, his single, green-flecked eye staring to the last as Finnoul slid her sword between his ribs.

The battle was done. No one spoke. Finnoul wiped her sword on her pant leg and sheathed it, then drew a knife and severed a small lock of orange-streaked hair from her own head and tied it to a strand of Lorcan's hair. Then she went to Aerath, placed her hands on his shoulders, and let her forehead rest on his. They exchanged no words but Raef could see much passed between them in that moment. When they stirred, Finnoul knelt beside Thannor's still form. Annun did the same and closed his friend's eyes, then he rose and stepped in front of Raef. The alf's eyes searched Raef's face as his hands detached a second sword, still nestled in its scabbard, free from the stains of battle, from his waist. It was the blade Raef had found in Finnoul's mountain hall. Annun held it out for Raef to claim.

"It does not belong with me," Raef said, his voice quiet. "It belongs here."

"But it found you," Annun said, his forehead creased with a frown.

Raef placed his hand on the hilt but did not let his fingers curl around it. He missed the feel of his old sword, of the smooth, plain shaft of an axe wrapped with strips of leather. "It was never mine. Keep it."

Only then did Finnoul stand and look to Raef. Her face showed weariness and Raef knew the deaths of Lorcan and Thannor had cost her much. When she stood, her gaze shifted to the plateau in the distance.

"The First will never walk again," Raef said, pressing his palm to his upper arm to stem the bleeding caused by Lorcan's sword. The smoke-colored kin landed beside him and Finnoul did not have to ask for an explanation. "Let us finish this."

Finnoul nodded at a warrior behind Raef, who had just finished tending to another alf's wounds. Without a word, the warrior rushed forward and, with deft fingers, spread a thin salve across the bloody, broken skin, then cinched a clean bandage tight around Raef's arm. Beneath the bandage, the salve grew hot for a moment, then turned icy cold and soothing.

Only when he had finished did Finnoul speak. "Us, friend. Not you. This is our war. It is time you went home." She took a deep breath and seemed to gather her strength. "The Guardians will be mine. But your part is done. Go, before it is too late." It was not death in battle that she spoke of.

A part of Raef wanted to stay, to see it through to the end, but the pull of Vannheim was too great. He looked to Aerath and then nodded at Finnoul and extended his hand. Finnoul clasped his forearm. There was much they might have said, and Raef knew in his heart he would never see Finnoul again, but the moment passed in silence.

The kin was as eager to fly as Raef and they took to the sky. Finnoul and her warriors followed, their sights set on the plateau to the south. Raef watched them grow small in the distance and then headed east to where the lonely mountain waited.

NINE

THE MOUNTAIN WAS shrouded in clouds but the smoke-colored kin did not hesitate when Raef urged her to descend into the mist. She made a smooth landing in the bowl but seemed uncertain when Raef dismounted, sunset eyes darting, wings spread as though she might take to the air at any moment. Raef did not know what he was looking for, but he began a thorough search of the bowl, the kin watching with unblinking eyes.

The clouds had lost their orange glow and darkness was creeping over the mountain by the time Raef completed his search, but he had found nothing, not even a crack in the rock that a man might slip through. At last the veil parted, revealing a starry sky above, and Raef retraced his steps though he had no more light to search by. Only when he had been over every inch of the bowl three times did he let doubt slip into his thoughts. Finnoul would not have led him astray, but that did not mean the gate between worlds still existed. There might be no leaving Alfheim. And yet, he had come to Alfheim, surely that meant there was a way out. Raef thought back to the attack that had brought him there and wondered again who might have sent him on a ship and if they had intended this course.

Raef began to pace, his steps aimless, his mind filled with thoughts that he could not piece together. His journey might be the work of a god, but which one and why he could not fathom. The world tree was home to other powers besides those that resided in Asgard, mysterious ones Raef had little knowledge of. Raef took a deep breath and tried to chase these thoughts from his head. Speculating about why he had been plucked from the world of men would get him nowhere.

The kin waited, curled now on the ground, wings tucked close, but her eyes never leaving Raef. Raef went to her and stroked the side of her neck. She butted against him until his hand rested on her nose. She closed her eyes and Raef wondered what would become of her when he left. He did not like to think of her enduring grief over the loss of a second rider, a rider she had chosen. Under his touch, the kin relaxed further and Raef felt her drift into light sleep.

Raef stood vigil as the stars turned in the sky and under his watch the darkness bloomed with color, spreading from the north and reaching over the lip of the mountain. Finnoul had called it the aurora, though the sky filled with bursts of red and orange this time. The colors played out over the bowl and Raef began his search again, looking for something, anything that might send him home.

Halfway across the bowl, Raef stumbled upon it, his foot striking against a barrier he could not see. Reaching out with his hands, Raef touched something solid. It was cool and smooth, like glass, but it pulsed beneath his fingertips, beating faintly as though the heart of it was far away. Using his fingers, Raef found the edges of the barrier, his arms stretching as they might to accommodate a large tree trunk. It was thin, the edges rough beneath Raef's fingers and it extended upwards out of his reach. But Raef discovered, reaching up, his fingers tracing the edges, that it also curved away from him as it rose to the stars.

Taking a step back, Raef circled, trying to catch a glimpse of what it was he had encountered. One step, two steps. There. A glittering curve, a glimmer of substance caught between the moonlight and the light of the aurora. Another step and it was revealed, a strange arcing thing that reflected starlight, moonlight, and the light of the sun that had sunk below. Between all that, somehow, was color. Every color that might be imagined. The colors pulsed and changed in time with the beat Raef had felt. And Raef understood. It was a bridge.

The bridge curved into the sky but seemed to trail off at the height of a tall tree. What lay beyond that point, Raef could not tell. The initial slope was steep but Raef used his hands to help him up until it leveled enough to stand straight. The bridge thrummed and vibrated beneath him, glowing brighter where his feet made contact. The kin, awake now, came close. She seemed nervous and a single stroke of her wings brought her to Raef's height. She hovered there, her eyes dark in the night, and when Raef took another step, she flew in front of him as though to block his path.

Raef reached out and placed his hand on her head. "I must." He stepped forward and she rose higher, letting him pass. On Raef went, climbing higher and higher until he was but steps away from where the bridge seemed to disappear, from where the lights went out. The smoke-colored kin stayed close and he smiled. "You will catch me if I fall, I know."

Another step took him to the edge and the air in front of him flashed with light and then seemed to split, severing itself before Raef's eyes until a shimmering, sparking ring lay before him. Inside the ring, all was as it should be. Sky, stars, darkness. And yet it seemed faint, as though Raef looked at it from a great distance. Beside him the kin shrank back and Raef, though he could see the sadness in her eyes, knew she would not or could not follow.

Turning his back on the end of the bridge, Raef looked deep in the kin's eyes. "Remember me as I will you." Keeping his eyes on hers, he stepped backward over the edge and she was gone.

He did not fall. He hurtled through the night sky, everything a blur of starlight and brilliant color, the breath sucked from him, and his body pummeled about like a leaf in a violent wind. For a moment, no more than a heartbeat, there was respite, and Raef knew he was somewhere in the vast sky, far, far above, caught in the middle of streaking stars. And then he was gone again, plunging through space, his body beginning to crackle with strange energy, and he felt himself a bolt of lightning descending toward earth.

The sensation ceased as suddenly as it began and then he did fall. The distance was short, too short to right himself, and Raef landed hard flat on his back. For a moment, he knew only the thudding of his heart and the desperate catching in his lungs as he tried to take in air. The pain came later, only when Raef was able to take a deep breath, and shivered across his back and out into his limbs. As it faded, lingering only at the point of impact, Raef flexed his feet and wiggled his fingers, relieved to find that everything functioned as it should, and then got to his feet.

The air was cool but not cold, the ground rough, rocky, and free of snow beneath him, and there were no silhouettes of trees against the sky, but all else was veiled by the darkness. He would have to wait for the dawn to see what corner of the world he had landed in. The night passed with fits of pacing and quiet moments. Sleep was out of reach. When at last the dawn broke over the horizon, pale light washed over Raef and revealed a grey, harsh place, so bleak and broken that for a moment Raef thought he was once again in the barren land of Alfheim. But this was beyond even that place. The landscape was dry and rocky, with no sight of vegetation. Mountains, bald and foreboding, rose in the distance and, between them and Raef, the land was pocked with spires of rock jutting to the sky.

Here and there, plumes of vapor puffed ashy clouds into the air, masking the feeble early light.

Raef had not traveled to every corner of Midgard, had not seen all the world of men had to offer, but he knew in his heart that this was not Midgard, that the bridge had not taken him home.

In vain he searched the sky for some sign of a way back. The hazy, thick air revealed nothing, not a glittering bridge, not a circle of light he might crawl through. Raef wanted to shout, to scream his anger and frustration, but he steadied his mind and looked to the sun. Fingering the Thor hammer that still clung to his neck, he asked the thunder god for strength and, leaving the small rise that had been his perch in the night, began to walk toward the rising sun.

Raef's path was not an easy one, taking him over blade-sharp ridges, under crumbling arches, and across deep rifts. The plumes of vapor spewed foul-smelling air that felt rough in Raef's lungs when he passed too close. His eyes grew irritated and his throat became caked with dust. He longed for water but the land was drier than a horse's bones left too long in the sun.

The sun was high, though weak behind the fume-filled air, when Raef saw the hall on the horizon. At first it seemed no more than a great, hulking rock among many, but as he approached, Raef saw it was hewn from a towering cliff, and there, nearly hidden in its own shadow, was a door. It was cracked open just far enough that a man might enter.

The door was five times the height of a man and carved with scenes of battle that gave Raef pause for all showed men dying in agony at the hands of unseen foes. To enter this hall might invite death, but to turn away from the only sign of life might bring the same. He could not just wander on toward the horizon. Raef touched the hammer one last time and then slipped between the slabs of granite.

The hall was cold, a deep, bone-chilling cold that pressed in from all sides and up from the stone floor, seeping into Raef's skin to take up permanent residence. Cold and dark. The rock walls were solid, without even the narrowest of windows to let in light. As Raef's eyes adjusted, he began to see the shapes of pillars holding the granite sky and a smooth, polished floor that spread far into the darkest recesses of the hall. And yet there in the distance, the floor was interrupted by a violent gash that cut deep into the ground. Raef approached with caution and felt dread turn his heart to ice when he peered over the edge. The pit was full of bones.

ᚠ ᚠ ᚠ

"I smell you."

The voice was deep and grinding and it echoed off the walls. Raef spun, trying to pinpoint the source but saw only shadows. "Not a bird or beast. You do not have the smell of feathers or fur. Bones to crunch and flesh to bleed, yes, but not feathers to stick in my teeth or fur to choke me." Raef, hoping he had only been smelled, not spotted, sprinted to the closest pillar and took shelter behind it. "A man, then." The voice laughed, a harsh, splintering sound. "Long has it been since I tasted the flesh of man." Raef eyed the door and was about to bolt for it when the floor trembled beneath him and a mountainous shape came into view, blocking his escape.

The giant, for Raef could not deny that this was what it was, cracked his massive knuckles. "Come out, come out. Let me see what I have caught." Raef stayed close to his pillar and held his tongue. "No?" He turned and pulled the stone doors shut. "I can wait. Can you?"

Raef knew he did not have the strength to open the doors on his own. He would need the giant to do so willingly. He could be patient, too. The giant, secure in the strength of his doors, seemed to lose interest and walked the length of the hall. Raef kept still but soon heard the sounds of fire preparation and a warm red and orange glow brought life to the dark stone. Cold to the bone, Raef longed for the warmth of a fire, but he dared not move.

In time, the hall grew quiet but even then Raef waited until he heard the sounds of snoring. Raef's legs, cold and cramped from sitting so long in one position, protested his sudden movement, but Raef managed to move in silence from pillar to pillar until the sleeping giant was in sight.

The fire had burned low but the embers were still bright. In its light, Raef could at last clearly see the giant, his massive head, long, scraggly hair, and monstrous features. He sprawled beside the fire, his length at least four times that of a tall man. His shoulders were boulders, his legs trees, his feet the size of farmhouse doors. But there was no time to stare. The remains of food and drink were on the floor, but Raef could not know how long the giant would sleep.

A tower of unburnt wood stood nearby and Raef selected a slender log the length of his arm that was tapered at one end. Stoking the coals just enough to revive them, he buried the pointed half of the log in the red-hot depths and waited. The giant turned in his sleep, groaning and flopping over onto his side. Raef, parched and in desperate need of water, picked through the giant's leftovers, but every cup was drained and dry. Risking further movement but realizing that the giant must have stores somewhere in the hall, Raef roamed further afield until at last he found a cache of barrels and a dipper strung up beside them. Sniffing the contents, Raef decided they were safe and took a long drink, wielding the immense dipper with some difficulty. Water spilled down his chin as Raef took gulp after gulp.

When he returned to the fire, he judged the log ready. Shrunken but not yet ready to break apart, the wood glowed red and Raef hefted the log to shoulder height. Approaching the giant with caution, Raef readied his grip and positioned the log over the giant's face. Steeling himself with a deep breath, Raef mustered his voice.

"Here I am," Raef shouted. As he had hoped, the giant's eyes fluttered open and Raef plunged the burning wood into one eye.

The roar was deafening and the giant's flailing arms nearly knocked Raef over as he fled to the safety of the pillars. Screaming, the giant came to his feet and tried to remove the hot coals, but the wood began to crumble and his colossal hands caused more damage as he smeared the coals across his face and into his other eye. Blinded, he reached out and stumbled forward, his hands searching for the culprit, but finding only empty air.

"Curse you, scum of Midgard. I will flay the skin from your body for this."

Raef, deep in the recesses of the hall now, cupped his hands around his mouth and let the echo do the work for him. "Silence, fool," he said, letting that rumble across the walls before continuing. The giant slowed his frantic movements. "You dare call me scum? You dare call me a man?"

"I smell man!" the giant shrieked.

"You smell the guise of a man." This seemed to give the giant pause and Raef, taking a deep breath, went on. "It is Loki and I have come to you in a man's skin."

"You lie, you lie. Loki has no business with me."

"My business is my own. But am I not often a friend to the giants, do I not travel here to Jötunheim and walk amongst you? And yet you threaten to eat me."

"No, no, you are not Loki." But the giant seemed less sure. "Loki would not blind one of his father's kin."

"I do as I wish. Now, will you open your doors or must I take your life?" Raef held his breath, for surely Loki would be able to open the doors himself.

"No, no, I will not. You must pay for what you have done to me."

"Should I summon the wrath of Odin? The retribution of Thor? Must I bring the strength of Asgard to your doorstep?"

The giant, standing in the middle of his hall, harms hanging at his sides in defeat, eyes raw and bleeding, quailed at this. "Asgard will pay, Asgard will pay," he said, though he no longer roared and the words were like an oath to himself rather than a threat to Raef. But defeated he was, for his blind, awkward steps took him to the immense doors and they ground open, letting shining moonlight spill across the threshold.

Raef began to creep toward the doors, giving the giant and his pit a wide berth, but when he was close enough to feel the night breeze on his face, the light of the moon was cut off by a shadow and Raef froze.

"You scream too much, Mogthrasir," the newcomer said. Stepping through the open doors, a second giant hefted a club and clouted the unsuspecting Mogthrasir across the jaw. His head flew back and he fell to the ground, twitching.

Though Raef was in the shadows, the second giant's gaze seemed to find him with ease. "Come out, Midgardian. I am not so easily fooled."

Found and with nowhere to run, Raef crossed into the moonlight, his heart pounding in his chest.

The new giant was not so tall as Mogthrasir and his face was fair and strong. His hair, black with streaks of silver, was pulled back and his dark beard well trimmed. He kept a steady gaze on Raef, showing no signs of malice.

"A clever trick. But Mogthrasir was never the brightest of our race."

"You killed your own kind. Why?"

"Our feud was long and fierce. But why do you judge me so? Do you not kill men?"

"In war." Even as he said it, Raef knew it sounded hollow.

The fair-faced giant laughed. "A nice story to tell your children. Men kill men when it pleases them to do so. As it pleased me to see Mogthrasir's head snap back and his brains shake in his thick skull." Raef did not argue but his eyes betrayed his thoughts, flickering to the door and then back to the giant's face. It did not go unnoticed.

"You are free to try, but you know it is foolish. Every step I take is ten of yours. I will catch you without even trying."

"Are you going to threaten to eat me, too?"

The giant smiled. It wasn't pleasant, even though his teeth were straight and white, his skin smooth, and his eyes blue and bright. "Not yet." He beckoned for Raef to come closer and bent down to take a better look. "I am Hrodvelgr. What are you called?"

Raef answered without thinking. "Einarr." Why he gave his father's name, he could not say.

The giant seemed to find this amusing. "Just Einarr?" Raef said nothing further. "Very well. Come, let us make use of Mogthrasir's hall." The stone doors slid shut once more, but it was not long before the darkness was chased out by three roaring fires that Hrodvelgr lit in three stone hearths, one at each end of the hall, and one close to the bone pit in the middle. Raef huddled near one, glad for the warmth, his eyes never leaving his new captor as he tried to determine how he might escape. Making short work of Mogthrasir's stores, Hrodvelgr produced a meal fit for a band of ten men and loaded a wide table down with it. Sizzling chunks of meat dripping fat onto the fire, loaves of dark bread, whole fish charred black, plums the size of a man's fist. Hrodvelgr popped these into his mouth by the handful and spit out the pits a moment later, washing it all down with great swallows of sweet mead.

Hrodvelgr beckoned for Raef and bade him sit. "Eat. Drink."

Raef did as he was told, though the table was far too tall for him to eat at. Instead, he climbed up and sat cross-legged at the end farthest from the giant. For a moment, there were no sounds but those made by chewing and swallowing as Raef and the giant gorged on the food before them. Only when Raef felt the hunger pains in his belly abate did he venture to speak. "Your land is barren and empty. How is it that you can build fires, drink sweet nectar, and feast on deer and fish?"

"All that you see is given to us. The gods think to keep us," the giant smiled a horrible smile, "content. They feed us meat and mead, gorge us on rich delicacies, and all the while, they sit in their golden halls and tremble out of fear of us."

"If you are so mighty and if they fear you so, why have you not already stormed the gates of Asgard, brought ruin to those halls and death to the gods?"

The giant's smile twisted. "Ours is an ancient race, the first to slink into being, the first to feel the light of the sun on our faces, possessors of bygone wisdom. The gods are children to me, bright things who live for youth and love and idle fancies. They are weak."

Raef persisted. "Tell me, great Hrodvelgr, if they are so weak, why do you not bring them to their knees?" Silence. The giant would not meet Raef's eyes. "I will tell you why. Mjölnir."

Hrodvelgr cast his head back and roared as though the very mention of Thor's hammer caused him pain. "Do not speak that name in my presence! The foe-smasher, the lightning-bringer. That is an ill, vile word."

"You fear it and you fear Thor who wields it. And you fear Odin, Allfather, Flashing Eye and Spear Shaker."

"Silence! Or I will put you over that fire."

Raef matched Hrodvelgr's stare but knew not to provoke the giant further. He kept his tongue behind his teeth, waiting until Hrodvelgr had satisfied his enormous appetite. Raef sipped mead and watched the giant devour the entire feast and empty a full barrel of mead.

"I wager you could not finish another barrel," Raef said.

Hrodvelgr laughed. "Done." He grasped a barrel in his hands, raised it to his mouth, and did not bring it down until it was empty. Not even a trickle ran down his chin.

"Another then?"

Hrodvelgr's face darkened. "You think to make me drunk? To rob me of my wits? You would regret that." Nonetheless, Hrodvelgr helped himself to more, though this time dunking his cup in the new barrel instead.

"What do you want?" Raef was tired of the giant's game.

Hrodvelgr did not answer right away, did not even acknowledge the question.

"If you mean to kill me, at least have the honor to tell me."

"Honor. The gods would have you believe we have none."

"Then show me the gods are wrong."

Hrodvelgr hammered his fist on the table, sending shudders down to the end where Raef sat. "I could crush you, smash you, in an instant. Is that what you want?"

"I asked that question first. Answer me."

Hrodvelgr sat back in his chair and studied Raef for a moment. "I want the world at my feet. I want my enemies slaughtered. I want to restore the rule of my race. Can you give me that?"

"You know I cannot."

"Then I think I will find a use for you. Men make for good sport, you know." Hrodvelgr rose, his eyes free of any humor.

Raef drew back, scrambling for words that might slow the giant's blood lust. "If you touch me, you will never know what I know."

"What could you, puny man, possibly know that would interest me?"

"Promise me my freedom, my life, and a way home and I will tell you."

Hrodvelgr grunted and sat back down, his blue eyes dark and thoughtful. Raef could see the distrust there, see that Hrodvelgr wanted to turn his back. But he also saw greed.

"You must give me some assurance that your knowledge is worth all that," Hrodvelgr said, and Raef felt his heart leap for the giant had not denied knowing how Raef might return to Midgard.

"I swear it. On the life of my father, the lives of my brothers, the life of my son," Raef said, hoping Hrodvelgr could not see the lie he spoke. He had no father, no brothers, no son. The oath was meaningless.

"You men and your vows. Words are but breath, breath but wind, and wind is nothing to me."

"Then what might I say to ease your suspicious mind?" Raef knew he was treading in deep water.

"There is nothing you can say." Hrodvelgr stood again and this time did not hesitate. In three strides, he crossed the length of the table and snatched Raef up in his mighty grip. "You are mine," he said, grinning and squeezing just enough that Raef had to work to draw breath. Leaving Mogthrasir's hall empty and his body at the door, Hrodvelgr took Raef into the night.

Outside, a pack of monstrous, wolfish creatures bayed at the moon and lunged at each other, teeth snapping. Only the stiff harness that bound them together kept them from ripping each other apart. Attached to the beasts was a sled and Hrodvelgr tossed Raef among sacks of something that smelled rotten, then tied him by the wrists to the sled's stout iron rail. Taking up the reins, Hrodvelgr bellowed a command and the sled lurched forward. The beasts, barking and snarling, were fleet of foot and Raef watched Mogthrasir's hall disappear behind them as they hurtled through the broken landscape of Jötunheim.

# TEN

R AEF HAD THOUGHT Mogthrasir's hall large; it was
nothing when compared with the vast network of caverns
that Hrodvelgr called home. The walls of each cavern were
carved in intricate detail, spirals in one, sunbursts in another, a third
covered in stars, and each was linked to the next by a tall, narrow
arch. Hrodvelgr pulled Raef through these seemingly empty halls
and the air grew thick and foul with every step until Raef found it
hard to breath. Eyes watering, Raef stumbled along, his arm held in
Hrodvelgr's vice-like grip, until the giant flung him into a tiny cell
and barred the way with an iron gate. Hrodvelgr's footsteps faded
away and Raef thought himself alone in the dark, his wrist burning where the giant's fingers had burrowed into his skin. But his
eyes were not the only things that adjusted to his new surroundings
and it was not long before Raef began to hear the sounds of living
things. Heavy, ragged breathing was the sound closest to him, but
in the distance Raef could also hear whispers and something that
might have been whimpering, though it sounded more animal than
child. There was no light to see by, only the faintest of differences
between black and blacker.

"Hello? Is anyone there?" The noises ceased at the sound of
Raef's voice and all was quiet. "I heard you. You need not fear me."

The breathing was the first to resume, though quieter and more restrained than before as though its owner was desperate to keep quiet, and Raef pressed himself close to the iron bars. "You are close. Will you not answer?" Raef waited and considered the possibility that whoever he spoke to could not answer, rather than would not.

"My name is Raef," he went on. "My home is green and bright. The trees grow tall and the mountains stretch to the sun. My waters are clear and cold and the sea beats upon my shore." Silence. "It is winter there. The snow will cover the land, the trees will drip with icicles, the sun will hang heavy on the horizon, casting long blue shadows. My people will look to the stars and dream of a warm summer night." Raef closed his eyes, his words bringing sadness to his own heart as he wondered if he would ever see his home again, or if the world would see another summer twilight. Lost now to his own mind, Raef grew quiet.

How much time passed before the voice answered him, he could not say. It belonged to the ragged breathing, of that he was sure, and it was so faint, so whisper-thin, at first, that Raef had to strain to hear it.

"Your words are like rain on the dry earth." A violent, dry cough followed but when the voice continued it was stronger. "Long have I dwelt in this darkness, but I see it now, light and beauty untouched by shadow. Tell me more."

Raef wanted to ask questions, wanted to know so much, but he did not want to frighten his listener, so he complied, reaching deep for words only to find them ready and waiting at the tip of his tongue. "A swift, joyful river jumps with silver fish, the birds call to each other and to the sun, their voices carried on the breeze. Wolves roam my forests, strong and silent in the shadows, and the meadows bloom with color. High above, kings of mountain and sky, the eagles soar." Raef trailed off, unsure how to continue.

"I can see them. I can hear them. I can smell the good earth." The voice was wistful and full of yearning, but there was gladness there, too. "Thank you for these words."

"Will you give me your name?"

There was a pause and then, "Skarpi was the name I knew as a child, sharp-boned and skinny. Skjaldi when my shoulders grew broad and I became a man."

"And now?"

"Now I should be Staeinn, for my limbs have turned to stone and my strength has left me."

"Where are you from?"

"Hullbern was my home."

"I have seen Hullbern," Raef said. In truth, he had seen it empty and broken, its fortress ruined at the hands of Torrulf Palesword and his devastating army. Better not to say that. Raef asked the question that was most dear to him. "How long have you been here?"

A longer pause this time. "At first I kept count as best I could. But I no longer know. Long enough to know I have grown old. I think he has forgotten me, or I would be dead."

"Forgotten you? What do you mean?"

This silence was the longest and Raef began to fear the man would not answer. "Our keeper craves blood sport. That is why we are here. We fight, we kill, to survive. He plucks us up from our tombs, brings us to the great arena, and pits us against the captives of others. Some return, some do not." Skjaldi heaved an unsteady breath, his voice growing weaker. "Long has it been since I was in the arena. I was young, then. If he chose me now, I would die." Raef heard something akin to hope in the other man's voice.

"Have you ever tried to escape?"

There was a sound Raef thought might be a feeble laugh. "Yes. Once. Everyone tries once."

"Why only once?"

"The giants, they know things, they can learn who we are, where we came from." A deep breath. "Who we care for."

Raef understood. "Hrodvelgr threatens our families."

"I could not risk my daughter's life. She was so small. Such a tiny thing."

"But he can travel to Midgard." Silence. "He must have a way. All the giants must. What do you know of it?"

"Please. I am tired."

Raef bit his lip to keep from persisting. He was desperate to know more about how the giants journeyed to Midgard and how often. It had to be seldom, or men would know of it and tongues would carry the tale far and wide, but it meant there was a way. Raef waited and then called again to Skjaldi. There was no response. Sliding down against the wall of his cell, Raef slumped to the stone floor. There was one small thing to be glad of: it was not cold.

Raef had no sense of time. The sun did not rise, did not cross the sky, did not set. There was only his growing hunger to measure time in the darkness. He had eaten well in Mogthrasir's hall so when his belly came to life he knew much time had to have passed. Of his neighbors, he heard little. The occasional scuffle, a whisper here, a cough there. Of Skjaldi he heard nothing, though if he strained his ears he thought he could make out the man's troubled breath. Raef stood, paced, sat, relieved himself in a corner of his cell, and slept.

When the darkness fled before an oncoming torch, Raef had to shield his eyes from the fierce light but he sprang to his feet and clutched the bars of his cell.

"Hrodvelgr!" Raef shouted. The footsteps and the torch came closer but it was not Hrodvelgr's face that peered into Raef's cell. Another giant, this one old and bent, scowled down at Raef.

"Silence, scum. Hrodvelgr does not wish to hear from you."

"I want to speak with him," Raef said, ignoring the giant's words.

"Get back," the old giant said. "Get back or you will get nothing to eat." He waggled an iron key and a platter stacked with wooden bowls in front of Raef.

Raef wanted to defy the orders, but his stomach protested and he knew he needed to eat and keep his strength. It would do no good to grow weak and witless. Raef went to the far wall of his cell. The giant opened the door and shoved a bowl inside. Sprinting forward, Raef tried to rush the door but the distance was too great and the gate clanged shut again, beyond the reach of his outstretched arms. The giant chuckled, a wet, hacking sound, and spit a gob of phlegm that Raef had to duck to avoid.

"Hrodvelgr cannot ignore me forever," Raef said, but the giant paid no attention and turned his back. He and his torch moved from cell to cell, distributing bowls of food to the other prisoners, then the light disappeared.

In the blackness, Raef used his hands to find the food. He sniffed it, was glad to discover it did not smell rotten, and then scooped it into his mouth with his fingers. The substance was pasty with pieces of something that tore between Raef's teeth as meat would. He tried not to think about what it was and ate quickly until the bowl was empty. Swallowing the last, Raef would have given much for a drop of water.

Clearing his throat, Raef called out into the darkness. "Do they bring water?" His voice rolled off the stone.

"Sometimes." The answer did not come from Skjaldi. The voice was farther away, but clear, and Raef found he was unsure if it was male or female.

"Who are you?"

"I am one of them."

"Why would they imprison one of their own?"

"Why is anyone ever imprisoned?"

"Will you give me your name? You heard mine already."

"Bara."

"A daughter of Aegir?" Raef could not keep the surprise from his voice.

"One of nine, yes."

"And Jötunheim is your home."

Bara snorted in derision. "My home is the sea and the foam and storm."

"But you know Jötunheim."

"I do. And I know what you would ask of me."

Raef asked anyway. "Will you tell me the way to Midgard, the way home?"

"Why?"

There were so many reasons but Raef could think of only one that might appeal to the giantess.

"I could tell you that I will kill Hrodvelgr and all those who put you here. I could make promises that I might not keep. But I will say only this instead and let you judge my worthiness." Raef took a deep breath. "You will help me because the end of all worlds is at hand. Because this and all else will come crashing down. Because we will burn at the hands of fiery Surt and then the sea will rise and swallow us all."

Bara was silent.

"Balder is dead and everything that follows has been set in motion." Still she said nothing and Raef began to feel he had misjudged the giantess.

When Bara spoke, her voice was strong. "If death nips at our heels, as Skoll does the sun and Hati the moon, what difference does it make if you die here or in your homeland?"

"None," Raef admitted, "and yet all. In all the nine worlds, I have one purpose left to me. I walk a path of vengeance and I would see it to the end before the fires come." Raef had not intended to speak of his father for he had thought the giantess would care little. But it was the truth and it had come out.

"I know something of vengeance. I will tell you what you need to know. But not now. Now they come for you. If you live, we will speak again."

Raef did not understand and he began to protest, but then he, too, heard the sounds of heavy footsteps on stone.

Three giants burst into the cavern, torches blazing. Hrodvelgr led them. "Midgardian," he roared. "It is time we knew the color of your blood."

ᚾ ᚾ ᚾ

The arena was vast, meant to confine much larger occupants with ease, and thundered with the voices of giants calling for blood. Raef stayed close to the stone walls that dwarfed him, gaze roving the arena for the first sign of attack. The light was feeble and four geysers that spit plumes of hazy, ash-filled clouds made visibility even worse. Raef shifted his grip on the sword that had been thrust upon him, his only weapon. It was bent and so brittle Raef feared it would break at the slightest touch, but it was sized for a man and there was some measure of sharpness left in the blade. He could kill with it, given the chance.

The giants were deafening as they screamed for death. If Raef had cared to look, he would have seen great treasures and riches, gleaming gold and flashing gems, pawed over by grasping hands and lusted after by greedy eyes, and all wagered on his life. But he did not look. Instead he let the lump in his chest swell until it consumed him, and there, there he found the battle-joy. His every muscle tingled with anticipation, his vision narrowed, shutting out the bloodthirsty spectators, and his heart sang of victory.

At last the gate at the far end of the arena opened and, through the smoky air, Raef saw his opponent.

The figure was thin, small, shrunken. A man, Raef decided, though wilted from hard use and long years. He carried a sword, a blade as rough as Raef's, but it hung low, as though he did not have the strength to wield it. His steps brought him closer to Raef but his gaze hugged the ground, his face hidden from Raef by a matted beard and long, tangled hair.

When he came within five paces of Raef, he stopped and raised his head, his eyes listless but for a glimmer of pain, pain that had been long-endured and thrust into a bleak corner of the mind and body. Raef saw nothing in his opponent to give him pause. He was neither strong nor nimble, angry nor scared. He was there to die and he knew it.

Their eyes met as the uproar around them reached a new frenzy and for a moment neither man moved, then the other man lifted his weapon, his arm shaking with the effort, and Raef knew it was time.

The blades clashed once and even that was too much for the stranger to bear. The sword dropped from his hand, clanging to the ground, and he stood defenseless in front of Raef, swaying. The giants roared, calling for Raef to take his eyes, break his fingers, make him run so he could be hunted down like prey, but Raef would not give them the satisfaction of such cruel sport. Retrieving the sword, Raef pressed it back into the man's palm. His fingers only curled around the hilt partway, so Raef held it there with a firm grip. Stepping close to the stranger, Raef whispered in his ear, "Go in peace and drink with my father in Valhalla."

Raef's bent sword slid between the man's ribs with ease and Raef watched life fade from his eyes. He went limp and Raef lowered him to the ground, hoping his final moments had been easier than those that came before. The giants were furious and shouted abuse at Raef, but his own fury burned bright.

"Hrodvelgr! Is this how you think to break me? By making me strip the life from those who cannot defend themselves? You think to kill me with my own compassion? I am more cruel than you know."

"You know nothing of cruelty, filth," Hrodvelgr answered. "I was born in it."

"If it is sport you want, send me someone worthy of me and I will give you a good bleeding."

The giants muttered to each other and Hrodvelgr shouted a command. The gate opened a second time and a pair of giants prodded a creature into the arena with sharp spears. The beast, the height of a horse but built like a mountain and covered in coarse, dark hair, growled in protest, teeth snapping. As the giants backed away, the creature stalked them, gnashing a great curved pair of teeth that hung out of the upper jaw, but it made no move to attack. When the gate shut, the beast snarled and at last Raef became the focus of its attention.

Man and beast circled, gaze never straying from the other. Raef's steps narrowed the gap between them even as he continued to move to his right, and the creature grew more infuriated with every move.

The charge was strong and thunderous, but slow and Raef evaded with little effort. Sliding on the worn rock, the creature spun to advance a second time. This time, Raef sidestepped and slashed at its rear legs. The damage was not great and the creature only grew more inflamed. The third attack was just as fierce and again Raef's sword bit into the beast's exposed flesh, but the fourth was more calculated as the beast churned toward Raef once more, matching Raef's footwork and succeeding in pressing Raef back.

Off balance, Raef ducked and rolled to avoid the slavering teeth. Reaching up, he stabbed into the creature's underbelly but the creature's weight and momentum tore the bent sword from Raef's grasp and Raef found himself weaponless as the beast gathered itself for another run. The sword dangled from its belly and blood dripped down the hilt and to the ground.

Before the creature could charge again, Raef was on the move, his feet carrying him over the smooth stone. As he closed the distance, the creature lumbered forward and at the last instant Raef dropped to the ground and slid. The beast ducked its head, trying to catch up its prey in its massive jaws, and one long tooth grazed Raef's right forearm as he shielded his face from damage. With his other hand, he reached for the hilt, grasping tight despite the hot, slippery blood. Wrenching hard, Raef drew the blade through the beast's belly as he continued to slide, and then he was out from under it. The creature roared and twisted, trying to attack, but its legs faltered and it fell forward on its face. Leaping forward, Raef jumped on the creature's back and plunged his sword down into its neck. Life left in a flood of gore and the body fell limp to the ground but Raef wasn't finished.

Raising his blood-streaked arms, he called to the giants in the arena. "Is this enough blood for you?" Sliding off the creature's back, Raef hacked and hacked with the battered blade until he had severed the head from the body. Dipping his fingers in the blood that pooled on the stone, Raef wiped them down one side of his face and then the other, his eyes locked with Hrodvelgr.

When the pair of giants lifted him up by the arms, he did not protest but let them carry him from the arena amid the shouts of the giants who bellowed for revenge for their fallen creature. He was tossed back into his cell with more force than was necessary but he did not let the giants see his grimace as he rolled off his bruised shoulder and got back to his feet. "Tell Hrodvelgr my offer still stands," Raef called to the backs of the retreating giants, and then darkness fell once more.

Only then did Raef use his fingers to assess the damage the creature's tooth had done to his arm. Though he had no light to see by, gentle prodding revealed that the slash was short but deep. There was nothing he could do and he slumped against the wall of his cell, weary and desperate for water, his forearm burning with pain. Closing his eyes, Raef drifted in and out of sleep as the blood, both his and the creature's, grew sticky and tight on his skin.

When he became alert, he did not know how much time had passed, only that a voice seemed to be calling to him. At first he thought it was Eira's voice and then it seemed to be Siv, but as his eyes and mind focused, he knew it was Bara's. Lurching to his feet, Raef found the bars of his cell.

"I am here," he called out into the black.

"Then you have not died of your wounds." The giantess sounded pleased.

"No. It is thirst I suffer from." Raef licked his lips.

"How many did you kill?"

"A man, old and beaten, a husk of what he used to be. And then a creature of some kind. Never have I seen its like."

A pause lingered in the blackness. "Did it have a pair of long teeth?"

"Yes."

"Then you are not likely to see the light of day again."

"What do you mean?"

"Once, my people kept many of those creatures. Though strong and ferocious, they could be controlled and they did hard labor. But a sickness swarmed through their ranks and their numbers dwindled. The strongest survived and these were carefully bred, but time was against them. Only one remained and he stalked Hrodvelgr's halls like a king, the mightiest of champions. Now, he is dead and Hrodvelgr will never forget who wielded the sword that took the life blood from him."

"If he was so precious, Hrodvelgr should have kept him out of the arena. Let Hrodvelgr challenge me himself. I will earn my freedom."

"You should not wish for such things."

Angry and reckless, Raef shouted, "I would wish for anything that would bring me home."

Skjaldi's voice broke in, faint but strong enough in the silence. "Please. Be careful of what you say. You do not know who might be listening."

Raef took a deep breath and fought to calm himself. "Bara. You promised me the knowledge I seek should I survive. Here I am. I ask that you speak and fulfill your promise. Tell me how I may leave this forsaken place."

The silence dragged on and Raef began to despair of hearing the giantess' voice again. The pain pulsing from the wound on his forearm had lessened, but now it flooded back. Raef's fingers tightened over the iron bar he had been clutching.

"I beg you." Raef's voice drifted into the darkness and still nothing answered it. He closed his eyes and rested his forehead against the bars of his cell.

"The way is ancient and perilous. I do not know that a man would survive it." Bara sounded reluctant.

"And yet I must try."

"From Hrodvelgr's halls, travel north for two days and two nights. There you will see a labyrinth of sharp rock. Look for the gate wreathed in smoke. Only there can you enter and you must follow the red stones, nothing else. Do not stray from the path. If you do, you are lost."

"Sounds simple enough."

"A fool's words. The very air you breath will wreak havoc with your mind and draw you astray. There is nothing simple about the labyrinth."

"Then how do your people traverse it?"

"Because we must. It is our last possession from a more ancient world. It was not made by the gods, does not answer to them. The labyrinth is ours, a reminder of past glory, and so we cling to it even though it is not kind to us." Bara paused. "There, I have told you what I know. Think of me when you have your revenge and I will know sweet satisfaction."

"Why do you not escape?"

Bara did not answer right away. "Hrodvelgr keeps me here because I would not submit to him. I have not seen the outside of this cell once during my captivity. He does not bring me to the arena, he does not attempt to win me over. He keeps me here in darkness and waits for me to die."

"Perhaps I can help," Raef began, but Bara cut him off.

"No," she said, her voice fierce. "If your chance comes, it will be brief. You must not waste it on me. Or anyone here."

Raef kept his thoughts to himself and sat down on the floor of his cell. Time passed in darkness and in doubt. He knew only a growing thirst and weariness that ragged fits of sleep could not overcome. The cells around him were quiet and Raef, when he was conscious, did not feel like speaking. Though he tried to banish them by thinking of home and Eira, his thoughts were dark and full of images of battle and fire and death. Once, he woke himself from a fitful sleep, the dreadful eyes of Fenrir the great wolf burned into his mind and across his eyelids. Though he had not cried out, his heart pounded and sweat glazed his face. He did not sleep again for a long time, but kept his eyes, wide and staring, fixed on the floor of his cell.

# ELEVEN

HOW MUCH TIME passed, Raef could not comprehend but for knowing it had to be a matter of days. At last a flicker of light returned and Raef was glad to see the old giant's cracked and crumbling face, glad of the sloppy stew that was pushed into his cell, and most glad to see a cup of precious water. Raef fell upon the food like a ravenous wolf and gulped the water down, his tongue probing the cup for each and every drop. When the bowl was wiped clean, Raef flung it against the far wall of his cell and groped among the shards until he found one that was sharp and as long as his hand. This he tucked between his pants and belt, then rolled the wool down over the belt to hide the sharp pottery. The food, poor as it was, signaled that he was not meant to die just yet and that gave him strength beyond nourishment.

But the brief light brought by the giant's torch had shown him something that gnawed at his mind. Unwashed and untended, the angry wound on his arm was oozing blood and puss. And the heat he had at first felt only in the skin surrounding the slash was spreading, coiling its way up to Raef's elbow. Had he been more careful, he might have saved a splash of water to wash the wound, but in his heart he knew it was not enough.

Sleep came, and with it a fever. Raef jerked awake long enough to know the sensation of sweat beading on his forehead and chest, to feel the frantic fluttering of his heart as it fought against the invading heat, but then the fever sucked him back down into the depths of unconsciousness. And he began to dream.

The nightmares wracked through him with far greater potency than before. No longer did Fenrir come alone to torment him. A pale face that Raef knew to be Loki's joined the wolf, but the god's presence was not what brought screams to Raef's lips. He saw his father, alive despite the gaping wound in his belly, an accusation on Einarr's tongue. But before his father could speak his condemnation, he vanished, replaced by Vakre, pierced with arrows, Siv, impaled on a spear, Eira, her heart carved from her chest. A moment's reprieve as Raef surfaced, awake, gasping for air, and then he was lost once more. Again and again Raef watched his friends die, watched his home burn, watched the forests of Vannheim wither and die, watched a great wave rise up from the ocean, until at last the world that came to him when he closed his eyes became too much to bear. Though exhausted, though the fever beckoned him, he did not sleep, but Raef knew it was only a matter of time before the images invaded his waking eyes as well.

When the jailor came a second time and deposited food and water in his cell, Raef crawled to it on hands and knees. He downed half the water and spread the rest over his wound with trembling fingers, but only managed to force down a few swallows of the meager stew before he set the bowl down, drained and sick to his stomach. When Bara called out to him once, her voice seeming very far away, he did not answer, for all his strength was concentrated on staying awake. Of Skjaldi there was no sound but for the broken, ragged breathing that seemed to come and go, at times filtering into Raef's embattled consciousness.

When the light came a third time, Raef did not remove his gaze from the wall of his cell and at first did not notice that the old giant had stopped at his door. Only when the keys came out, jangling in the silence, did he shift his glance to the bars.

"Time to go. Up with you."

Raef's muscles obeyed, though they were clumsy and slow, and he stumbled to the door.

Sneering, the giant picked Raef up by his ankles and dangled him upside down. He lifted Raef until they were eye to eye. "Men are weak."

As they moved between the cells, their way lit by torchlight, Bara's voice came to him.

"Remember who you are. Remember what you have promised."

"Silence," the jailor yelled, but Bara would not be subdued.

"Courage, Raef, and remember."

The stone door ground shut behind them, leaving Bara in darkness. Raef tried to cling to her words, tried to imagine them an ember that he could hold in his heart. He closed his eyes and saw not the world's ending, but a spark of light, faint but steady. It seemed to pulse in time with the beating of his heart. When he opened his eyes, the spark vanished but, though he was drenched in fever and devoid of strength, there was something new deep in his core, something that felt like hope.

The old giant deposited Raef on a stone floor. At first he crumpled, then fought through dizziness to raise himself to his feet. The fever that had burned so bright still ate at him but Raef forced himself to master the heat, pushing it down until it only crackled beneath the surface of his skin, until he could think clearly. Before him rose six massive steps and at their peak sat Hrodvelgr in an iron throne. The air was fresh in this cavern, free from the ashy plumes that had fouled Raef's lungs in his cell and Raef took as deep a breath as he dared. As the giant watched Raef sway and struggle for balance, he could not keep a satisfied smirk from marring his handsome face.

"Not so bold, now? A pity. I rather like it when they want to fight." Hrodvelgr rose and descended the steps. He circled Raef once. "I am unarmed. Would you like to strike me down, draw my blood? I know you want to. Your hatred burns within you. Go on," Hrodvelgr spread his arms, "do your worst." When Raef did nothing, the giant let loose a rumbling laugh, then peered down into Raef's eyes. "Perhaps you burn less bright than I thought. Perhaps the darkness took too much from you."

Raef did not look away from Hrodvelgr's face, but it was not the giant's straight nose and dark blue eyes that he saw. Instead he looked inward and saw the spark, brighter than before. "You have broken me, Hrodvelgr. I admit that I am no match for you."

Hrodvelgr laughed again. "Spoken like a true waste of flesh and blood. At last you know your place in this world. But tell me, what am I to do with you? You are too weak to fight in my arena. Perhaps I can yet make a slave of you. Would you like to pour my mead? Wash my hair?"

"Do with me as you will, only grant me one thing."

Hrodvelgr's eyes narrowed slightly. "What do you speak of?"

"Your knowledge, for I have been awed by your mighty race and surely you must be wiser even than Odin himself."

The frown grew but was at odds with Hrodvelgr's swollen pride. The giant's vanity won. "What would you know?"

"Three things, only," Raef said. The giant smiled, showing his teeth. "But," Raef went on, "if you cannot answer one of my questions, you must grant me a favor." Again Hrodvelgr's face grew dark with suspicion. Raef held his breath.

"Agreed. But if I answer you, you will be my slave and I will hunt down all those you cherish in Midgard and bring them here to die."

Raef swallowed and blinked, seeing the blood of his dying friends once more behind his eyelids. "Agreed."

"Then ask your first question."

"Dew gathers in valleys and low places. Where does it come from?"

Hrodvelgr did not manage to hide his surprise from Raef. He stomped up to his throne and sat down again before answering. "Hrimfaxi the stallion draws night across the sky. Foam falls from his mouth at dawn when he has reached the end of his labors. This is the dew in the dales. What else would you know?"

"Wind travels over waves and whistles through the mountains. Where does it come from?"

"The great eagle, Hraesvelg, the Corpse Eater, sits at the end of the world. Wind is born from the flapping of his mighty wings." Hrodvelgr looked impatient and less sure of himself now. "Come, be done with it. What is your third and final question?"

"Your hall is home to a man. Skjaldi he is called. What was the name he knew as a child?"

Hrodvelgr was still on his throne, his face rigid, and Raef knew the giant was caught in his own arrogance. A vein at his temple pulsed and at last Hrodvelgr burst to his feet. "You are false! This is no question."

"Answer me." Raef held his ground as Hrodvelgr pounded down the steps and came to a halt in front of Raef. The giant towered above but in his bewilderment did not strike. "Answer me," Raef repeated.

Hrodvelgr began to pace, his hands clenched into fists. "What name, what name," he muttered to himself. He rounded on Raef, his posture proud but his eyes betrayed his doubt. "Do not think to deceive me. His name was Skjaldi then as it is now."

"Wrong."

Hrodvelgr howled and charged, but Raef seized on the spark that had swelled into a flame and found strength yet in his limbs. Throwing himself out of the giant's path, Raef retrieved the shard of pottery that he had hidden at his waist. Small it was, but sharp, and it was enough to give the giant pause. Hrodvelgr pulled up, his gaze flickering between Raef's face and the tiny weapon in his hand.

"Would you violate our agreement, Hrodvelgr? You made a deal and if you do not fulfill it, Odin will strike you down and all the nine realms will know you to be a liar and an oathbreaker."

"Odin has no power here," Hrodvelgr shouted, but he made no move and the doubt grew.

"Would you risk all over me? Would you risk the wrath of Thor? Or would you rather grant me the favor you agreed to?"

Hrodvelgr's handsome face was twisted with anger, his jaw clenched tight, his nostrils flared. When he spoke, his voice was hard and tense, his words pulled taut over his teeth, as though he had to force the breath from his lungs. "What do you want?"

"You will free the prisoners, each and every one, and grant them safe passage from your lands and the lands of all your kin."

"You do not ask for your own freedom?"

"No. But mine will come to me." Raef could only hope he was right, but he heard Bara's warning ring in his ears and wondered if he was making the wrong choice, if he should have escaped on his own. Only time would tell.

Hrodvelgr remained suspicious but put on a pleased front. "You will regret that. I will spill your blood painful drop by painful drop. You will die in slow agony. But before your eyes grow dark, you will know that I have brought destruction to all you cherish."

Raef said nothing and did not look away from Hrodvelgr's face. The giant turned and bellowed. The jailor who had brought Raef to him answered his call. "Free the prisoners. Leave this one with me."

The wait seemed interminable but at last the ragged life forms that had long dwelt in the darkness and despair of Hrodvelgr's halls came forth. Men, giants, beings Raef did not know, and still others with bronze skin and pale, colorless eyes. Some showed joy, others shuffled their feet past Hrodvelgr as though they feared a trick, a cruel joke, was being played upon them, that they might reach the outer doors and feel the fresh air, only to be yanked back into the depths of the blackest of Hrodvelgr's caverns.

Raef watched them go. It seemed to him that none dared look him in the eye, though he caught many glancing away when he looked at them, and he began to fear that he had misjudged, that he would die as Hrodvelgr said. One by one, they filtered by until the footsteps ceased and the hall grew quiet. Raef was alone.

The scream came from behind Hrodvelgr's throne and Raef and the giant whirled together but it was too late for Hrodvelgr. The spear took him in the chest and he stumbled backward, surprise chasing away pain. A second pierced his belly and he doubled over, clutching the wooden shaft. He found his voice, then, though it was only a senseless roar as he fell to his knees. Raef had to jump out of the way to avoid Hrodvelgr's flailing arm.

The attacker stepped forward, a third spear in her hand. She leaned in close to Hrodvelgr's face, her other hand pulling his hair back to expose his throat. She pushed the tip of the spear up against his neck. Hrodvelgr growled, his eyes burning with hate, but the spears had rendered him weak and he could not defend himself. She did not curse him, did not revel in his defeat. Instead she slid the spear into his throat and did not stop until the head had exited out the back of his neck. She held him while he twitched, blood pouring from his throat, then removed the spear. Tossing the weapon to the ground, she dropped Hrodvelgr's body to the stone and turned to face Raef.

"Bara." For there was no doubting who stood before him.

"You should not have done that." The giantess, her hands covered in Hrodvelgr's blood, was dressed in what Raef could only say was sea foam and her long blonde hair cascaded over her shoulders. She was beauty and danger. She was the harsh and ever-changing sea.

"I could not leave you to rot. Any of you."

"Did you stop to think that some of his prisoners deserved death?"

"Perhaps. But that was not for Hrodvelgr to decide."

Bara cocked her head to one side. "You may be right." She turned to leave, then looked back. "Skjaldi remains. He will die this night."

"I will get him."

"Leave him." Bara was firm and faced him again. "It is not safe to roam these halls. Not now. There is no telling what might lurk in the dark." Her face softened a bit as Raef hesitated. "He dies a free man and he knows you have given him that. It is enough." This time Bara did not look back and stepped into the sunlight that waited for them. She closed her eyes and Raef watched the light, feeble and grey as it was, grow brighter in her presence.

Raef followed the daughter of Aegir and took a deep breath as he crossed the threshold into freedom. "Where will you go now?"

"The sea is calling to me. You must face the labyrinth."

"If I can reach it." In the sunlight, Raef saw himself for the first time. Skin blackened with blood and dirt, hands trembling, the angry wound on his arm red and oozing. He did not think he could stand much longer.

Bara held out her hand and reached down to touch Raef's cheek. Her fingers were cool and Raef closed his eyes as he felt a rushing wave splash over him and soothe his dry lips and parched throat. When he opened his eyes, he was not soaked to the skin as he might have thought and there was no water to be seen, but his desperate need had vanished, taking with it the fever in his skin. He could not have said for certain, but even the wound on his arm seemed less threatening in the wake of whatever Bara had given him.

Bara took her fingers away. "It is the best I can give you. Though it may not be enough." She looked to the sinking sun and then back at Raef. "You have done me a kindness, Raef. I will not forget it. Even if it was foolish." A hint of a smile made her even more beautiful, but no less deadly. "Keep to the path and you may yet see your home again."

"I will." They parted with a nod, Raef to the north and the peril that awaited him there, and Bara to the east and the rising moon.

# TWELVE

FOR TWO NIGHTS and two days Raef traversed the endless, barren landscape, traveling in as straight a line as possible, resting when he found the cover to do so safely. Of life he saw little. At dawn, a scavenging, bear-like creature kept its head buried in a mutilated carcass when Raef crept by. On the second night, a beast with tawny, moonlit fur stalked a ridge just above Raef's intended path. Raef skirted around and kept out of sight, resuming his northern trail only when he was certain the creature had not picked up his sent.

Bara's parting gift sustained him, keeping the thirst at bay, but on hunger it had no effect. Raef ignored his protesting stomach and the fatigue as best he could, pushing north, one step followed by another.

There was no mistaking the labyrinth as the sun set on the second day. Stretching east and west as far as Raef could see, it towered over him, sheer rock cliffs spiking to the sky, jagged and threatening, as hostile a place as Raef could imagine. Three gates Raef could see, but only one was wreathed in smoke and Raef approached it as the vent in the earth spewed forth another cloud of ash and hot air. The gate was taller than a giant but was no more than a crude hole in the rock as though the missing stone had been ripped and torn from its home. Just beyond the threshold, Raef could see a single stone the color of old, dried blood. It stood tall and straight and he knew he had found the way Bara had described.

With a single step, Raef crossed through the gate. The air was putrid and stank of dying flesh. The whisper of wind that wafted across Raef's cheek seemed somehow full of malice. Raef touched the hammer that hung around his neck and asked Thor for strength and endurance. Without looking back at the bleak, grey land of Jötunheim, he plunged onward.

Beyond the first blood stone, perhaps fifteen paces, was another, and a third stood in the distance, sentinels to whatever might befall those who walked the path. After the third, the way turned out of sight and Raef slid down a steep descent, nearly colliding with the fourth stone as he fought to catch himself on the loose rock. Finding his balance, Raef saw that two paths diverged, one twisting and narrow, the other straight but dark, hooded by a shelf of rock that hung over it. Barely visible, the next blood stone lingered in the darkness of the straight path. Raef scanned the rock shelf above, saw nothing to suggest danger, and continued on.

The moment he crossed into the shadow of the overhang, strong, icy fingers scrabbled to grip Raef's throat. Tearing at the invisible hand, Raef pushed forward but the cold fingers tightened and Raef had to struggle to take in air. Dropping to his knees, Raef fought on, the ice spreading up his neck to his face until Raef could see frost forming on his eyelashes. His vision grew dark with each choking breath, but there, there in the rock, was a sword, just out of reach in a path that had been hidden to Raef. If he could only take four steps, he could grasp it and fight off the frozen menace. And yet the blood stone, it lay ahead and Bara had promised death if he strayed from the path.

Raef fell to his hands, the last air fading from his lungs as he fought the urge to crawl to the sword. Gaze fixed on the blood stone, Raef edged forward, the cold seeping into his mind and through every vein, chilling his blood. A lifetime seemed to pass as Raef struggled on hands and knees but somehow the blood stone came in reach and Raef brushed his fingertips against its rough surface as he collapsed.

The pressure on his throat and the cold vanished in that instant. Raef gasped air into his burning lungs, seeing nothing but flashing stars though his eyes were wide open. He lay still; the will to do anything but breathe had fled. How long he remained facedown on the rock he could not say, but his fingers did not leave the blood stone. When he felt himself again, he got to his knees and looked back. The hidden passage in the rocky wall and the sword were gone and Raef knew he had been right not to succumb.

One at a time, Raef lifted his fingers from the stone, expecting to feel the icy grip again upon losing contact but nothing happened and he got to his feet. A gradual, curving slope rose up in front of him and Raef walked on, passing two more blood stones until the path ended, cut off by a cliff. High above, a blood stone jutted out of the cliff face, beckoning, and Raef began to climb.

At first, the handholds were many and easy to reach. Raef pulled himself up to a ledge no wider than his feet, then shuffled to his right, his gaze fixed on a curving crack in the rock that he could scuttle up. Beneath him, the ledge dropped away and Raef stretched out until he felt the crack beneath his fingers. Taking a deep breath, Raef pushed off the ledge and scrambled up with his feet until his other hand could find refuge in the crack. His fingers burned with the effort of holding his weight, and Raef wasted no time in traversing the crack. When at last he obtained more solid footing, Raef took a moment to breathe, but he could not afford to linger and waste his strength.

The holes and rock teeth grew scarcer the higher he went, but Raef persisted, knowing he had no other choice. As he neared the blood stone, arms shaking with the effort, his foot slipped and he dropped, caught only by his left arm. Raef's shout of desperation echoed around him as he dangled against the cliff. Gritting his teeth, Raef began to pull himself up, reaching with his other hand to find something, anything, to grab onto. His right hand gripped stone just as his left arm gave way and again Raef swung against the cliff. But the slight shift in position was enough for above him now was a clear path to the top.

The final part of the climb was agony. Raef's fingers were raw and numb, his arms loose and exhausted, only his feet remained strong and Raef relied on them to propel him to the top. When at last he crawled over the edge, Raef stretched out on the flat rock and felt his heart pound against the stone. After a long moment, Raef rolled over on his back and opened his eyes.

The sight made him forget to draw breath. Above him hung a luscious, green canopy. Air ruffled the leaves, sending two falling to the earth, and sunlight peeked through, warm on Raef's face. The ground was soft and mossy, damp with fresh rain, and Raef breathed in the scent he knew so well. It was Vannheim. He was home. Rising to his feet, he turned back to the cliff, only to find it was no longer there. This was a problem, he knew, the treachery of the labyrinth at work. But the voice that told him this was small and annoying and Raef pushed it away, letting birdsong take its place.

Turning again, Raef saw a small wooden hut thatched with earth and long grass, the kind a woodcutter might use deep in the forest, and he knew at once where he was. Raef closed his eyes and took another deep breath and when he opened them again, she was there, just as he remembered. The small voice returned, telling him she could not be there, telling him this was not real, but it seemed to him now like a whisper of water flowing in the distance and Raef let it wash away.

The girl was lithe and dark of hair. A band of flowers woven together rested on her head and her feet, pale and bare, caressed the damp grass.

"Svanja."

The girl smiled, her face bright and full of youth and yet her eyes were a woman's. "You are late."

"Will you forgive me?"

"Perhaps. Come closer and we will see." Raef did as she asked and reached out to touch her cheek. Svanja cast her eyes downward. "Is that the only place you wish to touch me? You were so bold last time."

"My father will be looking for me." The words were wrong. His father was dead. And yet if he was there at the hut with Svanja, then he was a boy again and Einarr Skallagrim lived.

"Let him look." Svanja took Raef's hand in her smaller one and began to walk backward to the hut, her eyes not leaving his. When they reached the door, she stopped and leaned forward, rising up on her tiptoes, to kiss him. Raef closed his eyes and let himself fall into the memory of that kiss, light and sweet, raw and inexperienced despite her words. She sank back down to her heels. "We should stay here forever."

The wreath of flowers had slipped to one side and Raef removed it from her silky hair, turning it between his fingers. She was right. They should stay there. Svanja tugged on his hand and Raef wanted to go with her but something kept his feet planted.

"I must go." He heard himself say it and then wished he had not, for Svanja's face fell, her disappointment plain. Raef extricated his fingers from hers and took half a step back. He looked at the flowers but they fell from his hand. He took another step back. "I must go," he repeated.

"Will you not stay with me?" Svanja's eyes were wide and blue and sad. "Please?"

The ground seemed to tilt beneath Raef's feet and he took

another unsteady step backward though every fiber of his being screamed at him to do the opposite. Raef looked over his shoulder and memory slammed back into him as the labyrinth revealed itself. There, just past those trees. A blood stone. He looked back at Svanja but she was gone. The hut remained and the green trees of Vannheim still beckoned. Raef fought the urge to take refuge in the forest, fought the urge to give in and turned his back on the hut, striding quickly toward the blood stone lest he lose his resolve.

He was five paces from the stone when the scream split the air. Whirling around, Raef saw the hut was in flames. Svanja's screams continued, piercing and full of terror. She called his name and Raef sprinted forward three steps before pulling up.

"You are not real. I am not here. This is not happening." Still she screamed and the hut was bursting now with impenetrable flames. Raef's breath caught. "Forgive me." He turned his back on the blaze and walked to the blood stone. Raef reached out and let his hand hover over it, its blood-red color holding new meaning, and closed his eyes. He dropped his hand to the stone.

Silence. Raef opened his eyes and he was back in the labyrinth. The cliff lay behind him; the dark, rocky landscape stretched out in front of him and another blood stone was in sight. Raef made his way to it and the one beyond, his feet continuing while his heart lingered. It was memory and madness and the work of the labyrinth he knew, but it had splintered him, leaving him feeling lost and forsaken in a way he had not felt even in his darkest hours in Hrodvelgr's prison.

How long he wandered from blood stone to blood stone, Raef could not have said, but at length he found he did not have the will to go on. There was nowhere to shelter, nowhere that might be safe, so Raef curled up against the next blood stone and fell into an exhausted, wretched sleep.

Of dreams Raef had no memory when he woke, but his mind

felt so scarred, so beaten down, that he was certain dark thoughts had assailed him in sleep. He trudged onward, the sallow sun crossing overhead, sending shadows spinning across his path. Twice he thought it twilight only to find the sun overhead and then off the eastern horizon as though it were but the break of day. Raef cursed the labyrinth, cursed his journey, and followed the blood stones. He grew weak with hunger as time seemed to drag by and then race forward. The moon rose once, twice, maybe three times, Raef could no longer be sure, and cold stars burned above him, callous watchmen indifferent to his plight.

A red sun rose, waking Raef from fitful sleep on a precipice above a deep, narrow canyon. He had dreamed of the deaths of his friends, not once, not twice, but endless in their agony, and for a moment he could do nothing but lie still, wondering if he might will his heart to cease beating. But then he was on his feet, swaying over the empty air that spread out in front of him. Raef imagined what it would be like to fall, to let go. But the next blood stone lay below, calling to him, and Raef reminded himself that he already knew what it felt like to fly, then began a slow, tricky descent into the depths of the canyon. At times the trail wound downwards, a progression of steep switchbacks, at times Raef had to lower himself down sheer walls to reach the next stone, but at last he reached the bottom, a dark, dusty place hidden from the faded sun. The air seemed sparse, thin, and Raef struggled to fill his lungs. A stone was in sight and Raef approached, only to see it was not saturated with the same blood-red color as the other stones had been. It was tall and straight, but it was grey and plain.

Turning, Raef backtracked but the canyon had changed. The rough walls he had scrambled down had turned smooth, polished even. He had lost the path.

A part of Raef wished to sink to the canyon floor, to let the labyrinth take him to oblivion, but a greater part of him would not give in to the labyrinth's demands. The path was gone and he would not find it again. Bara had said as much. But he refused to believe all was lost. He would not curl up and wait to die. He would wander until he met death head on or found another way out.

In his heart, Raef knew death would find him soon. He was weak in body and mind. But he had made a vow before the gods and he would honor that vow until his last breath.

The canyon twisted onward, meandering in darkness, at times so narrow Raef had to turn sideways to pass between the walls. He looked for a way out, but the walls remained smooth and impassable until the canyon gave way to emptiness. The walls dropped away, leaving only a flat expanse of rock in front of Raef. Winds swept across the stone, unhindered, battling themselves for supremacy, and buffeting Raef from all sides, immobilizing him. Raef ducked his head and tried to continue, but half a step proved too much and he dropped to his knees. The winds roared on, ripping across Raef's skin, and he brought his hands to his ears in a futile attempt to shield himself.

Raef pressed his face against the cool stone, seeking peace where none could be found, his body battered down by the relentless wind until he was stretched flat but still vulnerable to all. So this was to be his death, then, mired in an unceasing windstorm, stripped of dignity. Raef fought to cling to himself, forcing his mind to chase after memories of joy, of life. But he could hold on to nothing, not the battle-lust, not his father's laugh, not the sunlit trees of Vannheim, it all flitted away even as he reached for it. Siv's face flashed before him, a bolt of lightning gone too soon, and Raef found he could not conjure Eira's image, or Vakre's. They were shadows, untouched even by starlight.

Raef touched the hammer at his neck. Odin, Allfather. He should pray. He should beg. But the words would not come. Raef closed his eyes and wondered if he would become part of the wind.

He saw himself get swept away, piece by human piece, until the world was grey and quiet and he knew it was over.

ᛉ ᛉ ᛉ

And yet there was life still in Raef. Somewhere. His heart beat on, low and steady, and it seemed to grow in strength, refusing to let Raef float away, until he could ignore it no longer and opened his eyes.

At first, all was white, bright, shining, vibrant white, and Raef blinked away the darkness of the labyrinth. He was standing, though he did not remember getting to his feet, a wooden floor stretching out beneath him. The boards were wide and smooth, streaked with golden hues, and Raef followed their lines until his eyes took in pillars, strong, straight, and flawless, worked from wood and metal. Of walls he saw none, and where the roof should have been, there was only a sky burning a more brilliant shade of blue than he had ever witnessed.

He stared up at the vast expanse of the sky, lulled into its beauty and unable to tear his eyes away. If this was death, it was beautiful, but it was not Valhalla. Unless Heimdall had already sounded his horn and the great hall of dead warriors had emptied out to fill the plain of battle, this was some other place. Raef raised a hand to shield his eyes from the fierce light of the sun and saw that his skin was clean, saw that the slash on his arm was gone as if it had never been. Raef looked down at his body, searching first for the slice on his upper arm earned in the battle in Alfheim, then for the burned scar Vakre had given him to heal the wound in his side. They, too, had disappeared, replaced by smooth, unblemished skin, and Raef did not need to look further to know every scar on his body had vanished.

Raef turned, aware now of being watched. He thought the eyes on him were not malicious but he could not discern a figure among the pillars.

"Who is there?" His own voice was bright and sharp. It sounded foreign to his ears, but strong. "Show yourself."

"Here, Skallagrim, I am here."

The speaker's voice was fluid and unhurried, full of quiet strength, and Raef felt his heart miss a beat. He hesitated, though he could not have said why, before turning to confront the voice. What he saw took all breath from him.

"This is a dream. This is inside my head," Raef said when his voice belonged to him again.

"It is."

"Then you are not here and this is not real."

"Do not be so sure."

"Allfather." The name whispered across Raef's exhaled breath.

The god studied Raef, his single eye unblinking, hands resting on his mighty spear. "You do not fear me."

"I am beyond fear, Allfather. Death is seeking me and soon I shall be found. Fear will change nothing."

Odin's expression remained stern. "And what of those you love? Do you still feel fear for them, for their lives?"

Raef's heart leaped in his chest. "What do you know of them?"

"You are bold. Seldom do men make demands of me." Odin was motionless and yet the unblinking eye grew dread and fierce and Raef felt the urge to flee from the Terrible One. He stood his ground and let the wave of terror abate. At last Odin blinked and the fire shrank to a spark. "We have met before, you and I." The Allfather's gaze drifted past Raef. "In the snows of Darfallow. Do you remember?"

Raef frowned. "It was Loki I met in the mountains."

"Yes, him you know. But there was another. One you built a funeral pyre for."

"Tormund," Raef said, his mind revisiting the empty halls of Darfallow. Odin nodded and to Raef he seemed sad. "Why?"

"I knew you sought the Deepminded. And so did I know you would find only the illusions of Loki. I shrouded the true Darfallow and its lord and replaced it with my own, meaning to keep you from him, to turn you back. But I did not know you then, as I do now. I did not know the strength of your resolve." Odin's single eye stared hard at Raef. "Perhaps even you did not." The Allfather came closer to Raef. "You are strong of will, Raef Skallagrim. It has served you well. I can end your suffering." When Raef did not speak, Odin began to pace and he seemed to circle the world with every step.

"Hear me well, young Skallagrim. There is no place for you in Valhalla. I have touched the runes the Norns carve for you and, though your fate is shadowed, there is no doubt in my mind. You are not meant to walk the field of Folkvangr and the heroes of old will not welcome you with thundering cheers and precious mead. You must follow another path, one I cannot see, and though I would wish to have you among the Einherjar, it was not for me to decide. It never is."

Odin's words seeped into Raef like a morning chill that no warmth could draw out. To know that he would be denied a place beside his father and the other Einherjar and that even Odin was powerless to change this fate was worse than any death Raef had imagined for himself, worse than the labyrinth.

"I have an offer for you, one befitting a man who has battled Loki and survived to tell of it, and one that thwarts the runes the Norns have made in Yggdrasil. All this," Odin waved his hand and the white hall vanished, leaving Raef once more in the grey world of the labyrinth, "all this shall pass. You have suffered enough. Let me give you a new home."

The windstorm was no less violent and yet Raef felt as though it passed over him, kept at bay by a hidden barrier. "What home do you speak of?"

"The farthest stars play host to a hall of unsurpassed beauty, a green, fair realm free of pain and free of the fate that awaits us all in these nine worlds. Neither giants nor gods made it and neither race can set foot there. Yggdrasil, for all the world ash tree's mighty reach, cannot touch it."

"How?" Raef asked.

"How can I give such a gift? At a cost, of course." The Allfather removed one hand from his spear and brought it to the patch over his missing eye. His good eye stared past Raef.

"What cost?"

Odin was quiet for a long moment and when he did speak, his voice was soft and weary. "One you need not burden yourself with."

Raef stared into the Allfather's good eye, but it revealed nothing.

"You would find peace."

The peace Odin spoke of reached Raef on a breath of warm, fresh air, a gentle breeze on an unending summer's eve. Raef closed his eyes and inhaled, and though he could see in his mind's eye this flawless realm with its golden twilight, its pure, sprightly streams, its nimble shadows and bright stars, he had his answer ready.

"You speak of a home any man might wish for, Allfather. You honor me and I should find joy in this. But in my heart I smell the salt shores of Vannheim, I hear the waves pounding against cliffs I climbed as a boy, I hear the birds in the forests I know as well as my own hands, and I see the sun sparkling off the deep fjords that taught me to swim. That is my home, Allfather, and I do not want another. And though you will not speak of the cost, I know enough to know it would be great indeed. I will not ask such a sacrifice of you."

Odin was silent for a long moment and Raef felt the wind begin to rip through the barrier.

"You reject what I can give you, what is surely a better fate than any that awaits you?" Odin's voice revealed wonder rather than anger. Raef nodded. "You understand what I have told you, that you will not ride with the others to the last battle? That Valhalla's gates will never open for you?"

"I understand. And though this gives me endless sorrow, I still choose Vannheim in the hopes that I might see it again and take up my father's seat in his hall." The chill ate at him still, threatening unspeakable doom, but Raef meant every word.

"I do not promise that you will."

Raef nodded. "I know. Do you think me foolish?"

Odin's eye burned bright once more, though this time not with wrath but with life. He stepped closer to Raef. "I hung myself on Yggdrasil for nine days to sate my lust for knowledge. That was foolish beyond measure. And yet I knew no other course. My blood demanded it and my bones sang of it. We gain nothing without risk and sometimes we must risk all. I will see that they sing of your courage, Skallagrim, no matter the fate that befalls you."

Raef bowed his head, expecting the Allfather to end the conversation, but Odin seemed to be waiting. "May I ask a question?" Raef said.

"You may ask." Odin's eye flashed and Raef thought he saw a touch of laughter in the blue iris.

"Did you send me here? Did Freyja? Frigg? Loki? Did you send me to Alfheim?"

The hint of laughter faded. "No god has had a hand in your journey, Skallagrim."

"But you will not say more."

"No."

"Then answer this. Jötunheim is barren, a wasteland, and yet the giants feast on endless stores of food and drink mead sweeter and stronger than any hall in Midgard can offer. Why do you give them such bounty and treat them as kings?

Odin's face had grown still and suddenly Raef could see the cares worn into the Allfather's skin. "What would you do with a creature that does not know its own strength?"

The hair on Raef's arms stood up and a chill crept down his spine. "Has your grip over them become so tenuous?"

Now Odin did laugh, a deep, dreadful sound that shook Raef's bones. "It was always tenuous, Skallagrim." The Allfather held Raef's gaze, that single eye so dark and ominous and brimming over with terrible knowledge. "You know what comes. I can see it in your eyes."

"Then it is true?" Raef felt a knot of apprehension build in his stomach. A small part of him had clung to hope that the Allfather would deny him. "The end of all things has begun?"

"It has." Simple words, yet devastating in their finality. "It is time we both left this place." Odin stepped back and a shadow seemed to swallow him into its depths, leaving Raef alone in the wind.

In time, the web of dreamsleep fell away and Raef let the fog ebb from his mind until he was aware that he still lay pressed against the stones but the storm had shrunk to a whisper. If he had truly conversed with Odin, if the Allfather had offered him a place in a secret, hidden realm, if such a place even existed, Raef could not say. He only knew he was alive and that was enough.

Finding his feet, Raef looked to the dark sky, searching for a path he might follow. The stars were strange and unfamiliar, but a bright one hung over the horizon to Raef's right, twinkling with red and gold, and he did not take his eyes from it as he began to walk.

The landscape dragged on, unceasingly flat, until Raef caught a glimpse of something that broke the surface, a stone pillar growing taller with every step Raef took. When he reached its base, it reared up so high and straight that Raef could not see the peak and it stretched just wider than an eagle's wingspan.

Raef walked around the pillar and ran his hand across the rough, pebbled stone until his fingers found an indentation. To his surprise, he could make out the shape of a hand stamped into the stone. Placing his own palm into the smooth stone one, Raef found that it fit his hand and, as his heart beat faster in anticipation, he pressed hard, letting the stone fill each line and crevice of his skin. Nothing happened. Raef exhaled his disappointment, though he knew not what he thought should have happened, only that this pillar was surely the answer to something.

Raef slumped to the ground, his back against the cold stone, and closed his eyes to think. Drawing his knees up to his chin and crossing his arms over his shins, as though to ward off cold and retain his own ebbing strength, Raef felt a sharp prick on his hip bone. Unfolding the waist of his pants, Raef retrieved the forgotten shard of pottery, the one he had threatened Hrodvelgr with, and held it up to the stars. It gleamed like a black river at night and though it had not drawn blood, it was sharp enough to do so.

Getting to his feet, Raef held the shard between his fingers. Without thinking, he drew the sharpest point across the palm of his right hand, the movement slow, unhurried, the cut long and straight. He let the blood well and then pressed his hand once more into the stone.

For a moment, the pain of the self-inflicted wound was nothing beyond the ordinary. It stung, as it should, and blood seeped out from underneath Raef's hand until it dripped down the stone. But the stain had not spread far when Raef's palm began to burn and searing pain spread to each fingertip. Gritting his teeth, Raef kept his hand in place though every instinct told him to tear it away and end the agony.

Just as he reached his breaking point, a deafening crack shook the pillar and the stone began to tremble under Raef's touch. The vibrations shook Raef's arm and spread through each limb but he leaned into the pillar with all his strength, certain that his skin, his blood, must stay connected. Three more cracks sounded from deep within the stone and the fourth broke to the surface, sending fissures racing in all directions. And then all was still and Raef was left leaning against a broken pillar stained with his blood, nothing more.

Raef lingered, unwilling to break with the ancient power he had witnessed, unwilling to admit the pillar was yet another false hope. He could feel his blood, still warm, wet between his hand and the stone but whatever it had awakened had returned to slumber. Raef removed his hand and clenched his fist to stem the flow, then sank to the ground once more.

He closed his eyes and at first the roar in his ears seemed a thing of dreams, for Raef's exhaustion had him on the verge of unconsciousness, but it grew louder, more urgent, a wind rising from deep within the ground, a ferocious beast caged too long now sensing freedom. Raef pushed himself away from the pillar as the sound grew to a deafening pitch. The earth shook beneath him once more and then the pillar split apart, rent to pieces and dust. The force of the eruption sent Raef flying with the debris. When he struck the ground, he slipped into a world between life and death and all was darkness.

# THIRTEEN

RIP. DRIP. RAEF'S eyelids twitched, trying to rid themselves of the irritation on his face. More drips and Raef's mind fumbled for the word. Rain. Yes. This knowledge floated in his head as Raef felt the water splash against his skin. It seemed important, life-saving, but he could not remember why.

The drops fell harder and faster and Raef opened his cracked lips, his flesh drinking up the water and his tongue tasting its sweet relief. Only when the rain had soaked him did he venture to open his eyes. Blinking against the fat drops, he saw a grey sky, clouds in varying shades of darkness, their edges polished by the hidden sun. Raef knew he should move, should stand, but the effort required was unthinkable and it seemed enough to simply lie there.

The rain grew lighter and soon the drops were replaced with soft, whispery things. Snow. The flakes melted on Raef's cheeks and only at that moment did he understand he was cold.

Taking his eyes from the grey sky, Raef forced his unwilling body to roll onto its side. His vision swam, the extent of his weakness becoming clear to Raef, and it was with blurry eyes that he took in the pebbled, rocky shore, the rolling waves that tumbled in from the grey sea. Memory flooded back with each foam-capped wave. Beautiful, dangerous Alfheim and its dragon-kin. Finnoul and her rebellion.

Jötunheim, bleak and desperate. Mogthrasir, Hrodvelgr, the black cells and his escape. The labyrinth. Raef's mind seemed to shrink away from that last thought and he felt his body shiver and his breath catch, a visceral, violent reaction.

But this was not the labyrinth. His heart soared with this knowledge, bringing warmth to his cold flesh. He knew this place. He had nearly drowned off this shore as a boy, rescued only by his father's strong arms. He was home.

If he twisted his head and looked north, he would see cliffs, dangerous and battered in storms, bright and brilliant in sunlight. Birds would be flying to and from their hidden nests, seeking fish in the waters below. If he looked south, he would see the entrance to a fjord, Vannheim's deepest and longest. Fishermen would be trolling the waters there in search of silver scales. And if Raef stood and looked inland, to the east, he would see tall, tree-covered hills lining the fjord and stretching into Vannheim's interior. The deep forests would be filled with snow and yet alive with animals.

But Raef could see none of this, for each moment he grew more aware of his lack of strength and a dull pain that cocooned his entire body. The snow fell and Raef's mind wandered until a voice brought it back. It was a child's voice, shrieking in delight as a wave chased her across the pebbles. Back and forth she ran, drawing ever closer to where Raef lay, her cheeks rosy in the winter air. When she saw him, she stopped, the joy disappearing from her face. In its place rested calm curiosity. She stood still, her eyes on his, and then approached.

When she was close enough to touch him, she knelt down and studied him again, brown eyes taking in his bare chest, his ragged pants, his scars, the fresh blood on his palm. Raef tried to speak but his lips moved and nothing came out. She rose and scampered out of Raef's sight but it was not long before Raef heard her voice once more.

"Just there, Papa, come closer."

"Stay back, Eadilwif, he may be dangerous."

Raef heard boots scraping over loose stones as the man approached from behind him. Then a face loomed into the edge of Raef's view.

"Looks half dead," the man muttered to himself. He crossed in front of Raef and squatted down. "Can you hear me?"

Raef tried again to speak but had to settle with a simple nod.

"Here." The man unhooked a skin from his belt and held it against Raef's lips. The water dribbled down his chin but then Raef managed to swallow. "Shipwrecked?" Raef nodded again and the man mirrored him, sandy-colored, braided beard wagging, before mustering his wisdom. "Serves you right for sailing in winter. Aegir is a cruel god."

Raef thought of Bara, one of the sea god's nine daughters, and did not renounce Aegir his ways.

"Can you stand?"

Raef found his voice at last, cracked and broken as it was. "No."

The man scratched his head. "Wait here," he said, as if Raef might do otherwise. "I will return." He vanished from Raef's view and the boots retreated.

"Can I stay with him, Papa?"

"No, sprout, best you come with me." The sounds of their feet faded, leaving Raef alone with the waves and falling snow. Raef fumbled among the stones until his fingers seized on a smooth, flat one. He brought it up to his face and rubbed his thumb along the streak of white that split through the grey. Clinging to this piece of home, Raef drifted into unconsciousness. The tide rose, washing against Raef's feet, and snow settled in his hair.

The return of the fisherman disturbed Raef only a little. He was aware of hands, more than two but how many he could not have said, lifting him from the wet sand. Then he knew the warmth of a fire, distant, like the sun filtering through heavy clouds, and the feel of his soaked pants being stripped from his shivering skin, a wool blanket wrapping tight in their absence. A spoon to his lips and a hand to his jaw helped coax hot broth down his throat. He dreamed of ravens, a great flock of them, turning the sky dark with their black wings.

In time, the dream state slipped away and Raef, his frozen skin and bones thawed, knew pain. His entire body ached, dull in some places, sharp in others, and his stomach, awoken by the broth after long hibernation, raged to life, demanding sustenance. Faces peered over him, the fisherman, a woman, and two other men.

"Water," Raef said, his voice a croaking whisper. The woman complied and Raef took long swallows from the cup she held to his lips. When it was empty, she filled it again and Raef drained it once more. The broth returned, and this time Raef was able to consume a greater quantity, his head propped up on the fisherman's knees. When even this simple action of eating and swallowing exhausted Raef, they lowered his head to the ground and he slipped into a deep sleep, unmarked by dreams.

When he awoke again, his mind was clearer but the pain in his body stronger. He had been moved from his place on the floor in front of the fire and rested now on a bed of straw. The smell of cooking fish made Raef's mouth water but he lay still, listening to the voices around him and assessing the extent of his injuries.

To his relief, the broken ribs that had plagued him for so long were but a lingering memory. The worst of his pain was in his left leg, spreading downward from his knee. He remembered the pillar, the way it had shattered, sending him flying. His arms throbbed as well, the left one dark with bruises where he had landed on it, the right with a sharper pain where Hrodvelgr's creature had wounded him. The effort of holding his head up made his heart beat faster and he felt sweat break out on his forehead as his skull began to pound. Raef let his head fall back to the straw and closed his eyes until he had regained some measure of control.

His movement did not go unnoticed and the girl came to stand over him, her eyes still curious, until the woman guided her away and took her place.

"You have my thanks," Raef said. "I will repay you."

The woman smiled a little. "Do you feel well enough to eat? The stew is ready." Though the process was painful, the fisherman raised Raef into a sitting position. The blanket fell away, revealing Raef's pale skin beneath. Raef brought a hand to his chest, surprised at how small he seemed, how much muscle had melted from his bones. A bowl of fish stew was placed in his lap and, though his hands were unsteady, Raef began to feed himself.

"I do not think you have broken any bones," the woman said. She sat at a table with the fisherman and the small girl, breaking bread into large pieces to dip in their own bowls. "But I am not a healer."

"Nonsense," the fisherman broke in, a wide smile on his face. "If she says you have not broken any bones, it is the truth."

"I have treated the wound on your arm," the woman said, ignoring her husband. Her eyes said she did not dare ask what had caused it. "If you keep it clean it should heal, but there will be a scar."

Raef tried to smile but feared it came out as a grimace. "Another for the collection. Tell me how I can repay you." The woman rose and went to the hearth. Raef noticed for the first time that she was pregnant. "There must be something you need. Cattle? Goats? Coin?"

The fisherman looked puzzled. "How could we expect such great gifts? If you feel you must repay us, you may do so when you are able. For now, you must rest and regain your strength."

The knowledge that they did not know him was both a relief and a shame. Raef opened his mouth to identify himself but the words did not come. Instead, he ate in silence, the watchful eyes of young Eadilwif never straying far for long as her father and mother spoke of the day's work.

Night fell and with it came a cold wind, shrieking around the corners of the small home and trying, in vain, to slip through cracks.

The house was sturdy and well built, though, and the winter was kept at bay. The fire roared and sparked, a cheerful guard against the cold, and Raef knew he would not have survived this night had the fisherman's daughter not found him on the shore. The fisherman's wife brought him a drink of herbs that would still his pain. Its taste was familiar, a concoction Raef had downed more than once to ease the aches of rowing or battle. He drained it and then the last candle was blown out, leaving only the fire to burn down and light the night.

Raef slept, but peace and rest eluded him as his mind plunged back into the labyrinth. The visions of death, of all he held dear turning to dust while he stood by helpless, returned to him, riding the cloak of the wind but undeterred by the firelight. Raef's body became a battleground as his mind fought tides of darkness he could not overcome, and he awoke, screaming, sobbing, and gasping for air.

The fisherman and his wife knelt over him, her hands stroking Raef's hair, his holding Raef's shoulders as Raef, still blinded by the dreams, tried to wrench himself from the bed of straw. Deep breaths and the woman's quiet murmurs soothed him, calmed him, and all the while Raef watched their anxious faces and knew they wondered what madness they had brought to their home.

He did not sleep again that night, nor did the fisherman and his wife. The fire was stoked and the man brought Raef a small cup of mead, forcing it into his hand when he tried to protest. Raef took a sip and the sweet, strong liquid slid down his throat. It was good. And necessary. The woman, wrapping herself in a fur-lined cloak, ventured into the night, returning with more wood and a gust of wind that threatened the stubby candle burning on the table. The flame quavered, righted itself, and grew strong once more. His bladder bursting, Raef was forced to ask the fisherman to lift him from the straw and then, when Raef could not find the strength to stand, carry him from the house to the latrine out back. By the time they returned to the warmth of the fire, Raef was shivering violently.

"I am Brunn," the fisherman said, after settling Raef close to the hearth once more. He sat on a stool angled to face both the fire and Raef, though his gaze settled somewhere off of Raef's left ear rather than on Raef's face. "My wife is Sigrid." Brunn looked uncomfortable, uncertain what should be said. "Is Vannheim your home?"

"Yes."

"You have the look of a warrior. Did you fight with our lord in the east?"

Raef nodded.

"We heard rumor of battles hard-fought and fierce. They say three kings fought and two still live."

Raef was uncertain how to respond so he asked a safe question. "And Vannheim, how fares she?"

Brunn looked surprised and Raef saw him glance to Sigrid. "You do not know? We are in lordless lands. The son of Skallagrim is dead."

"How did he die?"

Brunn shrugged. "How else does a warrior die? In battle, I think. A great many warriors returned and spoke of a lake blazing with fire. I even heard one say he saw the Valkyries descend on the field of battle. But young Skallagrim was not among those who came back."

"His captains?"

Brunn shrugged again. "I am but a fisherman. I trade my fish at market. I listen to those who like to talk. But information is scare in these parts."

Raef asked the question he dreaded. "Who rules in Vannheim, then?"

"I could not say. Perhaps no one." Brunn looked again at Sigrid and gave her a smile. "Life goes on here. There are fish in the fjords and deer in the hills. Just as there always will be." Raef, beset with visions of a future that rumbled toward them like a storm, knew better but kept the darkness to himself.

They spoke only a little as they waited for the dawn. As rosy fingers of golden light began to spread from the east, the fierce wind dwindled, tamed by Sol and the coming day. Sigrid busied herself with the morning meal and little Eadilwif ran to the fjord for fresh water. They ate day old bread and a dish of cabbage and smoked sausages, though Raef found he did not have the stomach for more than a few bites, then Brunn set off for his boat and Sigrid filled a large, shallow bowl with water that had been heated over the fire. She knelt next to Raef's straw bed, a clean cloth in her hand and gestured to his face. Raef took the cloth, dipped it in the steaming water and wrung out the excess, then wiped his face. The cloth came away grey and grimy and Raef could see black flecks of dried blood. Hrodvelgr's creature, slain in the arena, and perhaps a bit of the giant himself, mingled with his beast in death. It seemed a lifetime ago.

Raef wiped again and again, turning the water black with filth, until Sigrid took the cloth from him, filled the dish with clean water, and began to wipe down the length of his arms, his neck, and across the part of his chest that was exposed to the air. Her touch was tender and sure, the water warm, and Raef closed his eyes, letting himself enjoy this small measure of comfort.

When she had finished, he was by no means clean. But a layer of grime had been lifted and Raef's skin prickled, cooled now by the water's residue. Sigrid helped Raef into a set of dry clothes borrowed from Brunn. He thanked her and pulled the blankets close and then, with the light of the sun filtering through the solitary window and settling over his face, he slept.

# FOURTEEN

"WHO IS HE?"

"He fought with young Skallagrim in the east."

"But his name?"

The voices tugged at Raef's ears and drew him into a sleepy wakefulness, his eyelids yet heavy and his limbs mired in straw. The first speaker was a stranger to him, the voice harsh and suspicious. The fisherman answered again.

"I have not asked." A pause. "He is very weak."

"He could be one of them," the stranger said. "Their ship wrecked somewhere to the north." Raef's drowsy mind tried to think whom the stranger spoke of but his thoughts were like scattered leaves blown out of reach by a stiff breeze.

Brunn's voice was stronger and more insistent now. "Look at him, Skarfi, he is just as you see him and he needs our help."

"You have always been so quick to trust, Brunn. And what has that brought you?"

Silence but for the sound of Raef's heart beating in his ears. It seemed a good time to open his eyes, before the conversation went further. He had intended to struggle into a sitting position so as to gain their attention, but the struggle was more real than he anticipated and he was glad of Brunn's strong hands helping him until

he could lean against the wall of the house, his lower half still burrowed in blankets and straw. The fisherman gave Raef water and
asked how he felt. The stranger, tall and dark of hair, eyebrows knit
together in disapproval, waited across the room near the ladder
leading to the loft where Sigrid, Brunn, and their daughter slept,
arms crossed over his chest.

When Raef had swallowed twice, the stranger seemed to think
that enough and came to stand over Raef, his bulk looming large
and no doubt meant to intimidate. Though it pained him to hold
his neck at such an angle, Raef titled his head up and held the man's
stare, keeping his own eyes blank.

"Do you have a name?"

Raef did not answer.

"Answer, cur. You are in my brother's house and I would know
your name and your father's before you."

The man was big and strong, with the look of a builder rather
than a fisherman like his brother. He might have been a warrior but
for the absence of three fingers on his left hand. He could never
have held a shield in battle. Raef wished for an axe and even a shred
of his former strength. He had to settle for words. "Vakre." Until
he knew the stranger's intentions it felt safer to cling to anonymity.
"My father is Gedda," Raef said, naming his grandfather.

Brunn's brother scoffed. "Never heard of him. What manners
did he teach you? To prey upon the kindness of others? My brother
has given you more than you deserve. It is time you left."

Brunn broke in, placing a hand on his brother's shoulder.
"Peace, brother. My house, my kindness. Do not forget it."

"How could I? Ever has your kindness plagued our family. It
will be the ruin of us all, the end of our line."

Brunn's eyes narrowed. "He stays if I say he stays."

Skarfi did not bother to hide his displeasure, but something
stilled his tongue. Brunn returned his attention to Raef.

"Sigrid has gone to visit her mother and Eadilwif with her. They will not return until after nightfall but do not think to lie here abed while the sun is out." Brunn smiled. "She has charged me with getting you on your feet. She says it is time."

"The sooner the better, that I may cease to burden you," Raef said, his gaze on Skarfi, whose lip curled in response.

"It is no burden, friend." Brunn got to his feet. "Brother, do you not have traps to tend and wood to cut?" Skarfi glowered but pulled his cloak tight across his chest and stomped out into the snow and the early morning sun.

"I do not wish to be the cause of anger between brothers," Raef said.

"There was anger there long before you washed up on shore. I should never have brought him here to see you." Brunn extended his hand and smiled again. "Come."

Taking a deep breath, Raef locked hands with Brunn, who also leaned down to lift Raef from under one arm. Together, they hauled Raef to unsteady feet, though it was Brunn who did most of the work.

The pain in Raef's left leg was fierce, the bones, tendons, and muscles protesting against the weight that bore down on them. He let his body sag to the right, easing the burden on his left leg, and did not let go of Brunn's elbow, hunching close to the other man's torso. With effort, he stood straight, forcing his shoulders back and his spine upright, though it cost him a great deal.

He was taller than Brunn, he found, and this surprised him for in his weakened state, Raef felt shrunken and depleted. That he stood a hand's width over Brunn's close-cropped hair was disconcerting when he felt only half himself, half a man. Down on the straw, Brunn and his brother had seemed as immense as Hrodvelgr, if not so fair.

Brunn said nothing of the white knuckles clenched around

his elbow, his voice remaining cheerful. "A step," he said, quietly demanding, and Raef complied, sliding his right foot forward. The left lingered and Raef dreaded moving it. "Another." Grunting with the exertion of so simple a thing, Raef dragged his left foot until it was nearly in line with the right, but even this left him sweating as his knee burned with agony. "Good. But this time, I want to see daylight between your boot and my boards," Brunn said, still smiling. His good mood was not infectious, for Raef was far from smiling himself, but it did feel indispensable, like water on a sweltering summer day.

Raef took his time before moving again and each step was agony but Brunn's guiding arm did not let him stop until they had crossed the length of the small house. Raef's reward was a sip of mead and a boiled egg but first he slumped in a chair, his knee throbbing.

"I should be dead," Raef said as he swallowed the last of the egg and washed it down with the mead.

"Perhaps. Perhaps not. Men drown in shipwrecks every day. Others survive." Brunn wiped his mouth on his sleeve, his own cup of mead half drained. "I see the bodies, both alive and dead, though," he added, "never have I seen a body as bruised and damaged as yours and still flowing with life-blood. But that is in the past. You must look beyond it."

Wise words but words Raef could not embrace with all his heart. He wondered what Brunn would say if he knew even half of Raef's true story, half of what he had seen and survived. Brunn emptied his cup and stood. "Again."

They walked the length of Brunn's house three times before Raef begged for mercy. He felt as though he had climbed a mountain, his legs crying out, sweat beads trickling down his chest, and blood pulsing in his ears. Brunn let him rest, offering water and broth Sigrid had left over the hearth, but making it clear that they would resume after he returned from checking on the pigs.

Raef leaned back into the straw and let his mind drift as clouds passed over the window, bringing the house in and out of shadow. The sound of a horse drew his attention and he opened his eyes when a second horse called out in answer. A voice, angry and harsh. Another chiming in. And then Brunn's. Raef could not make out words but the voices grew more heated and then the door banged open and Skarfi filled the doorway, blocking the sun.

"You, get up." He pounced on Raef and dragged him to his feet as a second man followed. "Three nights ago, thieves tried to make off with Hollof's sheep. Two escaped, and the third as well, but not before Hollof's dog got hold of him." Skarfi shook Raef and snarled, his red-rimmed eyes taking in Raef's bruises, the fresh wound on his palm, and the mark Hrodvelgr's creature's tooth had carved into Raef's arm. "That was you."

Brunn, protesting, stepped close but the other man, Hollof, punched him in the gut. Brunn doubled over, unable to speak. Skarfi shoved Raef against the wall and held him there, his forearm cutting into Raef's throat.

"Has the right look," Hollof said, peering at Raef with pale blue eyes. "Needs a good gutting." He spat and Raef flinched as the phlegm landed on his cheek. Skarfi's thick forearm bore down harder and Hollof drew a knife from his belt and held it to Raef's ear. Raef struggled for air, his hands reaching out to Skarfi's shoulders but pawing uselessly, as a weak animal might at the end of a hunt. He was prepared to give up his name, if it would stay their wrath, but he was unable to do more than grunt. The anger in their eyes, the glee at having prey at their disposal, shone bright and Raef did not think the name of Skallagrim would give them pause while their blood was up.

Beyond Hollof's shoulder, Brunn had risen, his face stricken but a crude hammer in hand. A single swing sent Hollof to the floor, blood sprouting from his temple, and Skarfi's grip on Raef slipped enough for Raef to duck and limp away. The brothers squared off, Skarfi all rage and brute strength, a knife flashing from his belt, Brunn less certain but the hammer held in a firm grip.

"You will not spill blood in my house, brother," Brunn said.

Skarfi bellowed in rage and lunged. Brunn sidestepped but Raef could see he did not have the training to win a fight against a bigger, stronger opponent. Skarfi circled again and Raef, his left leg a knot of agony, scanned the room for a weapon. Lurching to the table, he grasped a short, stubby knife.

"Stop this madness," Raef shouted, his voice raspy from Skarfi's hold. "The lord of Vannheim commands it." It was Brunn who looked at Raef, who dropped his guard, and Skarfi, whether deaf to Raef's words or choosing to ignore them, took his chance. He tackled Brunn to the ground, sending the hammer spinning across the floorboards. The smaller brother stood no chance against Skarfi's bulk and Raef tried to go to his aid, but Hollof, recovered, if woozy, beat him there and placed himself between Raef and the brothers sprawled on the floor. Hollof blinked away blood that trickled close to his eye and his gaze was unsteady, but the blade in his hand did not quiver and Raef knew his depleted strength and crippled leg made a fight foolish.

For a moment, there was silence but for the heavy breaths of each man. And then Hollof spoke.

"The lord of Vannheim, he says." A limp grin spread across Hollof's wide face. "I begin to think we should let you live."

Skarfi grunted from the floor. "Finish him."

"He may be worth more alive than dead, lord or not," Hollof said. "They will pay good coin for him."

Skarfi rolled off his brother but did not let Brunn rise. "And if not?"

"Then we can kill him later."

Skarfi got to his feet and advanced on Raef. Brunn rose and

made to follow but Raef held up a hand to keep him from coming closer.

"Will you come without a fuss?" Hollof leered at Raef.

"If you leave this man alone."

Skarfi scoffed. "Not worth the trouble, my brother. Never did have any ambition."

Raef looked from one man to the other, wondering if they would keep their word, but he knew he did not have any choice but to hope they would. He would not risk further harm to Brunn or his family and home. Raef limped to the table, trying in vain to keep upright and show himself to be stronger than he felt. The effort failed and his leg gave out after two steps, sending him careening into the table. Steadying himself to the sound of Hollof and Skarfi's laughter, Raef set the small knife on the table and caught Brunn's gaze. He tried to convey a great many things in that shared look, but most of all his gratitude.

"My fate is my own," Raef murmured, his mind on the words the Allfather had spoken. Raef turned to Skarfi and spread his hands. "I am yours. But if we must travel far, I will need a horse."

Skarfi scowled. "You will walk."

"Then the sun will set on us here. You have seen me fall after two steps. If you wish to travel, my legs cannot be trusted."

"Use mine," Brunn said. He did not meet his brother's gaze, but looked instead to Raef, who gave him a nod.

Brunn's horse was a shaggy-hoofed creature, big and strong for working the land. There was no saddle but Raef twined his fingers in the horse's black mane and pulled himself up, glad of the freedom of movement the horse could grant him and the muscles, rippling under a thick winter coat, that would carry him with ease. With only one horse between Skarfi and Hollof, they agreed to take turns riding. Skarfi, his fingers red from the cold, tied the horses together, then they set off, heading north and into the hills. Hollof led the way, his mount breaking the snow, Skarfi following on foot in his tracks, one hand on the rope, Raef bringing up the rear. Raef looked back at the small house on the edge of the fjord. He knew not what the day held for him, but better that than bring danger to Brunn's home. At least now Skarfi and Hollof would be far away when Sigrid and Eadilwif returned.

They rode in silence while the day passed out of its youth. The sun was bright, its light only broken by puffy clouds that skimmed across the sky. Snow crunched under the horses' hooves and Raef drank in the fresh air, even though it was cold and biting, sneaking its way under his borrowed cloak and the woolen layers Brunn had insisted Raef accept. When they paused to ford a stream, Raef ventured to speak.

"Where are you taking me?"

Skarfi and Hollof glanced at each other and neither spoke.

"Who do you think is going to pay you?"

Again there was no answer and Raef, urging his horse up the bank, decided to save his breath.

↑↑↑

They reached the second fjord as the sun slipped out of sight, casting deep shadows through the trees, but Raef did not need the sun to know where he was for every blade of grass, every tree, every rock was known to him. In the last of the light, he could make out the steep hills across the water, the snow clinging to the edge of the northern shore. And there, the walls that had stood in that place since his ancestors first called it home, two docks bereft of ships stretching out into the darkening water, and above it all, the Vestrhall. The torches outside the hall's doors were but pricks of light and Raef saw the sloping roof, the stone stairs, the great wooden doors with his mind more than his eyes. He was home.

But the joy Raef felt was buried deep under doubts and

misgivings as Skarfi and Hollof argued about whether they should stop for the night or continue on. Hollof wanted to press onward to the nearest ferry further inland, where the fjord began to narrow. Skarfi was adamant that they spend the night, grumbling that Hollof had taken far more than his share of the time on the horse and that he would not walk farther. Hollof cast more than one uneasy glance at Raef, though whether he was merely concerned that Raef might attempt to escape or whether he was having misgivings about holding the lord of Vannheim prisoner, Raef could not tell. In the end, Skarfi won Hollof over and they searched out a patch of ground sheltered by thick pine branches and largely free of snow.

Raef's leg gave out when he dismounted but neither Skarfi nor Hollof bothered to help him rise. By the time Raef managed to crawl beneath the pine boughs, Skarfi had tethered the horses.

"What about him?" Hollof asked.

"He cannot walk," Skarfi said.

"Fine, you stay up all night to make sure he stays put."

Skarfi glowered but took Hollof's advice. Though Raef tried to protest that he would not, could not run, Skarfi soon had him trussed around the waist to a slender pine, leaving Raef hunched awkwardly at the base of the trunk, his legs splayed out in front of him, his neck pricked by pine needles.

The night was mild but even so Raef knew the cold would sap what little strength he had regained in Brunn and Sigrid's care. To his surprise, after hearing Hollof and Skarfi muttering, a spare blanket retrieved from the depths of Hollof's pack was tossed through the darkness, landing just within Raef's reach. He draped it over himself, willing his body to find sleep.

He dreamed a new dream that night. A woman came to him, her face hidden in shadows, and he knew her to be his mother. She said nothing, merely came to sit by him, as though he were a small boy in bed with an illness. Raef wanted to speak to her, but his tongue was too heavy in his mouth, nor could he lift a hand to push away her hood and reveal her face. Just when he began to feel his tongue loosen, she vanished, slipping away like fog in the first light of day, and her place was taken by the same visions that had stalked him in Hrodvelgr's caverns and the labyrinth. Eira, calling to him, screaming for help. Vakre, dying in silence, his eyes accusing Raef of betrayal. Siv, drowning, gasping for air and finding only water and blood. And then he was alone in a crushing darkness.

If he cried out as he woke, Raef could not have said, but Skarfi was peering at him through a gap in the lowest branch and there was something uneasy in the big man's eyes. Raef's heart thudded in his chest in the wake of the dream as he met Skarfi's stare and he could feel sweat on his forehead. Skarfi said nothing and disappeared into the darkness once more.

Raef did not sleep again that night and was glad when his captors rose early, before the sun, and they began to trace the fjord's edge, dipping away from the water as the terrain required, but always heading east. Neither man said a word to Raef until the tiny village that had sprung up next to the ferry crossing was in sight.

"Not a word, understand?" It was Hollof who admonished Raef.

Raef had heard them arguing once more not long after sunrise about whether he might be recognized at the ferry crossing. Were it not for a bend in the fjord, the village would sit in sight of the Vestrhall. It seemed they could not agree and in the end did nothing to conceal Raef as they sought out the ferryman.

The ferry was no more than a sturdy raft outfitted with a small square sail and a few paddles manned by three skinny boys, the ferryman's sons. Hollof scowled at the ferryman's price, but he and Skarfi counted out grubby coins only to find they were still short. Skarfi began to reach for his knife, but the sharp-eyed ferryman spoke quickly and in the end offered to take Brunn's horse as payment.

Raef balked at this but the knife that had been aimed at the ferryman came to rest against Raef's ribs and he was forced to hobble aboard the raft. One of the boys watched with wide eyes but said nothing and soon they were underway.

The morning air was still and so Hollof and Skarfi took extra paddles and helped speed their progress. Raef, left alone by the mast, longed for the feel of an oar in his hands and had to settle for the hint of salt on the air.

The fever was raging again. He had eluded it since Bara had washed it from him in Jötunheim, but it had sprung to life overnight, overtaking the exhausted shell that was his body, and built as they made their way to the crossing point. Now he drifted in and out of consciousness as they crossed the fjord and Skarfi had to drag him onto shore when they reached the northern side. Left with only one horse, Skarfi had no choice but to lift Raef into the saddle, where he clung for the remainder of the journey.

When the Vestrhall came into view, Raef was blind to it. Only when they approached the gate and sentries called out did Raef manage to raise his head. The faces of the men at the gate swam in front of him, but he was certain they were all strangers.

"I am Skarfi, son of Eyvin. We seek an audience." Skarfi said in answer to one of the sentry's question.

One of the guards came close, inspecting their faces and their horse. "Your name?" he asked Hollof.

"Hollof, son of Bjormund."

"And this one?" The guard's gaze shifted to Raef, who could not focus on him.

"Our prisoner," Hollof said. "We come in search of justice for his crimes against us."

This seemed to satisfy the guard, who gave a nod at his companions. The gate was opened and they passed through, but once within the walls they were directed to leave the horse behind. Grumbling,

Hollof dragged Raef from the saddle. Somehow Raef kept his feet, though his left knee buckled. He opened his mouth and forced his tongue to form the words.

"My name is Raef Skallagrim." His voice was harsh and hoarse and weak, but even through his fever he could see the warriors squint and stare in surprise. Cursing, Hollof punched him in the gut and he reeled backward, falling, Hollof stalking after him. But it was enough. The guards descended on all three of them, spears bristling, and Hollof was knocked to the ground while Raef was pushed back against the gate, kept on his feet only by the hands holding him there, his teeth barred against the pain in his knee as his stomach roiled and his vision darkened. The horse skittered and reared, nearly striking a sentry in the head with a hoof.

"He lies, he lies," Skarfi said through gritted teeth, a spear point forcing his chin up, his hands stopped in the act of reaching for his knife.

"Quiet, whoreson," a guard said, but his face showed uncertainty as his gaze flickered between the three men. It lingered on Raef the longest.

"I am the lord of Vannheim and Einarr before me," Raef said, his voice stronger now. "Search out the captain of the gate. Ulfirth will know me."

"I am the captain of the gate," the man said, his gaze narrowing. "And I answer to one man. He will decide who you are." First sending a man up to the hall to announce their coming, he ordered them to be disarmed and their hands bound and then Skarfi and Hollof were marched up the rise, Raef half-carried, half-dragged in their wake, the village quiet around them save for the barking of a dog.

At the hall, three more guards stood watch, their faces blank and unfamiliar to Raef. The heavy wooden doors of the Vestrhall creaked open and a man burst forth.

"What is the meaning of this? Release him at once," he said, pointing to Raef. Then he held his arms wide and his face creased into a smile. "Cousin."

Uncertain and desperate for something to lean against, Raef swayed as the ropes came off. The man was a stranger to him, tall and broad shouldered, his orange beard tied into two tiny braids and the hair on his head wild and untamed.

Raef's reluctance did not seem to fluster him. He closed the space between them and wrapped Raef in his arms. "Thank the gods you are safe and have returned to us." He released Raef and held him at arm's length, his clear gaze taking in Raef's appearance and his cheerful face now showing displeasure. "Have these men harmed you? They will pay." He looked to the captain of the gate. "Take them away. I will deal with them later," he said, his voice earnest and dangerous. "And see that the villagers know this good news."

The warriors complied, leading off Skarfi and Hollof, who howled and protested but were rewarded with swift kicks to the shins. They disappeared, leaving Raef with the stranger and three silent guards.

The smile had returned to the man's face. He clapped Raef's shoulder and Raef felt his strength give out at last. Falling, he clutched at the man who called him cousin, then the orange-haired man was supporting him, strong arms under Raef's armpits, his face looming close and full of concern. "Come, come, let us get you inside, cousin." Raef tried to talk, to ask the questions that burned on his tongue, but, as the stranger and another man began to carry him over the threshold of the hall, found he did not have the will to speak. A sharp whistle brought servants running and at last Raef knew familiar faces. "Young Skallagrim needs rest and care. See that he does not want for anything."

Raef, his head spinning now, was carried to his chamber. The familiar bed rose up to catch him and there he lay, taking in the sights and sounds of home, aware that he should be demanding to know who was living in his father's hall, and yet losing himself to the simple fact that he was no longer alone. He searched for the orange-haired man among the faces that hovered over him, but the stranger had slipped away. In no time, a fire roared to life and his chamber came alive with its dancing light.

A pair of servants stripped the borrowed clothes from him, then removed Sigrid's careful bandage on his forearm and lowered him into a steaming bath. Gentle hands, those of an older woman he remembered was named Margeth, sponged the filth from his skin and cleaned the fresher wounds. When this was done, she washed his hair, her fingers kneading into his scalp with gentle pressure. When she finished, Raef sank back, letting the water come to his chin, and closed his eyes.

Margeth returned with a tray of food and drink, the stranger at her heels, his orange hair showing shades of red in the light of the fire in Raef's hearth. As Margeth poured mead, Raef tried to climb from the tub and failed, but the stranger was there to catch him, waiting until he steadied before wrapping him in a bearskin and helping him sink back onto the expanse of his bed. Margeth, her duties completed, left them.

The orange-haired man leaned over Raef, his eyes dark with concern.

"Sleep, cousin," he said. His face disappeared.

"Wait, wait," Raef said, his voice no more than a whisper. But the stranger was already gone and Raef was already asleep.

# FIFTEEN

"HOW LONG?"

"Two days."

Raef touched a hand to his forehead and found it dry and cool.

"Your fever broke early this morning."

Raef was propped in his bed, cushions supporting his shoulders and head so he could see the orange-haired stranger without straining his neck. The bearskin had been replaced with fresh linen and Raef could smell and taste the sharp tang of the salve that had been spread on his forearm and palm.

"Are you hungry?"

Raef was famished but he did not glance at the steaming broth the stranger had brought and set beside the hearth. His heartbeat was steady and sure for the first time in many days and Raef felt calm. But weak.

"Perhaps some mead?" The man filled two cups and settled one in Raef's fingers where they rested on the bed though he made no move to take it. He was not sure he was strong enough to lift the cup to his lips, but that was not the only source of his reluctance. The two men eyed each other, suspicion threading through Raef's mind. The stranger raised his own cup. "To your return and your health."

"Who are you?"

The stranger grinned. "I am Isolf Valbrand. The blood of Tyrlaug runs through both our veins."

"My mother was a daughter of Tyrlaug of Innrivik."

"As was mine."

Raef studied Isolf's face, wondering if there was something of his mother in his cheekbones, the shape of his nose, the tiny wrinkles at the corners of Isolf's eyes. "My father never spoke of relatives of my mother still living. Tyrlaug's line died with his son."

"This is true, and why would your father speak otherwise? My mother married a warrior of little repute and I was born in a wild corner of Innrivik. When our grandfather perished and our uncle with him, I was but a boy of nine. You could not have been more than four." Raef confirmed this with a nod. "Innrivik fell to the hands of Bjard Arvalungen, that brute and his four sons, and my mother kept me well out of harms way. I grew up in obscurity and it may well be that your father never knew of my existence."

Raef waited until Isolf turned his back to poke at the logs in the fire before trying to lift the cup. He failed and the mead sloshed over the rim. If Isolf noticed, he said nothing. "I am pleased to learn something of my mother's family, but your story does not explain your presence in my hall."

Isolf's face remained cheerful. "It does not. Only give me a moment and all will become known to you." Isolf took a drink and licked his lips. "As I grew to manhood, it became clear that I had something of a warrior in me, a remnant of Tyrlaug himself rather than my own father. I won renown in local skirmishes, making a name for myself, and men began to follow me, though I was no lord and the Arvalungen pups resented my growing reputation. They sullied my name in any way they could, blaming their thievery on me, naming me the murderer behind the deaths of their enemies. I wanted to fight them, to overthrow them and take up the seat in the

Styrkholm in Tyrlaug's name. But their forces were too strong and I lingered in Innrivik only until my mother died, keeping my head down at her insistence. That was three years ago, and I have wandered deep in the southern lands in the days since."

"And this war of the three kings? What part did you and your men play?"

Isolf shrugged. "None, if truth be told. When news of the war reached us, it was already stale. By the time we returned to Innrivik, Torrulf Palesword was already dead."

"Then why not throw your lot in with the Hammerling or Fengar?"

"These men are nothing to me. Names, that is all. Which should I have chosen to be my king? Which could I follow to death or victory?" Isolf poured more mead into his cup. "Imagine my surprise when rumor reached my corner of Innrivik of a young Skallagrim waging and winning a great battle to the east only to turn away from the war and return to Vannheim." Isolf grinned again. "I am a curious man and I knew you were my cousin. What sort of man was this, I asked myself. And so I resolved to travel to Vannheim, to meet you in your return, and see what we might make of our shared blood."

Raef was silent for a moment, soaking in Isolf's words. "And when you arrived and found me missing and presumed dead?"

"I was grieved to be sure. The last relation I had in this world, taken before I might see his face. But there were some who had traveled with you who spoke differently and it was their words that convinced me you yet lived."

"Who, who returned?"

"A young captain named Finnolf called Horsebreaker was chief among them. He said you had disappeared under strange circumstances. That there was no body, no demands of silver and gold in exchange for your life, no battle. What could I do, as your cousin, but hold the Vestrhall in your name, keeping the vultures at bay until you found your way back to us. And the vultures have come, Raef. They spit and scuffle at your doorstep, ravenous for a chance to take Vannheim for themselves."

"Do these vultures have names?"

"They do, names that will be familiar to you, I think. But you must be weary. You must rest and I will send the healer to examine you once more." Isolf frowned. "The war has taken its toll on you, that much is certain."

"The names, first, then I will rest," Raef said.

Isolf began to protest, but thought better of it. "Very well. The first to arrive was called Rudrak Red-beard but close on his heels was Snorren Thoken. They came sniffing for word of you but my men put them off. Since then, I have heard that they watch the most common routes in and out of Vannheim, searching for you so that they might kill you on the road."

"Not Tulkis Greyshield?"

Isolf raised his brows. "That name is unknown to me. You would expect him to prey upon Vannheim in your absence?"

"Long ago, before we kneeled to the first king, his ancestor was lord of Vannheim. The Greyshields have never forgotten this, nor forgiven the death of Thannulf Greyshield at the hands of Finnvold Skallagrim. Their grievance has passed to Tulkis and he bears it with great pride."

"Then I am sure he watches from the shadows, seeking his opportunity." Isolf took a long look at Raef, as though he was sizing up his cousin's ability to throw off those who would seek to supplant him. If Isolf found him lacking, his face did not betray his doubts. "Rest now, cousin. We will speak again this evening." Isolf rose from his chair and went to the door.

Raef closed his eyes, though he wished not to show weakness in front of Isolf. "What of my men? Those who went to war with me? We traveled apart. They made up the greater part of Vannheim's strength." He opened his eyes, though it was with effort.

"As far as I know, they have returned to their homes and fields, scattered into the far reaches of your lands. But information has been scarce." Isolf looked down at his feet. "My own men are not great enough in number to learn what I wish to know and I find your people do not trust me with what they know."

Raef smiled. "As they should, when a stranger walks among them. But I will see that they know what you have done for me."

"Till nightfall, then, cousin."

Raef nodded, his eyes half closed. The door closed quietly behind Isolf and his flaming hair, leaving Raef alone with the beat of his heart and the crackle of the fire. His mind drifted, though not into sleep, and he paid little mind when a woman entered and began to redress his wounds. Raef had known her since childhood, though she was only a few years older, and her hands moved quickly and deftly as she explained that, as best she could tell, his kneecap had come out of place and, though it had slid back in on its own, that was the cause of the pain in his leg. It would need rest, she said, and would take time to recover fully. She told him about the mixture of redtail and fox root she had given him for the pain, the smooth hazel oil she had spread on his bruises, the ice bath she had given him when the fever was at its worst.

"You have eaten nothing but a few spoonfuls of broth." She took her eyes off her work long enough to look Raef in the eye. "You must do better than that."

Raef nodded and did not protest when she carried the bowl Isolf had left to the bed and began to feed him.

"Some bread later, I think," she said. "Meat tomorrow."

But half the rich broth was still left in the bowl when Raef's stomach lurched and a wave of nausea churned through him. He leaned back against the pillows and swallowed hard. "Enough, Aldrif."

Aldrif frowned but set the bowl aside and pulled the blankets back over Raef's chest. "I will come back with something easier for your stomach." She stood but hesitated by the bed. "Did you go a very long time without food, lord?"

Raef met her gaze. "Yes."

Aldrif nodded, brisk and sure once more. "Then we will take it slow."

Raef thanked her but before Aldrif could leave, the door to Raef's chamber burst open.

"I must see him!" First through the door was a tall man, wrinkled before his time, the clawed, twisted fingers that made up his withered right hand reaching to Raef, but he was brought up short by Isolf's firm grip.

"He needs rest, priest," Isolf growled.

The wrinkled face turned on Isolf and the grey eyes narrowed. "And you need to keep your tongue behind your teeth before I pour molten gold down your throat. I must see him. Would you deny a priest of Odin?"

Isolf scowled and looked to Raef, who nodded.

"Let him in."

"And leave us," the priest hissed, still staring at Isolf. Another nod from Raef cleared the room.

"Fylkir." Raef pushed himself up against his pillows, trying to match the priest's height as best he could.

"I have not answered to that name since you were a child. Will you treat me with as much disrespect as your father did?"

Raef bristled. "There was no disrespect, priest. Not from my father or from me."

"And still you will not call me the name I am owed." Fylkir's twisted fingers clenched.

Raef kept his voice calm. "What do you want?"

Fylkir turned and paced the length of Raef's chamber, using his left hand to pry his fingers one by one out of the fist he had made. Only when this was done did he speak. "I had to be certain. Had to see you for myself."

"Certain of what?"

"Have you ever seen a shadow in a man's skin?" The priest sneered. "You are too blind to have seen it. But I am not. The Allfather has given me the sight to see what others cannot."

"And what do you see when you look at me?"

"Flesh and bone. No more."

"You sound disappointed."

The clawed hand clenched again, a reflex Fylkir could not control. Pain flashed through his eyes. "Do not play with me, boy."

"I am no boy, priest. Take care."

Fylkir lunged at the bed and for a moment Raef thought he might strike. "You should be more careful. The Allfather speaks to me, not you."

The laugh burst from Raef before he could swallow it down. Harsh and hoarse, it transformed into a shout of anger that caused the priest to draw back involuntarily. "Go back to your cave. Drink your sheep's blood and dance under the moon. I will not see you here again, Fylkir. Do you understand? Only Josurr is welcome in my hall if you have not already driven him mad. My father gave you far more respect than you deserved and I will not make the same mistake."

Fylkir stared at Raef, his jaw moving as though he were mustering a response. The fingers still clenched at his side were turning white.

"Leave," Raef snarled. "Or you will not walk out of here."

The priest left in a swirl of robes, the door thudding shut behind him, and Raef exhaled. His anger had awoken the pain that ate at his body and Raef clutched a hand to his traitorous knee until the throbbing dwindled. Forgetting his stomach, Raef swung out of bed and hobbled to the pitcher of mead Isolf had left behind. Ignoring the cup, Raef brought the cool stone to his lips and drank long and deep, swallow after swallow until he could take no more. The stone pitcher crashed to the floor, cracking open, as Raef doubled over and retched up mead and broth. He reached for the edge of his bed, missed, and fell, his knee giving out. His stomach continued to heave and Raef, his cheek pressed into the pool of spreading mead, brought his knees to his chest to try to still his shaking body.

It was Isolf who found him, who lifted him from the floor, who was the first to wipe the mead and vomit from Raef's face. Then Aldrif was there, pressing a cup to Raef's lips. He shook his head and tried to refuse it, but she murmured in his ear and he let the cool liquid slide across his tongue and down his throat. Her concoction stole through his body swiftly and soon Raef felt his muscles loosen. His stomach relaxed and even his knee no longer tormented him. He reached for the cup again and Aldrif gave him another swallow, then left at a gesture from Isolf.

In the wake of the pain, shame crept over him. He turned his head, taking in the mess he had made, saw the contents of his stomach soaking through Isolf's tunic.

"Forgive me," Raef said.

"You are ill, cousin, and injured. And you should not apologize to me in your own home."

"I let him anger me."

Isolf raised an eyebrow.

"The priest. I know him, I know his foul nature. I should not have let it happen."

"Shall I have him brought to you for punishment?"

Raef shook his head. "No. He knows he is no longer welcome in the Vestrhall."

"Will you not need him? He is a priest of Odin."

Raef sighed. "There is another. Josurr. Far more tolerable."

Isolf nodded his understanding. "I will have Aldrif bring you something to eat."

"Have her bring more of the drink she just gave me." When the door shut behind Isolf, Raef curled onto his side and stared out the window, past the dust filtering through the streams of sunlight, his gaze roving across the soft white snow and sharp black trees. Closing his eyes, Raef drew the covers over his head and shut out the light.

$$\xi \; \xi \; \xi$$

For four days Raef lingered in his chamber, drinking Aldrif's pain-killing brew, the sun shut out by heavy blankets Raef had ordered draped across the window. Isolf visited often at first, bringing matters to Raef's attention so he might fulfill his duties as lord of Vannheim. Engvorr, the shipbuilder, wanted to consult Raef on plans to refurbish one of the older longships. A pair of farmers trekked from their lands east of the Vestrhall to ask Raef to settle a dispute over a trade they had made. Ulli, the steward, wanted to know if Raef wished to sell excess wool to a trader from Danewyll or store it for the Vestrhall's weavers. Raef refused to see them. Once, he asked to see Finnolf Horsebreaker, the young captain, but Isolf could only tell him that Finnolf was away from the hall and had not said when he would return. Raef thought of Vakre, Eira, and Siv and wondered if they knew he lived. Isolf could tell him nothing of them. When the sun dropped below the sea on the second day and Isolf came to Raef's chamber, Raef sent him away with no more than a word. Isolf did not return the next day or the day after and Raef found he did not care.

His stomach grew stronger, prompting Aldrif to bring him bread, then tender bits of meat, but he made no attempt to test his leg. She was his only visitor and she began to speak less and less, though sometimes she lingered and worked a piece of embroidery with thread and needle while he slept. On the morning of the fifth day, she brought a small meal and began to leave as quietly as she had come but Raef stopped her.

"You have forgotten the medicine. For the pain."

"I did not forget, lord." She watched him from the door, deep brown eyes clear and determined.

"Please bring it." Raef flushed at the strain in his voice, the need.

"No. You have had enough."

"And if I demand it?"

Aldrif did not waver. "I would refuse."

The flush spread and Raef's stomach clenched in anger. "You wish to see me suffer?"

"I will not watch you drown in it."

Raef opened his mouth to rail against her, but nothing came out and the anger fled in the wake of his exhaled breath. He leaned back in the bed and closed his eyes. When he opened them again, Aldrif was sitting on the edge of the bed and Raef was suddenly aware of the disheveled blankets he lay in, his shaking hands, the smell of dried sweat on his skin, and the odor spreading from the chamber pot, poorly masked by sprigs of dried lavender and mint.

"Do you love Vannheim, Raef?" She had not called him by his name in all the time she had been tending him. Raef could remember her as a child, older by five years, quiet and confident. Seldom had she joined in the games the younger children played and Raef could only remember her using his name to scold him.

"The gods know I do."

"I do not pretend to know what god or curse or ill fate kept you from your hall and your people all this time. I do not know what is in your heart, what you have suffered. I can see the hurt in your eyes, the damage in your mind, just as well as I can see the pain in your body. But the boy I grew up with never wallowed in self-pity."

"Am I wallowing?" Raef felt a smile tug at his mouth and saw the same on Aldrif's face.

"You are."

Raef grinned but his good humor was only the work of a

heartbeat. "What was it all for, Aldrif?" He asked the question knowing she could not give him an answer.

Aldrif frowned. "I think that is only for you to understand."

Raef nodded, weary once more, the memories of Alfheim and Jötunheim weighing on him. "I do not think I will ever understand."

They sat in silence for a moment, Aldrif's hand resting on Raef's forearm.

"Do you wish to rest?"

"I think I have done enough of that."

Aldrif did not smile, but merely stood and offered Raef her hand. Placing his palm on hers, Raef sat up straight and lowered his legs to the floor. Taking a deep breath, he forced himself to stand, wavering for a moment. Aldrif did not step in and take his weight, did not offer her other arm, instead letting Raef fight for himself. When he was steady, she let his hand go.

His steps slow and halting, Raef rounded the end of his bed and reached the window, yanking aside the thick covering. Sunlight spilled in and splashed across Raef's chest. The day was still young. He let himself admire the light for a moment, then limped to his chest of clothes and drew out fresh things. A soft linen shirt and thick wool to layer over it. A sleeveless leather jacket fastened with thin cords dyed green and gold, the colors of Vannheim. Raef dressed himself while Aldrif watched and waited, ready to assist if he asked her. At last Raef cinched his belt and lowered himself to the chest to pull on a pair of boots.

When he stood again, he saw Aldrif suppress a smile. "Can I get you anything, lord?"

"A walking stick."

# SIXTEEN

A BITING WIND ripped across the steps that led up to the Vestrhall. The icy air was refreshing after the stifling warmth of his chamber and Raef, leaning on a tall, smooth ash staff, closed his eyes and sucked in a long, slow breath.

And yet the winter wind sapped what little strength Raef had in a single moment. As he glanced out on the village, the smoking chimneys and the snow-covered roofs, all bright and sharp under a clear sky, he felt dull, as though his body lingered still in the shadows of Jötunheim and the winter scene before him was but a memory.

"Cousin?" Isolf waited three steps down, his eyebrows raised as he wondered at Raef's hesitation.

Using the staff to take his weight, Raef eased down the stone steps and they began the descent down the slope, watching the people of the village go about their business. Some traded in the market, others tended hides, all watched him. Some smiled and he called them by name, others kept silent, noting his stiff, slow gait and the frequency of his need to rest the troubled leg.

By the time they had walked halfway down the gentle slope and back, Raef's limp had worsened and his mood with it. With as much dignity as he could muster, Raef climbed the steps to the hall, but it was Isolf's guiding hand that kept him steady. Raef paused on the stones that led to the doors and turned to face the man who called him cousin.

"I need proof, Isolf," Raef said. "You call me cousin and say we share the blood of Tyrlaug. Your story rings true, but I would be a fool not to question you."

"Question me? I have done nothing that would not bring you honor." Isolf looked wounded but Raef persisted.

"Proof, Isolf, that we are blood." Raef's voice rang out in the cold air, the only thing about him that had a sense of purpose. Raef took one ragged, limping step, drawing himself up to stare in Isolf's eyes. "I return from war, from the shadows of Jötunheim, to find a stranger in my home, a stranger who commands warriors and who has taken control of my gate. How can I not be wary?" Raef had not meant to speak of his strange journey beyond Midgard, but the words slipped out and there were more than Isolf's ears to hear.

"You are wary of good fortune?" Isolf cheeks burned to match his hair. "Think of what would have happened to your people had the vultures arrived here uncontested. Those loyal to you would be slaughtered, caught between the talons of one would-be lord and the teeth of another, and left to rot in the snow."

Raef, hand clenched on the walking stick, did not let Isolf's indignation sway him. But as he began to speak, Isolf held up his hands and sighed.

"You are right, you are right. No man would want less than what you have asked for." Isolf turned away. "I do not know what I can tell you." He pushed back the collar of his cloak to reveal a pin shaped like a snarling bear. "The mark of Tyrlaug, as you must know. It is all I have of him. But I might have taken it from a dead man, or had it made. It proves nothing." Isolf looked into the distance as if the fjord could hold an answer in its depths. "I never met your mother."

"This we have in common. She died at my birth."

"I was told she had the beauty of Freyja and Idunn. My mother was envious but spoke of her fondly. She could sing. And she danced like no other."

Raef closed his eyes, glad Isolf was not looking at him. The words called to mind his father's memories of Sunnlod, rare glimpses into Einarr's past seldom shared with his son. Raef strained through the darkness of his mind to picture his mother, to see her as Einarr had seen her, as he had so often tried to do as a boy. Here and there a shadowy figure danced across his vision, long dark hair flowing, feet light and graceful, but nothing more, nothing Raef could grasp.

"We shall feast tonight, in your honor, cousin."

Isolf turned, his face lit with gladness. But then his forehead creased and he took half a step forward. "Is it true?"

Raef knew what Isolf asked but he hesitated.

"You have seen Jötunheim."

"I have seen things only the gods can know, Isolf. And, yes, I have walked in barren Jötunheim." Raef turned away from the questions he could see forming on Isolf's lips.

The riders came at twilight, grey shapes streaking south down the narrow valley floor, then gliding along the edge of the fjord until they pounded through the gate. Shouts roused Raef from his chamber and he made it to the wide hall doors just as the riders came to a stop beneath the steps. At their head was Finnolf Horsebreaker and the young captain jumped from his saddle and bounded up the steps.

"Lord," Finnolf said, bowing low. The young man's gaze swept over Raef, showing a flicker of concern when it caught the walking staff clutched in Raef's hand. Then Finnolf looked Raef in the eye, though he seemed unwilling to do so. "We searched for you. There was no trace," he said, trailing off with only uncertainty left on his tongue.

Raef held up a hand. "Enough, Finnolf. You were not at fault." Raef reached out to Finnolf's shoulder. "Come. There is much to discuss." Raef looked out to the men who had ridden with Finnolf, hard, battle-worn faces, but familiar and loyal. Raef tried to wear a smile and forced out a laugh that he did not feel in his heart. "Come, all of you. We celebrate my return this night." The men cheered and soon the hall flowed with ale and rumbled with voices, the benches crammed with villagers and warriors intent on enjoying their lord's hospitality.

Raef sat at the high table, Isolf at one hand and Finnolf the other. He drank when they drank, ate when they ate, laughed at their jests and the unruly antics of the men, but all the while he felt distant, as though he watched the scene unfolding from far away. There was music, a single flute singing a cheery tune, reminding Raef of Gudrik. He felt ashamed at not having remembered the poet before then and turned to Finnolf on his left.

"Where is Gudrik? Where is the Palesword's poet?"

"My sister and her husband agreed to look after him," Finnolf said, his mouth full of roasted goat.

"And his leg?" Raef remembered the terrible break that had brought the poet so much pain and nearly claimed his life.

"It mends, but slowly."

"I will visit him tomorrow."

The hour was late when Raef limped from the hall and few eyes watched him go. In his chamber, Raef dreamed of spring, a whisper of green life hiding on the edges of dark winter. He seemed to be searching for something but could not name it. When he woke, his chamber burnished red with the faintest remainder of dying coals, the dream slipped away like a dark-scaled fish in a bottomless fjord and Raef sat up, his throat dry. Spinning his legs over the side of the bed, Raef got to his feet and lurched to the side table, his knee stiff and sore. Reaching in the darkness, Raef's fingers found the cup of water that had been left beside his washbasin. He drained it quickly but froze with the cup still at his lips as he heard a whisper of movement and then felt cold steel at his throat.

There was silence until Raef broke it. "What do you want?" If it was his life, he would be dead already, but the attacker made no demand. Instead, after a moment of hesitation, the blade retreated from his skin.

"We had to be certain it was you." The voice was soft but unapologetic and Raef turned to see a hooded figure, face deep in shadow. The knife was still raised but Raef closed his fingers over those of the attacker and pried the handle free while his other hand reached out and plucked the hood back.

"Eira."

It was the same as the first time he had laid eyes on her. Her hair, dark and smooth, her defiant eyes, and her pale face wreathed now in shadow rather than the sun of their first meeting. The shadows suited her, Raef saw, and he leaned in close to kiss her.

When she pulled back, Raef paused and then persisted, hungry for her lips on his, but when she placed a hand on his chest and deftly stepped to the side, he drew himself up. Their eyes met, each sheltering unasked questions. Raef looked away first and, tossing the knife onto his bed, limped to the hearth, feeling a sudden need to banish the shadows. He stoked the coals, sending flares of orange light into the farthest corners of his chamber.

Eira spoke. "We heard the Vestrhall had a lord once again. Some said it was you, others a stranger. We wanted to know."

"And so you sneak into my chamber in the dead of night and put a knife to my throat?"

"I did not wish to be seen."

"And why did you so desperately need to know if I was alive or if some pretender stood here in my stead?" Raef knew what he wanted to hear and knew she would not say it.

Eira retrieved the knife and sheathed it, returning it to her hip. "Your lands are in chaos. There has been fighting to the north between men who seek power and riders from Silfravall to the south have been seen patrolling your border. They can smell weakness and will strike if they catch the scent of Vannheim's infighting. At the very least, they will raid and plunder the farms that are in easy reach."

"What does it matter to you? This is not your home. You could be far from here, winning glory for yourself." As he said it, Raef realized part of him wanted this, wanted her gone and out of sight. And yet the far greater part of him yearned to hold her close and kiss her.

Eira looked as though she, too, wanted to be gone. "I made a vow."

"I will release you from your vow," Raef said, aware of the hurt in his voice and wishing he could keep it away.

"Quiet," Eira hissed, clearly uncomfortable with his words.

"You are free to go," he went on, but she cut him off with two quick strides and kissed him deeply. And though Raef knew the kiss was meant only to silence him, he took her in his arms and let the kiss burn away his other thoughts like the sun does a morning fog.

When they broke apart, she did not retreat but Raef could feel distance between them nonetheless. He cursed himself for wanting her, for wanting her to care for him, and wrapped a strand of her silky hair around his fingers, then brought it to his lips. Releasing her, Raef sighed. "You speak of we. Whom have you been scouting my land with? Vakre and Siv?"

Eira nodded. "When you disappeared, we searched for days without ceasing. When hope was lost, your warriors moved on and crossed into Vannheim. We followed. The young captain was kind and eager to give us supplies. But as word spread of your death, trouble soon followed. We felt we should stay and do what we could."

"To do what? Keep the peace? You let a stranger walk into my home." Raef let the bitterness creep into his voice but knew he was being unfair. Eira opened her mouth to answer but Raef waved a hand. "No, no, forgive me, protecting my home was never your responsibility." Raef sank into a chair by the hearth and put his head in his hands. "Where can I find Vakre? I would speak with him."

"How? You can hardly put one foot in front of the other." There was scorn in her voice. Raef wanted to silence her with another kiss. He did not respond to her insult.

"Tell me."

She studied him for a moment as if gauging what he would be willing to do if she refused, but then she answered as though it mattered not at all. "We made camp not far from here. In a ring of stones."

"I know the place. I will ride at first light." The visit to Gudrik would have to wait. Raef stirred the charred wood once more and a few feeble sparks cracked the silence. Raef leaned back in the chair and looked into her eyes. "I must ask, Eira. Did you see anything that night?"

She shook her head. "Nothing."

Raef sighed and returned his gaze to the fire, though it wandered, then, to the window and the dark night that lay beyond. "Why was I set adrift on the sea? Far easier to slit my throat and let me bleed into the snow. But if I was meant to live? Why?" Raef looked to Eira once more but there were no answers in her eyes. "Do you stay or do you go?"

"That has the sound of a challenge."

"If you like."

Eira came close and traced her finger down the thin, still-healing mark across Raef's palm. It was pink and fresh, the self-inflicted cut that had propelled him from the labyrinth. She moved on to the wound on Raef's upper-arm, sustained in battle in Alfheim. It had mended well but had never been serious. She came at last to the bandage wrapped around his forearm. The deep slash caused by Hrodvelgr's beast was knitting closed, the skin itching as it healed. Whatever Eira read from these marks and scars, some new to her eyes, some well known to her fingers, they seemed to make up her mind. She met Raef's gaze. "I will stay."

⟨ ⟨ ⟨

They were in the saddle with the first light of dawn. The hall slumbered still, remnants of the feast snoring peacefully with half-full cups of ale still at hand, and the only eyes that watched Raef and Eira ride from the gate belonged to two silent warriors. They were Isolf's men, strangers to Raef, and he did not tell them of his intentions.

The space between Eira's arrival and the dawn had been short and sleep had escaped Raef. His troublesome knee had protested the walk to the stable and brought sweat to his skin, and Raef had been glad to cast aside the walking staff in exchange for the horse. For a moment, as they moved swiftly over snowy ground, headed for the hills, Raef felt himself again. The brisk air, the horse moving beneath him, the ever-growing light on the eastern horizon, all served to shed the weariness that had plagued him for so long. But as they slowed their pace and began to climb into the hills, the sense of distance from himself returned, as though he were an eagle high in the sky, peering down on a man who moved toward an unknown fate.

The edge of the sun burned over the horizon as Raef and Eira approached the ring of stones. Two figures slept encircled in its grasp. Raef was tempted to let them sleep. Vakre was stretched out, limbs and blankets entangled, while Siv was curled tight, her braid nearly the only thing visible. They looked peaceful and Raef envied that. Eira spared no thought for her companions, though, and roused them loudly.

Siv was first to rise, her hand reaching for a knife until she saw Raef. A smile grew on her face as Vakre, cursing the blanket for snaring him, got to his feet. When his gaze, too, found Raef, he froze, disbelief etched on his face. Then he grinned wide and, laughing and closing the distance between them, first grasped Raef's forearm and then pulled him close in a strong embrace.

"It seems you have some life in you yet, friend," Vakre said as he released Raef and held him at arm's length. The grin faded. "We had begun to lose hope."

"He did," Siv broke in, her face impassive but a twinkle in her eye. "I held true."

Vakre rolled his eyes at her. "Forgive me, steadfast one, the error of my ways has been revealed to me."

Siv grinned and then made her way to Raef, the merriment on her face turning to an inquisitive look as she wrapped her arms around his shoulders. Her hold was without Vakre's vigor and Eira's unwilling, fiery passion, but there was solace that Raef found surprising. She stepped back.

"Are you well?"

He might have said yes, given any passing answer, but as he looked into Siv's eyes he heard himself say, "No." It was a simple thing and yet to him it conveyed a great deal more. She did not question him further and her eyes did not convey pity, and Raef was grateful for both of these things.

"What happened, Raef?" Vakre's question was soft but insistent.

Raef looked at Vakre, the burden of his journey heavy on his shoulders, but when he opened his mouth to begin the story, he said instead, "There will be time enough for that."

The four of them shared a morning meal of hard bread and dried meat and between bites they exchanged information. Raef told them of his new-found cousin, Isolf, then Vakre and Siv took turns telling what they knew of Vannheim and the growing sense of unrest. Eira kept silent.

"My cousin said two warriors are actively seeking my hall, Rudrak Red-beard and Snorren Thoken," Raef said. "Both fought at the burning lake."

Vakre confirmed this with a nod. "They arrived at your hall within a day of each other, but your cousin had beaten them there. They were surprised to find it defended and have avoided it since. We have seen Red-beard's men to the north. They watch the road to Finngale and prey on innocent travelers. As for this other one, Snorren, we hear he has retreated to his land in the south of Vannheim, but I do not trust what my own eyes have not seen. Neither has ventured close to the Vestrhall again."

"And Tulkis Greyshield? Has he come forth?"

Siv shook her head. "But you are not the only one to wonder. Not two days past, I heard villagers in the market speak of this Greyshield. They seemed surprised that he had not shown his strength." Silence from Greyshield only made Raef uneasy.

"What will you do?" Vakre's question lingered as though suspended on the rays of sunlight that stretched across the sky and crept along the snow.

"I do not know," Raef said. He looked from one face to the next and knew behind each one were unspoken thoughts and suggestions. He was glad they remained unspoken. "I should return. My cousin will wonder." Raef, stood, pausing as his knee threatened to buckle, grimacing at the soreness, wishing for Aldrif's draught only to remind himself of what it had done to him, and remounted his horse. The others watched him, waiting. "I expect nothing from you."

"You would cast us off?" Vakre said this lightly and with a small smile but Raef could hear the hurt in his voice.

"I only mean that Vannheim is mine to defend and her fate need not be entangled with yours."

"I cannot speak for Siv or Eira, but you need not be concerned about my fate." Vakre's good humor vanished and his voice became sharp, reminding Raef that this was the son of Loki and that there was much he did not know about Vakre.

"We are coming with you," Siv said.

They rode from the ring of stones, but Raef did not lead them back the way he and Eira had come. Instead, they traveled in a northwesterly direction, staying deep within the folds of the hills and treading a path not yet lit by the rising sun. Here the world was still and rooted in deep winter. An army of pine trees ruled here, each weighed down by thick snow, warriors stooped and bent by time. It seemed a forest of death to Raef, but he persisted in his course until they reached a boulder-strewn stream, frozen over and quiet. Here they turned north again, winding here and there until the trees thinned and a hut came into view. It had been abandoned long ago and the turf roof was crumbling in on itself, but Raef knew it well.

Raef pulled up his horse and held her steady for a long moment, the others fanned out behind him. Vakre asked him what they were doing there but Raef's only reply was to slide from the saddle and take slow, lurching steps through the clearing until he was ten paces from the hut. With each step he took, the world around him faded, his companions all but forgotten, leaving only the hut, Raef, and a woman's screams inside his head.

Raef sank to his knees, oblivious of the snow and the pain in his knee, seeing the hut wreathed in fire, seeing Svanja smile at him and then burst into flames, her hair blazing as she screamed his name. Raef stared, his heart pounding, the labyrinth crushing him once again. At last he forced his eyes closed and, though he still saw the flames in the darkness behind his lids, he was able to reclaim a hold on his true surroundings.

When he opened his eyes, the hut was nothing more than a wooden ruin, unscarred by fire, unblackened by smoke, and Svanja's voice had faded into the snow. His companions had dismounted and stood behind him. He turned to them, half-dreading and half-hoping they would demand an explanation. They kept silent and Raef mounted his horse once more. He quickened their pace, eager to put distance between himself and the hut. The labyrinth had found a crack in Yggdrasil and reared an ugly head into Midgard, relentless in its conquest of his mind.

But distance was not enough, for their path out of the trees took them to the narrow end of a snaking lake, a place populated by a smattering of buildings and more sheep than men. Here they met with a well-traveled, snow-crusted road and a single cart loaded down with wood and drawn by a pair of sturdy oxen. No matter how the oxen strained, the cart was stuck in mud hiding beneath the snow and an older man, his beard thick and grey and his cheeks ruddy in the cold air, struggled to push the cart free.

Raef pulled up and the four of them helped the old man push and twist until at last the wheel broke free and the oxen were able to pull the cart away from the mud. Only then did Raef look under the old man's hood and, though the other man's face lit up on sight of Raef, Raef had to remind himself to draw breath.

"Lord, you have done me a great kindness," the old man said, beaming. "Do you know me, lord? Long has it been since I last saw your face, but I would know it anywhere. I am Beomir, lord, and my—"

"Your daughter," Raef broke in, "yes, Svanja." He tried to smile.

"Never long separated, the two of you in your youth," Beomir said. "I never regretted moving away from the shadow of your hall, but for the loss of your friendship, lord. She missed you for many seasons."

"And now?"

Beomir's smile turned sad. "Now it is we who must miss her, lord. She died not twelve days past."

Raef's heart turned to stone, his already cold skin freezing as a knot of ice spread from his stomach through all his limbs. "How?"

"Caught in a fire," Beomir said, shaking his head. "House burned down around her before she could get out. One of the children, too, though her husband and the older girl made it out."

"I am sorry," Raef heard himself say, a faint voice beneath the thundering in his ears, the helpless screams rising again until Raef could bear it no longer. "I am sorry," he said again, turning, fleeing, to his horse. He pulled himself up into the saddle and with a furious kick they were off, the mare bounding through the snow, the icy lake but a blur alongside them.

He rode until the horse began to weaken and they found him high in the hills, seated above a cliff that in spring would be awash in waterfalls. Here the wind was fierce and snow began to swirl, some falling from swift grey clouds, some picked off the ground in puffs of white. And yet Raef paid it no mind and he sat with his cloak hanging loose rather than pulled tight, his gaze on the far horizon. He heard his friends approach, heard their horses snorting hot breath, heard feet crunch to the ground as they dismounted.

It was Vakre who approached alone. He sat by Raef, perched on a boulder that brought them to eye level. "Who was Svanja?" he asked.

Raef kept his eyes fixed on the streaks of sunlight that split through the grey clouds in the distance. "Her father lived in our village. We grew up together. She was the third girl I ever kissed, but kissing her taught me what it was all for. When her uncle died, her father moved them out to the family farm. I saw her twice, perhaps three times, after that."

Vakre waited.

"I think," Raef began, unsure, "I think I could have saved her. But I let her die."

The wind gusted and snow settled on Vakre's eyelashes. He blinked the flakes away. "Tell me what happened to you, Raef."

And so Raef took his mind back to that fateful day in Axsellund, when the crescent moon had drifted on the sky like a boat upon the sea, and he began to tell his story. He left nothing out. He began with the ship and his first moments of consciousness. He took Vakre to Alfheim, aware then that Siv and Eira were listening, and told of its strange forests and stranger inhabitants, of the Guardians and Finnoul's rebellion, of the dragon-kin and his near-death in the barren land. It was hard to find the words to describe how he journeyed from Alfheim to Jötunheim. The glittering bridge, the doorway to another set of stars, were vivid in his mind and yet paled when spoken of. Vakre listened, his face still. Raef told of tricking Mogthrasir, of Hrodvelgr's prison and arena, of Bara and the aid she lent, of Hrodvelgr's death. When at last it came to the labyrinth, Raef paused to steady his racing heart, and then he pushed back into the darkness. As he told Vakre of that bleak place, of what he had seen, of how it had eaten at him until he began to crumble in mind and body, he slipped back among the blood stones, closing his eyes without even realizing it.

He related the vision of Svanja in a quiet voice and might have stopped there but Vakre's eyes encouraged him to continue, and he told of Odin, the grim confirmation of the coming battle that would consume the nine realms, and the dire, unknown fate he had foretold for Raef.

When it was finished, Raef's words taken with the wind,

they sat in silence until Vakre spoke. "Svanja's death was not of your making."

"And yet, if I had," Raef began, but Vakre cut him off.

"No."

"And what of you? And Eira? Siv? I watched you die a thousand deaths and stood by helplessly. Is that to be my fate, then?"

"I would not claim to know your fate, but there are times we all must watch those we care for suffer. That is the nature of life."

"You should go. There is only darkness ahead of me. Spare yourself from that."

"There is nothing to spare myself from, Raef. Darkness is ahead of us all and the final battle looms. Distancing myself from you will make no difference." Vakre leaned forward, his voice solemn and earnest. "You are not at fault."

The snowstorm had settled and big flakes fell undisturbed by wind. Raef, feeling the cold now, pulled his cloak tight. Vakre's words seemed to delve into the dark corners of his heart, bringing faint hope of light.

"You survived a crucible, Raef, one that most would not. There is no shame in fear, but what matters most is what you do now with the life that you have carved out of the clutches of death. Or would you linger in doubt, caught up still in the web of this labyrinth for the rest of your days?"

Raef was quiet for a moment. "One thing sustained me. I made a vow before the gods to avenge my father."

"I will help you however I can."

Raef shook his head. "I am no closer to knowing the truth behind his murder than I was the day he died."

"Would you give up, then?" Vakre spoke quietly but there was an edge in his voice.

The sky broke above them, casting light through the still falling snow. A shadow crossed over the sun and Raef looked up to see a raven, black wings spread wide, riding the air. It circled and descended, settling into a tree. It cocked its head to the side, giving every impression it was waiting for Raef's answer.

"No." And with that simple word Raef felt a heaviness lift from his shoulders. He had found his purpose again, had reclaimed something that pulled at him stronger than the darkness.

Vakre went to his horse and lifted something from the saddlebag. "I kept this, in case." He handed it to Raef, who unwrapped the cloth to find the broken axe and the hilt of the sword that had shattered at the burning lake. The grip was smooth beneath his fingers, familiar in all the right places. It only lacked the steel to become part of Raef once again.

# SEVENTEEN

T HE HALL WAS full to bursting when Raef returned at sunset. Warriors spilled out onto the steps, flowing down around Raef and his companions, their eager faces shining with pride. They called to him and he answered. All their faces he knew well for they had fought with him at the burning lake and more than one had healing burns to prove it. But their purpose there was unknown to him until Isolf, a wide grin on his face and Finnolf at his heels, stepped from the hall.

"Cousin," Raef said.

"I have summoned these men in your name, lord, to ask but one thing of you. Finnolf sent riders before the break of day to spread the word and they have only just arrived, thirsty for sight of their lord and strong mead to share. And more will come." Isolf spread his arms. "You were lost to us, taken from your proper seat before your time, and yet the gods have returned you to Vannheim. What greater sign could we ask for?"

"What do you speak of, cousin?"

Isolf waved his hands. "No, no, I am not the one to say it. Let it be their voices you hear." He stepped back, leaving Raef alone on the steps, and the men gathered close about him, shouldering past Vakre, Siv, and Eira.

A single warrior pushed forward. He was built like an ox and bore scars all over. His head was shaven on the left side, leaving the right long and tied back in thick, twisted ropes, and the bare skin was inked with three crows pecking the flesh from a corpse. His beard hung in a single, heavy braid that reached his belt and was tied off with a band of gold, the only decoration he allowed himself for he scorned the wearing of arm rings. He was Dvalarr the Crow and his reputation had been built on the bodies of many men.

"What need has Vannheim for the kings who war in the east? They squabble in the aftermath of the great victory you won, lord. The glory is yours. We ask that you take what you have earned, that you show Vannheim's strength. We name you king!" This last Dvalarr roared and the men echoed him, their cries fierce and full of battle-lust.

Raef let the cheers die before answering their call. He held out his hands and was glad when they did not tremble. "What king could ask for more loyal men?"

The chorus was deafening as the warriors bellowed their approval. The armed guards at the top of the steps beat their spears against their shields while those who stood in the snow stomped their feet, making the earth shiver beneath Raef. Raef let the cries wash over him, clasped forearm after forearm, and did not protest when Dvalarr hoisted him onto one shoulder. He was carried into the hall and set down on a table. One by one, the men knelt and swore oaths of loyalty, mixing their words with blood, their faces solemn now, each touching the hammer amulet he wore after nicking the skin of his palm. Raef nodded his thanks to each until at last only Isolf knelt before him.

"Cousin," Isolf said, holding out a clenched fist that dripped crimson blood, "a great fate has led me to you in this hour. By the blood we share, by the love between our mothers, I swear to you my endless loyalty. I will be your most faithful servant and if I do you wrong, let the gods strike me down and deny me Valhalla."

Raef stepped down from the tabletop, his knee aching and weary though he fought to hide the pain, and lifted his cousin from his knees. "From this day forth, you are my cousin no longer. You are my brother." The warriors cheered and Raef embraced Isolf, then drew back and called out, "The ale will flow this night."

Behind the crowd, a single face, impervious to the tumult, caught Raef's eye. Josurr, the second priest of Odin, younger and gentler than Fylkir, but no less devoted to his duties, the telltale signs of recent sacrifice still staining the curve of his ears and tracing the length of his jaw. The priest watched Raef with quiet eyes that betrayed nothing and Raef wondered if the Allfather had given some sign, some indication that a king would be made that night.

ᚱ ᚱ ᚱ

The night was clear and brittle, the stars burning hot and searing the dark sky. Raef had found peace and quiet outside the hall, seeking the steps to a small terrace at the rear of the hall where he might observe the stars, and they him. Finnolf had tried to follow his new king, intent on keeping Raef in sight, but Raef had gently turned him aside and asked that he search out Vakre, Eira, and Siv, who had not made their presence known in the hall.

Only Siv and Vakre arrived, taking the stairs without hurry, their boots scuffing the stone. They paused on the threshold of the terrace.

"Shall I kneel as they did?" Vakre asked, his voice tight, his words clipped.

"I did not ask them to kneel."

"And yet you did not stop them."

"What could I do?" Raef's voice rang out across the stone. There was no good answer and none was offered. "If I had refused, Vannheim would be ripped from me. They would have slipped away, their disappointment keen, their anger at being slighted sharp. And they would have sought out the vultures who already covet this hall, strengthening them until one rose above the rest. My place is on a rowing bench with the sea road ahead of me and the sun rising at my back, not atop a mound of corpses who have died to make me king. But I will not be the Skallagrim who loses Vannheim and the Vestrhall. If I must be king to secure my home, then so be it."

"Being king may not keep you lord of Vannheim," Siv said.

"What do you mean?"

"A king must face his foes in battle. You will be drawn from Vannheim, forced to meet the Hammerling or Fengar in the field. And when you are gone, the vultures will descend for they know they have gone too far to escape retribution. They must see you overthrown, or see their own deaths."

"There are many hands I trust to keep Vannheim safe should I be absent."

"Whose? Your cousin's? Blood he might be, but loyal he is not," Vakre said.

"Take care of what you say," Raef said, his anger rising. "He is my family, the only blood I have left to me."

"I do not trust him."

Raef stepped close until only a hand's width separated their faces and grabbed Vakre's collar. "Isolf has shown his loyalty. He might have had me killed the moment he saw me. Give me proof or do not speak of that which you know nothing of." Vakre did not flinch, did not look away, but neither did he speak. At last Raef broke eye contact and looked to Siv. "Where is Eira?"

"I do not know."

Raef wanted to rage, to fight, but he swallowed it all. "Find her," he said. Siv placed a hand on Raef's arm and looked as though she might speak. "Find her," Raef repeated, his voice harsh. Siv's hand retreated and the warmth that normally lingered in her eyes vanished.

She descended from the terrace without a word. Raef waited until she was out of sight, keeping his gaze averted from Vakre, though he could feel the son of Loki's eyes burning into the back of his head, then traced Siv's steps and withdrew to his chamber.

He spent the night staring into his empty hearth, the ashes raked clean. Though he could feel exhaustion behind his eyes and longed for sleep, it was a comfort that danced out of reach. When this became clear, he gave up the chase and began to work on strengthening himself. He had eaten well in the past few days, had begun to see flesh fill back into the places it had inhabited before, and a mirror revealed that he looked the part of a king even if he did not feel it. Beneath his skin, his muscles ached merely from riding a horse, and his troublesome knee quivered when asked to bear his weight. And so Raef made it quiver as he squatted on that single leg time and time again. Twice it gave out on him and he fell to his chamber floor and felt a burn course up and down his entire leg, but as the sweat dripped down his forehead Raef felt something akin to satisfaction as well.

When he had done enough, he burst from his chamber and found Finnolf, as he knew he would, half-asleep outside the door. The captain blinked bleary-eyed at Raef.

"Long has it been since I crossed blades. I am out of practice." It was only a half-truth. He had battled in Alfheim with a strange-shaped blade and he had fought in Hrodvelgr's arena with a sword that threatened to break with every swing, but he felt an urgent need to hold a true sword in his hand once more and to rediscover his bladework and battle skills.

In his father's armory, Raef passed over the sword that Einarr had used, though he was glad to see it resting there, returned to its home. Instead he chose a simple sword, the kind granted to the warriors who watched the gates and walls of the Vestrhall. It was made for this purpose and would serve well enough. Raef hooked the scabbard on his belt and made for the yard, grabbing a shield on the way.

Finnolf waited there. He yawned once, but his sword and shield were at the ready. The yard was unlit by torches, the moonlight turning the snow to silver.

Raef started slow, taking note of the precision of each step he took, of the extension of his sword arm, engaging his shoulders and the muscles of his abdomen. He and Finnolf established a rhythm, a slow dance that neither knew the next steps to. They flowed across the snow, a sword thrust there, a shield raised there, a spin and sudden slash there. When they paused, each man's breath came faster, puffing into the winter air.

With a nod, they began again, but the dance was ended and Raef's attack was swift and furious. Finnolf fell back, momentarily off balance, but soon found his footing and they exchanged blows until Raef caught Finnolf's shield on the hilt of his sword and ripped it from the captain's grasp. His own he cast aside and pressed forward on Finnolf, a storm gathering deep in his chest. His onslaught was short and brutal and Raef was blind to how Finnolf fell back, how the captain deflected now in desperation, how his eyes showed real fear. It took only three slashes of Raef's flashing sword to put Finnolf on the ground, and even then Raef did not stop.

"Lord," Finnolf cried as Raef's sword descended.

Raef pulled up short, Finnolf's voice breaking through at last. He took in the sight of the young captain sprawled at his feet and saw he had drawn blood across the muscles of Finnolf's upper arm.

Horrified, Raef dropped his sword arm. He knelt at Finnolf's side and saw alarm still burning in the captain's eyes. "Forgive me. I was not myself," Raef said, his voice stumbling. "Forgive me." His own pain roared to life then, his left knee a ball of agony somehow drowned in the fury of swordwork. Together, they sat in the snow, their heartbeats slowing to a normal pace, and watched the sun rise over Vannheim.

When he felt he could manage it, Raef struggled to his feet and offered his hand to Finnolf. The captain took it and their eyes met.

"This was not my intent, Finnolf, believe me."

"I know." The captain had lost his fear and regained his natural trust and for that Raef was grateful beyond words.

"How many riders did you send across the land?"

"Twenty. Six returned with the warriors who answered the summons yesterday. I expect we may see five or six more by nightfall, though no doubt they will return with far greater speed than the men they were sent to find. The warriors will trickle in at a much slower rate. The rest ride to the farthest reaches of your lands, lord. It will be days before we see them."

"And how will we be alerted should an attack come from Redbeard or Thoken?"

"I have men patrolling the second ring of hills, lord. We will see them if they come."

"Good." Raef looked again at the wound he had given Finnolf. The young captain was pale. "Get that taken care of," he said. "I will have need of you in these coming days." Finnolf grinned and disappeared through the hall's wooden doors leaving Raef relieved to know he had at least one loyal warrior.

ᚠ ᚠ ᚠ

It was early yet, but Hoyvik the village smith was hard at work, bringing his sleeping forge to life again, his young apprentice scampering about to obey his every soft-spoken word. Hoyvik's work was renowned in the western lands and men sought him from distant homes in hopes of receiving a blade of his making. His work was costly, but the results were worth every coin. Hoyvik, his father, and his grandfather before him had been making swords on the edge of the fjord for more than one hundred years and Raef's first blade, sized and weighted for a youth, had come from this forge. There was no other smith he would rather trust the making of a new sword to.

Hoyvik did not seem surprised to see Raef and he did not hurry to greet him. Hoyvik never hurried and Raef was content to wait, hovering just outside the heat of the forge until Hoyvik came to him.

"A new sword, for a new king." This was spoken without reverence or much emotion at all.

Raef remembered the borrowed sword that had taken him from prisoner to the burning lake. He remembered the blow that had shattered it, the cruel eyes in the face of the Valkyrie who had wielded a sword of sunlight. Raef handed the smith the broken hilt of his old sword.

"Use this, if you can."

The smith took the hilt and turned it between his fingers, nodding to himself. "Five days. No more."

Raef frowned, knowing the smith could not make a blade of quality and still do other work in that time. "But your other work."

"Five days, and hope I am not too late. I think soon you will have need of a good sword."

Raef could not deny this and he thanked the smith, promising double in payment. At this, Hoyvik shook his head.

"The same payment as the last sword I made for your father, no more, no less. I will not have people call me greedy."

Raef agreed, then walked through the village, one more destination in mind before he returned to the hall.

The house of Finnolf's sister sat at the base of the gentle slope, close to the edge of the fjord and the docks where the timber walls protruded into the water. Her husband, a fisherman, was outside, so bent on his task of mending nets that he did not at first notice Raef watching him. When he did, he scrambled to his feet and stammered for words.

"I understand you have given the hospitality of your home to a stranger called Gudrik," Raef said.

"We have, lord."

Raef smiled. "I am glad of it. You have my thanks. I wish to see him."

The interior of the house was warm and cheerful. Finnolf's sister tended a pot over the fire but it was the figure resting in a corner, his nimble fingers carving a shaft of wood, who drew Raef's gaze.

"Gudrik."

The poet smiled and got to his feet. Raef could see he did it with difficulty and kept his weight off the healing leg. "I had heard of your safe return. The gods have smiled on you, Raef Skallagrim."

Raef smiled in return, but he could not agree. "Forgive me for not visiting sooner." The smile drifted away. "I was not well."

"A king has more important things to do than visit a crippled poet." It was said with ease but Raef could hear a hint of bitterness in Gudrik's voice. With the aid of a crutch, Gudrik limped from the house. They walked to the water, and Gudrik settled onto a log that had washed up on the pebbled beach.

"How is your leg?"

"As you see it." The bitterness was still there.

"You have seen Aldrif?"

"Yes. But far too much time had passed between the injury and when she got her hands on me. There was little she could do." Gudrik tried to smile, but there was no truth in it.

Raef realized he had hoped to find Gudrik in good spirits, had sought the poet's calm nature to sooth his own troubled mind. To find Gudrik shadowed in melancholy was unexpected and Raef did not know how to make it right. "You will have a chamber in my hall, if you desire it. We need music, good music."

Gudrik was quiet, staring out across the fjord. "I will never stand in a shield wall again. I will never know the joy of victory, feel the tremor of battle fill my limbs, or wield a sword again. I will never shout the battle cry alongside my brothers and face death with a laughing heart."

"You have words and music, Gudrik. These are gifts given only to a few, granted by the Allfather himself."

Gudrik turned his head to look up at Raef, his eyes burdened with tears. "I was a warrior, Raef. It is not enough to sing the songs of ancient battles. I have lost a part of myself, lost the part that matters most."

"Gudrik, I always valued your mind more than your sword. One warrior is much like another. But one poet, who can weave words and draw the hearts of men into their throats, who can bring tears to the eyes of the gruffest warrior with a simple song, this poet is worth so much more." Gudrik stared at the grey stones beneath his feet, unresponsive. "You are the bones of the land, Gudrik. You give life to our history. You keep the gods close to us. You bring people together as no warrior, no matter how strong and skilled, can." Raef held out his hand. "My hall awaits and I need you there." After a long moment, Gudrik met Raef's gaze, and though his eyes were troubled and full of guilt and longing, he took Raef's hand and was pulled to his feet.

Together they climbed to the Vestrhall and Raef instructed servants to show Gudrik to an empty chamber and fetch his few belongings from the house of Finnolf's sister.

"Rest, friend, and make this place your home," Raef said, glad to see Gudrik muster a smile that reached his eyes. "Then join us this night." Raef left Gudrik in the care of the servants and then sought out his father's vacant chamber.

It was as Einarr had left it. The heavy curtains hung askew, casting slanted shadows across the floor and the massive bed draped with furs. A pair of boots rested by a trunk, one standing upright, the other toppled as though it had been tossed to the floor in a hurry. Mud, dry and crusty now, stained the leather. A candle, stubby, well-used, sat on Einarr's table, the drips of its last use long hardened on the wood. Raef picked at the wax until it loosened.

There was dust, though not as much as Raef had expected. He blew a coating off the papers on his father's table and it hung in the sunlight for a moment before drifting to the floorboards. The papers were dry and brittle under Raef's touch so he looked with his eyes and used his hands only a little.

The papers were mundane. Lists of goods traded, inventories of the hall's warehouses and valuables, receipts of coin spent and gained. Raef searched a small wooden chest filled to the brim but found only more of the same. Sighing, Raef sat in his father's chair and massaged his fingers against his temples. He had hoped for something that might point to a conspiracy against his father, whether a direct threat or a warning from a third party. If Einarr had received any such correspondence in the days before they traveled to Balmoran for the gathering, he had destroyed it.

Raef sat in the half-lit chamber for a long moment, plucking idly at a cushion until he had extracted a downy white feather from the stuffing. He ran one finger along the feather's edge, then blew it across the room and watched it drift to the furs that covered the bed. He closed his eyes, acutely aware that this chamber and the sword in the armory were the last things of his father left to him. Raef inhaled but there was nothing, not the scent of good, worn leather, not stale ale, not a hint of beeswax soap, or anything else Raef remembered lingering about his father. He felt tears prick at the back of his eyeballs, itching to spring forth, and for a moment his vision grew watery. But not a single salty tear fell and the indulgence in self-pity passed. It would do no good wishing a king's burden had fallen on his father's shoulders instead of his own. Tears would not alter the past.

Raef sealed his hurt inside his father's chamber and sought out the hall's steward, finding him deep inside one of the underground storehouses, on his tiptoes on a rickety stool, counting withered winter apples. He started at Raef's appearance, knocking his head against a hanging side of beef.

"Lord, have you come for a report?" His inky fingers reached for his scroll even as he lost his footing on the stool. Raef caught him by the sleeve and steadied him.

"No, Ulli, I am sure the numbers are in order. I come on other business. I owe a debt to a fisherman and it is time I paid it." Raef ordered three fine pigs and a strong horse to be sent to the small house near the seashore where Brunn and Sigrid had given him life. "Send them at once by cart. I want two warriors to accompany the driver. Under no circumstances are the pigs to be left with anyone but Brunn," Raef added, his thoughts straying to Skarfi, Brunn's vindictive brother. Ulli took the order and the directions to Brunn's home without blinking, but before he scurried off to find a man to drive the cart, Raef stopped him, a question half-formed on his tongue. "My cousin, when he arrived, what was he like?"

"Courteous, lord, in every way. Respectful. They fed themselves from the forest and the fjord, making no claim to our winter stores. There were no demands, no threats." Guilt flashed across the steward's face. "When some of us began to lose hope, it was your cousin who insisted you were yet alive and gave us the will to believe."

"And when word came that Rudrak Red-beard and Snorren Thoken were of a mind to take the Vestrhall?"

The little steward's face was very grave. "Even then he spoke only of keeping Vannheim safe for you."

Raef nodded, glad he had asked. "Thank you, Ulli."

Raef returned to the hall. The vestiges of the previous night's kingmaking revelry were being scrubbed from the floor but a stale smell still hung in the air. Raef watched the servants go about their business, heads bent, only quiet murmurs passing between them. He ordered the doors be kept open to freshen the air and a large fire was soon blazing in the first of two fire pits in the floor, both to keep the hall from growing too cold and in hopes that the smoke might drive away the unpleasant odors. Raef lingered at the high seat, the chair his father had occupied with such ease. He had yet to sit in it, choosing instead among the stools and benches even during the kingmaking, and he traced his fingers over the carved wood. The chair was decorated with many scenes of old, all telling the first days of Vannheim's history. It was a bloody history and Raef knew the stories well.

His fingers had just found a particularly gruesome depiction of brothers mauling each other to a grisly ruin when Isolf appeared at his shoulder.

"This chair was born in blood," Raef said.

"As are kings."

"This story," Raef tapped the wood with one finger, "one of the more violent ones, which is saying something." He bent down behind the chair and gestured for Isolf to do the same. "Here," Raef pointed to one of the brothers, "Ulflaug has set his brother's hair on fire. Kell-thor responds by chopping Ulflaug's balls off."

"I would say Kell-thor got the better end of it."

"Perhaps. Unless you knew that in the end Kell-thor was murdered by his nephew who was in truth his own son. The boy knew nothing of his parentage but Kell-thor," Raef looked at the carving of the wild-haired warrior drowning in his own blood as a boy looked on in triumph, "Kell-thor knew." Raef rose and bit back a grimace of pain. His knee ached. "The mother killed herself for grief. The boy is remembered for nothing but wielding the blade that slew his father."

Isolf seemed unperturbed by the glum story. "And yet he endures, carved into a chair that will seat a king. That is something, is it not?"

Perhaps it was, perhaps not. Raef no longer wished to dwell on the brothers Kell-thor and Ulflaug.

# EIGHTEEN

FOR FOUR DAYS Raef received warriors in his hall. Men, fresh from the battles in Gornhald and Solheim, were eager to show themselves to their new king and pledged their oaths with solemn words and faces. One by one they knelt before Raef and he acknowledged them with his thanks and gave them promises of renown. The village and the Vestrhall were overflowing but the warriors kept coming, making camp outside the walls despite the cold and snow. It was an encouraging sight, those makeshift shelters, fires dotting the land at night, horses gathered in a circle against the wind. Each night, a portion of the warriors were feasted in Raef's hall and each morning, he sent most of them home again to await further word. He kept some of those with horses outside the walls as deterrence against an attack from Red-beard or Thoken.

As the numbers grew, Raef sent Finnolf and another captain, Yorkell, to scout further afield so that they might know where the traitorous warriors gathered. One went north, the other south, with strict orders to engage only if necessary, and with numbers great enough to discourage an ambush. And so Raef waited, Isolf and Gudrik at his side, Vakre and Siv nowhere to be found, as the warriors of Vannheim, young and old, man and woman, brought him their spears.

Not all came. There were absences Raef could not help but notice, men he had thought loyal to his father. He said as much to Isolf, but his cousin did not seem concerned.

"They will see the error of their ways when we rout Red-beard and Thoken in battle. And they will crawl back to you and beg to join your shield wall."

Raef was not convinced. The men he looked for were battle-hardened and not likely to crawl or beg.

It was twilight on the fourth day when Raef received a final group of warriors who had made the last push to the hall before night fell. They were weary but no less proud and each received a cup of ale and a place by the fires. As the men fell away, eager to eat and drink, a single boy, slight and skinny-armed, remained in the center, unnoticed in the crowd but now alone and exposed. The boy kept his gaze down, his arms straight at his sides.

"Your name, boy?" Raef's voice carried over the murmurs of the warriors and all eyes turned to middle of the hall.

The boy looked up but did not yet meet Raef's stare. He swallowed. "Ergil."

Raef smiled a little. Nerves had stilled the boy's tongue and he not given his father's name. "Come closer, Ergil." The boy did as he was told and Raef could see that his hair, shorn at the back of his head but longer at the front, was damp with sweat. He stopped perhaps five paces from the base of the stairs leading to Raef's chair and the high table.

Isolf stepped forward, his orange hair wild, his gaze fierce. The boy seemed to shrink within his skin. "What brings you before the king?"

"I wish," Ergil began, his voice so quiet Raef had to strain to hear him, "to give my oath."

"How old are you, Ergil?" Raef asked.

The boy's chin came up just a hair, a shred of defiance working its way to the surface. "Fifteen."

He was older than he looked, then, for Raef had thought him scarcely more than twelve. Either that or he lied.

"Ergil," Isolf said, "look around you. This hall boasts a hundred warriors and all have watched men die next to them in the shield wall. Their strength is great, their chests broad, their arms thick. The king has no need of you." It was unkindly said and not entirely true for there was more than one young warrior who had not yet seen battle. Raef saw Gudrik, leaning on his crutch just to the left of the high table, flinch. Raef frowned at his cousin and rose from his seat.

"What I need, Ergil, is for you to hone yourself into a weapon of war until your skills are unmatched and your strength is legendary. Then, when you are ready, return to me and I will place you by my side in the shield wall."

Ergil looked to the floor again and sucked in his bottom lip. "May I still give you my oath?"

"If you wish." Raef took his seat again and Ergil approached the steps. He paused before the first but did not kneel, instead continuing on, nearly tripping on the third step.

"That is far enough, boy," Isolf said, his voice a low growl. Raef raised a hand to silence him, but still Ergil came on. When he mounted the top step, he looked straight at Raef and then launched himself through the air between them, a snarl on his face and a knife, flashing suddenly from his sleeve, in his hand.

Raef and Isolf moved as one, Raef twisting from the chair and his cousin tackling Ergil to the ground. It was over in an instant, the boy pinned beneath Isolf, the knife out of his hand and out of reach, Gudrik lurching forward and falling to his knees in an effort to reach Raef, before the hall full of warriors could react, but then they were on their feet and calling for death.

"Silence," Raef called. "Silence." The noise quieted and Raef looked down at the would-be assassin, wrestled now to a seated position, his arms held behind his back. Ergil seethed, his eyes ripe with hatred, a far cry from the timid boy. He nearly looked a man, but his fury was useless against Isolf's strong arms.

Raef turned first to Gudrik, helping him rise to his feet. The skald accepted Raef's arm, but his face burned with shame and Raef, aware of all the watching eyes, could say nothing, could only grip Gudrik's hand and know it meant little.

Leaving Gudrik, Raef gestured for Isolf to bring the boy to his feet and then stepped close, forcing Ergil to accept his stare, though Raef towered above the boy.

"Let me deal with him," Isolf said through gritted teeth, a knife of his own now pressed to Ergil's ribs. "He is beneath you."

Raef did not answer his cousin. "What offense have I done you, boy?" His voice was soft but saturated with menace. He grasped Ergil's neck with one hand, his thumb pressing hard against the boy's throat. "Answer me."

Ergil tried to spit but the phlegm only trickled down his hairless chin. The warriors rumbled with laughter and Ergil's cheeks flushed with embarrassment. "You killed my father," he shouted. "And I have come to avenge him." The laughter ceased and the hall was quiet.

"I have killed many men in battle. If we all sought reparation for such deaths, we would walk this earth no more."

"I am Ergil Thrainson, and Jarl Thrainson was my father." The boy's words washed over Raef and for a moment he was looking at Jarl in his dying moment, not the son. "You robbed him of Valhalla," Ergil cried, near to tears. Raef was back in the Great-Belly's hall, the hilt of his knife slick with blood, the blood of Jarl Thrainson, who fell to the floor, staining it red. Jarl's last act had been to reach for his weapon, to secure a hope of Valhalla, but Raef had denied it. And the whole world knew it.

"He deserved it," Raef said, his voice a snarl of rage, the words passing through clenched teeth. The two sons of murdered fathers stared at each other, and Raef saw his own hatred and guilt burning back at him from the depths of Ergil's eyes. Raef thrust the boy away and took a step back. He gave a nod to Isolf, who dragged Ergil, cursing, from the hall.

In a matter of moments, it was as if Ergil had never been there. The men returned to their food and drink, their voices low at first, and then rising. Laughter burst forth from one corner, then more, and all was as it had been. Except Raef. His chair, the one carved with the bloody stories of Vannheim, was removed, pushed to one side of the raised platform, and Raef took a seat among his captains at the high table. Food was brought, quail, fish, mutton, venison, steaming bread, and roasted root vegetables, but he only picked at his portions. The ale he drank greedily and his cup was never empty. At length, Isolf returned to the hall and joined the high table. Raef did not catch his eye, did not ask what he had done with the boy, did nothing but swallow down more ale and watch the warriors below.

When he rose from the table, the hour was late and his head was thick with ale and mead. Music had broken out and the men sang a lurid song, their voices rising to the rafters in disjointed melody. Raef blinked and steadied himself, then, with four of Isolf's men at his back, strode from the hall. The cold air in the rear passage served to wipe away some of the haze in Raef's head, but it was with unsteady steps that he sought his chamber. Isolf had stumbled after him and caught up at Raef's door, his cheeks ale-bright.

"Does my king want for anything? A woman to warm his bed?"

Raef thought of soft skin, long hair, and a warm body to share the night with. Someone tender, smooth, and lacking Eira's sharp edges. But then he felt a surge of nausea, his belly heavy with liquid. "No." He waved a hand at Isolf. "No, nothing."

Isolf grinned. "All the more for me, then." He grasped Raef with brotherly affection and then they parted ways, the guards remaining outside Raef's door. In the darkness and silence of his chamber, Raef sprawled on the bed and let his thoughts ebb away on the tide of drunken sleep.

ᚾ ᚾ ᚾ

The morning came roaring upon Raef, the sunlight screaming through the glass of his window, his tongue thick, his throat fuzzy, and his stomach heaving. He tried to lie still, eyes shut to ward off the light, but such concentration only set off a hammer in his head. Groaning, Raef lurched to his feet, eyes only squinting open, splashed water from his basin onto his face, and then vomited clear liquid into the basin. Clenching the edge of the table, Raef felt his stomach heave again, but nothing further came up, leaving Raef panting and dizzy.

Dropping slowly to the floor, Raef leaned back against his bed and stared up at the ceiling, his head pounding and his rebellious stomach threatening further turmoil. He had been a fool to drink such quantities without eating a morsel of food, but the fault was his alone, even if he would rather blame the boy, Ergil. And in his heart Raef knew he had wanted the oblivion of drink to take him, to shut out Jarl Thrainson and the blood on his hands.

A servant, a boy of nine, stepped silently into the chamber. He paid his king no mind, avoiding Raef's outstretched feet as he took the soiled washbasin and emptied the contents into a bucket. He straightened the blankets and furs on Raef's bed, set a new candle on the table, and then raked the cold ashes from yesterday's fire into the same bucket. Darting out into the hallway, he returned with a new washbasin and then disappeared as quickly as he had come. All the while, Raef kept his eyes fixed on the ceiling, partially out of embarrassment, partially to keep the world around him from spinning.

At length, the sunlight seemed less violent and Raef ventured to his feet, pleased to find that his stomach had given up its protests. In return, though, his skull was thumping, his knee was cramped with stiffness, and it was a slow march to the hall with fresh, clear-eyed guards on his heels.

The hall was much as he had last seen it, only with more eyes closed than open. Men slept, faces in the remains of their meals, slumped on the shoulders of their comrades. So great was the disarray, the servants had not yet attempted to begin to clean. A rustling in one corner drew Raef's attention and he turned to see a blonde woman, a shieldmaiden whose name had slipped under the hammer in his brain, stretch and disentangle herself from the sleepy embrace of a black-bearded warrior. She was naked but for a pair of old boots and she squinted at Raef, no shame in her nakedness or drunkenness. With a yawn, she tugged a cloak over her shoulders, exposing the bare chest of her unconscious companion in the process, and went back to sleep.

Raef surveyed the disaster that was his hall, found he could not stomach it, and went out the wide wooden doors. Only there, under the blue winter sky, did he feel he could speak and he turned to one of the guards.

"Find Ulli," Raef said, keeping his voice quiet for the sake of his own head. "I want this," he nodded back at the hall, "taken care of by the time the sun reaches its peak. And tell him there will be no feast this night." The guard scurried off and Raef turned to another. "Bring bread and water."

"Here, lord?"

"Yes, I will eat out here." Raef did not much feel like consuming anything, but he knew he had to. Within the span of twenty slow, deep breaths, the second guard had returned, bearing a tray and Raef sat down on the stone steps and convinced himself to nibble on the loaf of bread. The guards withdrew to the doors, leaving him to eat in peace.

It was there that Eira found him. He spotted her as she approached the Vestrhall on foot but he continued to gnaw on the loaf, sipping water here and there, until she stood before him, their eyes nearly level.

"What do you want?" The sun was behind her but Raef was trying hard not to squint.

"To make my oath, of course."

"I think I have had my fill of oaths."

"You do not wish to be king? It has only been five days." If it was an attempt to make him smile, it did not succeed.

"You would know what I wished if you had been here."

She said nothing at first, gave no explanation for her absence, as though daring him to demand an answer. Then she came close and sat sideways on the step below him. "Forgive me," she said. Her hair fell away from her face as she looked up at him. He looked into her eyes and took a deep breath, for she smelled of green grass and heather on the moors and pine trees in high summer. All of which was impossible under the shroud of winter, and yet he breathed it in, his eyes drawn to the wildness in hers, tempered, it seemed, by a promise of spring. And Raef found himself taking her hand in his, the loaf of bread forgotten, the pounding in his head reduced to a gentle swell of the ocean tide.

Raef brushed her chin with his thumb and touched a finger to her earlobe, then brought his face close to hers. He paused, taking in every tiny feature of her face, the delicate scar above her eyebrow, the flecks of deep blue in her grey irises, the curve of her cheekbone, and it was Eira who brought her lips up to his. It seemed to Raef the kiss could heal him, mind and body, but it was all too fleeting for he had a prisoner to visit.

Raef rose, Eira's hand slipping from his, and turned to the guards. "Take me to the boy," he said.

Ergil was awake but listless when Raef entered the locked room in the stable Isolf had confined him to. His head was rolled to one side and his lips were parted and chapped. He had been crying, Raef could tell, sobbing even. His cheeks were dry but streaked with the remnants of tears and half-dried snot hung from his nose, out of reach of his bound hands. A welt had formed on his forehead and a cut blossomed under one eye, no doubt dispensed by Isolf. At Raef's entrance, he stirred only a little, but when Raef squatted down and the boy caught sight of his visitor, he scrambled back as best he could, scratching through the straw, until his back was against the wall. The hatred flashed into his face at the same instant and Raef could see the night in the cell had done nothing to quell it.

"I am going to speak, and you are going to listen. If you do not, I will instruct my cousin to cut off your ears and then the tiny thing between your legs, which he will gladly feed to the pigs. Do you understand? You need only nod."

Ergil shivered with anger but there was fear there, too, and he gave a reluctant nod.

"You have a grievance against me and I will not deny I am the cause of your grief and anger. We will deal with that in time. What we will deal with now is the reason for your father's death. He died because he was protecting someone, someone who gave him an order that he carried out. That someone watched me kill your father. That someone stood by and did nothing while a man under his command was deprived of Valhalla. Yes, I wielded the blade, but surely some fault lies with this person who sacrificed your father to save his own skin?"

The boy looked suspicious but he was still listening and Raef continued.

"I seek this coward, Ergil, and I have made a solemn vow to find him, for he is responsible for the death of my father, too. Perhaps you can tell me who this man might be?"

Ergil shook his head, lips clenched tight.

"Your father was a warrior of Finngale, bound to the Hammerling, but the Hammerling is not the man I seek. Who were your father's friends? Is your mother from Finngale, too?"

Ergil muttered something that Raef could not make out.

"Speak clearly, boy, or I will call for a knife."

Ergil glared at Raef but repeated his words. "My father was not of Finngale, nor my mother."

Raef frowned. "Tell me more."

Ergil grimaced. "There is nothing to tell. They came to Finngale when I was born and my father pledged to the Hammerling."

Raef's heart began to beat faster but he kept his voice steady. "What did they call home before Finngale?"

"It was no home!" Ergil burst out, fresh tears threatening to spill onto his cheeks. "They were chased out by their own kin."

Raef fought for patience. "Odin's eye, answer my question!"

Ergil sniffed, the snot running anew and a bubble of spit forming in the corner of his mouth. "Ruderk. My father was born in Ruderk."

# NINETEEN

RAEF STARED AT Ergil Thrainson, his heart in his ears.
"Say it again."

Ergil's eyes narrowed in confusion. "My father was born in Ruderk. As was my mother."

"Your father was sworn to Hauk of Ruderk?"

Ergil nodded, then bit down on his bottom lip. "Until my mother's family forced them to flee and seek a new home."

Raef hardly heard so intent was he on Ergil's revelation. It raced through him, a rock thrown into a still pool, ripples spreading unhindered. He bit back his thoughts and focused on Ergil.

"I meant what I said. Go home. Plant crops. Help your mother. Grow strong. And if, when you are older, you still find that vengeance burns as bright as it does this day, come to me and we will settle this score with blood. I swear it." It was both a threat and an invitation, for Raef understood what surged in Ergil's veins.

"You are not going to kill me?"

"No, not even keep you prisoner, my shame shut away from the world. I will not fight you. Not now. A man must live before he goes to his death and you have not lived. But neither will I deny you that which I seek for myself. Heed my words, Ergil Thrainson, and return to me some day if that is your wish."

"What if you die before that day?"

Raef shrugged. "Then you will either accept that you will not have your vengeance, or not. The choice is yours and the fate that follows it will be of your creation, not mine." Raef got to his feet and called for the guard outside the door. "Let him loose."

"Are you mad?" It was not the guard who questioned Raef, but Isolf, who was rounding the corner. "The boy must die."

"No, Isolf. Brother," Raef added in a hard voice when he saw disobedience in Isolf's face. "We have reached an understanding, and he is being allowed to return, unmolested, to Finngale. Save your breath. You will not convince me to do otherwise."

Isolf frowned, but his protest died on his lips. "As you wish. I only seek to protect you."

Raef softened and settled a hand on Isolf's shoulder. "I know." But his mind was already elsewhere for the ripples caused by Ergil had grown to a great wave and it was thrashing inside him, clamoring for release. Raef turned from his cousin and sought the winter sun. But it was Vakre he found.

The son of Loki had a doe slung over one shoulder, his bow in his free hand, and he and Eira spoke in quiet voices near the stables. For a moment, when their eyes met, there was a flicker of unease, a remnant of their last meeting. Raef felt it in himself and saw it in Vakre's eyes. Vakre let the doe fall to the ground.

"I heard what happened," Vakre said. "The boy got close."

"If that is the price for what he just revealed to me, I would gladly pay it a thousand times again."

Vakre's eyes narrowed and Eira looked to Raef with sudden interest, asking, "What do you mean?"

"We thought Jarl Thrainson a warrior of Finngale and he was, but not always. He was born elsewhere and loyal to a lord other than the Hammerling. By unhappy chance, he was forced to flee his home and start a new life, but I think in his heart he remained true to his first master. Perhaps the promised price for my father's death was triumph over Jarl's old enemies, so that he might return home and regain his honor." Raef felt a tremor in his chest as he said the words aloud. "I know who ordered my father's murder. I know the name of the scheming, treacherous, false friend who extended his hand to my father while plotting his death."

"Who?"

"Hauk of Ruderk."

Vakre's expression remained calm. "You are certain?"

"Can it be other than the truth?" Raef heard his voice rise and Vakre raised his hand.

"I do not know, Raef," Vakre said, his own voice steady, "but what tie do you have between Jarl and Hauk other than this shared past?"

"Is it not enough?"

"This is not the first time you believed you knew who was responsible for your father's death. Remember the Hammerling, Raef, remember what your hasty wrath wrought."

"What would you have me do? Live out my days waiting for a confession? The sword-age is coming, Vakre. The storm is upon us and the world of men trembles beneath us. I will not sit back and wait for all to crumble, not when I know the truth in my heart of hearts, and not while my father's blood still runs in my veins." Spinning on his heel, Raef turned his back on Vakre and Eira, jaw clenched against the sudden knot of agony in his knee. Ignoring all in his path, Raef readied his horse, mounted, and left the hall behind.

Outside the gates, Raef gave the horse to the wind, letting her run. They skimmed along the edge of the fjord, weaving through the trees, until the way grew rocky and unsafe to take at high speed. Settling to a walk, the horse carried Raef deep into the pines and bare-branched trees of summer, through narrow glens running between hills. At last, Raef brought her to a halt and dismounted. Fractured sunlight, fallen to the snowy earth, split the world into shadow and light. Rabbits had passed this way since the last snowfall, and a deer had stripped bark from a lone birch. His mind was clear, as unblemished as the untouched snow around him, all questions and doubts fled and gone. There, deep in his beloved forest, Raef dropped to his knees, raised his face to the sky, and made a new vow.

"Odin. Allfather. Hear my words. I am the serpent-breath, I am the wolf-song, and I bring you a promise of death. I name Hauk of Ruderk murderer and he will die by my hand. His is the blood I seek and I will stain the snow red with it. This I swear, in sight of all the gods."

His oath faded into the air, witnessed only by silent trees, but Raef felt as though he had branded the words into his skin, never to be forgotten. Yet the turmoil had passed, leaving behind only resolve, and Raef turned the horse toward home.

Vakre was right, he knew. There was no guarantee that Hauk had conspired with Jarl Thrainson. Their shared birthplace could mean nothing, but to Raef it was the key to all. He thought back on Hauk Orleson's actions in the days since the gathering, his gesture of alliance with Einarr, his place beside the Hammerling, the words that had passed between them now imbued with more meaning. It was the answer he had been looking for and his every thought was bent on how he would enact his revenge.

Upon returning to the hall, he tolerated Isolf's objections to his wandering off and promised not to do it again. Finnolf and Yorkell had returned with their warriors, and Raef heard their reports. Yorkell had observed a small party of men, no larger than his own group of twenty, taking a path through the northern hills. He had seen little else. Finnolf had been more fortunate and was certain that Thoken was holed up near the border with Silfravall with eighty spears at his side. The young captain was eager to return, but Raef had no ready order for him. As he sat in his father's chair, the faces around him earnest and proud, he searched in vain for the faces he most wished to see. Eira had slipped from the hall not long after Finnolf and Yorkell had arrived and of Vakre and Siv, there was no sign, not that evening, or the next. Once he thought he caught sight of Siv's red-gold braid in the crowd, but the face it belonged to was not hers. Raef did not ask after them, did not look for them. Instead, he told himself he did not need them and he drank mead with Isolf, telling his cousin of Hauk of Ruderk's treachery.

"Let us secure Vannheim, first, brother," Isolf said. His face and orange beard were lit with candlelight as they shared a skin of mead in Raef's chamber. "Once Red-beard and Thoken are brought to heel and punished, we can turn to Orleson and bring justice to your father."

"I do not wish to wait any longer," Raef said. "I have failed my father for long enough. It is time I acted."

"It is not my place to challenge your will, only hear my counsel. War is upon us. Here, in the heart of Vannheim, and out there. And what is out there will soon spread here, for the Hammerling and Fengar will not tolerate another contender. Yes, they snap at each other's throats and bleed each other, but one or both will ready to strike as soon as word of your naming as king reaches them. We must take care of your lands and we must reach out to allies, those who have not yet chosen a side and those who question their choices. Meet the Hammerling in battle, and bring Ruderk to his knees there, but only when Vannheim is safe."

"Your words are wise, but I must follow my heart."

"And what will your people think when their king abandons them, slips into the wild to fulfill his private need?" Isolf voice rose and his face was stiff with anger. "Red-beard will cut a path to your hall, lining it with the bodies of your people, and Thoken will spill their blood, bit by precious bit, until they collide, head-on, here in this very hall, their destruction complete. Is this what you want?"

"I will leave Vannheim in your care and I will trust you to keep my people safe." Even as Raef said it he knew the folly in his words.

"If this is your decision, I will do all in my power to protect Vannheim, but I am not the king, Raef, I am not the one your people have chosen. It is you who must keep them safe, keep their lands unburnt, their children alive."

Raef was silent. In his heart he was already riding, swift-footed, across the distance between him and Hauk of Ruderk, or, faster yet, hurtling through the sky on the back of a strong-winged dragon-kin, but his mind could not ignore the truth behind Isolf's words. Vannheim needed him.

"What would your father want you to do?"

Raef closed his eyes, silently asking his father for yet more patience. "My duty as Vannheim's lord." He emptied the mead skin and got to his feet. "It is time we showed the vultures what it means to defy a Skallagrim. Find Finnolf. And Dvalarr. We must make plans. I wish to ride tomorrow."

ᛉ ᛉ ᛉ

The pre-dawn fog was thick and damp, turning blazing torchlight into murky glowing orbs and muffling the sound of horses. Two columns of warriors snaked away from the hall and village, one to the south and one to the north, fifty in each. A small portion of Vannheim's strength, meant to move and attack with speed and without the encumbrance of larger numbers. In their wake, Raef steadied his horse, which danced away from shadowy figures moving through the nearly deserted camp, and relayed his final instructions to Finnolf, who would lead the southern-bound group.

"There will be no burning or looting or raping, Finnolf. This is our land, our people, and I will not bring destruction to those who are innocent, no matter how close their ties to Thoken and Red-beard."

"And those who are not innocent?" Finnolf's face was masked by the fog but Raef could see enough to know the young captain was eager to carry out his charge.

"I have no mercy for them."

"Shall I take Thoken's head myself?"

"You or any other man. I make no claim to it."

"It will be done, lord." Finnolf wheeled his horse and disappeared into the fog, riding to reach the head of his column.

Raef looked next to Isolf. "The Vestrhall is yours in my absence, brother."

"You need not fear." Isolf gestured to the camp of warriors around them. Another fifty warriors remained behind, and Isolf's own men, too. "We are too well protected and the enemy too few in number. They will not dare to attack."

Raef turned his horse but then looked back over his shoulder. "Keep an eye out for Tulkis Greyshield. Red-beard and Thoken are warriors, hard like steel and strong, but not clever. With them it will be battle and little else. When Greyshield rears his head, and he will, that will be a different matter."

Isolf nodded and raised a hand in farewell. "May Thor guide your sword and keep your shields strong."

Again, Raef made to depart but a voice calling through the fog held him back. Hoyvik the smith burst into the torchlight, panting and bearing something wrapped in linen. Gudrik followed the smith, limping forward on his crutch.

"As promised, lord." The smith handed his bundle up to Raef, who unwrapped the linen with care to reveal a simple leather scabbard, undecorated but for a single silver tree inlaid near the hilt. Yggdrasil. Raef ran his finger over the metal, curled his hand around the familiar hilt, and then drew the sword from its sheath.

The blade was beautiful death and felt as though it had been an extension of Raef's arm since the forging of the nine realms. The length, the balance, the weight, all tuned precisely to Raef, an instrument to sing the song of battle. It was the finest sword Raef had ever held.

"This will rival the famous blade of Torrulf Palesword. My thanks, Hoyvik. You have outdone yourself." The smith smiled and Raef knew he did not need to be told of the virtues of the sword. Raef exchanged it with the sword borrowed from the armory and strapped the new one to his belt. The smith withdrew, leaving Gudrik alone to look up at Raef.

The poet opened his mouth to speak but his words failed him and Raef knew what was on his tongue.

"I cannot take you with me, Gudrik."

It was the truth and Raef could see that Gudrik knew it. But he could also see the hope die in his friend's eyes. "I know."

Raef leaned down from the saddle and put a hand on Gudrik's shoulder. "The gods know your strength." The skald gazed up at Raef with empty eyes. Raef tightened his grip. "I know your strength. You do not need to prove it to me."

Gudrik nodded, his eyes brimming with tears of frustration, and stepped back. With a heavy heart and a nod at Isolf, Raef turned his horse, looking over his shoulder for one last glance into the fog in the hopes that a shadow might step forward in the shape of Vakre or Siv. Raef put his heels to his horse and they were away, the fog turning to water on his cheeks as they raced to catch up to his men and Eira, who had reappeared in Raef's chamber the night before, eager to join him as he traveled north.

His chosen path took them to the sea, and when dawn broke they had reached the coast, which they would follow until the next fjord split the land. The fog burned off quickly once light spilled over the eastern horizon, and they were left with gentle morning waves that seemed at odds with the brisk, winter breeze that came off the sea. The men rode with hoods pulled up or fur collars tucked tight around their necks and they kept a quick pace.

By mid-day, they had seen nothing but gulls wheeling overhead and they turned inland to trace the edge of the narrow, short fjord on the gentle southern shore. When they reached the apex of the fjord, they turned north again and began to climb into higher hills, passing a farm here and there, the stone walls crisscrossing the slopes but enclosing nothing except snow. Smoke could be seen rising from each farmhouse, but Raef did not disturb his people and they made camp in a small, curved valley that night.

The farm of Rudrak Red-beard was another day's ride north, if they held to their course, and it seemed likely that Red-beard would stick to the land he knew best until he was ready to strike. But as Raef warmed his hands over a fire that night under the stars, his thoughts were on lands to the west, rugged lands that hugged the sea and were the home of Tulkis Greyshield. To reach them would add another day of riding and Raef did not think he could spare so much time, not when Greyshield had made no threat. And yet he did not like the idea of passing up an opportunity to determine Greyshield's mind. Raef wrestled with his thoughts that night, the stars above offering nothing but their cold light, sleeping only a little. He half-hoped Eira would ask what troubled him so that he might speak his thoughts out loud, but she seemed tucked into her own mind, as he had so often seen her. When dawn came and the camp began to stir, he had made his decision.

Five men turned west when they broke camp, charged with being Raef's eyes and ears. "Under no circumstances are you to engage Greyshield," Raef told them. "You are shadows, nothing more. I want to know who he meets with, if has gathered men to him and, if so, how many. When you have done this, return to the Vestrhall. I will look for you there." Raef watched them ride away, five warriors he trusted not to be reckless, who were less blood-thirsty than others, and yet still he wondered if it was a mistake not to send more.

The day was dark, the dim, grey light of dawn staying constant even as the faint shadows shifted under the passing of the distant, shielded sun. Raef kept them to higher ground as much as possible so they might, as an eagle, catch early sight of their prey, but the land they crossed, one of the least fertile and least populated parts of Vannheim, remained empty. As they drew closer to Red-beard's home, they fanned out, splitting into three groups to cover more territory and yet all three parties converged on Red-beard's farmhouse with nothing to report.

The four buildings that made up Red-beard's farm were nestled against a stand of trees and built into the side of a rocky hill. Raef observed them from a vantage point across the valley while his men stayed out of sight. The farm was quiet and no smoke drifted from the roof of Red-beard's house. Raef watched until the sun dipped below the hills, then approached on foot with Eira and a handful of men as darkness gathered in the trees.

A closer inspection showed the farm was deserted, bereft of both people and livestock. The hearth was cold, the cupboards devoid of food, the house stripped of anything of value.

"Lord," a voice called to Raef, "over here."

Raef followed the voice around the side of the southern-most of the three buildings and wrinkled his nose against a foul odor that hung in the air.

The horse had been dead two, maybe three, days, it was hard to tell for the cold had delayed the rotting, but it was rotting nonetheless. The carcass lay in the snow, its neck black with blood where the axe had severed the head from the body. A crow had been at work there, tearing flesh from the wound in bits and pieces, and it took to the air now, cawing, as Raef and his men disturbed it.

But it was the head that drew the eyes of the warriors and caused many to reach for the Thor hammers they carried around their necks. Even Eira was not immune, her face paler than usual and her mouth tight.

The head was impaled on a spear, mouth gaping, teeth bared in a hideous, deathly grin, tongue flopping to one side. The eyes had been pecked out and the cheeks torn by savaging beaks. It was a grisly scene, but it alone was not what had made Raef's men stop in their tracks, unwilling to come closer.

The horse head faced south and just a little west and Raef knew this was not a matter of chance. If he flew, like a raven, in the direction the empty eye sockets were staring, he would come directly to his own hall.

"The nidstang," muttered the warrior closest to Raef.

Raef stepped close to the spear and its gruesome prize. The words were roughly carved into the spear shaft, but Raef read them aloud. "I curse the line of Skallagrim, the ancient dead, the unborn children. Darkness and death shall haunt them, Thor shall punish them, Odin shall keep them from Valhalla."

The crow, perched now on the roof of the barn, squawked, its call ringing in the air. The men were still, their faces betraying the fear the nidstang curse had unleashed in their bellies.

Raef drew his axe and hacked the spear in two. The horse head tumbled to the ground and came to rest by his feet while the spear splintered and scattered the words of the curse in the snow. The men drew back, unwilling to touch any part of the nidstang, but fury and Rudrak's barefaced threat had made Raef bold. Using his axe to hold the skull down, Raef wrenched the point of the spear from the horse's neck and held it out to the men. "Piss on these words. I will shove Rudrak Red-beard's curse up his ass." He removed his axe from the rotting wreckage and wiped it in the snow. "Burn it all."

In the growing dark, Raef's men went to work, distributing

the supply of firewood Red-beard had left behind, and soon the farm was in flames. Raef himself held the torch to the horse carcass and the leering head, and the stink of rotting, burning flesh filled the night. The men, even those who had not seen the nidstang for themselves, were nervous, the curse having worked under their skin. Raef admitted to no one his own discomfort at seeing the dead, empty sockets staring toward his home, their meaning and intent clearer than Mimir's well. The nidstang was an ancient curse, well-known but seldom used, and Raef could not help but wonder if some hand other than Rudrak's had carved the words, some hand that had the means to discover that it was not Raef's fate to go to Valhalla. The gesture reeked of the priests of Odin and yet Raef did not think even Fylkir, for all his discontent, would have reason to invoke such a malevolent threat. He would have to seek out Josurr upon his return to the Vestrhall and learn what he could.

The blaze was high and bright, leaping to the sky, sparks flying. Raef watched it burn, a beacon in the night that sent a clear signal if Rudrak or any who followed him were watching, but the satisfaction of destroying Red-beard's home only fueled his anger and left him wanting more.

"What now, lord?" The question came from a warrior called Elthane. He rested on his spear, his eyes moving from the fire to Raef's face, and other men turned from the fire, one by one, until all eyes were on him.

"I do not need a curse to bring down Rudrak Red-beard. He has shown his hand, he has shown the depth of his treachery. He has broken the deepest oaths a man can make and we will tear him apart." The men did not cheer, but their faces were grim and hard and Raef knew they felt as he did.

Wolves sang to the stars that night. Raef and his men camped in sight of Red-beard's burning farm, and the pack was close, their voices calling and answering from all directions.

"They are hungry," Eira said as she and Raef shared dried meat and cold, hard bread. They had lit no fires, wanting to keep all attention on the blaze on the next hill for Raef was certain Redbeard was watching.

Raef kissed Eira's forehead. "So am I." He tucked her against his chest, for warmth, if nothing else.

"When this is done, who will you march on first, the Hammerling or Fengar?"

"Neither. I will seek Hauk of Ruderk and finish what he started. If he is at the Hammerling's side, then so be it."

"Would it not be better to ally with the Hammerling once more and finish off Fengar together?"

"I have been named king and he will hear of it. Even if I dispute that, Brandulf Hammerling will never accept me back into the fold. He will regard it as a deep betrayal. I will be an enemy, just as Fengar is, perhaps even more so for having once fought at his side."

They were quiet for a moment until Eira spoke again. "My shieldmaidens fight with the Hammerling," she said.

"You know this? How?"

She did not answer right away. "When we rode west after the battle of the burning lake, I saw them. They told me they intended to swear oaths to him." She paused and Raef sensed there was more. "They said if I did not do the same and ride with them once more, they would choose a new leader."

"I am sorry."

"The choice was mine," she said, shrugging against him as though the loss of her warriors meant little. Raef did not believe it.

"When we go to war," he said, "you will command many spears and you will lead them to glorious victory." He felt her smile and kissed her hair, glad to be able to give her something that would please her and make up for what she had lost. But when Raef slept that night he dreamed a dream that had visited him more than once in Hrodvelgr's prison and again, a sleepless vision, in the labyrinth. In it, he watched Eira lead men to battle. Her blade flashed in the sun, the spears and axes around her were a bristling wave of death, and the battle-joy was etched on her face. And yet she stumbled, as she always did, and death came swiftly for her. This night, it was a spear to the throat and Raef watched her squirm, clawing at the unseen enemy whose spear had dealt the blow, but then falling limp. Some nights it was a spear, others an axe, or a sword, or even arrows, and but always the dream ended with Eira staring at Raef as her life bled out of her, her grey eyes calling for help. Raef woke with a jerk, his breath coming hard and fast, sending vapor into the night. Eira was still curled in sleep and he found himself touching her dark hair as though to reassure himself of her presence. Raef took a deep breath and then a long drink of mead from his skin. The sharp edges of the dream began to dull and Raef drifted back into sleep, hoping the dream would not return with the face of Siv or Vakre, as it so often did.

The morning brought fresh snow and it fell fast and thick. Raef relieved his bladder at the edge of camp and had turned back to ready his horse when the arrow flew past his shoulder. Ducking, Raef ran, aware that more arrows had been loosed.

"Shields!" he called. "Shields!"

The camp shuddered to life and Raef snatched his own shield from the ground just in time to take the next arrow in the wood instead of the neck. The warriors shuffled together, staying low behind their shields, until the wall had been formed. From there, Raef peered out, but there was little to see except snow. The arrows still fell, but they were harmless and soon ceased.

For a moment there was silence but for the breathing of the men around him and his own heartbeat, and then the war cry pierced the air and other voices rose up around it. The charge had begun.

The snowfall was so dense that the shapes of their enemy could not be seen until they were less than ten paces away, but Raef's men reacted quickly, moving their shields apart just enough to let the spears from the rear slide through, breaking the charge and impaling several warriors.

With a tremendous jolt, the two lines clashed, shield on shield, and the short swords and axes went to work, hacking, stabbing, biting through any crack in the wall. Raef, his legs braced, the man behind him pushing forward to keep the wall in place, found an opening and sliced at the knees of the warrior opposite him. The man went down and was replaced by another screaming wordlessly, but his voice died in his throat as Raef, propelled forward by the wall around him, hacked down his shield and sliced into his chest. The man tumbled beneath the momentum of Raef's wall and Raef finished him with a swift chop to the neck. Still his wall pressed forward, pushing the attackers back, and Raef, though he could see nothing but the heaving bodies around him, knew he had the advantage of greater numbers.

The attackers broke, their wall crumbling and Raef's men went on the offensive, breaking their own wall just enough to allow the freedom of movement they needed to secure victory.

Tucking his axe into his belt, Raef sidestepped a spear aimed at his chest, then switched his shield to his right arm and drew his new sword. It seemed to hum in his hand, ready to spill its first blood. Raef chopped off the point of the spear and then used his shield to throw his opponent off balance before plunging the blade into the man's belly. He had not fallen to the snow before Raef had moved onto the next, a yellow-bearded, bald-headed man with an axe. Raef knew that face. This was Gunbjorn, one of his father's warriors, stout and strong but with a laugh that could bring a smile to any face. All this Raef thought of as he rammed into Gunbjorn. They grappled for a moment, shield on shield, and then Raef dropped to his knees. Gunbjorn fell forward and Raef upended him with his shield. The warrior sprawled in the snow and Raef, without hesitation, stabbed Gunbjorn in the back.

Glancing around, Raef saw that his men were in control, that the fight was all but won. And then he saw Rudrak Red-beard wielding his massive axe, dealing death on all sides. Three bodies lay ruined at his feet and he held four more warriors at bay, spinning, cursing, raging like a corned bear.

Raef approached, the peace he found in battle worn about him like a cloak, his heartbeat steady, his sword held low. He reached the circle of his warriors and Red-beard snarled at the sight of him.

"This one is mine," Raef said, his voice level. The fury that had boiled over in sight of the nidstang now only simmered beneath his skin. This was battle, nothing more, and his opponent was a man with an axe, not a man who had followed his father into battle, had defended Vannheim with his blood.

Raef's warriors stepped back, giving their lord the space to fight, the rest now looking on as Red-beard's warriors had dwindled to only a handful held at sword point.

Raef circled left but he had gone no more than two steps when Red-beard charged, sprinting forward. Raef stepped sideways and the axe glanced off his shield, but Rudrak spun quickly and Raef had to dodge to avoid the axe again, almost losing his footing. Roaring, Red-beard pressed forward again, but the snow had grown slick beneath the trampling feet and his balance was off, leaving his shoulder unprotected. Raef's sword found its mark, slicing through leather with ease and opening a deep gash in Red-beard's flesh that he followed with a quick slash to Rudrak's exposed back as the warrior stumbled.

Raef gave him no time to recover, and Rudrak got his shield up just in time to stop Raef's arcing blade meant for his neck. The shield splintered and Rudrak dropped it, using his axe two-handed now to shield himself as Raef drove him backward. When the axe haft, too, broke, Rudrak howled and flung the head of the axe at Raef. It missed and fell to the snow. Rudrak went for his knife but Raef was too quick. His sword cut into Red-beard's thigh, biting deep into the muscle, and he dropped to the ground.

It was not a fatal blow, not yet, and Raef loomed over Red-beard. Their eyes met and there was no regret in either face. Raef kicked the knife from Rudrak's hand. "Your treachery is not deserving of death in battle." Raef raised his sword. "But I will take this," the blade came arcing down and sliced off Rudrak's right hand, "for with this you reached out to take Vannheim from me." Rudrak roared in pain and blood gushed from the stump of his arm.

Raef looked up. The snow fell still, dusting the shoulders of the men looking on. "Tie him up," Raef said, pointing to the trees not far from the battle site. Red-beard was dragged, cursing still, to the trunk of a wide oak, its bare limbs hovering over him in judgment. He was bound and then Raef stuffed Rudrak's hand into the bindings so the bloody fingers seemed to reach around Rudrak's throat. A final length of rope was wrapped around his neck and shoulders to hold it there, but even though he bled heavily from his leg and the severed limb, Rudrak's eyes still showed hatred and fury.

"The wolves were close last night, Rudrak. We heard them while we burned your farm." Raef leaned close. "How long do you think you will last?" Rudrak seethed but Raef turned his back and wiped his sword on a dead man's cloak. He surveyed the scene around him. Only a few of his men were dead. Others, bloody but satisfied, watched and waited for his command. By his estimation, Rudrak had attacked with no more than twenty-five men. A foolish decision and they had paid for it. Only eight lived yet, and they were on their knees, heads hanging. He might have asked questions about the nidstang, might have tried to discover if Rudrak had thought of the curse on his own, but he did not want to remind his warriors of the beheaded horse, not when victory, small as it was, had bolstered their spirits, nor did he wish to voice his suspicions about the priests of Odin.

"What of them?" Eira asked, her sword slick with blood.

Raef stepped close to the huddled prisoners. "Look at me," he said, for he would know their faces before he sent them to their deaths. The men did as he asked and he looked from one familiar face to the next. Three trembled, their fear visible for all to see, pleas of mercy on their lips. One could not hold Raef's gaze and his pants were wet with his own urine. The other four stared with dead eyes, knowing this fate had been of their own making. "Kill them," he said. He looked to Eira. "Make it clean and quick."

Only two babbled, trying to extend their lives, but Raef had already moved on and he did not watch them die. The fury of battle had held the pain in his knee at bay, but now it roared back, protesting the movement he had required of it. Raef limped to his horse, glad of its solid strength to lean on. He forced himself to draw breath as he fought to control the pain and busied his mind and hands with his saddle. The men stripped the dead of items of value, arm rings and amulets, and then gathered at their disheveled camp and collected the horses. They moved on, leaving Rudrak to die of his wounds or meet the wolves when night fell.

They spent the hours before midday searching the area for any sign of further followers of Red-beard, but they found nothing beyond some horses tethered not far from the site of the battle. Raef let the men rummage through the saddle bags for anything worth taking, then, tying the horses to their own, they turned toward home.

# TWENTY

"SO, RED-BEARD IS dead." Isolf passed a cup of ale to Raef, who had sunk onto a bench by the fire. He gave another to Eira. The hall was empty around them, the last warriors having trickled into the night. Isolf raised his own cup. "To victory."

"To victory," Raef said. They had returned with the setting sun, riding hard and through much of the night to speed the journey back to the hall. He was weary and ready to retreat to his chamber, but Isolf seemed eager to talk. "What news? Any word from Finnolf?" The young captain and his men were still in the south of Vannheim.

Isolf shook his head. "None. But warriors from Silfravall raided two farms four days ago. A single survivor carried word of the raid to me."

"There was no one to help them?"

"None close enough. They were isolated from other farms and none were warriors themselves."

Raef grimaced. "Silfravall's incursions will continue and they will grow bolder unless they are checked."

"Send warriors."

"I should go myself."

"It may be that you will be needed here."

Raef closed his eyes, and tried not to think of Vakre. If the son of

Loki were there, Raef would send him to Silfravall in an instant. "You then, brother." Raef did not look at Eira. He did not want to see if she was disappointed at being passed over.

"When?"

"How many men do you have?"

"Forty."

"The ones who rode with me need rest. Take your own and ten of those who remained here." He looked hard at Isolf. "Can you do what must be done with that number?"

Isolf grinned. "They will rue the day they entered your lands."

"Then I want you gone tomorrow." Raef leaned back in his chair. "Still no sign of Greyshield?"

"None." Isolf spat. "Coward."

"He will have seen what was done to Red-beard. It will fuel him."

"You still think he will come?"

Raef nodded. "I do not doubt it."

"Let him come, then." Isolf took a swig from his cup and wiped his lips on his sleeve. "You say you sent five men to scout Greyshield land?"

"Yes. I fear it was a mistake. They should have returned by now."

"They may yet." Isolf refilled his cup and Eira's. Raef had hardly drunk his and he felt his eyelids growing heavy. Excusing himself, Raef retired to his chamber, sure he would sleep deeply. But the gods gave him no respite and the dreams came once more, one after the other, horrible visions of death and destruction with Raef helpless against it all. There was a new dream that night, though, and he woke from it with a layer of sweat cooling on his forehead and chest. He had stood among the standing stones, the ring not far from the Vestrhall, but instead of stones he faced twelve nidstang poles and the horse heads, their eyeballs bloody, laughed at him, each with the voice of the Deepminded.

Upon waking, Raef could not seem to steady his heart. Long had it been since Loki in the form of the Deepminded had invaded his thoughts, and Raef was unsettled at the return. His chamber seemed small and unnaturally warm and Raef, his mind turning from the Deepminded to the visit he would have to pay to the priests of Odin, did not sleep again that night.

↑ ↑ ↑

Isolf led fifty warriors from the gates the next day, between the green and gold banners of Vannheim snapping in a stiff wind above the walls. Raef watched them go, torn between a desire to go after them, to show the Silfravall raiders the wrath of Skallagrim, and a desire to track down Finnolf in the south of Vannheim. He trusted the young captain to deal with Thoken. Finnolf had Dvalarr at his side, a seasoned, fierce warrior who would give his last breath to see the job done. And yet Raef itched to do something other than wait in his hall, wait for news of Finnolf, wait for news of Isolf, wait for the Hammerling or Fengar to fall on him with axes and spears.

Once, as a boy, Raef had watched his father wait when beset by an enemy, and he began to understand now, as he had not then, the patience and strength it took to not act.

Eira was worse than Raef. She paced in his chamber while Raef bathed in preparation for his visit to the priests of Odin. She strode up and down the hall, feral and restless, as Raef spoke first with his steward, Ulli, then Aldrif, the healer. Raef found he did not wish to watch and when at last he was free to seek the priests' cave, he was glad to be away from her.

He had visited the cave many times as a boy, often with his father but also in secret, eager to spy on their strange rituals. He had never seen more than the usual sacrifices, the familiar chants, and he soon grew out of his fascination, attending sacrifices only when his father required it.

The cave was not far from the Vestrhall. It sat among the hills just to the north, the entrance disguised by a grove of thick pines among the bare trees of summer. Even at a distance Raef could smell the peculiar smoke that wafted from the priests' fire. Once he had asked what they burned that was so strange but Fylkir, no older than Raef was now but already debilitated by the illness that would deprive him of the use of his hand, had refused to answer.

But it was Josurr who was there to greet Raef. The young priest was leaving the cave as Raef approached, two stone pitchers tucked into the crook of one arm, the other hand clutching a small axe with long, nimble fingers. If he was surprised to see Raef, he did not show it, though Raef had long suspected that an affinity for concealing emotions was the first requirement for being honored with the priestly robes.

"Skallagrim."

"Josurr."

The priest studied Raef for a moment. "I am fetching water. Will you help me?"

Raef followed Josurr to a nearby pool, frozen over, though the ice showed scars in many places where the priests had broken through before. Raef took the axe from Josurr and began to hack at the ice. Though he longed to ask if Fylkir was waiting in the cave, he knew the priest would not answer until the work was done.

No words were spoken until the pitchers were filled with icy, clear water, until they returned to the shadows of the pines and Josurr led the way into the cave. As Raef's eyes adjusted to the dim light of the wide-mouthed cave, he saw a smoking, earth-covered pit, heavy furs piled on two thin pallets of straw, a small iron pot heating over a fire, and crude shelves stocked with dried meat, hard cheese, pressed herbs, and honeycomb. The priests, recipients of gifts from those who wished to know something of the next harvest, of an unborn child's future, never lacked for food or delicacies. Farther back in the recesses of the cave, Raef knew he would find barrels of winter vegetables, dried fruit, and foraged mushrooms.

The animal sacrifices were always performed outside the cave under the open sky, but evidence of the rituals was everywhere. Slender knives wrapped in eel skins, antlers and small skulls with sharp teeth, the withering heart of a hare resting in a wooden bowl, waiting to be examined for signs from the gods.

There was no sign of Fylkir.

Josurr, after pouring some of the fresh water into the pot over the fire, placed the pitchers to the side and closed them up with wooden stoppers. Only then did he look to Raef, who felt the old, childish prickle of anxiety as he wondered if he had bathed thoroughly enough, if his hair was neat enough. The priests required cleanliness and had the right to turn away those they deemed polluted.

"Why have you come?"

"Is Fylkir here?"

"Eagle-in-the-Eye," Josurr said smoothly, using the name the other priest preferred, "has gone away."

"Away," Raef echoed. "Did he not tell you where?"

"He is my superior. It was not for me to ask."

"I thought priests kept no secrets from each other."

The mask of calm on Josurr's face twitched but he held his tongue.

"I am not in the habit of speaking ill of Odin's priests, Josurr, you know this. But we both know Fylkir to be ill-tempered and vindictive, no matter his skills." Raef paused, watching Josurr's face. Still the priest revealed little. "I need to know if he would go so far as to act against me."

It was the wrong thing to say and Josurr bristled. "A priest of Odin does not answer to men, even to a king. When a priest speaks it is with the weight of Asgard. He is not bound to uphold your will."

Raef raised a hand, acknowledging his misstep. "You speak true. But does it not trouble you to know that he did not trust you with details of his journey? Has he not forsaken the ties that bind him to you and you to him? When you pledged yourself to Odin, Fylkir became your sacred teacher. Has he not abandoned you? Has he not left your training unfinished?"

The mask had slipped again as Raef spoke, slowly, like warm wax, and Raef could see the uncertainty that hid beneath. Uncertainty and pent up bitterness. He shifted his approach.

"You are good with children, Josurr. Patient. Gentle. Firm. Perhaps I am wrong, but is it not time for you to take an apprentice? Are you not of age?" Raef paused and gestured to the cave. "But I forgot, there can only be two." Raef shrugged as though it meant little to him and brought a bunch of dried lavender to his nose, inhaling deeply while Josurr squirmed.

The priest broke his silence at last. "You will find boys for me to choose from? No older than ten," Josurr went on, the words tumbling out now. "Six or seven should be enough. Clever, but with flexible minds, and parents of good standing."

Raef smiled and spread his arms. "You shall have them." He strode to Josurr's side and clapped a heavy hand on the priest's shoulder. "I will make it known that wise Josurr is searching for his student." Raef made a show of scanning the cave. "Your pallets are looking worn. I will have fresh ones sent to you. New furs, the best mead in my hall." He looked to Josurr. "Do you like honey? I can have a hive of bees brought here after the spring thaw." Raef frowned. "And Hoyvik will make you a new set of knives, of course. I will have him fit some fine pearls into the handles. It will please Odin, no?" Raef smiled wide once more.

"And in return?" There was no reluctance in Josurr's voice, only acknowledgement of the yoke Raef was placing on his shoulders.

Raef's smile vanished. "You will lift up the name of Skallagrim. You will find signs of the Allfather's favor in the blood of a goat or a doe or a hare, or whatever pleases you. And you will speak of it."

"It will be done."

"Then tell me now, did Fylkir speak to you of Rudrak Red-beard?"

Josurr shook his head. "It is as you said. He left, confiding nothing, violating his sacred duty."

To know that the priest was still unaccounted for, that he might have made the nidstang for Rudrak Red-beard and then, after that traitor's death, gone in search of another who would rise against the name of Skallagrim, was disconcerting, but Raef was pleased to have broken through Josurr's righteousness and composed exterior to expose the resentment he harbored for his belligerent teacher.

"Then let us share a drink in Odin's name," Raef said.

Josurr scowled, all pretense of serenity forgotten. "He drank all the ale."

Raef's laughter filled the cave and Josurr's grimace twisted into a wry smile. Raef clasped the priest's forearm. "Another time. My hall is open to you."

Raef said farewell to his unexpected new ally and returned to the Vestrhall, his mind circling between thoughts of Fylkir, loose and unpredictable, capable of brewing turmoil within his lands, and the need to forge alliances with forces outside Vannheim, forces that would remain loyal when Brandulf Hammerling or Fengar brought the war into the west.

Shutting himself in his father's chamber, he pulled out the great map his father had kept and poured over the lands, near and far, wondering where he might find allies for the war. Karahull, perhaps. It had been Raef's words, not the Hammerling's, that had drawn out Karahull's warriors and convinced them to join against Fengar. Hullbern, if there was anything left of it. Raef thought of the lady Dagmaer and wondered if she had made it to Finnmark and found a measure of safety there. Then there were those who had as yet chosen no side, at least not that Raef knew. Bergoss, Axsellund, Innrivik, Silfravall, Ver, Freynor, Garhold. With Isolf at his side and the bad blood that lingered between him and the Arvalungen, there was little possibility an alliance might be had with Innrivik, and the raids from Silfravall would likely sour any chance at a relationship there. But that still left Raef with options. Balmoran, too, had been quiet, which surprised Raef. Thorgrim Great-Belly had called the gathering, had watched Fengar be proclaimed king, had seen the factions rise up in his very hall, and yet there had been no sign of Balmoran's banners on any battlefield. And then there was Ulfgang. Torrulf Palesword was dead and his army and allies would have scattered, but perhaps some might be persuaded to rejoin the fight under a different banner. Raef would have to reach out and soon. He did not wish to be caught without friends when the Hammerling and Fengar turned their hungry gazes to Vannheim.

Raef made his choices and wrote two letters, one addressed to Torleif of Axsellund, the other to Sverren of Bergoss. He sent two riders with the swiftest horses Vannheim possessed hastening across the narrow valley and into the hills. By nightfall, they would split, one headed to Axsellund, the other to Bergoss. Raef was left to wait again, wondering if he should have sent gifts, should have cajoled Torleif and Sverren with flattering words. His letters were blunt and honest. He made promises, of course, as a king must, but most of all he wrote of Fengar as an unlawful king, chosen without the voices of the warriors, and asked that Axsellund and Bergoss help him strike down this false king. On the Hammerling, Raef was silent.

Raef watched the riders disappear into the trees, Eira at his side. She wore a frown.

"These are not the allies you should seek," she said, keeping her gaze on the horizon though there was nothing left to see.

"Both border with Vannheim and peace has existed between all three for many generations."

Eira snorted, her disdain plain. "They possess no strength worth having."

Raef fought to keep his voice level. "They are small, yes, but I will not attract more powerful allies such as Thorgrim of Balmoran or Sigun of Ingis, if he has not already traded the Palesword for Fengar, without first building a foundation here in the west. I must begin somewhere."

Eira's scowl remained. "You seek out the dogs when you should be brothers with wolves."

"Wolves who would slash open my throat at the first chance? No, I will keep my dogs, and we shall be the very hounds of war."

Raef turned to go but Eira's voice stopped him. "It is the wolves who catch the sun and swallow the moon, not dogs. The dogs will die without a name."

Raef stepped close to Eira, her hair blowing in his face. He felt an urge to take hold of her, to squeeze something other than hatred from her, but clenched his fists at his sides instead. "Then I will die and take my name and the names of my fathers with me. I will not bed down with wolves just to carve my name into the world." Raef spun around and left Eira at the lookout, his hands shaking with his anger and uncertainty, her words spinning webs of doubt in his mind.

Raef shared a quiet meal with Eira and Gudrik that night. Little was said, the hall silent around them but for the footfalls of the pair of servants that waited on them. The loudest noises were the creaking of their chairs as they reached across the table to help themselves to more food and the sound of each swallowing in turn. The silence stretched on when the food was removed and it was only when Gudrik began to play his flute that Raef began to relax.

The melody was sad and slow, a frail thing, yet beautiful. Gudrik stopped and restarted more than once, changing it a little each time as though he were composing it in that moment. Raef closed his eyes and stopped pretending to be glad of the company around him, letting the music take hold.

He was jolted from his thoughts when Eira stood, her chair

scraping back across the floor. Her eyes were hollow, her lips tight. Gudrik's fingers paused, hovering over the holes in the flute.

"This song," Eira said, her voice rough, "where did you learn it?"

Gudrik looked surprised. "Learn it? It has been in my mind for some time, but it is my own."

Eira frowned and Raef glanced down to see a slight tremor in her fingers. She clenched her fist as though she felt his eyes. "I know it."

"Perhaps it is much like another song."

Eira looked at Raef and then away again, still uneasy. "Perhaps." She returned to her chair but her gaze was far away and troubled. Gudrik put the flute aside.

"A story?" The poet looked to Raef, who nodded. Gudrik closed his eyes and was still for a long moment. The fire crackled, sending a shower of sparks into the air. Raef watched them settle and burn out and only then did Gudrik begin to speak, his eyes still shut.

"Hail to those who listen," Gudrik began. It was the story of Eileif, called Sunchaser, who was born in the dawn of Midgard. Eileif's life was a tale filled with sorrow and loss, for he was tricked into slaughtering his family. In his grief, he went mad and clung to the false belief that if he could only reach the sun, he would find his family there and they would be restored to him. He climbed every mountain in Midgard only to find that the sun was always beyond his reach. In his desperation, he wove himself a cloak of eagle feathers and jumped from the highest peak.

Gudrik had just spoken of Eileif's leap, of the air underneath the feather cloak, of the moment when Eileif soared into the blue sky, when Eira rose again from her chair and paced toward the door of the hall. The door slammed behind her and Raef got up as Gudrik's voice trailed off in the midst of Eileif's plummeting death. Raef squeezed the poet's shoulder and went after Eira, though he could not have said why.

He found her on the stone steps, staring out at the black fjord, her eyes fixed on the east where the water curved out of sight. She clutched her arms to herself and did not react to Raef's appearance at her side.

"Do you fear your past?"

"I fear nothing," Eira snarled. But Raef saw her throat catch and knew he had guessed right.

"You told me once you did not remember anything of your life before you awoke in the far eastern mountains. I do not believe you." Raef saw no point in being gentle.

"I remember nothing."

"There is a melody in your mind and a memory that goes with it."

"No," Eira was shaking her head now, "no."

"What happened to your family?" Eira's whole body shook. Raef gripped her wrist. "What happened to them?" Raef was shouting, though why it mattered so much he did not know. "What happened?"

"She killed them!" Eira sobbed, her voice cracking, her eyes staring past Raef into the horror of her memory. "That knife. It slid into their soft flesh like a needle into cloth. So easy." She closed her eyes, her body trembling violently. "But they screamed." She put her hands to her head, covering her ears. She collapsed and would have dropped to the stones but for Raef's arms. He lowered her to the ground and she curled her knees to her chest, head bent, ragged sobs bursting from her. Raef took her shaking hands in his and held them still until the tears ceased.

Eira spoke, but did not raise her head and meet Raef's eyes. Her voice was dull, lifeless. "I remember children. Brothers and sisters. They were younger. They were happy, always laughing. My mother would sing them to sleep, every night the same song. One night, she took a knife from her sleeve and when the song ended she slid it between their ribs. They screamed but no one came to save them."

"How did you survive?"

"She was stronger than I was, bigger. But I was quick and she could not catch me. I took my father's axe and split her skull." Eira raised her head and looked at Raef. Her eyes were red and her cheeks streaked with tears, but she seemed angry that he was there, that he had witnessed her moment of weakness. Yanking her hands from his, Eira got to her feet and wiped her cheeks. "Never speak of this." She turned and fled like a startled crow. He let her go.

Raef lingered on the stone steps, wondering if he should not have ripped the memory from her. It had festered in her for far too long, that much he was certain of, but pressuring her to speak had not been done out of a desire to help her, but rather to satisfy his own mind. Nothing would change the words she had spoken and nothing would obliterate the pain she had unwillingly showed him, and Raef did not feel their relationship, such as it was, would be any better for it.

His gaze turned to the stars, glittering here and there through holes in the thick clouds, the only light in the absence of the moon. So familiar in their shapes and patterns. He wondered if one of those tiny pricks of light was the star Odin had spoken of, the one he might have called home but for the workings of his heart.

A distant light bobbed and flashed in the corner of his vision. Raef turned to the south but the light was gone. He scanned the dark southern shore of the fjord, searching. There. And another. Torches. By the time he counted ten, Raef knew what moved far across the black water, hugging the southern shore. But whether friend or foe, he could not tell. Then the torches went dark, extinguished as though on command and Raef had his answer. Finnolf would have no need to snuff his lights out, but would continue east along the shore until he could ferry across or ride farther to curve around the end of the fjord and set his course for the hall. This was not Finnolf. This was a raid and Raef did not need eyes to know that sleek ships were slinking across his fjord, masked by the night.

# TWENTY-ONE

SPRINTING BACK INTO the hall, Raef called the guards to him and told them what he had seen.

"Shall we meet them outside the gate, lord?" The warrior who spoke gripped his spear with eager fingers.

"No, they will not make land and come to the gate. They will come from the water." Lights bobbing on water were sure to draw unwanted attention. Raef could guess that the lights had been extinguished at the moment the ships had left the shoreline and struck out across the open water. Time was against them, but Raef still had extra warriors camped outside his walls. "Bring all the men inside the walls. Tell them they must move as quickly and quietly as possible. I do not want them to know we have seen them. They think to surprise us and slaughter us in our beds. It is they who will be surprised for we will spring like mountain cats the moment they make land."

The Vestrhall's walls were sturdy, the Vestrhall's walls were not easily breached, but the walls had one weakness. The tall timbers plunged out into the fjord matching the length of two docks, a narrow place, wide enough only for two ships to make landing, but there was no gate in the fjord and two ships full of warriors was more than enough to wipe out the village if defenders were caught unaware. His own ships, nine in number, were far away for the winter, nestled in a cove farther up the fjord, leaving the landing open. Raef had never seen the water entrance used against his father, had never had to fear attack from the fjord, but he had always known the risk of the walls and Einarr had told him this day would come. He only wondered which enemy had come, if it was the Hammerling eager to find retribution against his former ally, if it was Fengar, thinking to take control of the west, or if the threat came from within Vannheim.

The warriors gathered, grim shadows creeping against the walls on both sides of the water entrance and hiding behind the houses that had been built closest to the beach. The houses were emptied and those who could not fight were ushered up the hill to a place of safety. By Raef's count, he had more than sixty men. It was a good number and could hold the narrow place with ease unless the attackers vastly outnumbered them. Only the size and number of the longships would tell and they were still hidden from his sight, lurking somewhere out on the gentle swells of the fjord. Ten archers scrambled onto the grass roofs and pressed themselves flat. Twenty spears hid furthest from the shore, ready to press down on the attackers from the higher ground, the last line of defense. The rest found cover where they could, axes and swords at the ready.

The wait drew on and still there was no sign of the raiders, not a splash of oars in the water, not a voice carrying across the distance to the shore. They were either very cautious or Raef had guessed wrong. His heart began to beat faster and every instant he expected to hear a shout of alarm from the gate. Three men had been left to watch the gate. If they were silenced with swift arrows through the throat, the raiders could swarm over the wall and through the gate before Raef was any wiser. A bead of sweat trickled down Raef's temple and he had just stood from his crouch, his mind set on returning to the gate, when he froze.

The tell tale splash was unaccompanied but it was unmistakable. Raef felt the tension release from his limbs and his next breath was deep and steady. He had guessed right. Peering out from his hiding spot between the wall and Finnolf's sister's house, Raef could see the longships, two of them, one just ahead of the other, black shapes against a black night. It was with relief that Raef saw they were not the great warships, fitted with seventy oars and capable of carrying one hundred or more warriors. These were of middling size and Raef estimated they could hold forty warriors at most, though there was no way to know if these were fully manned.

Raef and his men held their ground and Raef heard the first ship slow between the two docks, the oars held steady in the water to keep the longship from running aground too hard and fast. Then the gentle scrape of the hull sliding into the shallows. And a low, watery thud marked the ship's arrival. Raef closed his eyes and listened to the second ship do the same. Only then did he hear men begin to disembark.

The raiders were skilled and careful but still Raef caught the sounds of feet shuffling against the pebbles and sand. A splash here and there. A rustle of cloth against shield. But not a single voice. Raef waited, tracking the raiders with his mind's eye until he judged the moment right.

When the dark figures of the attackers had gone far enough, Raef raised his gaze to the rooftop of the closest house and let out a low whistle, the call of the night birds that lurked and nested in the trees close to the water. In answer, an arrow was loosed and soundlessly pierced one of the raiders. He fell in the same moment Raef sprang forth, sword raised and a cry on his lips. Around him, his men swarmed from the shadows and fell upon the enemy with savagery.

Raef had cut down two men before the raiders began to fight back, their surprise turned to ferocity, but there was no chance for them to form a coherent defense for Raef's warriors pressed from both sides, pinning them into a narrow channel where every man had to fight for himself. Raef seized on his next target, his sword slashing down as he aimed for the warrior's shoulder. The man raised his shield in time to stop the blade from biting his flesh and Raef's sword caught firm in the wood. Without hesitating, Raef released his grip on the sword and whipped his axe from his belt with his right hand, chopping into the warrior's left side with a single swift motion. The axe went deep and the warrior lurched and arched his neck, a howl of pain forming on his lips. He was silenced with an arrow to the throat and Raef retrieved both axe and sword from the body, his sights already set on his next kill.

Three more men fell to his blades before the spray of blood caught Raef in the face, blinding him to the crush of battle. Raef raised his arm to wipe away the hot, sticky blood with his sleeve, but before he could see clearly, a small knife tore open the side of his thigh, thrown from a distance by a practiced hand. Raef roared against the pain and, dropping his axe, put his hand to the wound, whirling at the same time to raise his sword against the oncoming charge of an enemy warrior. Blade met blade and the force of the charge cost Raef his balance, sending him sliding through the slushy snow covering the beach. Yanking a knife from his belt, Raef thrust it into his opponent's neck just as they toppled into the icy waters of the fjord.

Raef sunk, the heavy weight of the dying warrior pinning him into the shallow water. The sudden cold had elicited a sharp indrawn breath and his mouth and nose flooded. Shoving the dead weight away, Raef surged to the surface, choking, gasping, and spluttering all at once. In vain, Raef's fingers searched the rocky bottom for his sword and he blinked away the water from his eyes only to see a figure leap from the nearest of the longships, sword poised to drive into Raef's chest. Throwing himself into deeper water, Raef eluded the death blow, and then both men were on their feet, submerged to the thigh and unarmed, for the impact against the water had cost the warrior his grip on his sword.

"Death to Skallagrim," his opponent screamed, then launched himself at Raef, sending them both under the water once more. Raef twisted and lashed out with his feet, one boot missing and the other making contact with something that felt like a skull. Hands grabbed at Raef's clothing, scratching, clawing, seizing him around his waist until they were tangled together, a mass of thrashing limbs. They tumbled for a moment and Raef felt his lungs begin to burn. They surfaced together, in shallower water now, and then Raef found the bottom with his feet. Planting one leg, he brought his other knee to the warrior's chest, felt the ribs crack, felt the breath burst from him in a sudden painful gust, and the warrior went limp just long enough for Raef to grab him by the neck with both hands. Raef kneed him again and then plunged him under the water. Tightening his grip, Raef pushed down until the warrior was on the bottom. The warrior kicked and lashed out with his arms, but already his strength was fading, throttled from him by Raef's hands.

When he was quiet, when the thrashing had stopped and the bubbles had vanished, Raef held on for a moment longer, then released the drowned man. The body floated up, the face frozen in agony, the dead hands reaching for Raef. Raef recognized that face. It was not one he knew well, not one he could put a name to, but it belonged to Vannheim, to his father, to him. And now that man had died cursing the name of Skallagrim.

Raef dragged the body from the water and let it fall on the shore, retrieved his sword from the shallows, then headed back into the killing ground. Bodies littered the snow, their dead limbs choking the living into a confined space. There was no more beauty, no more skill, only desperate bloodletting.

A voice sounded over the din of battle. "Skallagrim!"

Raef searched the melee while the voice roared twice more, and at last he knew who had brought death to the Vestrhall. Snorren Thoken had the broken shaft of an arrow protruding from his shoulder and his shield was a splintered ruin, but somehow he and a small circle of warriors held their ground, defying the efforts of Raef's men to draw them out from the safety of their comrades.

But the moment Raef's eyes locked with Snorren's, the dark-bearded warrior broke from the circle and began to close the distance between them, heedless of the danger around him. Raef took a deep breath and glanced quickly at the wound in his thigh where the knife had ripped open his flesh. The cold water and the battle-fire had numbed the pain but did nothing to slow the flow of blood. Tearing a piece of cloth from a dead man, Raef wrapped it around his thigh and tied a hasty knot, all while Snorren bore down on him with eyes blind to everything but Raef. The cloth would help, but it was a poor bandage and would not long stem the loss of blood. Raef needed to end this fight, and soon.

Raef adjusted his grip on his sword, wishing he had time to recover his axe from where it lay further up the beach in the snow, and plucked a shield from the ground as Snorren broke into a run, a snarl fixed on his blood-streaked face. They were but ten paces apart when a figure stepped from the shadows, sword raised in defiance of Snorren's charge, face obscured by the night. Snorren did not slow, but the unknown warrior did not shy away and he threw his shield, catching Snorren in the chest and throwing the bigger man off balance. Spinning away, Snorren kept his feet, but his eyes were on the new challenger now. His steps were quick and sure, his sword a dull gleam in the starlight as he charged the unknown warrior, who did not move. Raef could not understand why, and then, just as Snorren was in striking distance, the warrior took a single, limping, lurching step to the side, a feeble attempt to avoid the oncoming sword, and Raef knew.

He heard himself shout, felt the shield drop from his hand, felt his legs begin to churn beneath him, but he was too late. Snorren's sword stabbed into the man's belly and he dropped as a stone does to a river bottom. Raef was upon Snorren the next instant and he shoved his blade into Snorren's back and up through his shoulders until the tip protruded out of his chest, tickling his chin. Snorren writhed, his mouth working furiously but no sound came out.

Raef leaned in close to the dying man's ear and said, "My father waits for you in Valhalla, usurper, and will kill you a thousand times again."

Shoving Snorren off his sword, Raef dropped to his knees next to the warrior who had taken Snorren's blade for him. Blood poured from the wound, black like the night sky above, and though Raef put his hands to the ruptured flesh, he knew it was hopeless. The warrior looked up at him, a feeble but content smile on his pale, sweaty face.

"Why, Gudrik?" Raef's voice tumbled out of him, ragged and broken.

"Do not be angry with me, Raef." Gudrik spoke quietly but his voice was as calm and fluid as ever.

"Never. But why would you throw your life away like this?"

Gudrik's breath caught and blood trickled from the corner of his mouth. "What is my life worth if I cannot defend my friend?" Raef began to protest, but Gudrik persisted. "I made this choice, Raef. Now I may go to my fathers in Valhalla and know I am worthy of a place there."

If words could heal Gudrik's fatal wound, if words could make the poet see Raef's grief, see that there was no shame in living a life of music and words, crippled as Gudrik might be, he would have poured them out of his heart. But he would not tarnish Gudrik's final act. With a shaky, bloody hand, Raef touched Gudrik's cheek.

"Then go in peace, friend. Look for my coming." It was a lie. Raef knew he would never join Gudrik in Valhalla, but he kept that to himself.

Gudrik tried to smile again, but it turned to a grimace and the poet coughed, his body wracked with the grip of death. Seizing Raef's hand, Gudrik squeezed, his eyes going wide as he stared into Raef's face. His body gave two tiny jerks and then Raef saw the spark of life slip from Gudrik's eyes and the hand that gripped Raef's went limp.

A violent, angry roar filled Raef's ears and he realized it was his own howl of grief as he tipped his head back and screamed to the stars.

Around him, the battle was ended and his men were victorious. To a man, the raiders had been slaughtered, though the cost to Raef's men was high. Only half of his warriors were on their feet. The other half lay in the snow with the dead.

"Lord." A warrior looked down on Raef, who was not yet ready to let go of Gudrik. "What should we do with the bodies of the enemy?"

Raef was weary of death. "Burn them. Give them the honor they might have earned, had Snorren not turned their ears and hearts against me."

"All?"

Raef's gaze slid to the corpse of Snorren Thoken. "Take his head. Put it above the gate. Let Snorren's skull serve as a warning."

"And the body?"

"Throw it in the fjord. The fish can fight over his flesh."

"It shall be done, lord."

With the fire of battle burned out and Raef's soaked clothes freezing in the air, the cold had begun to sink into Raef, and yet still he knelt beside Gudrik, the tears he felt in his heart remaining unshed.

One by one the bodies were carried through the village and out the gates, then laid to rest in a heap, awaiting the flames. With the help of the villagers, Raef's men worked through the night, felling trees, erecting five pyres, and dividing the bodies among them. Raef placed Gudrik's body on one, and, as the sky began to lighten in the east, set the torch to the oil. The other four pyres were lit as one and the hot blazes brought a different kind of dawn to Vannheim. By then, even children had come to witness the funeral. The villagers, solemn faces reflecting the flames, stood in silence and Raef knew they were watching friends, brothers, and sons burn. Above it all, Snorren's head sat atop a spear, his dead eyes rolled up, staring toward the breaking day.

Raef watched the fires burn until the smoke made his eyes sting, his clothes half frozen from the fjord, half dried by the heat of the pyre. But as he turned to the gates, intent on shutting himself in his chamber and drinking mead until he no longer saw Gudrik's face, he saw movement to the east, horses breaking out of the trees and rounding a curve in the fjord's shoreline, Vannheim's banner streaming in the wind. They grew closer and Raef saw Finnolf Horsebreaker at their head and Dvalarr the Crow just behind.

Finnolf pulled his horse up hard in front of Raef, his eyes reflecting the fires and then looking up to the top of the gate to rest on Snorren's head. Raef did not need to tell him what had happened. Finnolf jumped to the ground and took a knee at Raef's feet.

"Lord, forgive me. They slipped through our noose and vanished. We rode through the night in the hopes of catching them."

Raef felt anger bubble up inside him, though his mind told him Finnolf could not be blamed. "Did you think to look to the sea?"

Finnolf's face fell and he closed his eyes. "Ships," he said, almost to himself.

"We would all be dead if not for a stroke of luck."

Finnolf lowered his head. "I have failed."

Raef wanted to rage at the captain, but he bit back his words and turned away. It was only then that he saw Siv and Vakre, their faces two among the many that had returned with Finnolf. He slowed only a step, his relief at seeing them unharmed overwhelmed by his sudden anger at their disappearance and failure to bring Snorren down, then brushed past the onlookers and returned to his hall. He spent the day in solitude with only a cask of mead for company. Three times there was knocking on his door and three times Raef did not even give the disturbance a flicker of thought as he sat in his chamber before the empty hearth, ensconced behind the walls of his own mind.

Only at twilight did he emerge from the darkness of his chamber and allow Aldrif the healer to clean and stitch the wound in his thigh. When she had finished, he wiped the dried blood from his face and hands and left the hall without a word to any who saw him. In the village, Raef sought out an old woman who had lived in a tiny hut near the gate for as long as anyone could remember. She had a name but to every man, woman, and child in the village, she was simply known as Grandmother.

She was at home, as Raef expected, bent over a cooking pot, her white hair falling over her shoulder in a thin braid. For a moment, he thought of Siv, and wondered if her red-gold braid would look like this when she was old. Grandmother turned at Raef's entrance, a ladle in her hand, and she blew on the soup and tasted it twice before acknowledging his presence.

"Best I ever made," she said with a wink as she returned the ladle to the pot.

The smell of the soup cooking and the warmth of the fire seeped into Raef's senses and he felt himself relax for the first time since listening to Gudrik tell the story of Eileif the night before. Exhaustion set in, taking the place of some of the anger that festered in him, and for a long moment, Raef was content to stand by her hearth and Grandmother let him do so as though having the lord of Vannheim staring into her fire were a nightly occurrence.

She hummed as she went about her business, the sound so light and faint that Raef could not pick up the tune, but the sound of her voice was welcome. Only when she had ladled soup into two bowls and poured ale for them both did she speak again.

"Eat. Before it gets cold." Her face creased in a gentle smile and Raef did as she instructed. The first spoonful burned his tongue but it awoke his hunger and he began to eat with abandon, slurping and swallowing until his bowl was empty. She refilled it and by the time Raef had emptied it again, her own bowl was still half full. She smiled again. "And now you will wait," she said, and Raef felt himself a child, admonished for eating too quickly and forced into patience as penitence. The thought brought a hint of a smile to his face, no doubt as she had intended, and Raef knew he had been right to seek her out.

When Grandmother finished, she set down her spoon with precision and drank the last sip of her ale. Then, folding her hands in front of her, she looked at Raef, her eyes still kind, but with new vigor in the blue depths. "Now," she said, "what would you like?"

Raef inhaled and spoke. "Therein lies the problem, Grandmother. I do not know. And yet I feel I want to do this, to mark this day in some manner."

She nodded. "Tell me, then, what your heart feels."

Raef was unsure where to begin, but the words began to fall from his lips. "I am not the man I once was. That man was a warrior, a sea-farer, strong and skilled. He was a son, young and content with the world."

"And what are you now?"

"I have tasted bitter sorrow and burning pain. I have a promise of vengeance in my bones. I have flown with the wind in my face and the sun in my heart. I have walked in barren Jötunheim and lived to tell of it. I have looked into the eyes of a Valkyrie and the Allfather himself has shown me the stars."

She did not seem disconcerted by Raef's revelations. "But what are you?"

Raef was quiet for a moment. "I am a named king. I am a lord. I am surrounded. And yet I am alone."

The old woman smiled, but her gaze was lowered and the smile was for herself, it seemed. "I know what to do. But why now, young king? Why this day when you have never come to me before?"

"I lost a friend last night. Not the first, and likely not the last. His was a brave death, a sacrifice, and yet a senseless waste. He had words and music to make remembrances. I do not."

She nodded. "Then let us begin." They cleared the table and Raef watched as the old woman collected her tools. Then he stripped from the waist up. She ran a hand up his shoulder blade. "Here. So grief, joy, and memory are always looking over your shoulder." Raef nodded and stretched out on the table, propping up his upper body on his elbows.

She went to work, wielding the ink and fine bone needles with precision, the gentle tune again murmuring through her lips. The work went on for hours. Raef drifted in and out of something akin to sleep, but always he was aware of the old woman's tune and the tiny pricks of the needles into his skin. The dawn was approaching when she sat back and returned her tools to the table. Her thin, delicate hands were smeared with ink and she smiled to herself again.

"It is finished."

Raef twisted his neck and peered over his shoulder to see what she had created. The wolf rendered into his skin, climbing up his shoulder blade as though readying to leap over his shoulder, was snarling back at him, and yet if he hunched his shoulder a different way, the ferocity was replaced by sorrow. It seemed a perfect reflection of himself.

"Thank you, Grandmother."

She smiled, pleased with the work she had done. "It is time you slept."

Raef cocked his head. "And you?"

"Sleep is for the young."

Raef thanked her again and returned to the hall, the stillness of the sleeping village a welcome peace that Raef felt he could breathe in. When he reached his chamber, he sprawled on his bed, careful to keep off the fresh tattoo. Sleep overcame him in an instant.

## TWENTY-TWO

WHEN RAEF AWOKE, it was a slow extraction from the depths of sleep, the sunlight pulling, pulling at the edges of his eyes until at last he opened them. Even then Raef kept still, content to breathe. He knew now that the death of Gudrik had entwined in his heart with his father's death. Raef remembered Einarr's death as though he had been a watcher from afar. He had stood at the funeral pyre, he had done his duty as a son, but he had raced straight from shock to vengeance and never truly had a chance to grieve as the land erupted in war. But with Gudrik there had been no distance, it was all glittering sharpness and pain, dampened not at all by Raef's swift retaliation against Snorren Thoken. But it seemed some of that sharpness and pain had been eaten by the wolf that now prowled Raef's skin and it was with a clear mind that Raef rose from his bed.

The hour was late. Past mid-day. His chamber was cold, having been deprived of fire for two days and Raef padded across the floor to crouch before his hearth. A fire was born in moments, sending tongues of warmth snaking out to touch Raef's skin. He had Aldrif change his bandage and inspect her stitches, then called for bread and meat, hard cheese and winter apples, and a fresh cup of ale, and ate on the small ledge outside his window.

It was from there that Raef saw the riders at the same moment the horn sounded at the gate to give notice. It was not Isolf. A banner, no more than a blur at that distance, was strung out at the front of the pack and Raef had not given Isolf a Vannheim banner to carry. It was a small party, though at that distance Raef could not count them. If foe, they could not threaten the walls. Raef thought of his letters to Axsellund and Bergoss, but it seemed too soon to hope it might be Torleif or Sverren with an answer.

Raef watched the riders draw closer and calmly finished his meal, washing down the last crumbs of bread with the ale. By then, the knocking had begun and Raef, still wrapped in his fur robe, went to the door.

It was Ulli, the steward. "Riders, lord."

"I have seen them."

"The gate insists it is the banner of Garhold."

Raef kept his surprise to himself. "Whoever they are, keep them outside the gate. I will have no strangers pass these walls without my permission." Ulli left to deliver Raef's order and Raef looked once more out his window before dressing in clean clothes.

By the time he reached the gate, word had spread and a crowd of warriors and villagers had gathered. On Raef's command, the gate was opened and Raef and ten heavily armed warriors stepped out.

The banner of Garhold, blue and white against the blue sky, flapped in the wind, but all else was still as the warriors faced each other. Raef recognized Uhtred at their head and the older lord dismounted and approached on foot.

"Not the warmest welcome I have known." Uhtred's voice was level and unthreatening but his blue eyes stared hard at Raef.

"I will decide the manner of my welcome when I know your purpose here." Raef did not flinch away from the older lord's gaze.

"Are you so quick to turn away a friend?"

"Friend, no. And if I had wanted to turn you away, you would know it. But is Uhtred, lord of Garhold, my friend?"

"He is, if you would let him."

Raef felt his heartbeat quicken but the treachery of his own warriors had made him wary. "Then tell me the manner of your friendship." It was perhaps too much to ask a lord to pledge himself before giving him welcome, before sharing mead, before letting him pass the gates. Uhtred was a proud man and Raef's insistence on a demonstration of loyalty could chafe at him. But a true ally would swallow it and prove himself before all watching eyes.

The blue eyes did not flicker as Uhtred drew a small knife from his belt. The warriors behind Raef tensed, ready to defend their king, but Raef did not move and kept his eyes fixed on Uhtred's, showing that he could trust if he chose.

Uhtred brought the knife to his palm and drew it across the skin. Blood rushed to the cut and Uhtred raised his hand so all might see. Then he went to one knee and shouted, "Hail, Skallagrim, king!" Uhtred was echoed by those who had ridden with him and then again by Raef's warriors and the watching villagers. "Garhold is yours," Uhtred said. "I swear it on the Allfather's spear."

Raef grasped Uhtred's unbloodied hand and, with a wolfish grin, raised him up to his feet. "Then you are most welcome."

"There is one I would have you meet," Uhtred said, gesturing to the riders behind him. Raef nodded so he might continue. Uhtred turned and signaled and one rider, a young woman, dismounted and approached them. She was not dressed as a shieldmaiden, but her demeanor was commanding all the same. Her stride was confident and her eyes, the same piercing blue as Uhtred's, were undaunted as she came to stand in front of Raef. She allowed Uhtred to take her hand, and there was no soft smile for either man, no meek downward glance.

"My daughter," Uhtred said.

"Your name, lady?" Raef asked.

"Aelinvor."

"You are welcome to Vannheim, Aelinvor."

Uhtred's daughter responded with a slight smile. It warmed her face without diminishing her boldness. "My king is kind." Her dark, curly hair, long and unbound, swirled about her face in the wind.

At Uhtred's signal, the remaining riders dismounted and one by one gave Raef their oath of loyalty, and there, before his gates, Raef gained his first ally.

The visitors from Garhold were given guest quarters in the Vestrhall and preparations began for a feast that night. To solidify their alliance in the sight of the gods, Raef and Uhtred shared a cup of mead and broke bread together, establishing the men of Garhold as guests in Raef's home. As Raef passed the mead to Uhtred, he caught sight of Eira at the back of the hall. She had been absent since the night of the battle and Raef had begun to think he had driven her off. Their eyes met and she seemed calm but distant. He wondered why she had returned, why she kept returning. He could ask the same of Siv and Vakre, who he had thought long gone only to see them return from Finnolf's failed journey to the south of Vannheim. He knew not whether he was angry that they had chosen to go with Finnolf or relieved that they had not yet abandoned him.

Uhtred had drained the rest of the mead and Raef turned his attention back to the other lord. "It is time we spoke away from the others," Raef said. "You have spent many days in the saddle. Can you bear another hour?"

Uhtred grinned. "I am not so old as that."

Five warriors went with them but kept their distance as Raef and Uhtred rode through the gate and curled around the north of the walls and the hill that stood at the Vestrhall's back, then turning west to pass between the hills to reach the sea. Leaving the horses, they walked on the shore, watching the unrelenting waves batter the rocky coast. The salt spray leaped into the air, catching them in its fine mist.

"What brought you to my gates, Uhtred? Why align yourself with me?"

Uhtred was quiet for a moment. Gulls circling overhead tried to speak for him. "Your father might have been king, Raef. That day of the hunt in Balmoran, I was preparing to bind myself to him, to grant him the voices of Garhold's warriors. He was a good man, strong, just, undaunted by lying tongues. Many things the last king promised to be and, we learned too late, did not deliver. Brynvald of Kolhaugen lived more years than most men and spent twenty of them as our king, but only because the lords were too busy fighting each other to bother with him. I watched your father navigate those feuds with skill and cunning, and through it all, Vannheim prospered, engaging in battle when necessary, letting lords tear at each other's throats when it suited him. And I waited for the day that I could support him at a gathering and see him rise above all others."

Uhtred looked out to sea and Raef knew the older lord was watching a future he had worked for slip away. "That day in the forest, I might have been able to save him."

"Or you would have died at his side and not be standing here with me today," Raef said. "Is it my father that brought you to me, then? And perhaps a nagging guilt?"

"I kept Garhold from the war because I would not support the manner of Fengar's choosing. And yet what lord would I turn to in place of him? The Palesword I knew little and the Hammerling and I have never been friends. Should I make my own claim, then? But I have never craved power as some men do. Give me Garhold and I am content."

"I have only ever said the same," Raef said.

"Then I think you have the makings of a king, Raef Skallagrim. A man who seeks to be king with ravenous hunger is not the king we need. But I have not answered your question. A rumor came, on the heels of the news of the great battle in the east, a rumor that said it was not the Hammerling who had won victory over the Palesword, but rather it was the young lord of Vannheim who had triumphed against a terrible darkness. And then you vanished from the world of men, seemingly lost even as your star was born. Some said you were dead, betrayed by one of your captains. Some said you were the traitor, turning your back on the Hammerling and seeking Fengar instead that you might pledge Vannheim to him. But these rumors are nothing when compared to what I have heard of your absence and unexpected return." Uhtred looked at Raef with a curious eye. Raef kept silent. "Perhaps one day you will tell me the truth. But it matters not for I am not blind. A strange fate guides you, Raef. I know not what it is, if it is darkness or light, if it will tear a hole in the world of men or return us to the golden age of heroes. But whatever it is, I have chosen to follow it. Too long has Garhold been idle, too long have I watched and waited in the shadows. No more."

It was more honest an answer than Raef could ever have asked for, but Raef grew uneasy as Uhtred spoke of fate, the words of the Allfather burning in his mind. "And what would you have of me in return?"

"You are the last of the line of Skallagrim. My daughter is my only surviving child. I make no demands. I have already given you my spears and nothing you say will change that. I only ask that you consider tying our families and our lands together."

Garhold and Vannheim shared only a small border at the edge of the sea but joining them together would create a tract of land larger than any claimed by another lord. Raef placed his hand on Uhtred's shoulder. "You have my word, I will consider what you ask."

They watched the frothing seas as clouds blew across the sun, the high winds driving the shadows unceasingly. Finally Uhtred broke the silence. "Whose head is above your gate?"

"A warrior who broke his oath. He was not the first. There has been trouble in Vannheim. Men sought to replace me in my absence. They have been dealt with, though I think they are not the last." Raef looked hard at Uhtred, waiting to see if the other man might question his decision to support Raef now that he had the knowledge of unrest in Raef's own land. Uhtred showed no such doubt.

"What would you have me do? My warriors await word from me."

"And I await word from Axsellund and Bergoss. Send for two hundred of your men to meet us here, have the rest watch your borders and prepare to march."

"It will be done."

ᛋ ᛋ ᛋ

The lone rider was spotted coming down from the north as the sun flared over the sea that evening. Four warriors rode to meet him, wary of strange visitors, and Raef, alerted by a watcher on the wall, went to the gate to await their return, Finnolf a quiet but persistent presence at his side.

The horse was a farm beast, heavy-hoofed and shaggy, and the rider was slumped over its bare back, clinging to the horse's mane with raw, wind-bitten fingers, his hair hiding his face. He wore only a thin shirt and his clothes were torn in several places.

"He has not spoken, lord," said one of the four warriors.

"Get him down," Raef said. The rider was lowered to the ground and stretched out on his back. Only then did Raef recognize him as Thorvin, one of the men he had sent to scout Greyshield. Bruises colored his face and his eyes were listless and unfocused. "Odin's eye, get him inside."

Finnolf unhooked his cloak and settled it over Thorvin, then he and another carried the unresponsive warrior through the gate and into the guard house. A fire blazed there and Thorvin was laid in front of it. In the light of the fire, Raef could see his skin was deathly pale and his breathing shallow. Blankets were fetched and hot broth made ready, but once they had wrapped Thorvin up, there was little they could do but wait.

Raef watched the man's face for signs of renewed life. His eyes were closed now, the eyelids fluttering, but his cheeks were still cold to the touch. Too cold.

"He does not shiver," Finnolf said quietly, voicing what each man was thinking. Shivering was a sign of life, a sign that the body was fighting the cold. A body that did not shiver was as good as dead.

Raef rose. A feast and his new ally awaited, though leaving Thorvin did not sit well with him. "Keep him warm. Do everything you can. And find me the moment something changes." Finnolf nodded to show his understanding and Raef returned to the hall.

After the solemn faces and silence of the guard house, the light in the hall seemed too bright, the music too loud, and the faces too cheerful. But Raef could not dampen his new alliance so he forced a smile onto his face and greeted Uhtred of Garhold with enthusiasm. If he grasped Uhtred's forearm too hard, if he held onto his smile too long, the other lord did not seem to notice.

Raef handed Uhtred a glass of mead and raised his own in the air. "With the gods as my witness, I welcome Uhtred, lord of Garhold, to Vannheim and into my home. May the gods bring you long life and prosperity, my friend." This was met with a cheer and Uhtred thanked Raef with a nod.

Then the lord of Garhold raised a hand to quiet the crowd. "Remember this day, for this day I make a promise to you, my king, and to all of you." Uhtred gestured to the eager faces. "The promise of fire and blood and victory, and the promise that this man will rise above all others, that his name will endure, that his song will be remembered in years beyond our reckoning." Uhtred's words quickened Raef's heartbeat and he felt the hair on his arms rise. The crowd erupted, hammering the tables with their hands and cups, their voices threatening to bring the roof crashing down. Uhtred and Raef drank and the feast began in earnest.

Among the benches, one figure stood out from the rest, Josurr in his long robes, his face marked with the blood of a recent sacrifice. Raef could not hear the priest's words as he drifted from table to table, but the faces of the warriors who listened told of promises of fame and riches for those who followed the name of Skallagrim. Once, Raef caught the priest's eye, but only the slightest glance passed between them and it was not long before Josurr disappeared into the night.

Aelinvor made a late appearance, one that drew the eyes of every man in the hall as she made her way to her father's side at the high table. She was dressed as a wife of a king, luminescent in dark blue that contrasted her pale skin. Her hair, so loose before, was pulled up in intricate braids, not a lock out of place, revealing a slender neck and straight shoulders. A single gem, a blazing star, sat on her neckline, pulsing in the firelight. The effect was mesmerizing and Raef was sure she knew it. She greeted him with grace and her father with affection, seemingly oblivious to the shameless stares of the watching warriors. Only when she had taken her seat and accepted mead from Raef did the hall return to its natural state.

Every smile, every word, every turn of her head was meant for him, he knew, a display to convince him to make her his wife. It was not deceitful, though, but bold and honest. It was not unwelcome. Raef wondered if Eira was present, if she watched Uhtred's beautiful daughter, if she felt even a sliver of jealousy in her volatile, changeable heart, and then he pushed Eira out of his thoughts and let Aelinvor seep into his senses.

They did not speak more than a few words to each other until Uhtred went to relieve his bladder. Aelinvor leaned over the empty space of her father's chair and poured herself more mead.

"You are very beautiful, lady."

Aelinvor smiled a smile that said she did not need to be told. "You are kind."

"Your father wishes to see us wed." Raef was pleased that this blunt statement brought the barest hint of hesitation to her eyes. She banished it quickly.

"My father is a wise man."

"How old are you, Aelinvor?"

She looked away, as thought she might refuse to answer. "I am not yet eighteen."

"I am older by seven years. Does this trouble you?" Raef leaned close, his hand brushing against hers.

"I do not wish to wed a boy."

"Then you do not care for love?"

She deftly stepped around that question. "Would you see me the plaything of an unbearded youth, valiant but less than skilled? Or would you see me rule at your side, mother of your children?"

"So that is what you want. To be wife to the king."

Aelinvor smiled. It was not the smile of a child. "I will not deny it."

"I like an honest woman."

"Then you think me a woman?"

Raef looked into her eyes and traced the side of her neck with the backs of his fingers. "Without a doubt." He wanted to kiss her and it was clear she would not refuse him. But he hesitated, he knew not why, and then Finnolf was there, hunched beside his chair.

Raef looked to the young captain, aware that Aelinvor had sat back in her chair and her gaze was now on the crowd of warriors. "Thorvin?"

Finnolf shook his head. "He is dead."

"He never said anything?"

"Nothing."

Raef stood. "Prepare wood and oil. I will see him." What he hoped to glean from the dead man, Raef could not say, but if nothing else he felt he owed it to Thorvin to say farewell. Raef could only imagine what had happened to the other four who had ridden to Greyshield's lands.

In death, Thorvin's pale, cold skin had turned grey and stiff. He was still stretched before the fire in the guard house, tucked beneath the blankets as though the heat might still deny death, might bring color to his cheeks. Raef pulled the blankets off.

"Did he have family?"

None of the warriors present answered. Finnolf finally spoke up. "He came from the north, lord. I knew him only a little but he seldom spoke of it. He always called the Vestrhall his home. Perhaps he had no one."

Raef looked over Thorvin's body then leaned down and pulled aside the neck of his shirt. A burn, raw and angry-looking, covered his shoulder. More bruises, dark now in death, colored his chest. A ring around his neck showed he had been strangled, at least for a time. "He was beaten. Badly. Greyshield wanted information."

"He escaped. The horse was not his own," Finnolf said.

"Escaped? Or turned loose? Why would Greyshield let one injured man, a man he easily could have ridden down and slaughtered, return to me?" Raef looked down at Thorvin's face. "Perhaps he did escape. But I must believe that Greyshield let him go, that Tulkis wanted me to know the fate of those five men." Raef nodded to the watching warriors. "Give him to the fire. See that it burns hot and true." Then he gestured to Finnolf. "We will await Isolf's return, then ride to Greyshield lands."

"Shall I call more warriors?" Most of those who had camped outside the walls and survived Snorren Thoken's ambush had been sent home.

Raef shook his head. "We will have enough to show Greyshield he has made a grave mistake."

❬ ❬ ❬

Eira came to him that night. She said nothing but slipped into Raef's chamber and began to undress in the light of his lone candle. She stopped only when she saw he stood yet by the door, unmoving.

"Are you ill? Wounded?" she asked, scorn in her voice and derision in her eyes. She did not seem embarrassed.

"Only tired." It was a bad lie but Raef did not know what to say.

Eira laughed, a surprising sound, but not pleasant. "You think of that bitch, that daughter of Uhtred, with her fine cloth and her blue eyes."

"Yes, I think of her." Raef's defiance lashed out, his words more heated than he intended.

"You would rather have that girl in your bed? You want to hear her cry your name when you put a child in her? She is nothing. You will regret it the moment she spreads her legs and then you will crawl back to me." Eira's face was twisted, an ugly combination of rage and contempt.

"Are you jealous? Am I yours to do with as you wish? I made you no promise and you made me none. One moment you are as cold and distant as a silver fish in the sea, the next you melt against my skin, a scorching, wild thing. Always, always this has been on your terms. We have fucked more times than I can count, but you remain a stranger to me and I have had enough." The words were out before Raef could stop them. He could feel his heart pounding and his breath trembled against his lips. He had not meant to go so far, had not meant to chase her away, and yet he had spoken a truth he had denied himself.

Eira's chin was raised, her eyes hard. Her scorn for him was writ in every bone, every muscle of her body. "You still want me."

Raef's voice fell to a strained shadow of what it had been. "You are right, by the gods, you are right. But I will not have you and you will not have me."

Their eyes did not unlock as Eira put her clothes back on. She did it slowly, teasing his resolve, but when she stood before him fully clothed and he still had not moved, she spit at his feet and left the room, the door closing heavily behind her.

Raef stood in the darkness of his chamber, immobilized. He wanted to go after her, to forgive her and himself, to wash away their hasty words with tender kisses. He wanted to see her destroyed, brought low by her own arrogance, cast out and left to wither away in isolation. The truth he had spoken hung about him, a heavy burden that seemed to fit in all the right places, as though it had been molded long before and only needed forging. Eira was fierce, Eira was strong, and he had been drawn to her, sure that they might do great things while they stood at each other's side, but she was not a partner, not even a friend.

If they met again, he knew it would lead to bloodshed.

The knock on his door was abrupt, an unwelcome interruption from the conflicting thoughts that swirled in his heart and mind. He reached for a knife and opened the door only a crack, wondering if Eira had come for vengeance so soon. Vakre's face stared back at him. Raef hesitated, then stepped away from the door and let the son of Loki enter.

Vakre glanced at the exposed blade in Raef's hand and grinned. "Expecting trouble?" Raef did not answer and the grin slipped away. They had not spoken since Vakre had cautioned Raef against turning on Hauk of Ruderk without proof that Hauk had conspired to murder Einarr. "I am sorry for Gudrik's death. And I am sorry we did not discover Snorren Thoken's ships."

"It was a good death. The one he wanted." Raef returned the knife to its sheath. "Do you bring news?" He did not trust himself to speak of anything more with Vakre.

Vakre held out a roll of parchment. "This."

It bore the mark of Axsellund. Raef took it. With a deep breath, he broke the seal and unrolled the message. The paper was blank.

"What is the meaning of this?" Vakre had no answer. "Where is the messenger?"

Within moments Raef and Vakre were in the hall and a pair of warriors hauled the messenger in. He was shoved to his knees in front of Raef.

"Why is this blank?" Raef brandished the parchment in front of the messenger.

"For the sake of caution, lord." The man did not appear dismayed at his position. "Torleif did not wish his answer to fall into the wrong hands. The guards at the gate did not give me a chance to explain."

"Then speak." Raef tried to remain patient. He could not fault the lord of Axsellund's caution.

"I am meant to give you this." The man reached for his belt and the warriors lunged, ready to kill if he went for the knife that hung there. The messenger held up his hands and looked to Raef.

"Disarm him." The knife was stripped from the belt and the folds of his cloak were searched, revealing no threat. "Continue."

The messenger delved into a large pouch at his waist and withdrew a tiny, round wooden capsule, so small it fit comfortably in his palm. Raef stepped forward and retrieved it. The lid twisted to the side, revealing the lord of Axsellund's message. Raef took it between his fingers and held it aloft. His eyes met Vakre's and he saw his own hope mirrored there. "Cedar." The sprig of green was small but identifiable.

"Faithfulness and friendship," Vakre said, his voice quiet in the large, empty hall.

"Endurance and loyalty." Raef turned his gaze back to the messenger.

"Torleif is with you, lord, and names you his king. The strength of Axsellund is yours."

# TWENTY-THREE

THE NEW ALLIANCE with Vannheim's eastern neighbor held Raef's impatience at bay for less than a day. Raef and Vakre celebrated it quietly with mead that night, the easiness between them stealing back into the folds of their conversation and the silences between words, and Raef took satisfaction in sharing it with Uhtred at the morning meal, and again with Finnolf and three other captains by the still waters of the fjord as they, along with Engvorr the shipbuilder, assessed the two ships Raef had acquired on Snorren Thoken's death. One was an old longship, repaired many times, and Raef knew Snorren's family had lovingly cared for it for three generations, a valuable possession that hinted at wealth they did not possess. The other was smaller but younger, perhaps only a season or two old, and Raef suspected Snorren had stolen it. But even amid the familiar scent of greased sails, even with a sheer strake under his fingers and smooth boards beneath his feet, the need to take action against Tulkis Greyshield gnawed at Raef as the sun climbed higher into the sky and he looked for Isolf's return with eager eyes.

But Isolf did not return, not that day, or the next and Raef began to wonder if his cousin had met with an ill fate in the wild woods that marked Vannheim's border with Silfravall.

Eira had vanished. The gate guards saw her leave and take to the hills, her horse in tow. The loss of her was both a relief and a burden. He was glad when Vakre did not question her absence, though he could feel the son of Loki's eyes on him.

He entertained Uhtred and Aelinvor as best he knew how, taking the father hunting and the daughter fishing. Uhtred's spear remained unbloodied and his arrows in his quiver while Raef took down a skinny brace of snow hares. Aelinvor took to the water with ease, at home in the small boat as though it were a high seat. And yet when Raef might have fished in silence, mesmerized by the shifting reflections in the waters and the fresh snow swathed over the trees, Aelinvor questioned him with unrelenting precision about his plans for the war, the beauty of the living, breathing land around them seemingly lost to her.

When they gathered that night for the evening meal, Aelinvor resplendent in onyx and silver, the captains lively and boastful of the glory they would win in battle, Raef saw in his mind's eye a different gathering, one tucked on the edge of a secluded stretch of fjord, the waters darkening as the late summer sun slipped behind the hills, a single campfire flaring up to light the night, and fresh-caught fish cooking over the flames. Raef closed his eyes and let his mind go. He could smell it all, the fish charring, the wood burning, the damp earth. The faces in the twilight were cheerful, content. His father, tending the fish. Gudrik, a song on his lips. Siv, laughing and dunking Vakre's head in the shallows of the fjord. There was no talk of war in that place, no alliances to be made, no battles to win or lose, no burden of doubt, no fate surfacing from the deep, only life.

"More ale?" Aelinvor's voice broke into Raef's dream and her blue eyes brought him back to his hall. Raef nodded and she refilled his cup. "Your mind is elsewhere," she said, resting her hand on his forearm.

"It is."

"Tell me."

Raef studied her face for a moment, tracing the line of her nose with his eyes, the curve of her cheeks, the arch of her dark eyebrows. "Tulkis Greyshield is much in my thoughts."

"Do you still wait for your cousin?"

Raef sighed. "Another day, but no more. I cannot allow Tulkis to go unmolested any longer for inaction will show him to be strong in the face of my weakness. Men whose loyalty wavers will flock to him and subduing him will only become more difficult."

"And yet you wait."

"I sent five men to learn what they could. One is dead and four are missing and I know nothing. I do not wish to march to Greyshield land blind, but if I must, I would do it with more men than I have here. I need the men who left with Isolf. To gather others would take days. Isolf may return at any hour. And I would not leave without knowing if the raiders from Silfravall have been dealt with, or if they might spring up in my wake in search of a far greater prize."

"Vannheim is vulnerable." Aelinvor's expression was unreadable but her voice betrayed something Raef could not name.

"Does this worry you? Do you question your father's desire to wed you to a king whose fist does not grasp his own lands? Your own desire?"

"What is power worth if it does not threaten to slip between our fingers?" Aelinvor arched her back and Raef could see the pulse in her throat beat faster, the pale skin above her neckline mirroring it, as though the rise and fall of kings stirred her blood. "I mean to have what I seek," she said, her voice quiet and fierce. Then she laughed, almost a child filled with delight, and her eyes turned bright. "You see, you cannot fail."

In spite of himself, Raef laughed along with her and felt some of the weight lift from his mind. His good humor did not go unnoticed. Vakre, when the company parted ways under the moon, lingered, a cup of ale still in hand, and they traced the path to a quiet garden, bare in winter, behind the hall. The son of Loki seemed hesitant to speak, but Raef, his spirits still high and Aelinvor's eyes still in his thoughts, ventured to do so for him.

"Speak your mind, Vakre." Raef tossed back the contents of his cup. "I will not bite."

Vakre smiled a little but turned serious again. "Uhtred would part with his daughter for you?"

Raef nodded. "And even if he would not, she would convince him it was his fondest hope. I think it as much her notion as his." Raef took a deep breath, filling his lungs with winter air. The night seemed alive, the stars so close he could reach up and seize them. "What do you think of her?"

"She is fair, that I will not deny."

"To say she is fair is to say a sword is sharp. She is a raven-haired Freyja. I could not ask for a more beautiful woman."

"You mean to do this? Marry her?" Vakre was all surprise.

"I do not see why not. It would honor my first ally above all others who might seek to join their banners to mine."

"Yes, and make you unavailable to the daughters of other lords."

"She seeks power and does not try to hide that. Surely that is to be admired."

"Perhaps. And yet you say nothing of your own heart."

"My heart is not king." Raef relented and looked at Vakre. "This troubles you."

"The decision is yours, but I would not see you choose as a king. Choose as a man."

Raef was quiet for a moment. "I have not yet made up my mind." This seemed to satisfy Vakre, but he was not finished.

"What of Eira?"

The words did not bring a surge of anger, as Raef had expected they might. His good spirits reigned yet. "She will not be returning."

Vakre raised an eyebrow. "And I am glad of it." It was difficult to say, but Raef meant it. "Tell me, though, will Siv follow her?"

"They are not such good friends as that," Vakre said, a slight grin showing teeth in the moonlight.

"No, and as different as Frigg and Freyja."

"But which is which?"

Raef laughed, throwing his head back, his mouth so wide he might catch a fallen star. "Neither one nor the other, but both, and as unknowable as the goddesses themselves." Vakre grinned wider but Raef sobered quickly. "Where can I find Siv? I would speak with her if she will let me."

"Your smith gave her a place to sleep at the forge."

"At the forge? We have room here." The moment Raef said it he knew the fault lay with him. "I have been a poor host. I never offered. And you? Have you been sleeping with the pigs?" Raef tried to smile but knew it lacked conviction.

"Finnolf brought me to one of the common rooms shared by others." Vakre said nothing else.

"We will remedy that. I have treated you ill of late, both of you." Raef was no longer filled with good cheer. The stars, so bright before, now seemed dull and foreboding in his eyes.

"You have much to occupy you, Raef. A king is more than just a man."

"No," Raef said, his voice firm, "make no excuses for me, Vakre. A king is only a man and a man does not treat his friends as I have." He looked Vakre in the eye. "We have walked this path together and you have asked nothing of me, made no demands, only been steadfast and true. At times I have been too blind, too angry, too caught up in my own mind to see it. Isolf means well and he is my family. But you are the brother I would share my blood with." Raef let out an unsteady breath in the wake of the words that had sprung from some place deep within him.

Vakre smiled, though it seemed to reflect inward rather than at Raef. "And you are the brother I would choose. Though," the grin flashed bright, "I do not think my father would commend my choice."

"Nor mine," Raef said. He did not smile. "My father told me once that the children of the gods are not like other men."

"Your father was not wrong."

"He also said he would never name one friend."

"Fathers need not always be right."

"No," Raef said, "no, they do not." Raef exhaled, sending a puff of white vapor into the air. "When this is done, when Vannheim is secure, I will go in search of Hauk of Ruderk. I will scour every cave, every mountain, every glen of Midgard until I find him."

"What of your people? Your warriors? They have named you king and they sing the song of war. They will expect you to meet the Hammerling and Fengar in battle."

"I will not leave my father unavenged, Vakre." Once, Raef might have spoken those words with heat on his breath and anger in his gut. Now he felt only calm certainty and knew that Vakre did not question his resolve. "I would gladly trade what I did not ask for and do not crave in return for the traitor of Ruderk's blood on my hands. Being king means nothing to me."

"And the alliances you have made?"

"Let them band together, let them name Uhtred king, let them go to war under my banner if they wish while I hunt him down, only let me do as I must. It is selfish and negligent, and more than a little rash, I know, but I cannot live another way. I will not."

"You do not have to explain yourself to me, Raef. Only answer this. Will you seek Hauk of Ruderk alone?"

Raef grinned. "And deny you the chance to use that flaming cloak? Never."

ᚱ ᚱ ᚱ

At sunrise, Raef found Siv outside the walls. She was perched on a stone at the edge of the fjord, her hair vibrant in the purple and orange light of morning. When Raef approached, her eyes were closed, and he waited, hesitant to disturb her. But his footfalls had made enough noise in the snow and she opened her eyes and looked over her shoulder at him.

"If I were a deer, I would be long gone," she said, grinning. "Your footsteps are those of a giant." And she hopped from her rock and mimicked a lumbering, stone-footed giant, closing the distance between them with heavy, hulking strides. Raef laughed, but Siv placed a finger over his lips, her eyes beyond him. "There, at last."

Raef turned. The ice bear drank from the fjord, its white coat blending with the snow. Siv watched it, her eyes bright.

"I have watched for him these past three mornings," she said. "Your smith, Hoyvik, he told me men had seen him by the water four mornings past. I wanted to see for myself."

The bear raised its head, looked up and down the shore, then resumed drinking.

"Seldom do they venture so close to the hall," Raef said. "They keep to the high hills in summer and deep valleys of the north in winter."

"He is beautiful. A fine prize for a hunter, but even finer in a moment like this, full of life, a lord in his domain."

Raef watched Siv watch the bear, taking delight in her smile and the joy in her eyes. Their green depths seemed more vivid than he remembered and he caught flecks of gold and blue, calling to mind the skins of the dragon-kin of Alfheim.

"Tomorrow we ride north to confront Tulkis Greyshield, whether Isolf has returned or not," Raef said. "Will you come?"

Siv tore her eyes from the bear. "How could I not?"

"Any number of reasons. Because you long to rejoin your fellow shieldmaidens. Because I have not treated you with the respect you deserve. Because the nine realms are in their last days and this is not where you wish to make your end."

Siv smiled a little. "I will come, Raef."

Her words made him glad but there was little else he might say, and yet he did not wish to return to the Vestrhall. Siv seemed to sense this and, taking his hand, drew him back to her rock. They sat side by side and watched the ever-changing sunlight conquer the waters of the fjord. The ice bear wandered back into the trees.

"See that point that juts out, just there?" Raef pointed to the east where a short cliff, perhaps the height of three men, rose out of the fjord. "I nearly drowned there once. We would jump from the top and then race back to shore. I remember diving in, but when I came up, another boy landed on me. I lost consciousness. They told me later that I was sinking. Two of them lugged me to the shore. I remember waking there, spewing water from my lungs. I was only six. I asked my father if I would have gone to live with the stromkarls, and he laughed and said they would not want the likes of me, but I remember now the relief in his eyes that I had lived." Raef did not know why he told Siv the story.

"Stromkarls are very particular about their victims," Siv said with mock seriousness. "When choosing boys, they only take the best and brightest, those destined for renown, so, yes, you were safe."

Raef laughed. "Did you believe in the creatures we were told about as children? Or were you much too clever for that?" Raef asked.

"I was sure we had a nisse on our farm," Siv said, smiling. "And a very good one, too. I would hide in the barn late at night, determined to catch a glimpse of him, but I always fell asleep and my father would find me, covered in bits of straw, in the morning. He would scold me, but always with a smile." It was the first time Siv had spoken of family to Raef. He found he wanted her to continue.

"Your father sounds like a good man."

"He was. He was no warrior and held no standing among other men, but he worked hard and loved his family, and he always helped those in need." Pride rang out in Siv's voice.

"If he was no warrior, what drew you to the sword and shield?"

"He died when I was nine. My mother and younger brother, too. A fever took them all. My older sister and I were spared. My uncle took us in. He did what he could for us and was not unkind, but I learned quickly that we were a burden."

"Where was your home?"

"I was born in Wayhold, in a valley by the sea. My uncle lived two valleys to the east."

"What happened?" Raef asked, sensing there was so much more to Siv's story.

"A year after my parents died, my sister had just reached her thirteenth year and my uncle began to speak of finding her a husband. He never had the chance." Siv paused, her green eyes now dark with sadness. "The raiders came. They took her and my aunt. They would have taken me, too, had I not hidden in a woodpile. My uncle had three sons. They were slaughtered. When I had the courage to climb out of my hiding place, I found the farm burned, the livestock killed or stolen, my cousins dead, and my uncle lying in a pool of his own blood. He could not speak but I could see the fear in his eyes and, I think, relief that someone had survived. I held his hand until he died." Siv went quiet, her gaze fixed on the water. She blinked. "There, kneeling in my uncle's blood, I made a vow to search for my sister, to become strong enough to take her back. I wandered to the closest village, and there, Frigg took pity on me, for I found a warrior who was willing to teach me what I desired to know. And so I became as you see me today." She looked at Raef and smiled.

"And your sister?"

"Twelve years have passed. I have traveled through many lands, first on my own, then with Ailmaer Wind-footed's band. Then at last

I joined the shieldmaidens just before Eira became our leader. I do not know who the raiders were or where they came from. In all likelihood, my sister is dead, raped and beaten by the raiders and left to die in some lonely place. But if not, I mean to find her. It may be that she lives and is happy, the wife of a strong warrior, the mother of four fine children, with good earth to work with her hands. If so, I only wish to see it with my own eyes. Then I will leave her be."

"And if she is not happy?" Raef almost did not want to ask.

"Then death will come to those who have done this to her." For the first time since she had begun her story, there was fire in Siv's voice, and deadly intent in her calm face.

"Do you linger in Vannheim when your heart has already gone, then?"

Siv smiled again. "I linger in Vannheim because it is a part of the world I had not yet seen. My sister may dwell in some corner of your land." She seemed to understand Raef's growing sense of guilt. She touched his shoulder. "I am here because I want to be here, Raef."

"You do not owe me anything, Siv. I will not keep you here against your will."

"Have you heard nothing I just said? If you held me against my will, you would know it." Her fingers lingered on the fur collar of his cloak. "Twelve years of wandering has not granted me many friends. Ailmaer Wind-footed was good to me, an older brother I never had, but theirs is a brotherhood not easily breached, and so I moved on. With the shieldmaidens, I found a better reflection of myself, and yet," she paused, "even there I was most myself when I was alone." She looked him in the eye. "As I was the day we met. For the first time since my sister was taken, perhaps even since my father died, I have found, here with you and Vakre, something I value as much as the vow I made to the gods."

"You told me once you have not been lonely, but I do not see how this could be the truth."

Siv cocked her head, the corners of her mouth lifting in a smile. "I have been alone, yes, but not lonely. Look around you," she said, a wide gesture taking in the sparkling fjord, the green pines standing tall above the snow, the hills rising up to the cloudless sky. "With all this around me, I am never lonely. The eagle, there, is my brother." The bird soared high above them, a black shape against the bright sky. "The sun, my father. The ice bear is a silent friend, the trees, the valleys, the peaks, all are my constant companions." She looked at Raef, her eyes clear. "And I have you."

Raef could not help but marvel at the woman next to him, her pure joy in the world around her, and the confidence that burned within her. "The gods have done me a great kindness, Siv, in bringing you into my world."

They enjoyed the peace and quiet of the fjord in silence, the rock warmed by the sun even though the air was cold. Only at the sound of horse hooves did Raef stir.

Aelinvor, mounted on a white horse and accompanied by two of her father's men, approached, her dark hair sleek and silky in the sunlight. She pulled her horse to a halt and Raef got off the rock to face her.

"You are out early," she said, her gaze flickering to Siv and then back to Raef. It was so quick, so innocent, Raef might have thought he imagined it.

"As are you, lady."

Aelinvor dismounted, her slender figure draped in voluminous folds of grey wool. She walked to the water's edge. "The fresh air is invigorating, after being shut inside. Will you walk with me?"

Raef found himself looking to Siv before answering Aelinvor. Her eyes twinkled and she looked ready to burst into laughter. Instead, Siv managed a nod. Raef fell in beside Uhtred's daughter and they turned west to venture along the shore. Raef looked once over his shoulder and saw that Siv still sat on the rock, legs crossed.

He was sure her eyes were closed again but a smile lingered on her lips. Aelinvor's hand on his arm drew his gaze forward again, and he helped her step over a fallen log.

They spoke of many things, her home in Garhold, the ship her father had built for her, the brothers she had lost, one to childhood illness, two to the sea. She asked about the gathering and the war, and Raef answered as best he could. She showed great interest in Finndar Urdson, the Far-Traveled, and Torrulf Palesword. She was curious and eager to learn, not shying away from questions. And yet Raef felt there was a question she did not ask.

At last, when they had nearly walked the distance to the walls, Aelinvor stopped and turned to Raef. "Is she a shieldmaiden?"

"Yes." He could not see why Siv would occupy so much of Aelinvor's thoughts.

"You have fought beside her?"

"Yes."

"She does not look very strong."

"Strength can be deceiving. But why do you ask of Siv?" Aelinvor bit her lower lip and Raef could see her youth in that moment. Then the proud woman returned, but it was too late, for Raef understood. "You are jealous?" Raef took Aelinvor's gloved hand in his, feeling unexpected warmth toward this young thing, so sure of herself, so bold, and yet faulted by this one weakness. "Come, little night bird," Raef said, giving her the name without thinking. He tucked her arm into his and they turned and retraced their steps back to her horse. When they reached Siv's rock, the shieldmaiden was gone. Raef returned to the hall with Aelinvor, but he could not help but wish he might stay in the wild with Siv.

# TWENTY-FOUR

RAEF TURNED IN his saddle and looked back at the walls. Winter fog swirled at the base of the timbers, but the rising hill behind the walls and the rooftops were visible in the grey dawn. There was no sunrise this day, only thick, white clouds and pale light brushing against the shadows of the night.

Isolf had not returned, depriving Raef of fifty warriors. But Greyshield could not wait, and so they rode north, leaving twenty men to watch the walls. It was far fewer than Raef would have liked, but he trusted Dvalarr the Crow to hold the walls at all costs, should an attack come in Raef's absence. As Raef's band of warriors crested a small hill, the Vestrhall dropped out of sight, and he turned to the path ahead. Uhtred rode at his side, as was his place. Finnolf and Vakre roamed ahead with a handful of men. Siv was close, Raef knew, though seldom in his sight. She wove between the trees, keeping to the fringes of their column.

Aelinvor remained behind. She had seen Raef off that morning with a smile and a bold kiss on his cheek. Of Uhtred's warriors, half rode north with their lord, the other seven remained to protect Aelinvor. In the event of an attack on the walls, Raef knew he could not count on those seven to assist Dvalarr. Their sole purpose would be to get Aelinvor to safety.

They followed the coast, cutting inland only where the landscape demanded it. It was not the fastest route, but it would allow them to arrive at Greyshield's home from the south, across beaches and a shallow river mouth. The easier land route would have brought them to the eastern edge of Tulkis's boundaries, but that approach was more easily watched. In spring or summer, Raef would have come by the sea, unseen until it was too late, beaching the ships in the dark of night and surrounding Greyshield's home before an alarm could be sounded. But the angry winter seas were treacherous and impulsive, and he did not wish to risk even two of Vannheim's smaller ships for such a short journey up the coast.

On the second day, snow fell from dawn to dusk, sometimes small and swift flakes, sometimes fat, slow ones that left wet smears on Raef's cheeks and melted in his hair. They crept on, seldom out of sight of the sea and never out of reach of its salty scent, and only when they had made camp that night did the snow cease and the stars come out. The night was cloudless and the air frigid. Sea winds blasted at their stone shelter as they took refuge in small caves and crevices along the beach and cliffs. Fires sprang up any-where the men could coax a flame into life and Raef was glad they faced the sea for only a ship out on the waves could see the flames in the night.

Uhtred ducked into the cave Raef had chosen, a grim smile on his face. "I have not seen the sea froth and churn like this yet this winter. Jörmungand must be restless." Uhtred took a seat by their small fire. "But then, the children of Loki are always restless."

Raef looked to Vakre, who stifled a grin and spoke. "I have heard that a son of Loki walks in Midgard."

Uhtred scoffed. "A tale for children."

"They say he has a cloak of fire but does not burn." Vakre's eyes brimmed with laughter and Raef was glad Uhtred's gaze was turned to the fire.

"Loki's children are all monsters. He would never father something so common as a man."

"If you say so," Vakre said, grinning as he took a bite of dried meat. Raef tried not to laugh and was glad when Vakre kept his mouth shut. The truth of Vakre's ancestry had become known to some in the east, and still more had seen his cloak, Loki's cloak, flame to life, a wondrous thing to watching eyes. But if the stories of Vakre Flamecloak had not yet reached the west, Raef was glad. He did not wish to explain to Uhtred why he trusted a son of Loki.

The watches were set. Siv drew the second shift. Raef was still awake when she left their cave to take her place out in the cold and had only slept a little by the time she returned. He watched her stir the fire, drawing out more flames and heat, then settled close to warm herself. Raef rose and draped his blanket over her shoulders. She smiled.

"The wind is biting." She peeled her sheepskin gloves from her hands and held them over the flames.

"Here, let me." Raef took her right hand in both of his and rubbed gently with his thumbs to bring life back into her skin. He did the same with the left and did not let go even after he felt warmth return to her veins. They sat in silence as the fire smoked and spat and gusts of wind threatened their shelter. "You have not asked after Eira." The thought had been with him on the journey north.

Siv looked at him, her eyes tired. "What happened between you and Eira is not for me to know."

Raef made circles on her palm with his thumb, only half aware he was doing so. "Then you will not hear me speak of her again."

Siv yawned. "You should not say such things when they will not hold true. I think your paths will cross again." She leaned back against the cave wall, her gaze not leaving Raef's face. At length, her eyelids closed and Raef watched the rise and fall of her chest slow into the even rhythm of sleep. The dull orange light of the dying fire played across her face, sending shadows dancing. Raef watched and wondered at the song in his heart.

When he awoke, the air was quiet, the winds no more than a soft, salty breeze, the dawn already bright and clear, and his fingers still brushed against Siv's, who slept yet, slouched against the stone in such a manner that would surely bring a sore neck and cramped muscles. Raef fought the urge to wake her and instead left the cave and relieved his bladder. The men were stirring, woken by the cries of gulls, and the horses stamped their feet and snorted frosty breath, eager to stretch their legs.

They would be in sight of Tulkis Greyshield's home by midday, so Raef allowed a morning meal around the fires rather than in the saddle, and set an unhurried pace after they had doused the fires and mounted the horses. Even in winter, the coast thrived, a haven for birds of all kinds and game both big and small could find nourishment closer to the sea than deep in the winter forests.

As they neared the heart of Greyshield land, a strange shape, growing in the distance, caught Raef's eye and he, Vakre, and Siv rode ahead to inspect it.

It was the remains of a ship, the burned, gutted bones of a hull. No more than half remained, the rest washed away. Raef dismounted and kicked one of the beams. It crumbled at his touch, rotted from the damp air and sea spray.

"Strange, to burn a ship," Vakre said.

"An accident, perhaps. Ships are too valuable," Raef said.

"My father told me a story once," Siv said, her voice quiet, as though she had not quite worked out in her mind what she wanted to say. "Two giants strove to win the heart of the beautiful Lisgothmir. One gave her riches and jewels. She turned him away. The other, who lived far away, came to her on his best and biggest ship, a wonder that the gods themselves envied. She thought he meant to make a gift of it, but when he stepped onto the shore, he set it on fire and it blazed for six days and six nights." Siv took her gaze from the charred wood and looked at Raef. "He did this to prove to her that he would never return to his land, that he was there to win her heart, not give her treasures."

"You think someone burned this to show they would not return to the shores they left behind? Show who?"

Siv shrugged. "Themselves? A man becomes desperate when he has no way but forward, when he cannot turn back." She shook her head. "It is only a story. I do not know what made me think of it. Likely it belonged to Greyshield and was wrecked as winter set in."

The host of warriors had caught up, so Raef remounted and continued north, winding along the shore, his thoughts on Siv's story. It troubled him, but he could not have said why.

Confronted with steep headlands rising in front of them, Raef turned his men inland and onto a smoother, gentler approach. They climbed off the beach and into a forest thick with pine, and there, well-concealed from watching eyes, the column drew to a halt. Raef rode onward with only a few warriors at his back, leaving Uhtred to watch the host.

Keeping to the trees, Raef headed north once more, pausing at any sound or movement, until he came within sight of the first of Greyshield's outbuildings, a storage house and a long, low barn for livestock. Pigs, grey, spotted shapes in the snow, were the only moving things in Raef's view, but he could hear sheep. Raef dismounted and handed the reins to the closest warrior, then crept forward for a closer look, Vakre at his shoulder, Siv just behind. When the farmhouse came into view, Raef stopped and waited. Smoke rising into the sky told of life within, but there was nothing to indicate if Tulkis himself was at home. Though the space between the farmhouse and the barn appeared to be no more than a field of snow, Raef knew it was littered with stones and broken foundations, the remnants of a time when the Greyshields ruled Vannheim from a long-forgotten hall. Raef settled into his crouch and waited, determined to be patient.

His leg muscles were burning and his toes frozen when the call of the horse reached his ears. It went unanswered, but moments later five riders emerged from the trees east of the farmhouse. Even at a distance, Raef could see it was Tulkis Greyshield who led them. Raef watched the men dismount, tie the horses, and shut themselves inside the house, the sound of laughter trailing after them. Only then did he rise from the snow and retreat to his horse. Leaving Vakre and Siv to watch should the situation change, Raef and the others returned to Uhtred and the host, speaking not a word until they were well away from the Greyshield farm.

"Greyshield is there," Raef said as he rode up to Uhtred. The other lord tossed his skin of ale to Raef, who took a swallow. "The land is in our favor. We can surround them easily."

"How many?"

"I am certain of five, including Tulkis."

"Could there be more?" Uhtred wiped ale from his beard with his sleeve.

"Perhaps. But the house is not large enough to hold more than twenty. If Tulkis has gathered men to oppose me, he has not done so here."

Uhtred grunted as he mounted his horse. "Clever."

Giving Uhtred, Finnolf, and Yorkell each command over a portion of his warriors, Raef gave instructions for the approach and encirclement of the farmhouse, and then the host moved in on its prey, dark shadows stalking among the trees. Vakre rejoined Raef, reporting that no one had come or gone.

Moving as one, the warriors burst from cover and formed a ring around the farmhouse. Those who had bows knocked arrows on their strings. Spears and axes bristled. For a moment all was quiet but for the stamping of hooves. A cloud passed over the sun. Then Finnolf's voice broke the peace.

"Tulkis Greyshield, you are summoned to answer the Skallagrim in Vannheim." The captain's voice rang out and the cloud scuttled away from the sun as though it fled at the sound. "Come forth!"

Raef's heart beat no more than five times before the door swung open, but it felt far longer. At first, only a shadow filled the doorway, but then a figure stepped out, a hand raised to shield his eyes from the sun. "What is the meaning of this?" Tulkis Greyshield came forward another two steps, his left leg dragging slightly in a limp, and lowered his arm, his gaze finding Raef. Even with the space between them, Raef could see the other man's eyes narrow, could see his shoulders and neck stiffen.

Raef urged his horse forward until he was eight strides from Tulkis. "I come in search of answers, Tulkis."

Other men had filtered out of the house now, and stood behind Tulkis, their faces grim. They were armed with swords and one had a bow, though no steel or arrow was yet shown.

Tulkis gave a small bow, but the courtesy did not mask the scowl on his face. "And I shall give them to you if I can, lord."

"Five men came to your land on my orders. They were no threat to you, but four are missing and one dead."

"The wolves are hungry, lord, and have grown bold. My corner of Vannheim is a wild, dangerous place. Or perhaps it was Rudrak Red-beard. He has grown restless."

"Red-beard is dead, by my hand. He had no part in this." Raef was pleased to see the flicker of unease in Tulkis' eyes.

"I see your mind, Skallagrim. You think me a traitor."

"Are you?"

The arrow was on the string before Raef could flinch, but Tulkis' strong arm came down on the archer's hand, dragging the bow downward until the tip of the arrow was buried in the snow. "No,"

Tulkis growled at the archer, his gaze taking in the many arrows now aimed at him, "you will kill us all." Tulkis straightened and looked at Raef. "My cousin is thoughtless and rash. I am no traitor, lord, and I will prove it to you." He drew a knife and turned as though to plunge it into the chest of his cousin, the man who would have shot at Raef.

"No," Raef shouted, halting Greyshield's arm in mid-swing. "His death will not convince me."

Tulkis lowered the knife, though he looked reluctant. "Very well. Then bind my hands, take me to your hall, and I will swear my oath to you in front of any you would have as witness."

It was an unexpected offer and Raef did not answer right away. Tulkis emphasized the silence by tossing his knife into the snow. He gave a nod to the four men around him and they disarmed themselves. Raef looked over his shoulder at Vakre.

"Take them," he said. Vakre nodded and he led a group of ten warriors forward. They collected the weapons and bound the wrists of the five men, then got them mounted onto their horses, which were then secured to the saddles of five of Raef's men. Through this all, Greyshield said nothing and looked straight ahead, and Raef watched, trying to read the other man's thoughts.

A quick search of the farmhouse and outbuildings revealed no trace of the four missing men, dead or alive, but Raef had one last question for Tulkis before turning south.

"Where is your family, Greyshield?" He knew Tulkis had a wife and children, two sons who had reached fighting age, and two daughters, one still very young.

"Saegertha has gone to visit her ailing mother, and the children with her."

"Even your sons? Are they not too old for such visits?"

Tulkis did not look away from Raef. "They love their grandmother very much."

That Tulkis lied, Raef was sure, but tramping across Greyshield land in an attempt to find the sons would be useless. He gave a nod to Finnolf, who shouted for the warriors to fall in line. Raef waited until the column had filed past, and took up the rear with Siv and Vakre.

"I do not trust him," Vakre said, bringing his horse alongside Raef.

"Nor I, but what can I do? I cannot leave him here, untouched. I cannot kill him, for he has done nothing wrong, violated no oath, and killing him would only turn the minds of other men against me. Bringing him to my hall is what he wants, but I see no other way."

They returned to the Vestrhall by a shorter, more direct route, avoiding the winding coast in favor of the inland hills and valleys. A rear guard stayed alert to the possibility of retribution at the hands of Tulkis' sons and a watch was set that night, but the land around them was peaceful and a farmer was glad to shelter as many of Raef's men from the cold as he could. The family had little to offer, for the winter had claimed half their sheep and an early frost had shrunken their last autumn crop, but Raef's men had more than enough to share. Tulkis and his companions were allowed to join them, for Raef had no cause to punish them, but the five men kept to themselves, spooning their broth in silence.

The farmer's children, a flock of faces ranging from wide-eyed twins who could barely walk to a lean boy of eleven who could not take his eyes off the sword at Raef's side, filled the small house with eager voices as ale was poured and bread passed.

The men were fed in shifts, then sent back out to claim whatever corner of the barn and storehouse they desired. At length, Raef sent Tulkis away, entrusting him to the care of his captain, Yorkell. When the last of the men trickled into the night, leaving Raef, Vakre, Uhtred, and Siv behind, Raef leaned back in his chair, his toes stretched toward the hearth, and allowed himself to relax.

With the men gone, the family settled into its nightly routine. The oldest boy dumped food scraps into a bucket for the pigs while the farmer scolded a younger boy for poking one of the twins until he cried. The mother comforted the red-faced child and spoke to Siv, who was helping the two girls comb their hair.

Raef watched Siv's deft hands untangle the long, loose locks and wondered if this home reminded her of the one she had lost. Siv glanced his way and smiled, a quick flash gone all too soon as she returned to the task at hand.

When the other twin started crying, the mother handed the first off to Vakre, who took the child with surprising ease, finding just the spot to tickle him and turn his tears into fits of laughter. For a moment, Raef could only marvel at how the house could contain the son of Loki and an orphaned, battle-hardened shieldmaiden and still be so full of laughter.

"I would ask you what you think of my daughter, Skallagrim, but I think your thoughts are elsewhere." Uhtred had pulled his chair close to Raef's and leaned in to speak quietly in his ear.

"Your daughter is beautiful," Raef said. But Uhtred was not looking at him. Raef followed the older man's gaze and saw it led to Siv.

"She is. You are not the first man to say this," Uhtred said, looking at Raef now.

"I would be a lucky man if she were my wife. But I have not yet made my decision." Raef's gaze slid back to Siv and her red-gold hair.

"Oh, I think you have." Uhtred's voice was quiet and hinted at a smile. Raef looked back and found himself caught in the blue depths of Uhtred's eyes. He felt heat flush his cheeks. "There is no shame in following your heart, Raef," Uhtred said, speaking now as a father to a son, rather than a lord to a king. "I made no demand, my warriors are yours, marriage or no marriage. If Aelinvor is not the woman you wish to share your life with, I ask only one thing of you."

"Name it."

"That you tell her this the moment we return to the Vestrhall. I would not have her thoughts linger on what has slipped beyond her reach."

"I will." Raef hesitated. "Thank you."

Uhtred smiled and got to his feet, letting out a belch that sent the younger children into peals of laughter. Uhtred pounded his chest with one fist. "Even Thor is no match for me in matters of wind-making," he boasted. More laughter. "But if you will excuse me, good hosts, I think I will retire and refrain from challenging the god of thunder just yet." The farmer tried to insist that Uhtred remain, but the lord of Garhold overruled him, and swept out into the winter night, leaving grinning faces in his wake.

Not long after, Raef excused himself to take a piss. The night was clear and cold, but calm. Not a breath of wind stirred Raef's hair as he rounded the corner of the house to empty his bladder. After checking on the horses, the watch, and Tulkis, Raef returned to the farmhouse to find Vakre out beneath the stars as well.

"These are good people," Raef said. "I will send them wool and food and new sheep when we return to the Vestrhall."

Vakre nodded but was quiet.

"You are troubled?"

"I look at them, that family, poor in wealth but rich in happiness, and I wonder that will become of them when the final battle comes. When flaming Surt stirs from his blazing throne in Muspelheim and marches on Asgard, when Jörmungand raises the oceans and Fenrir breaks free, leading the nine realms into chaos. They are ignorant of the destruction that is at hand, of the numbered days before them, but they deserve a better fate."

"They do."

Vakre looked up at the stars as though he expected to see them fall and go dark at any moment. "Sometimes I think of sharing what I know, what we know. Of warning people." His gaze returned to earth and he shook his head. "But it would not matter in the end, and it would only strike terror into hearts that should be glad."

They were quiet for a moment, neither quite ready to return to the warmth of the farmhouse. "What becomes of the son of Loki when the seas rise and the giants go to war with the gods?"

Vakre shrugged. "The same will befall me as any other man, I think." He met Raef's look. "Except you, son of Einarr. You will not fight beside us at the last battle."

"No. My fate remains in the shadows. And yet I can only think of one thing that I would wish for. That I could stand beside you and Siv, that we might draw our swords together and sing the song of battle one last time."

# TWENTY-FIVE

THE VESTRHALL WAS no longer empty when Raef and his warriors returned. Isolf, his face bright with a wide smile, rode out of the gates to greet them.

"I rejoice at your return, brother. Has Greyshield bent to your will, or is he food for crows?" Isolf's horse pranced in new fallen snow as Raef's company came to a halt.

"Greetings, brother," Raef said. He gestured to Tulkis, whose horse was tethered to Uhtred's. "He comes to give his oath in the Vestrhall, before gods and men."

"Then today is a good day, for I have a gift for you as well."

"I trust the raiders from Silfravall have known my brother's wrath?" Raef urged his horse forward and Isolf fell in beside him to cover the remaining distance to the walls.

"They have, but rather than fall to our swords and spears, they have parted ways with their lord, Harbjorn. I have brought you thirty warriors to join your shield wall." Isolf could not hide the pleasure he took in his accomplishment.

Raef was surprised. "They will renounce their oaths to Harbjorn and make one to me and then fight against their brothers in Silfravall?"

"If it comes to that, yes, they will fight against Silfravall. But they do not think Harbjorn will risk open war for the loss of thirty men."

"Open war will be upon Harbjorn soon enough. The kings will demand his spears or take them by force."

Isolf shrugged. "They wish to be men of Vannheim, now. They wish to follow you. They await you."

Raef's hands clenched on the reins. "In the Vestrhall? You have brought them into my home?" He kept his voice low, not wanting to shout his irritation in front of the warriors.

Isolf frowned. "They have left their weapons at the gate."

"Even so, the Vestrhall is my home, Isolf." Raef urged his horse forward, separating himself from the column. The gates swung open for him and he raced up the hill, jumping to the ground at the base of the stone steps. He heard horses behind him but did not wait for Vakre and Siv to catch up before throwing open the doors of the hall.

Men sat at the long tables. A pig roasted over the open fire pit. Ten armed men of Vannheim were present, standing aloof from the strangers. All conversation and movement ceased at Raef's entrance, and all eyes went to him. A stool scraped against the floor as one man stood, and then all the benches were pushed back and the warriors of Silfravall got to their feet. One by one, they took a knee, just as Vakre and Siv came up behind Raef, Isolf at their heels.

"You see? They swear themselves to you," Isolf said.

Only then did Raef see Aelinvor at the far end of the hall, seated alone at the high table. She came to her feet slowly, her gown a whisper against the floor.

Raef did not trust himself to speak but the hall waited for his word. "You are welcome to Vannheim."

The Silfravall warrior who had stood first rose from the floor and approached, then took a knee again in front of Raef, his disheveled blonde hair hanging over half his face. "I am Lingorm and I speak for these men. We pledge ourselves to Vannheim, lord, and name you our king. We are but thirty in number, but what we lack in numbers we make up for with loyalty."

Isolf thrust a cup of ale into Raef's hand, and gave another to Lingorm. Raef raised his in Lingorm's direction and took a sip. The warrior of Silfravall did the same and his men gave a shout. The formalities done, the Silfravall warriors relaxed. Raef set his barely touched ale on a table and strode the length of the hall, past Aelinvor, and left.

Isolf was on him, but the moment the door closed, Raef rounded on his cousin, his hand shaking as he fought the urge to seize Isolf's shoulder. "You had no right to bring them into my home, into my father's hall. Blood you may be, but lord you are not."

Isolf's face was red with anger. "I did what I judged to be right. Should I have turned them away, sent them back to Harbjorn with resentment festering in their hearts? You wish to win your neighbors to your side, and I have done so."

"Thirty men," Raef shouted. "Thirty men do not make an alliance. And they were raiding my land, Isolf, burning farms, raping women. What loyalty can they bring me, they who change lords so easily? I never intended to ally with Harbjorn and his raiders."

Isolf was quiet for a moment. "Had you but shared your plans," he began.

"But I did not and you acted beyond your right."

The anger drained from Isolf's face. "Then I ask you to forgive me, brother, and know that I only did so with you in mind, with Vannheim in mind."

Raef stared into Isolf's eyes, still trembling. "I understand," he managed to say. He could understand, but he could not remain in Isolf's presence a moment longer and took refuge in the solitude of his chamber.

It was Aelinvor who sought him out as the day turned into twilight. She stood just outside the doorframe, as though she hoped to draw him out. "My father wants to know if you intend to feast the men of Silfravall and if Greyshield should join."

"Let Isolf do the honors of the feast. I have no stomach for it." Raef returned to his seat by the window. The eastern horizon had faded into purple and grey. "No, no." Raef sighed. "I will do it. I will not insult them because Isolf has displeased me. Tell your father to begin preparations. And that Tulkis must be included. He will give me his oath this night." Aelinvor nodded and turned to go but Raef remembered his promise to Uhtred. "Wait." Her dress swished against her legs as she halted and looked back. Raef beckoned her closer. "Come here."

Raef rose to his feet and reached out to take her hand as she approached, then thought better of it. Her blue eyes were dark, an ocean at dusk, and her face half in shadow. Her hair shone in the light of the single candle. He tried to find words that might suffice. "You are a lovely creature, Aelinvor, and any man should be honored to call you wife. But I am not that man. We are not going to be married."

He could see the disappointment flicker into her face and in the way she lowered her gaze and then, with a swallow, raised it again to meet his eyes. Whatever else she felt, she hid it well, no child to pout and cry despite her youth. She smiled a little. "I am sorry you could not see our future together. I saw it laid before our feet as clearly as I see you now in front of me," she said. "But a king does as he chooses."

"Bold to the last, little night bird," Raef said, almost smiling himself. She bowed her head and left him alone with his thoughts.

Raef started a fire in his hearth and called for a bath. He lounged in the iron tub until steam no longer rose from the water, relishing the chance to clean the grime of travel from his skin. Dripping, he stepped out and wrapped himself in a fur, then poured a cup of mead and drank while letting the air and heat of the fire dry him. His toes curled against the still cold stones of his chamber floor, but soon his lower legs were burning with the heat of the flames and Raef settled into a chair away from the fire to finish his mead before dressing.

The honeywine was soothing and began to melt away the raw edges of Raef's anger toward Isolf. His cousin had acted rashly, but with good intent, and though he might have to consider carefully what future responsibilities he would trust Isolf with, there was no point in berating the man further. Better to move on and make the best of the situation Isolf had created.

The thrum of noise from the hall had grown loud as the warriors awaited his presence and Raef knew he could put it off no longer. Dressing quickly in fresh clothes, Raef tried to be glad of the night's events, of thirty new warriors to add to his shield wall, of Tulkis Greyshield kneeling before him for all to see.

The hall came to life at his entrance. The warriors of Silfravall were clustered around the middle of the long tables, their unfamiliar faces turned toward him with cries for Vannheim. His own men filled the remainder of the benches and cheered as he approached the high table and accepted a cup of ale from Uhtred.

"Men of Vannheim, of Silfravall, and of Garhold," Raef shouted, "remember this night, for this is the night we become a band of brothers. Soon all the world will tremble before our roaring cry of war." He raised his cup high. "To victory."

The very air seemed to shiver as the warriors echoed Raef, their voices sure to reach Asgard itself. From the side of the hall, Finnolf prodded Tulkis Greyshield forward. The hall quieted and all eyes watched Tulkis limp to the center of the hall. He took a knee before the high table, and Raef could see the action pained him. Tulkis fought back a grimace.

"See what I have already given you, lord?" Tulkis said, gesturing to his left leg. "A leg, ruined while fighting under your banner at the battle of the burning lake."

"Yours was not the only wound sustained, Greyshield. Come, is this not what you wanted? To kneel before me in my hall and give me your oath? Speak your words."

Tulkis looked to Finnolf, who handed him a small knife. His eyes fixed on Raef, Tulkis drew the blade across his palm and made a fist, letting three drops of blood fall to the floor before speaking. "I, Tulkis Greyshield, swear by the shaft of the Allfather's spear, by the heartwood of great Yggdrasil, and by the blood of my sons, to live and die in service of Skallagrim, king. May Thor strike me down a thousand times if I am disloyal."

The oath rang out and Raef nodded in acceptance of it. Tulkis rose and the feast began in earnest. Of those sitting at the high table, only Uhtred was in good spirits. Aelinvor, seated next to her father, ate, drank, and smiled, giving every appearance of happiness, but Raef was not fooled. Her laughter was too bright and her eyes did not smile along with her mouth. Isolf, on Raef's left, was quiet, and spent much of the meal refilling his cup. Raef could not be sure if his cousin was sulking, or merely trying to keep the attention away from himself. Raef wished for Vakre and Siv but their faces were not among those growing red with drink in the hall and he did not blame them for their absence.

Raef endured the feast for as long as he could and left once there was no danger of insulting anyone. A hearty rendition of an old fighting song had just broken out as he slipped away into the night. He was weary, but not ready for sleep, and his feet took him down the hill, winding through the village, until he reached the shore. The pair of men watching the ships and the water entrance nodded at his approach and Raef strode down the length of one of the docks until all that was before him was the dark fjord.

The night was dark and quiet, the gentle lapping of the water against the shore the only sound to reach Raef's ears. One of Vannheim's smaller ships had been brought over from its winter home down the fjord, ready to carry word to Garhold if necessary, and Raef climbed aboard, wishing for a moment that he was out at sea, a stiff breeze in his face and the fierce sun dazzling the waves, far from the reach of Tulkis Greyshield. He looked west, where the sun had disappeared, and saw the sea road stretch out before him, saw storms and wide open skies, saw gulls lead him to strange shores. The dream of such a journey, long buried, reared up, and Raef would have given much to feel an oar beneath his hands once more, to sweat and row and then at last catch the wind in the sail. But the sea road was not his fate.

Raef walked up to the prow of the ship, running his hand along the smooth wood as he went, then climbed up and perched beside the dragonhead, whose black eyes stared unblinking at the fjord, as if it, too, dreamed of the open water. Raef put his hand on the beast's long neck, his fingers remembering the smooth skin of the dragon-kin in Alfheim, the way the wings unfolded just before flight. They were not much alike, he saw now, the wooden image and the full-blooded creature. If he ever had a chance to build a ship, he would give his dragonhead sunset eyes. The likelihood of that was slim, he knew, for winter was not the time for building ships and unyielding fate bore down on Midgard.

Raef stared out across the water, the blind wooden dragon his only companion, and before his eyes, the dark waters of the fjord began to glow, faint at first, a hint of green. Raef raised his eyes to the sky and watched, his breath caught in his throat, as the sky above Vannheim came alive with swirling blues and dancing greens.

It did not last long, and soon the sky was nothing but stars and darkness, but Raef could not doubt the beauty he had seen. What the aurora of Alfheim was doing in the Midgard sky, he could not say. He could only think of Finnoul, brave Finnoul, and her dream for the future.

# TWENTY-SIX

THE SUN, NEWLY risen, shone in Raef's eyes as he surveyed the bloody scene outside the armory, crimson stark against snow. Finnolf had found the warriors at dawn. One was slumped against the armory wall, the other was face down in the snow. Raef used the toe of his boot to lift the corpse by the shoulder and turn the dead face to the sun.

"Brogund, lord," Finnolf said, identifying the Vannheim warrior. "He was Thorald's brother." Raef frowned. Thorald had been a good captain, his father's right arm and Raef's, too, before falling to Fengar's army in Solheim. Thorald deserved a brother who might carry on their family name with honor and pride, not one who would bleed to death after a drunken quarrel.

"And the other?" Brogund's opponent in the fight had the badge of Silfravall worked into his belt, a silver stag. He had been stabbed in the gut.

"Lingorm has named him Freyvind."

"Do we know what they fought about?"

Finnolf shrugged. "They argued when leaving the hall. Yorkell heard something about a wager. Perhaps one refused to honor it."

Raef squinted into the sun to look at his young captain. "Be on your guard, Finnolf. These deaths may spark something greater.

See that there is no further violence. And get this mess cleaned up." Finnolf nodded and left just as Vakre and Siv arrived.

"A sour way to begin with Lingorm's men," Vakre said.

Siv knelt and pried open Brogund's stiff fingers, withdrawing a gold ring from his grasp. "Perhaps this was the cause." She handed it to Raef.

It was a fine piece. If either man had been foolish enough to offer it up in a wager, he was right to lose it. But not so fine to be worth dying for. Raef tossed it to the waiting guard, who snatched it from the air, a grin on his face.

Raef looked to Vakre and Siv. "I do not wish to loiter in my own hall today. Will you hunt with me?"

They rode east, taking to the hills until they reached a tiny lake, a blue gem set among the trees, the shore home to a long, low barn and a single snow-capped house where Finnolf had spent his childhood. The captain's father and mother still lived there with their youngest child, an eager girl of ten with a fondness for brushing horsetails and tying flowers in manes. Her father, who bred hunting dogs and horses, was accustomed to Raef's visits and waved from the barn door as the three of them wound through the trees to reach the lake.

"Any good game today, Kolbrand?" Raef called as he dismounted.

Finnolf's father shook his head. "Nothing, lord." He strode through the snow to meet them. "A large herd of deer came through yesterday, though. Set the dogs off. Might not have gone far. But with the fresh snow," Kolbrand shrugged, "could be hard to track."

Raef nodded and then grinned as Finnolf's sister burst out of the house. She dashed into the snow, stopping only when she was close enough to press her face to Raef's horse's nose.

"Am I to watch the horses, father?" she asked, breathless.

Kolbrand smiled at his daughter. "He has not asked yet."

The girl turned her large brown eyes up to Raef, who laughed.

"What would I do without you, Tolla?" He leaned in close and whispered in her ear. "This one thinks he can fly, so keep a close eye."

Tolla nodded, her solemn face betrayed by a twinkling in her eye.

Raef ruffled her hair and then went through his hunting gear to be certain he had what he needed before they left the horses under Tolla's care. Vakre and Siv did the same, securing knives and bows and a bit of food to sustain them through the day.

"You should visit in the spring, lord," Kolbrand said as Raef checked the bowstring coiled in a pouch at his belt. "The foals will be good this year. I can feel it."

"You know I cannot resist your horses, Kolbrand," Raef said, the words out of his mouth before he remembered that there would not be a spring, that there would not be foals to birth and raise. He kept his smile fixed to his face. "We will return before dark."

Kolbrand nodded and Raef turned to go as father and daughter led the horses to the barn, a song on Tolla's lips and her fingers twisting a hunk of mane into a braid even as she walked.

On foot now, Raef turned north and they trekked up higher into the hills, looking for signs of the deer Kolbrand spoke of. They found snow, broken only by the tiny footprints of birds, and heard squirrels chastising them from the safety of tall pines, but nothing worthy of the hunt and so they rested in a grove of bare birch trees and ate the cheese, dried apples, and carefully wrapped bread that had still been warm from the oven when Darri, the old kitchen woman, had handed it to Raef that morning.

"Was there snow in the other realms, Raef?" It was Siv who asked the question. She was perched on a fallen log, her legs crossed under her. She took a drink of water from her skin and handed it to Vakre.

Raef had not spoken of his journey to Alfheim or Jötunheim since the day he had learned of Svanja's death. Siv and Vakre knew only what they had heard in that telling but Raef found his reluctance to speak of it had faded.

"No. Alfheim was in early summer. Everything was lush and green, flowers everywhere. Except for the barren place. There the earth was dry and hard, a wound wrought by giants in a nearly forgotten war."

"And Jötunheim?"

Raef did not have to reach far to dredge up the sights and smells of Jötunheim. "A dead place," he said, his voice quiet. "But not winter's death. True death. The very air was poison and the sun was dull, as though all the brightness had been sucked from it."

Siv nodded and was still for a moment, the cheese forgotten in her hand. "What was the Allfather like?"

Raef opened his mouth and found the words he was about to speak to be a lie. He hesitated, his eyes on Siv, then spoke. "Old. Weary." The words were heavy on his tongue. Raef shifted his gaze to Vakre. "Sad. There was power in him, yes, and terrible strength, of will, of mind. He was just as he is in the stories we learned as children. And yet so much more." Raef took a drink from his own skin. "At least, that is what I saw. It may have been nothing more than a dream. I was not," Raef paused, "my mind was not well."

Vakre stirred. "You do not believe it was a dream."

"No."

"Nor do you wish you had accepted the Allfather's offer." This from Siv.

Raef smiled a little. "No. But I do wish I might understand why. Why I landed on Alfheim's shores. Why, then, did I go on to Jötunheim? And how? The giants may have a way into Midgard, but only the gods can traverse the nine realms at will." Raef shook his head. "None of it should have happened. I should have died at sea, swept overboard by tall winter waves, or dashed against the rocks of an unfriendly coast. Or better yet, I should have died in Axsellund. None of it makes sense."

"Might the Allfather be mistaken? He told you no god had led you on your journey," Siv said, her gaze flickering to Vakre, "but Loki breathes deception as we do air."

"Odin knew Loki was the Deepminded. I must believe he would know the truth of this as well."

Vakre broke in. "Perhaps you were not meant to die." He frowned. "Perhaps you were meant to disappear, just as you did. Death is final. A body is final. But absence is something altogether different. It breeds confusion, disorder, uncertainty."

Siv asked the question on Raef's tongue. "To what end?"

"Rudrak Red-beard and Snorren Thoken might have wished for my absence, but they would have killed me and made the world know it."

"And Greyshield?" Vakre asked. "Would he have done the same?"

Raef could not say with any certainty. "He might have understood the power to be found in disorder, but I cannot even prove he killed those five men and he has made no overt action against me."

"Whoever cast you off in that boat may not have wanted your body found, but surely they expected you to die. Perhaps he thought he had more time."

"And then there was Isolf. No one who wanted the Vestrhall could have anticipated his arrival." Raef found his appetite had diminished and he tucked the uneaten bread back into his pack.

"And still there are others who might have desired your death but never with an eye on the Vestrhall as a prize," Siv said. She, too, was no longer eating and her gaze, when it met Raef's, was troubled. The names were left unspoken but they were loud and clear in Raef's mind. The Hammerling. Fengar.

Vakre got to his feet. "I do not think we will find answers here."

They abandoned the birches and pushed onward. Siv soon

spotted recent deer tracks that led further east, and not long after they crested a rise to find a herd meandering down a bald slope. The open ground was a challenge, but the herd was not yet alert to their presence, giving them an advantage. Raef exchanged looks with Vakre and Siv, and they separated. Raef crept to the right, taking the steep descent head on, while Siv held the middle ground and Vakre followed the shoulder of the hill to the left so he might get ahead of the herd.

As he watched Vakre drop out of sight, Raef slid down through the snow until he reached a knob in the slope that provided some cover. Peeking over, Raef saw the herd tense, heads up, tails flicking. Their attention seemed to be on something further down the hill. Raef watched, his breath even and slow. At last the herd began to move again, but now they traversed across the hill, rather than angling down into the valley. Raef crawled forward, trying to close the distance to the herd. When he came within easy bowshot, Raef stopped and drew the bow over his shoulder, staying pressed to the hill, and knocked an arrow on the string.

Raef took a deep breath of cold air and let it out, then in one swift motion, he got to one knee, drew, and loosed. His aim was true. The arrow sailed, struck home, and then he heard the snarl behind him.

Scrambling to his feet, Raef spun just in time to knock away the leaping lynx with his bow. The large cat landed, digging into the snow with its claws to keep its balance, and came at Raef again. He dodged and drew the axe from his belt as the cat crouched for another attack, but then an arrow pierced its neck and it slumped to the ground, one last snarl escaping from between its teeth. Raef looked up to see Siv, still far away, lowering her bow.

The herd was long gone, racing down into the valley and the safety of the trees, but Raef's kill remained along with another deer that had fallen to Vakre in the moment the herd fled. Raef approached the lynx, ready to end its dying if it yet clung to life. There was no need. Siv's arrow had severed a large artery, killing it instantly.

Siv approached and knelt beside the cat, placing a hand on its head. "Her den must be close, or she would not have attacked you."

They followed the lynx's tracks through the snow, Vakre catching up to them as they went, and came to a ledge protruding out of the hillside. In its shelter were slabs of broken rock that formed a half moon, shielding a pair of lynx cubs wrestling in the dirt. They skittered away to the far corner of the den at the sight of Raef, but peered out at him with wide eyes, curiosity mixing with fear.

"They are smaller than they should be," Vakre said. "She birthed late." The cubs were lanky and long-limbed, but lacked the muscles and strength they would need to hunt and survive on their own.

Siv looked at Raef and then Vakre, then drew a knife from her belt. "I will do it. It was my arrow that took their mother." She stepped forward and prepared to crouch down under the ledge when Raef laid a hand on her shoulder.

"Wait."

"I will not leave them here to die of starvation."

"Perhaps they need not die." Raef returned to his deer and slung it over his shoulder. When he reached the den again, he dropped it in the snow and started skinning it. At first, the cubs remained hunched in their corner, but the smell of fresh meat made their noses twitch and one, then the other, crept to the edge of the den and watched Raef with hungry eyes. The skin removed, Raef carved a hunk of flesh from the doe's shoulder and tossed it at the cubs' feet. They jumped back and then stretched their necks out, ears quivering. The larger of the two pounced on the meat, sunk her teeth in, and dragged it back to safety. The cubs tore into the flesh with eager growls.

"One meal is good, Raef, but what of tomorrow? And the day

after? Will you butcher a deer for them every day?" Vakre leaned on his bow and watched the cubs fight over the final bite.

Raef rose. "No, you are right." He heaved the rest of the deer carcass onto his shoulder and began to climb the hill. He did not look back, but at length he could hear Siv and Vakre follow. They had begun the descent on the other side of the hill, retracing the path that would take them back to the lake, when Raef saw the cubs dash into the closest trees on his left. He stopped. The cubs did the same and crouched low, only their eyes and ears visible above the snow that came halfway up Raef's calf. Keeping his gaze on the black-tufted ears, Raef continued on. The cubs mirrored him, the larger female leading the way, the smaller male on her heels. They kept their distance, careful never to come closer than twenty paces, but their first true hesitation came when they reached the lake and caught sight and scent of the horses and dogs on Kolbrand's land.

The cubs hunkered down behind a berry bush and watched as Raef and Vakre loaded the deer onto the backs of their horses. Tolla was delighted and insisted that Raef take the cubs home to the Vestrhall.

"They are already farther from home than they have ever been," Raef said, plucking a twig from her honey-colored hair. "But then, they have followed us this far. We will see." She grinned and climbed onto her pony. She would accompany them back to the Vestrhall and spend a few days with her older sister in the village.

The cubs did not move as Raef and the others rode away from the lake. He looked once over his shoulder and saw the female watching them, but then he lost her in the trees. They might die, or they might survive. Perhaps Freyja would be kind to them, for all men knew the lynx was dear to her.

They had made the final descent out of the hills and the Vestrhall was in sight when Finnolf's sister let out a shriek. Raef spun his horse, reaching for his bow, but froze when he saw the female cub bound out of the trees. She slid to a halt when she saw them watching her, but then, to Raef's astonishment, she trotted forward until she was far closer to them than she had been before. Raef scanned the trees for her brother and the cub seemed to do the same.

"A brave little thing," Vakre said, grinning. "Her brother seems to lack the courage." But no sooner had they turned the horses back to the west than Raef spotted a smaller figure slink out of the trees and scurry to catch his sister. They continued in this manner back to the Vestrhall, a strange procession, the male cub stopping often and murmuring plaintively, and then carrying on when his sister chattered at him.

As they neared the gate, even the bold female came to a halt, ears swiveling as she processed a new world of sounds and scents.

"They will never pass through the gate," Vakre said. "Nor should they. Let me see if I can draw them into the trees there." He gestured to the west and north, where the hills hugged the far side of the walls. The pine forest was dense there, and the steep slopes and hidden bowls between the Vestrhall and the sea were rich with rabbits and other small game. Raef nodded and Vakre took the partially butchered deer carcass from behind his saddle. The female cub latched onto its scent and followed Vakre with eager steps. The male, far more cautious, slunk after. Raef watched as Vakre and the cubs followed the curve of the wall and then disappeared.

After accompanying Tolla to her sister's house, Raef and Siv began to climb the hill, their horses in tow, stopping to greet Hoyvik the smith at his forge. A guard from the gate caught up to them there.

"Lord," he shouted, out of breath, "a messenger from Bergoss is here." Raef exchanged a look with Siv, then handed his reins to the guard.

"I will see him at the gate. Take the horses to the stable," Raef said.

The messenger was armed with axe and sword. A short sword and broad shield hung from his horse's saddle, and at least two knives were nestled in his belt. He waited outside the gate, head held high, not looking at the four Vannheim warriors, Finnolf among them, who, suspicious of the stranger bristling with weapons, watched with narrowed eyes, their fingers wrapped tight around their own weapons.

Raef slid past his men, placing a hand on Finnolf's shoulder as he went. Siv followed. The stranger from Bergoss continued to stare straight ahead as Raef approached.

"Greetings," Raef said.

"I come from Bergoss." There was no salutation, no show of respect for Raef's authority.

"What does Sverren have to say?" Raef opened his palms up to the sky, skin stained with the blood of the doe.

"Only this. Bergoss will never kneel to Vannheim." The warrior puffed out his chest as though his strength alone could defend his lord and home.

The words came as no surprise, not after setting eyes on the warrior-messenger. "He pledges to the Hammerling, then? Or is it Fengar who has swayed Sverren?"

"Sverren Red-tail chooses no king." Pride shone on his face. "Bergoss will kneel to none."

"Then Bergoss will be obliterated," Raef said, letting his anger show for a single instant. He stepped closer to the man and lowered his voice. "The fire of three kings and the rage of three hosts will descend upon Bergoss and every man, woman, and child will be put to the sword. Your land will be a ruin, an empty, barren place, bereft of all life." He was pleased to see apprehension in the warrior's eyes. "Be gone. Before I choose to send your head back to Sverren."

The warrior did not hesitate to climb back into his saddle. He put his boots to the horse and raced away. Raef watched until he was out of sight, swallowed by the wilderness.

Finnolf and the other warriors were pleased with their lord's response, he could see. They grinned and made lewd gestures at the retreating rider, speaking of the death and sorrow they would bring to Bergoss. Siv was quiet.

Raef turned his back on the gate and walked to the fjord, his mind a muddle of thoughts. A light snow started to fall, the flakes soft on Raef's cheeks, the waters of the fjord grey and calm under a bleak sky. Raef reached the shore and clambered onto a rocky shelf that leaned out over the water. He tried to think of his father, to gather wisdom from Einarr, and determine what his next course of action should be, but he could conjure no more than his father's image, and even that was rimmed in shadow.

A boot scuffed on rock behind him and Raef turned to see Siv.

"Not the time for a swim, I think," she said as she came to stand beside him. Raef could not help but smile. "But then, perhaps kings have odd bathing habits." She turned serious. "Those were strong words."

"Words are only words. Sverren would be a fool to expect nothing less from me."

"Sverren is bold to refuse to kneel to any. Though if he is brave, or mad, I cannot say."

Raef put a hand on Siv's shoulder. "I do not wish to speak of Sverren Red-tail, or Bergoss, or the war." His voice was quiet and he looked into her eyes, those green eyes that had become a part of him. She did not look away. "They are far away. But you, you are here, Siv, and that is all that matters to me." He leaned in, eyes still locked with hers, and kissed her. There was no more sky, no cold air, no birds singing in the trees, not even rocks beneath his feet. Raef knew only the feel of her lips on his and the sensation that raced across his skin. He was fire, he was air, he was life itself, and every breath was joy. He drew back, knew he was grinning like a child, and did not care. Siv grinned, too, and they both laughed, then her arms went around his neck and she kissed him again. Raef held her close and when the kiss ended, he pressed his forehead to hers and their fingers entwined at their sides.

If there were words, Raef could not find them, and in not speaking, found he did not need them.

The snow fell, faster and thicker now, catching in their hair and coating their shoulders. Raef tapped his thumb on Siv's nose, then murmured in her ear. "I could toss you in the water."

Siv laughed. "Try."

"I would have to jump in after you, you see, to save you."

"Is that so?"

"And then we would be soaking wet. And cold. And we would come down with a chill. Perhaps even fever."

"So you will spare me, for the sake of your own health?"

Raef made a show of deliberating. "Yes, I think so." Then without warning, he seized her at her waist and threw them both off the edge. They tumbled, then splashed into the fjord in a tangle. Raef surfaced and shook water from his hair as Siv sputtered, laughing and wiping water from her eyes.

"I thought you were wary of stromkarls," she said, grinning.

Raef laughed, then pulled her close and gave her a quick kiss. They swam to shore, weighed down by their heavy, waterlogged cloaks. Siv was shivering but she never lost her smile as they raced back to the gate and up the hill, oblivious to the onlookers. Raef skidded to a halt in front of his chamber, his expression serious as Siv nearly collided with him, her wet boots slipping on the floor.

"You are wet. And cold."

She rolled her eyes at him. "Am I?"

"Let me remedy that." And he pulled her into the chamber after him.

# TWENTY-SEVEN

I T WAS VAKRE who came knocking when twilight began to settle, when long purple shadows started to creep across the snow, when the birds grew quiet and the stars emerged. Raef, half dressed, opened the door.

"One of Finnolf's men has come in from the hills. You should hear what he has to say," Vakre said.

The hall was quiet but for the sound of Raef's footsteps and the crackle of the fire. A single man, hooded, with cloak pulled tight, waited at the bottom of the steps. Isolf and Uhtred of Garhold stood to the side, watching Raef with keen eyes. Vakre and Siv followed and waited by the high table. The man cast off his hood and went to his knee in front of Raef.

"Rise. You have been watching the hills for trouble?"

"Yes, lord. I am Urlach, son of Farold, and I have come from my father's home."

"And what have you seen?"

"Riders, lord, twenty riders. They bear a banner of black and gold. They will not be far behind me."

Raef thanked and dismissed Urlach, then poured himself a cup of mead. "The Hammerling," he said. "Too small for a war party."

"Could the Hammerling be seeking peace?" Isolf asked.

"I do not know. In his mind, I am an oath breaker. I do not think he would forgive that." It was more than an oath that had passed between Raef and Brandulf Hammerling. The Hammerling had spared Raef's life when he had every right to claim it. Raef looked to Siv and Vakre and knew they were thinking the same. "I will meet them outside the gates. Isolf, find Finnolf and see that he has thirty men, armed like Thor himself, ready and waiting."

Raef returned to his chamber and gathered his sword and fur cloak. Siv secured a pair of knives to his belt for him, then tightened the end of her braid and armed herself. Raef watched her run a finger along the edge of her axe blade, then stepped close and kissed the back of her neck as she placed the axe at the small of her back. The fine hairs on her neck stood up at his touch.

"The war may yet be far away, but the Hammerling's envoy is close," she said, turning to face him.

Raef wrapped his arms around her and held her close. "I know," he murmured into her hair. He took a deep breath and released her. "There. I am ready."

A line of torches blazed outside the gate, tall ones, thrust into the snow and flickering beneath the dark sky. The warriors Raef had requested waited, Finnolf at their head. Raef was surprised to see Aelinvor with her father. She did not look at him but kept her eyes forward. Isolf lingered near the gate, his hair flaming in the light of the torches. Ten of his own men stood with him

They waited. The warriors stamped their feet to keep warm. Raef stood shoulder to shoulder with Vakre and looked back, finding Siv's dark figure at the top of the wall, bow at the ready, the western sky a faint glow behind her.

They heard the riders before they saw them, and then dark shapes came to the edge of the circle of light, horses snorting, faces in shadow. Only one came closer, and he dismounted, then shed his hood. Raef knew that face.

"I seek Raef Skallagrim, lord of Vannheim."

"You have found him." Raef took two steps forward.

"Greetings, lord," he began, but Raef cut him off.

"I know who you are. I remember you. We met at the gathering. You came to my father's tent on behalf of the Hammerling. Now you come to me. But the last time we met, you did not give me your name."

"I am Edvard."

"You are no warrior. Nor farmer. You were with us when we drove south into Solheim, but not when we traveled north again to meet the Palesword. Tell me, Edvard, what are you and what place do you hold with the Hammerling?" Edvard was quiet, his expression resentful. "Answer me, tell me why the Hammerling trusts you to speak for him when you do not fight beside him in the shield wall?"

"Must a man fight to prove his worth? I do not carry a sword. Does that make me unworthy to speak to you?"

"No. Far from it. I have known many good men and women who do not carry swords. They work the earth in spring, reap the harvest in fall, and their labor feeds us through the winter. They brave the fickle seas to bring us fish. They cut wood to fuel our fires. They do honest work. Do you do honest work, Edvard?"

"I do as the Hammerling bids."

Raef understood at last. "Because you want to rule Finngale after his death. Am I wrong?" Edvard's face, wreathed in shadows as it was, had grown dark. "You are his son, his first-born, but born at the wrong time. And you watch him, your father, raise up his other sons, those boys, and you do what you think you must to raise yourself in his eyes."

"What difference does it make to you, what I am?" Raef could hear the anger, the snarl in Edvard's voice.

"It makes no difference. Except that I have stripped you of what dignity you have mustered, of the strength you hoped to show me. You might as well be standing there naked, such is the position you are in. And that makes all the difference. Now, tell me, what does the Hammerling have to say?"

Edvard was quiet and Raef could see him swallow back his pride and anger. "He wishes to come to an understanding."

"Not peace, then, but a truce. That we might fight Fengar together. And when Fengar is dead, we will go to war."

"He did not say."

"No, but that is what lies in his heart, Edvard. There is no other way." Raef turned to Finnolf. "Give them the guest right. Then we will talk."

Bread and ale were brought, and Raef retreated to Vakre's side to wait while a pair of servants distributed the symbols of hospitality, the bond between host and guest, to Edvard and the nineteen other riders.

Raef took his share and held his cup in the air. "Drink with me and no harm will come to you while you are my guest." Raef took a swallow. "You," he said, looking to Edvard, "you and I will speak more." He began to turn back toward the gate at the same moment that some of those that followed Edvard stepped into the torchlight. A single face seemed to leap out of the shadows. Raef froze, his heart pounding, hammering in his chest.

"Murderer!" he shouted, his hand going to his sword.

Hauk of Ruderk did not shrink away from the light that had revealed him, but looked at Raef with steady eyes.

"I am your death!" Raef screamed, his voice hoarse with fury. He drew his sword but Vakre put a heavy hand on his arm.

"No, Raef, you cannot."

Raef shrugged him off, but Vakre grabbed on and held him back. Uhtred came forward and did the same. "He is responsible for my father's death. I will have his blood." Raef lurched forward half a step and saw Eira step out from behind Hauk. He heard a roar of anger and knew it was his own.

"You gave him the guest right, Raef. I will not let you violate the thing that is most sacred to the gods," Vakre said.

"The gods can rot," Raef shouted, trembling with anger, straining still against the arms that held him. "Do you deny what you have done?"

Hauk of Ruderk shook his head, the calm in his face infuriating Raef further. "I am what you say I am, Raef, son of Einarr."

Raef lunged forward, but still he was held back. "Do not speak his name!"

Vakre's eyes loomed close and Raef could feel heat coming off the son of Loki. There were flames in his eyes, and they did not reflect the torches. "I will not let you stain yourself for him. You will kill him, and you will keep your honor. But not this night." Beyond Vakre's face, Raef could see Hauk of Ruderk looking on, a satisfied smile on his face. Eira's features were impassive. "Trust me, Raef. You must trust me."

Raef's heart screamed for vengeance and death, though his mind knew Vakre spoke the truth. He hesitated, and then a shout broke through the night air and chaos reigned.

The attackers came from the north and the shadow of the wall, swift riders on horseback, steel flashing in firelight. Men were dying. His men. Raef ducked and rolled away from a blow aimed at his head. His sword arced out and caught the horse's back legs, sending the animal tumbling over its own neck. The rider flew out of the saddle and Raef descended on him with a savage swing that split open his chest. He whirled, drawing out his axe, unsure where the next attack would come from, and saw Edvard, fear on his face, scramble onto his horse. The other Hammerling men did the same, though one was pierced with an arrow that sailed out of the night and took him in the throat. Hauk of Ruderk caught Raef's gaze and then he was gone, urging his horse away, Eira close behind.

But there was no chance for pursuit. Raef's warriors were besieged on both sides, caught between a press of men and horses. Only Uhtred, Vakre, and Raef were free from it. The screaming continued, and Raef, to his horror, saw smoke rising over the walls and knew that his people were dying. He scanned the wall for Siv but had no time, for a warrior was on him. Raef deflected the slicing sword, spun, and hacked upward into the man's ribs with his axe.

"Isolf," Raef shouted, for he had seen his cousin by the gate. Isolf, his face bright in the light of the torches, did not move, and his ten warriors beside him might as well have been stones. "Isolf!" Raef was screaming now. He lashed out with his sword at the closest attacker and finished him off with his axe. "You swore!" Through the smoke of the torches, Raef saw Isolf smile and give a command to the ten men beside him. They entered the fray, and Raef did not need to watch to know that his men were their targets.

Finnolf staggered out of the battle, his face spattered with blood. He screamed for Raef to get to safety, but there was no safety. The gates were closed now, and barred by Isolf. Another figure joined him and Raef recognized Tulkis Greyshield. His limp was gone and his face burned with satisfaction. Fires raged inside the walls. No doubt his warriors within were being slaughtered, if they were not dead already, caught by surprise and struck down by men whose faces they knew, the Silfravall warriors, betraying their unsuspecting hosts.

Rage burned across Raef's skin and he advanced, eager to put himself in the thick of the fight, but then Finnolf was at his side.

The young captain could barely stand, but his words were clear. "We can fight another day, lord. They are too many. Our king must live. Get out of here." Raef pushed him aside but then he saw Vakre fall to the snow, a knife slipping from his gut. Raef burst past

Finnolf cleaved his axe into Vakre's attacker, but the son of Loki was not getting to his feet. Raef knelt, his eyes locked on Vakre's, whose face was contorted with pain, and then Uhtred was there, a horse in hand.

"Go," Uhtred shouted. "We will be right behind you." Raef mounted, still searching in vain for a sign of Siv. Isolf, seeing Uhtred urge Raef to escape, was advancing now, Greyshield a step behind. Uhtred lifted Vakre onto Raef's lap and with a slap, sent the horse out into the darkness. The lord of Garhold squared his shoulders and turned back to meet Isolf.

They hit the trees before Raef realized he was gone. He yanked the horse to a halt and slid from the saddle, taking Vakre to the ground with him. Raef lurched to his feet and looked back at his home in flames. The battle was over and Isolf stood the victor. The bodies of Raef's men were scattered before the gate and Uhtred and Finnolf were on their knees. Tulkis Greyshield was holding Finnolf by the hair and Isolf had his sword pointed at Uhtred's heart.

Vakre moaned and Raef went to his knees at his friend's side and pressed his hands to the wound, trying to stem the flow of blood.

"I know you are out there, Skallagrim," Isolf shouted. "I will find you and my sword will send you to your death." With horror growing in his heart, Raef watched Aelinvor step close to Isolf and even at that distance he could see the triumph in her face. "But you are done," Isolf went on. "Vannheim is mine." He slid his sword into Uhtred's chest. Without a sound, the lord of Garhold went limp and slumped forward as Tulkis drew a knife and sliced open Finnolf's throat, then pushed the young captain into the snow.

Silence pounded in Raef's ears. He could see Isolf talking, could see shouts of victory on the faces of those around him, could see the gates open to let Isolf in, could see Lingorm, the captain from Silfravall, clasp arms with Isolf. But all was soundless.

Vakre shuddered under Raef's hands and Raef forced himself

to look away as the gates closed behind Isolf and Greyshield, shutting him out. His hands were covered in Vakre's blood. The son of Loki was pale and sweaty, his eyes half open, his chest heaving with ragged breaths.

The sound of a horse snorting reached Raef and he looked up, scanning the trees for an attack. But there was none. Instead, he saw Hauk of Ruderk and the rest of the Hammerling's men. They lingered in the trees, less than a spear's throw away, unaware of Raef's presence, their eyes on the gates. At last, Raef's quarry was within killing distance.

And yet he could not go, could not leave Vakre, who would die without Raef's hands stemming the flow of blood. Fury rose in Raef's throat and he wanted to scream his anger to the gods, but he kept silent and hot tears of frustration burned in his eyes as he watched Hauk of Ruderk ride away, out of sight and out of reach.

Numb, Raef pressed his shin to the wound, to provide pressure in place of his hands. Using a knife, he cut away the bottom of his wool overshirt, wet and dirty as it was, and wrapped it around Vakre's torso, cinching it with a tight knot. Then he sat back in the snow and stared across the narrow strip of open land that lay between him and the Vestrhall. It seemed to him a void, a great expanse, as wide as the sky above but without the stars to guide him. He should have died with Finnolf and Uhtred. He should have given his life for Vannheim. He should have stayed with Siv. Instead he lived, stripped of all that mattered.

Everything was lost. His vengeance. His home. Siv.

# TWENTY-EIGHT

THE STARS TURNED overhead and still the smoke flourished above the village.

Raef watched, waited, desperate to change the dark fate that had crept up behind him and settled over his home, unwilling to look away. Whether he waited for a sign of life or for Isolf to come for him and bring death, he could not say. The cold seeped into him, but he did not feel it. The wind whispered that he should flee while he had the chance, but he did not heed it.

It was only when Vakre's breathing, shallow and weak as it was, went silent that Raef tore his gaze from the walls around his home.

"No, no," Raef murmured, fighting the panic that rose in his throat, his hands hovering over Vakre's chest. "Do not leave me here alone." The silence dragged out and then at last Vakre's ribcage rose once more and a shaky breath slipped out into the cold air. In his relief, Raef pressed his lips to Vakre's forehead. "I must not let you die," he whispered.

With purpose steadying his heart and his mind, Raef got to his feet and went to the horse that had carried him from danger. The mare was unknown to him, ridden into battle by a traitor who wanted to drive the line of Skallagrim from the Vestrhall. But she was strong and clear-eyed, and Raef was grateful to find a blanket rolled behind the saddle. He pulled it free, then led the horse close to Vakre's body, rubbing her nose as he went. "You must be sure-footed, friend," he said. "The burden you will carry is all I have left in this world."

Raef knelt once more next to Vakre to check that his makeshift bandage held. It was poor but he had nothing better. He adjusted the knot and brushed sweat from Vakre's forehead. "No way but forward now," he said. "Just like Siv's story of Lisgothmir." Raef closed his eyes, remembering the remains of the burned ship on the beach. He knew now in his heart who had abandoned it. Opening his eyes, he lifted Vakre from the ground and managed to settle him onto the horse, then swiftly pulled himself up before Vakre could fall. He shifted Vakre's weight until it rested against his chest, wrapped the blanket around Vakre's torso, and took up the reins. "She was right. Isolf had to show his men that there was no going back, that they would take the Vestrhall or die trying."

Raef took one last look toward his home, wondering when he would see it again, then turned the mare east and urged her deeper into the trees. "You did not trust him," Raef murmured, his mouth close to Vakre's ear, "and I should have listened. Everything was a lie."

He was not without friends. Kolbrand, Finnolf's father, would shelter him without a thought for his own safety and his home was not far. But thoughts of Kolbrand reminded Raef that Finnolf was dead, and Tolla and her sister, if they had not perished in the fires, were at Isolf's mercy. He did not have the will to face their father.

There was Axsellund. His new, untested ally. But the journey to Torleif's hall was too far for Vakre and Isolf might think to look for him there.

Others in Vannheim would gladly take him in. His childhood friends, the brothers Rufnir and Asbjork. Svanja's aging father, Beomir. Countless warriors who had bled with his father and again with him, who were loyal to the name of Skallagrim. Josurr, bound now to Raef's fortunes, would not hesitate. But Raef feared what Isolf might do to those he suspected of aiding Raef, even for one night. He would not risk it.

There was one place he could go. One place Isolf would not know to look. There, he could gather fierce-hearted friends. There, Vakre would have time to heal. There, he could hone his fury and his sorrow into a weapon against Isolf's betrayal.

Raef glanced to the dark sky and the stars burning bright above the silhouettes of the trees.

"Odin. Allfather. Give me time," he whispered. "Darkness is coming, I know. But I must do this, not for myself, but for those who died for me this night. Before Fenrir comes for you, before the stars begin to fall and the sun and moon vanish, caught up in the jaws of wolves, I will bring death to Isolf Valbrand and I will take back what is mine." The trees were still, the forest quiet. The very earth was listening. "And then I will go to the fate that awaits me, the fate even you cannot name, Allfather. I will go with a glad heart. Only give me time."

There was no answer, but Raef did not need one. He had only one way forward. Vakre shivered against his chest as the grey mare snorted out hot breath, and then the forest swallowed them into its heart.

# List of Characters

Raef Skallagrim, lord of Vannheim

*Alfheim*
Aerath, troubled
First Guardian
Second Guardian, tricksy
other Guardians: the kind one, the angry one, the strong one, and the forgettable one
Finnoul, dreamer
Ylloria, never smiles
Annun
Thannor
Lorcan, sees much, despite missing an eye

*Jötunheim*
Mogthrasir, giant, not too clever
Hrodvelgr, giant, much more clever
Skjaldi, a dying, forgotten man
Bara, giantess, one of the nine daughters of Aegir, a sea god
Svanja, a memory
Odin, Allfather

*Vannheim*

Eadilwif, a curious child
Brunn, her father, a fisherman
Sigrid, her mother
Skarfi, Brunn's brother
Hollof, misplaced some sheep
Isolf Valbrand, Raef's cousin
Aldrif, healer
Fylkir, priest of Odin, cantankerous
Josurr, priest of Odin
Gudrik, skald, warrior, cripple, disheartened
Tulkis Greyshield, clings to the past
Rudrak Red-beard, a vulture
Snorren Thoken, another vulture
Finnolf Horsebreaker, captain
Eira, Raef's lover, a shieldmaiden
Siv, a shieldmaiden
Vakre Flamecloak, half god, son of Loki
Beomir, Svanja's father
Dvalarr the Crow, kingmaker
Hoyvik, smith at the Vestrhall
Ulli, steward at the Vestrhall
Yorkell, captain, sent in search of vultures
Ergil Thrainson, a boy seeking vengeance
Grandmother, an artist
Uhtred, lord of Garhold
Aelinvor, his daughter
Lingorm, a captain of Silfravall
Kolbrand, Finnolf's father, breeder of horses and hunting dogs
Tolla, Finnolf's youngest sister, more horse than girl
Hauk, lord of Ruderk
Edvard, Brandulf Hammerling's illegitimate son

*Off Stage*
Brandulf Hammerling, lord of Finngale, Raef's former ally
Fengar, lord of Solheim
Tyrlaug of Innrivik, deceased grandfather to Isolf and Raef
Brynvald of Kolhaugen, the last king, deceased
Torleif, lord of Axsellund
Sverren Redtail, lord of Bergoss
Harbjorn, lord of Silfravall

# About the Author

T L Greylock is the author of *The Song of the Ash Tree* trilogy, consisting of *The Blood-Tainted Winter*, *The Hills of Home*, and the forthcoming conclusion, *Already Comes Darkness*.

She can only wink her left eye, jumped out of an airplane at 13,000 feet while strapped to a Navy SEAL, had a dog named Agamemnon and a cat named Odysseus, and has been swimming with stingrays in the Caribbean.

P.S. One of the above statements is false. Can you guess which?

www.tlgreylock.com

 @TLGreylock

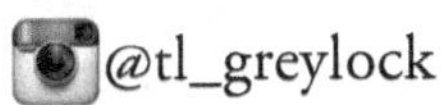 @tl_greylock

Look out for the conclusion to *The Song of the Ash Tree*

# ALREADY COMES DARKNESS

# ONE

THE HOUNDS CAME with the sun.

The day had dawned in shadow, the skies cluttered with writhing clouds, but at last the sun broke through following close on the breath of a stiff winter wind. The horse swiveled its ears, nostrils wide, at the first notes of the chorus, and Raef, cupped hands spilling the icy water before it reached his mouth, sprang to his feet. For a moment, he was as rooted as the bare oaks that towered above him as he sought to pinpoint their direction. The strong, eager voices of the hunters rose and fell on the air, and though at first they seemed to call from every corner of the world, Raef closed his eyes and soon knew they were yet behind. They had not flanked him. But it was only a matter of time.

Raef looked to Vakre, who sat limp and listless in the saddle, his face pale and slick with sweat. His eyes were open, but the fevered gaze gave no sign that he heard the hounds. He would not survive a fight. Raef wrapped the reins in Vakre's hands as securely as he could, then slapped his palm to the horse's flank, sending the grey mare reeling through the trees and leaving Raef alone with only his thudding heart and the knowledge that he might have sent his friend away to die. Turning east, Raef began to run in a desperate attempt to lead the hunters away.

His path was perilous and steep, the snow masking jagged spurs of rock, slick ground giving way beneath his boots. He sprinted when he could and crawled when he had to, but always he went up, and when he gashed his hand on a splintered tree trunk, he let the blood drip freely to mark his trail. The hounds would follow, but their progress would slow and the men that trailed after would have to abandon their horses and continue on foot.

The voices of the pack rose and fell, and more than once they went silent for stretches of time that dragged on Raef's nerves. But always they returned and he drew strength from the knowledge that it was his trail they followed, not Vakre's. Raef forced himself to focus on his pace and each stride as he pushed onward while the bright winter sun slid across the sky. Sweat dripped from his nose and his lungs began to burn with each breath of cold air that he drew in. The swords, his and Vakre's, banged against his legs, and his long cloak caught on the rough ground. He risked no glances behind, his mind bent only on moving forward.

The sun was sinking behind him, spilling his shadow across the snow, when he broke through the tree line and emerged onto the open slopes of the high hills. Behind and below him, the fjord was a dark snake, stark against the snow-covered slopes, stretching west to the hall he had lost and the sea beyond. Ahead and above, the darkening sky loomed. If he could reach the stones before losing the sun to the sea, the dark cloak of night would be his ally. Raef pushed on, ignoring his protesting legs, and climbed a rocky outcrop to gain his first look at his pursuers.

In the low light of dusk, there was little to see. All was grey and white and purple shadows, but, his skull thudding with rushing blood as he fought to slow his breathing, Raef picked out movement here and there. Two, three, six men. Perhaps more. As many dogs, though the swift-legged hounds were harder to spot even as the trees thinned around them. He could not fight them all. Taking a deep breath, Raef turned away and ran on, making his way toward a narrow spot between two peaks.

The statues were silent sentries under a deep blue sky and the light of the first stars by the time he arrived at the saddle between the peaks and stumbled upon the ring of stones. In daylight, Raef knew, the faces would stare down at him with bleak stone eyes, carved by ancient, unknown hands. Now, in darkness, they were only black shapes blotting out the stars.

The snow was thick here and Raef skirted the edge of the ring of statues until he stood between the eastern most pair, one, a woman who faced away from the rest, her gaze turned to await the rising sun, and the other, a stern man wielding an axe as tall as Raef. There Raef remained, letting the hunters come to him as the wind banished the last of the clouds, revealing the pale face of the moon.

The dogs came first, bounding through the deep snow as they finished the ascent. The men lagged behind, but the moonlight did nothing to hide Raef and a voice, heavy with ragged breaths, called the dogs off. The men slowed their pace and approached on foot, hungry eyes pinned on Raef. They were seven in number and sure of victory.

"Did you really think we would not catch you, Skallagrim? We would not hunt you down?" One man led the rest and Raef's heart burned with fury at the sight of him. "And this is how you have chosen to die. Here in the wild, a fugitive on the land your family ruled for more than five hundred years, without a friend to watch your back." Tulkis Greyshield spat in the snow. "At last the Greyshields will reclaim their rightful place. My sons will carry on our name while yours turns to dust and is wiped from memory."

"You are wrong, Tulkis." The arduous climb was but a distant memory, the exhaustion that had crept up on Raef for three sleepless nights was pushed away, forgotten. Raef put a hand on the hilt of his sword and felt the familiar anticipation of battle swell within him. This was blade-work, this was the steel song, and though the numbers called for his death, he knew he would not be the first to die.

Greyshield let out a barking laugh. "About what?"

"Everything. Your sons will die this night," Raef said, nodding at the young, freshly-bearded warriors who flanked Tulkis, "and I am not without friends."

Two of the warriors behind Tulkis glanced beyond the circle of statues, wary now of every shadow.

"Your friend? The one on the horse?" Greyshield's smile burrowed into the knot in Raef's stomach. "We have him, or will soon enough." Raef said nothing and Tulkis, grinning still, gestured to the axe-wielding statue at Raef's right. "Will he fight for you, Skallagrim? Will he strike us down with a single blow?"

"Even now, Isolf is sitting in my father's chair, Tulkis, tightening his grip on Vannheim. You will never have it."

"Vannheim or Garhold, it matters not."

Raef wanted to laugh. "If you think you will have Garhold, then you do not know Uhtred's daughter."

"The lady Aelinvor will do as she is told."

Now Raef did laugh, a bitter, scornful sound. "She craves power and helped murder her father to grasp it. She will not bend to you." Raef was glad to see a flicker of uncertainty in Greyshield's eyes, but words would do nothing to alter the situation.

"Kill him, father," one of the sons said. Raef could see fear in this one's eyes, fear masked by eager words.

"No, father, let me drain his life's blood." The other son was shorter and smaller than his brother, but his eyes were alive with the promise of bloodshed.

"Better yet, let me fight you both." Raef spread his arms wide, inviting them in. "I will gut you as Finnvold Skallagrim did

Thannulf Greyshield. You are boys still clinging to your mother's skirts, so weak the Valkyries will never carry you to Valhalla."

The brothers moved together, snarling and cursing Raef and all his ancestors, swords drawn. They raced into the ring of statues and Raef let them come.

Three strides later, they were screaming and the snow was bright with slick blood as the sons of Tulkis Greyshield impaled themselves on sharp stakes buried beneath the snow. The false cover of skins and branches broke and vanished, revealing the pit that stretched to the feet of the silent, stone onlookers.

Tulkis was as still as the statues, his mouth gaping as he watched his sons die. One went quickly, for he had caught a stake in the throat, and his corpse sagged into the snow. The other, the second, younger son who had been so eager to kill, writhed still, legs jerking, blood coursing from his mouth and seeping out around the stake buried in his belly. His screams turned to shuddering moans of agony, but he lingered and the smell of urine reached Raef, but he had eyes only for Tulkis.

The shock and horror frozen there thawed into rage and Tulkis' roar of anger drowned out the cries of his dying son. "I will cut off your cock and feed it to the crows, Skallagrim. I will flay you and make you eat your own skin. You will sob for death before I am done with you."

Raef kept his voice even. "You spoke true, Tulkis. Here in the wild we are and I am alone. But the wild is mine." Raef stepped behind the stony-faced woman who looked to the east and circled around to the north, every step taking him closer to Tulkis and the four warriors with him. He had hoped the pit might claim three, or even four, warriors, for now he was left with five men to fight, but seeing Tulkis watch his sons be ripped from him was worth it. He drew his sword in his left hand and the axe in his right, reveling in the calm their sharp edges brought to his mind.

"Greet the corpse maidens for me, Greyshield. I will send you to Valhalla."

Tulkis charged and his first swing was full of power and wrath, meant to slash Raef open across the ribs. He jumped back, the steel passing by harmlessly, and countered with a lunge of his own that Tulkis only just deflected away, heaving his sword back around in time to keep Raef's blade from burying itself in his gut, but the axe that followed was too quick and Tulkis could not prevent it from biting into his shoulder. Bellowing, Tulkis stumbled back, nearly falling in the deep snow, and Raef pressed on. The swords clashed again, Tulkis keeping his sword arm raised despite the fresh wound, but the snow claimed Greyshield's balance and Raef's next swing cleaved into his ribs, splitting flesh and splintering bone with ease. Tulkis dropped to his knees, his eyes staring, mouth hanging open, and he did not move, did not try to defend himself as Raef's axe came to rest against his neck. Blood began to spill from his lips, streaking down his beard, but their eyes locked, hatred and fury blazing in Tulkis' face. With a short, brutal chop, Raef hacked the axe into Tulkis' neck and watched the eyes dull, the skin grow slack, and then Raef knew Greyshield was dead. Wrenching his weapons from the body, Raef let it fall backward so the dead eyes might stare at the stars. Only then did he face the four remaining warriors, his heart heaving with the battle-lust.

Two were faces he knew, men who had fought with him at the burning lake. He focused on them.

"So ends the line of Greyshield. Would you suffer the same fate, Olaf? Or you, Hakon? If you fight me now, I will kill you and hunt down your children and my blade will know the taste of their flesh. Is this what you want, to die a traitor, unremembered by the gods?"

Olaf looked down to the snow as though he might find an answer or his courage buried there, but Hakon grimaced, his lips tugged sideways by an old scar, and Raef knew he would have to kill at least one more man that night.

"I broke an oath once, lord," Hakon said, "when I took mead from Greyshield's hand and drank for him. I will not break another, even if it means my death."

"You would stand by a dead traitor?"

Hakon shrugged. "It is all I have left, lord. What am I if I beg for my life now?"

"Then draw your sword."

There was grit and determination in Hakon's eyes, but also a measure of resignation. He was a strong man, and tall, but made for chopping trees and hauling loads, not battle. He had never been a skilled warrior, and Raef wondered what had tempted him to Greyshield's side, but found he did not wish to ask.

It was over quickly and Hakon fell not far from where the hounds crouched, whimpering now as the scent of the blood of men filled their nostrils. Olaf fell to his knees and begged Raef to spare him, or if not him, his wife and children. The other two warriors, unknown men from Silfravall, said nothing, though one fidgeted with his hands. He made a half-hearted attempt to draw his knife, but Raef hurled his axe and it sank deep into the man's chest. He fell heavy and hard and did not move again. The other warrior paled and Raef could see the fight had left his eyes.

"Go," Raef said, weary now, but his voice still sharp with anger. "Run, run back to my traitorous cousin. Tell Isolf he will never be free of me."

Olaf and the other man turned their backs and fled, the hounds at their heels, and Raef watched them tread the snow-sea until they disappeared down the slope. Only then did he allow himself to expel a deep breath, and he sank against the closest statue, resting his head between his knees, his cloak pulled tight against the wind.

The lone howl of a wolf jerked him awake. A quick glance at the moon told him he had not slept long, but it was not safe to linger. Rest could come when he was better sheltered. Raef hauled himself to his feet and walked to the edge of the pit that had claimed the sons of Greyshield. The bodies were stiff and cold and looked younger in death. With silent thanks to Odin, Allfather, Raef turned his back and began the descent, fixed now on finding Vakre, if the son of Loki lived.

www.ingramcontent.com/pod-product-compliance
Lightning Source LLC
Chambersburg PA
CBHW030659120726
47905CB00001B/279

9 780996 536639